ADVENTURES AT THE BOAT SHOW

"The Castro Diaries"

Dale Robbins

KDP

Copyright © 2025 Dale Robbins

All rights reserved

While there are true events portrayed in this book, there are also many characters and events in this book that are fictitous. Any unintentional similarity to real persons, living or dead, is coincidental.

No part of this book may be reproduced, or stored in a retrieval system, or transmitted in any form or by any means, electronic, mechanical, photocopying, recording, or otherwise, without express written permission of the publisher.

ISBN: 9798310634862

Cover design by: Art Painter
Library of Congress Control Number: 2018675309
Printed in the United States of America

Dedicated to the Staff and Management of the Boat Shows produced by the National Marine Manufucaturers Association (NMMA) - a team of trade show professionals, of which the author, in another llifetime, was proud to be a member.

PREFACE

The now world-renowned Miami International Boat Show was started as a small local event in 1941. In 2025, now in its 84th year it continues to be recognized as one of the premier gatherings of the Marine Industry in the world.

The author had the honor of serving as the General Manager of the show for three years during the 1990's - though there is a lot of creative fiction wove in this tale, there are many elements of truth sprinkled throughout. It is left to the imagination of the reader to determine when "artistic license" has been taken to enhance the story.

As for "the Castro Diaries," the author has never personally seen such documents. He will confirm that many boats built in Canada were indeed on displayed in the Main Halls of the Miami Beach Convention Center.

While the "adventures" begin at the Boat Show, this is only a starting point. In reality this tale is a complicated "coming of age story," "a romance story," "a mystery," and an all important discovery of religious conviction - as told through the lens of characters who are members of The Church of Jesus Christ of Latter-day Saints (Mormons).

Members of the LDS Community will immediately recognize

elements of their religion. For other individuals it will be an interesting view into one of the nation's most misunderstood Christian denominations.

Expression of appreciation is given to the town of Salisbury, North Carolina for serving as the backdrop for much of this story. Many of the characters are drawn from the recesses of author's memory, who did much of his 5th grade year as well as his first two years of college in that beautiful Piedmont, North Carolina town.

ADVENTURES AT THE BOAT SHOW
The Castro Diaries

By: Dale S Robbins

© January 2025 – All Rights Reserved

INTRODUCTION

As Alex Barton, Junior (or AJ) to friends and family, walked home that beautiful North Carolina spring afternoon he had many thoughts on his mind. Until last night, he had always assumed that his college professor father and charity fund-raiser mom were two of the most average, if not on the boring side, parents a boy could have. His wasn't a bad life – they lived in a nice home and drove nice cars in a nice neighborhood in a bedroom community of Charlotte, North Carolina. His hometown since his birth, Salisbury, had not always been thought of as a part of greater Charlotte, but as the city grew in every direction smaller towns (once with their own identities) simply became part of "greater Charlotte. Many times, AJ wished they simply lived IN Charlotte where they would be closer to the "action." But no, instead of being in a city that boasted an NFL Football and NBA Basketball team, as well as one of the larger campuses of the sprawling University of North Carolina system he lived in sleepy (boring Salisbury).

It was an old city – somewhere in the downtown area there was a plaque that proclaimed, "George Washington Slept Here!" Across from his old elementary school was once the site of a notorious prison (he had always found it ironic that his school was close to what had been a prison site). Charlotte's UNC campus had over 22,000 students – Salisbury's predominantly white college, Catawba, – named after some forgotten Native American tribe, had about 1,200; the HBCU college, Livingstone College had barely 1,000 students. In middle school he had once googled, "famous people from

Salisbury, N.C." The Google search returned the names of 30 people that perhaps even his history professor father would not recognize.

Last night, though, AJ made what was for him an eye-opening and even head-turning discovery. His family were very strong members of the local LDS Ward, Alex Senior had actually served as the congregation's Bishop until last year when he was honorable released and for the first time in his teen years his dad had been able to sit with the family during Sunday worship – instead of on the stand as the "presiding officer." AJ's youth group had been challenged to find out more about their family history. His queries to his parents had always yielded very brief answers. AJ had never met his grandfather – who according to what his dad had been willing to share must have been a real character in the years before Alex Senior was born – there were only vague references to "most of the first half of his life as a career criminal" – with the suggestion, perhaps even a gangster.

His Mom, who he considered not only the most important person in his life, but still in her early 50's one of the most beautiful women he had ever seen. Sure, he knew most boys thought *their* moms were beautiful – but, in his case Carmen Roja-Barton really was stunning. When AJ pressed her about his grandparents on her side the answers were even more vague. She had been born in Cuba and smuggled off the island to live with relatives in Miami when she was a small child. She would only say that her pa pa and ma ma were "no longer living." Likewise, the Tio and Tia [Uncle and Aunt] who had raised her from early childhood "had passed away." He thought his dad had been born a member of their church, but with no details on how the son of a possible gangster and a mother who was even less talked about, went on to become a missionary for his church.

There were a lot of unanswered questions in his parents' background. After his discovery last night while looking for family history information in the attic, there were even more questions. Like many LDS families, they had information on distant relatives – he knew he had some ancestors who walked across the plains with Brigham Young to re-establish the Church in the valley of the Great Salt Lake. He knew that he had relatives on his mother's side who, at one time, received land grants in Cuba from the King of Spain. But his immediate grandparents were never discussed, nor was his parents' courtship and marriage which had happened over ten years before he was born. After his birth, there was a five-year gap before his younger brother and sister, fraternal twins, were born.

The banker's box he had opened read simply, "The gap years 1994-2006." The box contained pictures, files, notes, fridge magnets from all over, some sort of trade show directory from the "Miami International Boat Show," and a thick bound copy of what appeared to be some kind of diary written in Spanish. His mother spoke fluent Spanish, and his dad spoke what his mom referred to as "gringo Spanish," from his days as a Church Missionary in South America. It was like a treasure trove of his parents' past, of which he had never heard them mention. What startled him most were the pictures – including some ancient Polaroids (he had seen a Polaroid camera only once in his school's 'cameras of the past display'). Aside from the age of the pictures was the shock of seeing his parents as he had never seen them (or even imagined). There were beach pictures of his mom, with long raven-black hair cascading past her shoulders – and a bathing suit so small he blushed. There was his dad, also with jet black hair as opposed to the salt and pepper he had always known – shaggy, and over his ears. Then there were other pictures, his mom with very short reddish blonde hair wearing a formal outfit again revealing more skin that he could have ever imagine her showing in public! One of the pictures was clearly a formal function and they both appeared to have mixed drinks in hand for a toast. He was left almost speechless – these were pictures of a Bishop of the Church and his wife. This was not the modesty and decorum he had lived with all his life.

Dad's Prius was in the driveway and his mom's hybrid Rav4 was gone. She was probably out with the twins on a Wednesday afternoon at whatever enrichment activity in which they were currently enrolled. AJ saw his father in his study, took a deep breath and figured it would be a good time to ask his dad about the treasure trove of memories he had uncovered. He knew that his dad did not have any classes on Wednesday evening as it was the last week of the Spring term. Seeing his dad in his study he called out, "Dad, I'm home...have you got a few minutes?"

He knew the answer before he asked the question – his father would always make time when one of his children needed to talk. "Sure son, pull up a chair – I was just working on "This Day in History." Do you know the significance of May 10th?" AJ didn't, but knew by the enthusiasm in his father's voice – and that every day was a significant day to historians like his dad, that he soon would know...

"On May 10, 1869, the Golden Spike was driven in Utah, marking the completion of the Transcontinental Railroad," he said with the unbridled passion that only a man with four degrees in history and several published books can explain!

AJ had inherited a lot of his dad's interest in history, but it never ceased to amaze him how his father could find and know so much knowledge about such a vast amount of information. Here he needed to tread carefully – too much excitement and he would get far more of what his dad called, "the rest of the story," and they would never get to the box, the memories, and the pictures.

"Now, I remember – Mr. Smith mentioned it in his class today..."

"Clarence is a good teacher, good man, I'm glad you have him this year – but something else is on your mind...what's up?"

"Uhh, I'm not sure where to start dad..."

"I don't know son; the beginning is usually not a bad place to start."

"OK, Dad, you and Mom rarely talk about your parents – we know more about your great-grandfather than we know about our own."

Alex studied his feet – as was normal in his home he was barefoot – his son had kicked off his own shoes right inside the door. "Aaaj (a nickname that had stuck since when his young sister was only a toddler; she couldn't form the letters A and J) is complicated – and I guess we have never felt you were really old enough or needed to know..."

"I know Dad, but it is almost like there is no history of your life prior to when I was born. No wedding pictures, no college pictures, nothing about your life; everything is after the twins and I were born. We now have family pictures every year; framed school pictures; videos of us – records everywhere..."

"Son, your mother and I had been married for 12 years

before your arrival – it is safe to say, we were different people than we are now..."

"I saw the pictures."

Puzzled, Alex looked at his son and asked, "The pictures?"

"I was looking for some family history stuff for our Youth Group at Church and there is a box in the attic."

Alex shook his head, offered an awkward smile, and asked, "The Gap Years box?"

"Uhh. Yeah. And, I guess I should have brought it to you when I found it, or least the things in it."

"It's OK. I guess the time has come to let you know some of our more immediate family history. Your mom and I have known someday you would find out that we indeed have what the world calls, 'a past.'"

"It looks like it was a very adventure-filled past..."

"AJ," he began, "it didn't start that way. My father was 42 when I was born; your grandmother was 40 – I was not a mistake – but certainly a surprise. For various reasons, their relationship didn't last, and I grew up with aunts/uncles/stepparents. If there was a good thing, one of these was an elderly aunt – my dad's oldest sister, who was a member of the Church..."

"But you have ancestors who walked across the plains..."

"True, several generations back we had relatives in Kirkland and Nauvoo. . .but a few generations later, their children had left the Saints and returned to the South, primarily Alabama and North Carolina. Some of our relatives on my mother's side had always lived there – hence why we also have blood kin who fought for the Confederacy."

"How, what…I'm confused."

"I'm giving you the big picture son – it'll take a long time to fill in all the details."

"OK, let's stay with you and Mom – you were a member, she wasn't, when, how, what, I, I don't know what ask first…"

"I was baptized when I was 14, the Ward had a great youth group and a Bishop who made this "cast off" kid feel like he had finally found home, found a family. When I graduated at 17, I took a year and a half at the local community college and finished my AA in history and then at 19 volunteered to serve a two-year mission for the Church. The mission in many ways changed my life."

"All I know about the mission is it was in South America and Mom, who I know was born in Cuba, says you still sound like a gringo when you speak Spanish."

Alex grinned and continued, 'She is right, two years in Paraguay – often in the village - did not really prepare me to speak Spanish with a native-born Cuban – also raised by a native-speaking Aunt and Uncle.

"So, how did you meet and why have I never heard the story?"

"That's where it gets complicated. To say the least..."

"Please Dad, more."

"I returned from my mission, the aunt who had introduced me to the Church was now in memory care. I applied for my first-choice school – the University of Alabama at Tuscaloosa. Our Alabama relatives were all big Tide fans, even though most of them had never finished high school. I had a 1295 on my SAT, a 3.9 with honors classes in High School, and a 3.96 for my associates from Community College. With scholarships and Pell Grants I graduated in 3 and half year's summa cume laude."

"So that history degree number 2"

"Yes."

"Have you always wanted to be a history prof."

"Gosh no. I wanted to be a history teacher on an Indian Reservation..."

"What??"

"Probably still in the missionary mind set of taking care of indigenous people..."

"So did you go for a teacher's certificate?"

"No, life kicked in – I was working part time as a theater manager, researching grad school and checking out what starting teachers were earning..."

"So did you go to grad school for your master's in history?"

"No, that comes later in the story, I lost the dream for a while – I took the LSAT, applied. and was accepted at the University of Miami Law School?"

"REALLY? Isn't that a weird switch?

"Not really, a BA in history works great to get into Law School."

"Miami makes sense now – but you've mentioned you lived in Miami though I know Mom lived there when she left Cuba – but like you, she has never talked about it. . .

"Get comfortable, son; this may take a while. It will answer a lot of questions, but in their place, you'll want to ask at least 100 more . . ." With that, Alex began the narrative that only he, Carmen, and a few others throughout the world knew about.

CHAPTER ONE

While his gaze was on AJ, in reality he was looking past his son and bringing up memories of over two decades in a hidden past as he started his story:

I had moved to Miami two years earlier and was then in my third year of law school; as I was driving home the moment I changed lanes, the distinctive sound of a Mercedes horn blared loud and long. Glancing in the rear-view mirror, I saw a beautiful, although enraged, young woman giving me the finger - and a piece of her mind. My first thought was what an amazing phenomenon it was that only beautiful women drove Mercedes sport coupes. Judging from the animated use of her hands and her raven black hair she was probably Hispanic.

Miami was then and even more now, one of the most cosmopolitan melting pots in the Western Hemisphere. As

I said, I was born and raised with relatives throughout the south, honors grad from the University of Alabama. With a two-year Church mission under my belt I knew that graduate schoolwork would be different - but nothing prepared me for the great cultural differences that abounded in that city. Even though I spoke passable Spanish after being a missionary for two years in Paraguay, the Hispanic and especially the Cuban speaking part of the community really confused me. Clearly the only thing that Asuncion, Paraguay and Coral Gables had in common was the locals both spoke Spanish. Even after a couple of years, it was an example of a cultural gulf simply being too much for me to fathom.

Glancing back in the mirror I saw the young Hispanic beauty in the Mercedes was still denouncing me with great vigor. It was a mistake, I hadn't meant to cut her off, but my mind had been wandering, and I hadn't realized till the last second, I was about to miss my exit off the turnpike. I'm sure to her I looked like just another rude guy cutting in and changing lanes at the last possible moment. As we crept down the exit ramp heading onto Kendall Drive, I spotted one of the seemingly ever-present street vendors coming towards me with a handful of fresh-cut flowers. Stealing a quick glance in the mirror I saw the Latin lady was still very upset.

Don't ask why but I quickly fumbled for a business card, grabbed one, and wrote on the back, "I'm sorry - give me a break!" Then I pulled a five-dollar bill out of my jeans pocket. As I rolled down the window the young woman with the flowers approached. The light would change at any moment, so I quickly shoved the note and the five-dollar bill in the vendor's hand and said, "Give'em to the lady in the black car behind me."

The flower seller looked puzzled and said, "perdon,

señor...no enteindo, no hablo ingles." [pardon, sir...I don't understand, I don't speak English]

Trying to switch and think in Spanish I said, "Señorita (I hoped) en coche negro. "Using my body as a shield I pointed to the car behind me. [the woman in the black car]

The vendor's eyes lit up as she said, "Si, si señor. Para señorita. Muy bien!" [Yes! For the lady. Very well!]

I watched in his rear-view mirror, and prayed as the flower lady approached the black Mercedes and motioned for the aggravated woman to roll down her window. At first, she tried to wave her off, but the flower lady was insistent. Just as the light changed the window of the Mercedes came down, and the driver managed to take the flowers and the card.

Miami had been hit with a wave of drive-by shootings, and I didn't at that moment know if it was a good move or not, so, I hit the gas and sped off to leave the lady in the black Mercedes stunned as she read the note. Regretfully, common courtesies were, like in most big cities, not really that common in Miami. And out-and-out apologies practically never happened.

At the next light she caught up to me and looked me over with those piercing black eyes. At that time, I was driving an aging Nissan 280zx, which had seen its better days. That was the moment that I got my first close-up look at your mom. The anger had at least melted off her face. My guess she was between 20 and 25 – I was close she was almost 23. Happily, I noticed there was no ring on her left hand. "Well at least there wouldn't be a mad husband to deal with," was my first thought.

Slowly she grinned and motioned for me to roll down the window. Even though she looked very Hispanic, she shouted without the hint of an accent, "Forgiven, pull in at the next gas station."

I was stunned, but my eyes lit up and I nodded in agreement. Two blocks later we pulled in at a Chevron station and drove to the back so as not to block the gas pumps. The black Mercedes 600 SL pulled up beside me. As the car door opened, I was almost stunned by the beauty of the driver as she got out of the car. At that moment, and until today, to me she is still the most beautiful woman alive.

Your mom was an absolute vision of loveliness. Her hair was jet black and fell halfway down her back. She was tall; the legs seemed to go on forever and her complexion was perfect. Walking over to the car she noticed the University of Miami parking decal on the front window. Still sitting there stunned with the scene unfolding in front of me, she asked, "UM student?"

"Law school, third year" I replied, "and you?"

"I take care of myself," she answered, "my name is Carmen Rojas, and yours Mr. Law Student?"

Alex, Alex Barton," I replied, almost stammering, so I babbled on with another apology, "Hey, I'm not or wasn't trying to hit on you. I just wanted to say I was sorry for cutting you off at the exit. You looked mad, and I just wanted to make sure you didn't shoot me."

Your mother is so quick on her feet, she knew that she

had a young Mr. Barton very much off guard, so she continued playing along, "Does that mean you are trying to hit on me now?"

"Well, I, I, uh..." I stammered.

Still being very formal she wet her lips and said, "Relax, Mr. Barton. I'm not going to bite you or shoot you. The roses are lovely, and I love roses. I just wanted to see someone who took the time to apologize for anything in Miami. Tell you what, buy me an espresso at the cafe up the road, and we can talk some more."

"Sure," I offered, "hop in."

"I'll meet you there."

As our two cars headed west on Kendall Drive my mind was racing a hundred miles an hour. The girl who promised to wait for me on my mission married my best friend six months before I came home. The college girlfriend (who was a professor's daughter) evaporated when I was accepted at the University of Miami. She made it clear that Miami was not her kind of town. This helped me make the decision she was not my kind of prospective wife, and so it ended. But it had been over two years since I moved here, and my love life was going nowhere. I had only dated a few girls I met on campus, but they all seemed interested in finding a doctor, lawyer or other rich professional, not an impoverished law student.

And yet here I was, getting ready to have a cup of coffee with one of the most beautiful women I had ever seen, who, judging from the car and the jewelry, already had plenty of money or at least access to it. We pulled up to Cafe Havana.

It was located in one of the endless number of strip malls that line the main roads of every suburb in America. The difference in Miami, unlike Birmingham, Atlanta, or Kansas City, was there would be a Cafe Havana. If not so named, there is something similar in every shopping center in Miami-Dade County.

The first year of law school is designed to make students' eyes bleed from the amount of reading that is expected of them. The rigors of study and picking up the habit of coffee to burn the midnight oil were the primary reasons I had drifted away from the Church. For this moment though I put the thoughts behind me. In Miami they give Cuban coffee to preschoolers, so to not drink and expresso with this young woman would have not served me well. I was wrong, but at that moment I didn't care.

AJ took his dad's confession with an open mind and heart – in his almost sixteen years he had never seen his father have a cup of coffee, smoke, have even a single beer even at faculty parties – and drugs were just out of the question. Seeing his dad as human with temptations and choosing not to follow the rules didn't diminish his respect for him. If anything, it made him feel a little older just knowing his father would share this with him.

So, I ordered two espressos, and we took a seat by the window. Up close, she was even more beautiful. She wore tight-fitting designer jeans, a simple red silk blouse, and very little makeup. I looked at her jewelry. She had the obligatory Rolex on her left wrist, three simple gold chains on her right wrist, large diamond stud earrings, and a heavy gold rope necklace. When I joined her at the table, your mom started the conversation by saying, "So, Mr. Barton, tell me about yourself. Do you always cut people off on the expressway; buy them roses; and then try to pick them up for coffee?"

My face turned red as I replied, "Well, no, I, well, never until today."

Slowly as the conversation progressed, I got used to her aggressive form of conversation and became less intimidated by it. We talked for almost an hour. During that time, I found out that she was turning 23 and very single; that she loved Cuban coffee, fine dining, exciting nightlife and lived in the Gables

Meanwhile, your mom brought out that I was pretty much a loner, and this was the most daring move I had ever made on a woman in my life. She knew I just turned 25; had grown up with several different families, the last one being a devoutly religious home - but that I hadn't practiced my faith since moving to Miami; that I missed the family that I was still in contact with; and I was having a hard time juggling school, and the law firm that I clerked for when I wasn't studying.

Since she had my business card, she knew the name of the firm I worked for, and I gave her my home number – remember this is when we still had landlines and answering machines -and my address. Realizing that she knew a lot about me, and I knew next to nothing about her, I finally asked, "What about you? I've done most of the talking, tell me about you."

She replied softly but firmly, "You know enough for now. I'll call you tomorrow."

She got up and walked to the door, leaving me somewhat dumbfounded. "Thanks for the coffee," she said as she walked out the door. Staring down at my cup, I asked myself, "What just happened?" All the way home, I replayed the morning events in my mind. Sure, I finally made a daring play on a beautiful woman; it turned out to be a great pick-up move; and then I didn't even get her number!? I was a third-year law student, not a high school sophomore. But I sure felt like one on the ride home.

AJ grinned at the thought – he was a high school sophomore and was almost afraid to speak to the cheerleader types in his own grade – even though he had known many of them since middle school. Maybe he came by it honestly, he thought to himself.

His dad then continued. Late that night, the ringing phone interrupted my studies. Rather than pick it up, I waited for the answering machine to screen the call. As the machine beeped, I heard a female voice that at first, I didn't recognize, "Alex, let's do dinner tomorrow night. Monty's in the Grove at 8:00 PM and be on time. I'm unlike most Latinas - when I say 8:00; I mean eight sharp."

Suddenly I realized it was Carmen's voice. I grabbed for the phone but all I got was a dial tone. "Damn. I still didn't know have her number," Alex saw the puzzled look and shot his son the answer, "Because we didn't have caller ID then," he said with a smile.

I knew we had a test the day after tomorrow, but I also knew I would be at Monty Trainers the next night. What I didn't know was that I would never get her number.

* * * * * * * *

The next few weeks proved to be some of the most

exciting and frustrating days of my young life. Carmen and I dated two or three times a week. But it was always on her terms. We found we could talk for hours and often did. The conversations spanned a wide universe of topics, but if it ever started getting up close and personal about herself, Carmen would find a way to take the subject in another direction. Alex smiled, recalling, "Even then, she always called the shots on when and where we would meet and destination."

It was so frustrating in so many ways! After six weeks, I still didn't have her phone number or address. I knew very little personal information about her at all. But she filled a major void in my life, and that she was the most beautiful woman I had ever dated certainly didn't hurt matters. In all honesty, I was smitten and falling deeper in love every day.

Many of the night spots we hit had, in the past, been way out of my league and out of my price range. On the other hand, your mom was well known in all these places, and usually, a bill never appeared. If it did, before I could reach for my wallet, her platinum, American Express Card was already lying on the table. I was on scholarships and student loans – these outings would have broken my meager savings.

We would go for long walks on South Beach and Key Biscayne. We would often stroll hand in hand or with our arms wrapped around each other's waist. We would kiss and embrace under the moonlight, with the waves gently breaking at our feet. As we embraced my resolve to stay chaste before marriage was being pushed to the limit. But if my hands attempted to stray below her neck or back, she would gently but firmly push me away.

Though I had abandoned many tenets of our faith, I

still felt very strongly against pre-marital sex, at least when we weren't in one of those embraces. Honestly, she was so exciting that, at times, I really questioned even this value. AJ looked down as his dad was explaining what every teen knew but couldn't imagine – his mom and dad having sex. The young man blushed as his dad continued the story and admitted, "Yes, I wanted to make love to this woman more than anyone I had ever known, but secretly, I was glad at least one of us had the control to stop."

"Sorry, son," Alex said with a smile while interrupting the narrative – I know every generation thinks they are the first ones to discover sexual attraction – but you and your siblings and all of us are proof that isn't true."

Regarding sex, your mom told me, clearly, "Only with my husband, and then not until I'm married." When I pushed for a reason she smiled and said with a half grin, "I promised my pa pa." It was the closest thing to a window to her soul that she ever allowed to open.

It was times like this that both father and son were grateful they had always been able to have open and honest conversations.

During his dad's narrative, AJ said practically nothing. Indeed, he was sitting in stunned silence as his dad opened up on the beginnings of a relationship until less than an hour earlier, he had no clue even how his parents at first met – and now, he was totally blown away as his dad continued.

Our relationship continued this way for several months. She was a beautiful, mysterious woman, and I was a handsome law student. Your mom always kept her cards very close to her chest. Every so often, a window would open; I would peek inside, and then she would close it again.

During Christmas break, under a full moon, sitting on the beach on Key Biscayne, I told her for the first time that I loved her. She was lying on the sand with her head in my lap. She looked up into my eyes and said, "I love you, Alex - but you don't know me - you can't love me."

"Damnit," I replied, "it's not fair."

"Life's not fair Alex. We found each other and we are together, well maybe someday..."

I implored her, "Let me know you. I want to know the woman I've fallen in love with!"

"Alex, you don't understand. I can't tell you. Not yet, but the time will come. Until then, let's enjoy what we have...

She reached up and kissed me. My hands wandered through her thick long hair and past her neck. She was wearing a backless dress when I gently touched her bare skin. Let's just say at that moment, I am grateful that your mom's resolve to do what was right was so much stronger than mine. Quickly, she sat up, took me by the hand, and we walked back towards her car. Let's just say it was a wonderful, and totally confusing time in my young life.

Your mom was on everybody's party list in keeping with her public lifestyle. Between Thanksgiving and the Super Bowl, we went to a party almost every night. She always picked me up and turned her keys over to me. I always drove until it was late into the evening and then by midnight, she always dropped me off at my student apartment. While I joked about her being my "Cinderella" I was grateful because it was the only chance I got to study. At the parties, recreational drugs were always present, but she never showed an interest, and her friends never pushed.

Once, when I was complaining about needing to stay awake to cram for a final, she said, "I can get you something for that - but in the long run, you'll be better off to stick with the espresso."

Alex got up walked around and put his hand on AJ's shoulder, and said, "I hope this isn't either disappointing you – or boring you to tears; you seem awfully quiet."

"Dad," he quickly answered, "it's the most amazing story I HAVE EVER HEARD; Mom and the twins aren't home yet – PLEASE go on!"

"OK, I guess here is where it will get even more interesting."

AJ simply shook his head in disbelief and asked, "EVEN more interesting?"

CHAPTER TWO

So, picking up where he left off, Alex continued his narrative.

The holidays were a blur; Thanksgiving was spent serving food at a homeless shelter in downtown Miami, just past Little Havana. It was her idea, but it reminded me just how much of a gulf there was between the middle class, the rich, and the very poor in South Florida. I made a short obligatory trip over Christmas to Alabama – though I would have much rather spent it with your Mom in Miami. As was expected, she was very vague about her Christmas plans – but we spoke several times by phone when I could track her down. Remember, these were pre-cell phone days.

After the New Year as January rolled into February, your mom told me she would be busy a lot during the coming month, but she'd "call me." She offered no details and when pressed for specifics she would only say, "Alex, its business - trust me."

For almost two weeks my phone didn't ring. Finally, one Friday afternoon I got a call at work, it was your mom.

"Come over to the beach at 5:45 and meet me at the Convention Center."

I thought for a minute and asked, "Isn't there a boat show in town this week."

"Yes, it's here. But don't worry. Come to the registration in the "B" lobby - look for me."

After several months of these types of adventures, this seemed almost normal. So, at exactly 5:45, I walked into the lobby and, to my surprise, saw your mom sitting behind a registration counter. She offered only the slightest smile of recognition. I glanced at her ID badge - it read Michelle Lewis.

I started to speak when I was greeted by a bubbly short Jewish lady who was explaining the show was almost over for the day, but I could get my badge, go in for a few minutes and come back tomorrow.

Your Mom spoke up and said, "I have his badge right here, Mrs. Curtis."

"Thank you, Michelle, you're such a dear," replied Mrs. Curtis.

Your Mom mouthed, "I'll meet you inside," as Mrs. Curtis

wasn't looking. Confused, but by now, at least accepting I would always be confused around her, I took the badge and walked in the door.

The show was overwhelming in size. At lunch, I read about it in a special section of the Miami Herald. The article explained that the main convention center building alone was over 500,000 square feet of display space, and there were another 1.5 million square feet of boats and accessories spread throughout the City of Miami Beach in various marinas and land displays.

Seeing boats up to 90 feet long inside a building was an awesome spectacle. I had heard this was the largest boat show in the world. It was held every year, but as a struggling grad student, it never crossed my mind to attend.

What was even more confusing to me was what was your mom doing here? Certainly, she didn't support her lifestyle working as a registration girl at trade shows. Thinking back, several times there were several times when we met on the beach, after six in the evening.

As these thoughts ran through my head, suddenly, your mom walked up beside me. As I started to blurt out a dozen questions, she put her finger to her lips and said, "Shhh - not now. Follow me and don't ask any questions."

Quickly we walked to a pod in the center of the building. There an escalator led up to a glassed-in crossover which connected the meeting rooms on the upper floors of the building.

Instead of taking the escalator, she quickly opened a

service door in the pod and motioned for me to follow her. We were immediately confronted with a set of steep cement stairs. This area was clearly the "back of the house." No paint, a lot of cobwebs, and a year-old folded newspaper.

"What are we doing, Carmen, or Michelle or whoever?" I asked with almost a demanding tone.

"Relax, these steps go up to a service corridor connecting the second floors. The public crossover is on the third floor."

"Alright, I repeat, what and why are we doing this?"

"Look, you wanted to know everything," she replied, "I had to get to know you. I had to know if I could trust you."

"I'll try again. We've done a lot of things - but never against the law. Now what are we doing?"

"Shhh - this isn't against the law. Well, not really. Come up the stairs. There's a storage room and I'll show you the big picture."

We made our way up the dimly lit stairs into another barren hallway with me muttering under my breath on every step. The area must have connected directly to the cooling system as it was as cold as a meat locker, and the air conditioning was blowing hard enough to lift your mom's hair. Turning down another side corridor, we came to a door. Reaching into her pocket, she pulled out a key and opened the door.

I shook my head in disbelief. Then she felt along the

wall for the light switch. She reached into another pocket and pulled out the special tool, which allowed her to turn on the lights. The bare fluorescent bulbs lit the room in pale white.

"All right, Alex," she began, "you've wanted to know about me for months. It wasn't supposed to be this way. I've got a cause that I'm dedicated to; I'm not supposed to fall in love. But I did. As I said, I had to know everything about you before I could determine if I could trust you. Alex, I'm into some heavy stuff - if you want to walk, now's your chance. You don't know where I live or anything about me."

"Is it drugs?"

"No."

"Is it illegal."

"To which government?"

"Carmen," I almost demanded, "is that your real name?"

"Yes."

I told her, "Carmen, I don't want to play twenty questions. I told you at Christmas, and I meant that I'm in love with you. Let me ask this - is your life in danger?"

"I'll give it to you in a nutshell with no specifics. Then if you want to stay, I'll give you all the details. But if I do, there's no turning back for either one of us. Deal?"

"Deal."

"My name really is Carmen Rojas. My parents had me smuggled out of Cuba when I was six months old. They stayed behind. A very rich Aunt and Uncle raised me. I've seen my natural parents three times in my entire life. But their quest has become mine since I was twelve years old. Alex, I want you to want me, but I'm afraid you'll run when I give you the details."

"Go on," I said without hesitation.

"Still in a nutshell. It involves Castro; it involves rogue elements of the CIA; it involves Alpha 66; it involves certain NY 'families'; and it involves the Kennedy assassinations. With piercing black eyes, she stared at me and said, "What will happen here tonight might change the face of our country and planet. If you stay, I can promise you that life as you know it will never be the same.'"

My mind raced back to high school. I had been the class valedictorian. I spoke of change and courage of conviction. I served for two years as an unpaid missionary for our Church in regions where no one has ever heard of our faith. There I stood up for my beliefs even though no one seemed to care. On to college, as the President of Student Government, I spoke of doing the right thing, at the right time, for the right reason.

But it was mostly words. I went to law school, to get my degree and practice International Law. Along the way, I planned on getting comfortably wealthy and having a magnificent home in a restricted upper-class suburb. Changing the world, literally, had not been in my plans.

But then, neither had your mom. I had always felt I would someday return to the fold, get my life in order, marry a "nice" girl, and have 4.2 kids with a minivan and a dog. She had shown me a side of myself I never knew existed. A side filled with passion and intrigue. The fact we hadn't made love just consumed me with even a greater desire for this mysterious woman. But change the world?

"So, Alex," her voice brought me back to the reality of the moment, "are you with me, or is this goodbye?"

I answered with the strongest words of conviction that I could muster – it sounds sappy now, but I said, "You're the most exciting woman I have ever known, but more important than that, is for the first time in my life I love someone more than I do my own goals and ambitions. Tell me where we're going 'cause I'm going there with you."

"Alex, my father is one of Castro's closest lieutenants. He was with him from the early days of the revolution. During one fierce battle my father was hit and seriously hurt. He was only 17 at the time. The others said, 'leave the kid.' But Fidel went back for him and saved his life."

"So, your dad's loyal..."

She went on, "In Latin culture, it is a sacred relationship with someone who has risked his own life to save yours. But after the Bay of Pigs, my Father began watching all that was going down in the Cuban government. He realized the 'revolution' was only a dream and that Castro himself had become worse than what they fought to overthrow."

"Why didn't he leave?"

"He couldn't betray the relationship. Without Castro, he

knew he would have been a dead man. So, he worked to try and make things better from within - but things just kept getting worse and worse."

My head was spinning, and I interrupted, "But I still don't understand. What is the cause? Why are we at a boat show, and how are we going to change the world by being here?"

Your Mom gave me that smile as she continued her story; "I've been waiting for this night for three years. During that period, I have worked for the lady you met tonight in registration at many shows; I've worked for the company running the concessions; and I even got my security guard license and worked overnight security in this building."

"But why?"

"Access." Reaching in her pocket, she pulled out badges and ID showing she was a boat show staff member, a Service America concession worker, and an Andy Frain security guard. "I've tried to space out the times I work here where no one will get suspicious. The show closes tonight at 6:00 - by 8:00, this place will be empty except for the overnight security guards. We can get past them with proper staff ID because this show brings new staff members in every year but doesn't give a roster of them to their security force."

"I'm still confused," I responded, "why do we want to do this?"

"This is one of the largest international gatherings held yearly in North America. People can get in and out of the country and not look out of place. Last summer my father smuggled some documents out of the country. He sent them with a Canadian tourist to Toronto. From there, they went to a boat-building plant not far away in Don Mills, Ontario. One of our operatives then hid them on a boat that was being built for display at this show. My job tonight is to retrieve those papers."

"What are the papers?" asked Alex.

"The Castro diaries. Written in Fidel's own hand. He is a proud man who relishes in his accomplishments, especially when it comes to defeating the United States."

"Excuse me, he beat us in the Bay of Pigs when we wouldn't provide air cover to a bunch of his ex-revolutionaries. I don't call that much of a defeat..."

"No, Alex," interrupted Carmen, "the diaries explain how rogue elements of your own CIA wanted John Kennedy dead because of the Bay of Pigs. Organized crime wanted him dead because of the crippling of their machine by his brother Robert Kennedy. Certain "agents" met with Castro in Havana and planned the assassinations of both John and later Robert Kennedy. My father was at those meetings. The assassins were trained on the Island.

Hoover knew some things and suspected a lot more, but in that era the CIA and the FBI didn't work well together. It is often whispered they kept Hoover and the FBI in check by threatening to expose Hoover's gay lover. The new chief of the FBI knows the diaries exist and is willing to let them be thoroughly vetted and at some later day even be made public.

The CIA, even though they have long since cleaned up their act, cannot afford for the documents to be made public because the outcry would be so strong the President will probably be forced to dissolve the agency.

Meanwhile, Castro didn't want the documents published when his government was teetering on the verge of collapse because he felt the President would have justification for an armed invasion. He knows he could not repel such an attack with the Russian army gone. Furthermore, he knows that the US would want to arrest him and try him for his involvement in the Kennedy murders.

Finally, the New York families don't want the papers revealed because they give the names of the young Mafia lieutenants who helped in the assassinations. There is also some evidence that Castro is involved with drug trafficking. Those men are now the bosses of three of New York's most powerful families."

"Please tell me there's a plan. Tell me this isn't a suicide mission," I pleaded.

"When I was younger," your mom said, "I would have thought about a suicide mission. No, there's a plan; the question is, can we pull it off?"

"So, what's the plan?"

Your Mom never missed a beat as she continued, "We shouldn't have any problems getting to the boat. I saw it during the move-in and know where the papers are hidden. The problem is Castro's agents, the CIA bad guys, and certain young men with Italian surnames have been tripping over themselves to follow me around for the past ten days."

"My uncle has been a major financial supporter of the anti-Castro movement in this country. Castro's men and others think my uncle is my real father. They all assume I'm meeting someone at the show who will give me the papers. It is thought we'll use the diaries to raise more money to overthrow Castro."

"My father alerted Castro the diaries had been stolen when it became obvious that he would be found out. Being the actor he's been over the past 30 years, he convinced Castro of his own innocence."

"Little do they know the papers have been here for a week. The boat they are in is in the Northeast Hall. My car is parked in the North lot, which is a secure staff-only area. I flirted with one of the boat show staff guys from the New York office and convinced him it wasn't safe for a girl to have to park blocks away. He got me a parking pass."

"We get the papers and drive across the Venetian Causeway. The Miami Herald is there, only two miles away. Sitting in the publisher's office, waiting for us, is the new director of the FBI. He has promised to call the President when I deliver proof. Of course, it'll take some time to verify their authenticity. But the moment they are in his hands, we go underground. Witness relocation. Carmen Rojas vanishes from the face of the Earth, as does Alex Barton."

Alex continued the explanation to his son, "Remember, this had been your mom's lifetime quest – and she had worked out the details over almost a year – I was only ten minutes into the plan – "won't they try and stop us when we leave the lot?"

"They might," said Carmen, "that's why we have a few changes to make, plus we'll ditch the Mercedes and take your car."

From out of the bag she was carrying, she pulled two red shirts like the boat show staff wore back then, a white skirt and a pair of white pants in my size. She had read me correctly, snd knew I would be on board and was prepared. "Put these on and turn around," she said, tossing me the shirt and pants.

I did, but before I could reply, she had stripped down to her bra and panties and was redressing in her red and white outfit. Next, she handed me a staff badge with Bob Black's name.

"Who the heck's Bob Black?" I asked.

"He's a nice old, retired guy, he still comes back to work this show. He always carries his badge in the outside pocket of his jacket. I lifted it from him one day when we were chatting."

Pinning her badge, she became Michelle Formisano. "This was the woman," explained Carmen, "who ran registration the first year I began casing the show."

It was now after 8:00 - looking like the rest of the boat show's famed "red shirts," we went back down the stairs to the main floor and over to the Canadian boat builder's display. Your Mom quickly climbed up on the boat and entered the small cuddy cabin to retrieve the package sewn in the master bunk's upholstery.

She excitedly whispered from inside, "I got it!"

As she was climbing down, one of the Miami Boat Show security guards rode over on his bicycle and asked, "You guys are here awfully late tonight. I thought the staff were all getting together down at Penrods'."

As always, quick on her feet, your mom replied, "Yeah,

we're there when I remembered this guy promised me he'd leave me some additional names for registration tomorrow, and Bob was kind enough to bring me back to get them."

"Oh well," said the security guard, "course with a young thing like you, I'd volunteered to bring'em to you if I'd known where they were."

"You're too sweet," she practically cooed. Motioning to me, she said, "Come on, Bob, let's go back and join the others."

"Smooth," I whispered under my breath as we walked away, "you're really smooth."

"Yeah, we're not there yet."

We walked quickly across the hall past the giant Hatteras, Viking, and Bertram Yachts and stepped out of the north end of the building onto the loading dock. Suddenly from out of the shadows stepped a young man and said, "Carmen, you have something that belongs to the people, let me have it."

Looking down at the man's hand, I saw the reflection of the nickel-plated .38 caliber revolver.

"Carmen, don't be a fool," said the assailant.

What happened next was just a blur. Another figure stepped from the shadows with a lead pipe and knocked the first gunman to the ground. Then suddenly, the boat show's security chief was behind him and, in his stern, firm voice, said, "Freeze, mister, or I'll blow your kidneys all over South Beach."

Your mom started crying hysterically and screaming, "Bob, please get me out of here!"

I turned and looked at Gary, the boat show security chief, and said, "I'll take her back to her room if you'll take care of these guys."

"I'll need a statement from her," said Gary.

Again, your mom wailed at the top of her lungs, "please take me out of here!"

"Well, I can get it later after I get the police to book these two," replied Gary.

Things were moving fast - within moments, we were in her car, abandoning the idea of using mine. Alex explained to AJ, "Though I had seen it before, that is when I found out that her dad wasn't the only good actor, as her tears vanished the moment we got in the car. Just as we were headed onto the Venetian causeway off the beach, what appeared to be a large black government car moved to cut us off."

"I spun the Mercedes around gave it the gas, jumped the curb, and headed for the bridge. Crashing through the toll booth with the black car in hot pursuit I realized the drawbridge was being raised to let a lone sailboat cruise thru."

Turning to your mom, I shouted as if I knew what I was doing, "Hang on!"

AJ continued to sit in stunned silence as his dad continued the narrative.

"By now," he said, "I am running on pure adrenalin, so without a moment's thought, I rammed through the olden wooden barricade and hit the bridge as it was being raised like a giant ramp. The sleek 600 SL went airborne over the 10-foot gap and landed on the bridge on the other side. The black government-issued Crown Victoria missed hitting the sailboat as it crashed into the water."

"Needless to say, I am not a trained stunt driver, and this is something you see in car crash movie scenes. I fought to regain control of the car. As I did so, I looked up and saw on the side of the building at the other end of the bridge the bright neon lights spelling out THE MIAMI HERALD & EL NUEVO HERALD.

As we pulled up in front of the building and stopped the car, men in dark suits surrounded us. Their leader opened the door and said, as he flashed his credentials, "FBI, ma'am - the Director is waiting for you upstairs."

Within an hour we had handed over the material and were on a government Gulfstream jet bound for a destination unknown. We were assured the proper action would be taken to bring all involved to justice. When? When the time is right. At that moment, your mom felt reasonably certain the diaries would bring Castro down and to justice. Knowing the publisher of one of the nation's leading newspapers had a copy and would print them if the government did not act promptly helped fuel that assurance, or so we thought. But as a last security blanket, she asked for and got her copy of the Castro Diaries. They are what you saw upstairs in the gap years box."

We were given a preliminary briefing on our new identities and circumstances on the flight. I was thrilled and delighted to hear in our new identities, we were already married. But so your mom could keep her promise to her 'papa' and me to my faith, we exchanged wedding vows at 30,000 feet with the captain (also an ordained minister when not flying) officiating.

So, then we adjourned to the back cabin of the plane, folded down the seats, and honestly, simply fell sound asleep – it had been a long day. The plan was that we would wind up somewhere in the west, not North Carolina, and up as just another married couple with a minivan, a dog, and at least three wonderful kids...

AJ was still too stunned to do anything but sit and stare at his dad trying to process everything he had just heard. Finally, he simply said, "And what about 'the rest of the story/'"

The rest of the story is the life that happened on the way to where we are now...

CHAPTER THREE

As the twins burst through the front door with Carmen with their ten-year-old voices at full volume it signaled that Alex and AJ's private talk was ending. AJ was still stunned at what he had learned about his parents' lives prior to his and the birth of the twins. As he got up to head to his room, he looked at his dad and said, "I am like totally blown away – can we talk later?"

"Sure, son, after dinner. Mom will be glad to fill you in even more..."

AJ swallowed hard, trying to get the image of his mom in the bikini out of his head, and only muttered, "Thanks, Dad."

Alex went to the kitchen and kissed his wife as she opened the pizza boxes she had picked up from Dominos.

Before he could say anything, Carmen started with her recap, "So, I picked the twins up at school, and we were going first to the bank, then their karate class, and on the way, I had to drop off the donations at Goodwill, the traffic was a mess with a wreck at Main and Innes – long story short..."

"Too late," he answered.

She grinned and said, "Anyway, that's why we are having pizza, I didn't want to cook."

"Please tell me there is a meat lovers in addition to your all-veggie pizza..."

"And Hawaiian," she answered, "AJ seems to have a sudden interest in the island since he learned there is a BYU campus on the North Shore of Oahu...'

"I'm glad he's already thinking about college while only a sophomore – but I suspect he had another subject he wants to talk to us about tonight..."

"Not girls! I'm not ready for that..."

"He is turning 16 in a few months, so I promise you girls ARE on his mind."

"I know, but I don't know, I just, I just..."

"MOM!" came the chorus of Jon-Mark and Sam, the two very vocal and hungry 10-year-old twins, "when can we eat?"

"Soon, let me finish talking to Dad..."

As the two disappointed tweens walked out of the

kitchen, Alex continued, "You know how the youth were challenged to work on family history?"

"Yes. . ."

"AJ found the 'gap years' box."

Carmen put the pizza box down and turned slowly to face her husband, "how much did you tell him?"

"I walked him through how we met, that we fell in love, the boat show, and that we went into witness protection. . ."

"How did he take it??"

"Startled; to say the least, I get the impression that he had assumed we were always Mr. and Mrs. Suburbia – or his unspoken expression said 'boring'."

"Is there a period in this conversation?"

"Not really. He is processing, but he has already asked if we can talk more after dinner. . ."

"We have always known this day would come. It may be my fault – I saw the box last week when I was up in the attic looking for the summer decorations. I pulled the box down and took a walk down memory lane. I left the box out without thinking. . ." answered Carmen.

Alex and Carmen both grew very silent. It was as if they had lived four distinct lifetimes: their lives growing up in such different places and lifestyles, the Miami years, the witness protection years, and then their life of the last 17 years as a devout LDS, mini-van (and now SUV) - driving family with three kids living in small-town America.

Like it or not, they knew the time had come to at least bring their firstborn into the inner circle of their lives. Their experiences had shaped them and prepared them for their current life roles. "AJ is very mature for his age—we have. Perhaps it was because he was our firstborn and only child for five years, treating him older than his chronological years," replied Alex, breaking the silence.

"So true," added Carmen, "let's eat, get the twins ready for bed, and then we can share some details with AJ…"

Soon the family was seated on the lanai directly off the family room. The waterfall had turned on, spilling into the pool. It was a beautiful spring day with the sun setting beyond a distant tree line. It was Carmen's favorite time of the day – and the poolside dining was where weather permitting, the family could usually be found every Monday night. It was a family time – a ritual they tried to do at least once a week when calendars and plans for the coming week were shared. Sometimes it would be an adventuresome new food night (time and again, weather permitting) or, on rushed days, pizza with ice cream sandwiches for dessert. Jon-Mark and Samantha didn't have a clue on what was going on in the mind of their older brother, who seemed more quiet and less engaging than normal, but they were too distracted by the thought of ice cream sandwiches to spend any real time worrying about it. They likewise did not notice that their mom and dad also seemed distracted. The evening clean-up with dinner served on paper plates was quick and easy.

As was the family tradition they gathered in the living room for family prayer at 8:30 before the twins headed off to their respective rooms. Also, as normal there was a plea for a few more minutes before bedtime – after all they were ten years old, certainly 8:30 was too early for young people now in their tween years. The plea went to dad first, who turned to Carmen with a questioning look.

"We've had this discussion," she answered, "over the summer, we'll discuss it. Next school year, when you start middle school, maybe pero. es tiempo de orar." [but now it is time for prayer] That ended the debate when either parent, especially Carmen reverted to Spanish – that was a signal it was the end of the conversation. For emphasis, she asked, "A quién le toca rezar?" [Whose turn is it to pray?]

As always, the family knelt for prayer, and Jon-Mark said the family's evening prayer – perhaps stretching it a little longer to push bedtime back even a few minutes. When the twins headed for their rooms, Carmen turned to her oldest son and stated, "I hear you and Dad had quite a talk this afternoon…and you might have a few more questions."

"Actually, Mom, like a few thousand more," he replied.

Carmen smiled as she answered, "Then this conversation will probably take several days…where do you want to start?"

Alex leaned back in his recliner. After the emotional discussion of the afternoon, he was more than willing to let Carmen answer some of the questions. AJ studied his toes for a few minutes, and then a whole rush of thoughts and questions flowed almost nonstop:

"Mom, Dad, honestly, as I was walking home, my mind was wrestling with this confused picture. Up until last night, while I have liked our quiet little life, I really thought you two were perhaps two of the most boring – and strict religious type people of any of my friends! We are like a postcard of the average – and somewhat boring, middle-class family. Don't get me wrong, I like our house, we have nice cars, you guys do good things for the city, the church, us, the kids, everybody. But... I don't know – I have friends whose dads have been deployed overseas;

Brother Wood in our ward once worked with the Secret Service—he's retired now—and personally knew four Presidents; Brett in my class at Church is the grandson of an Apostle. We just seemed like we were mundanely "average."

"Average is bad?" asked Carmen with a twinkle in her smile.

"Dad has always said 'average is where the worst of the best meets the best of the worst,' and that 'average is the cream of the crap...'"

Carmen shot her husband 'the look,' as if to say, "I told you those motivational sayings without context aren't always helpful." Instead, she answered, "So, what are you thinking now?"

"Mom and Dad, I don't know – the box, the pictures, the story is more than I could have ever imagined – I guess I just want to know who my parents really are."

"Fair enough," Carmen answered, "we are God-fearing Christians who, not in spite of, but because of our different life experiences, want to bring up children who love the Lord, do their very best, and become the leaders of tomorrow. Our goal is to lay perhaps a foundation for you that is more solid and different than we were blessed to have had. You have questions and are old enough to know much more than what we have shielded you and the twins from. You ask, we'll answer the best we can."

"I want to know about my grandparents – not just the great and great-great ones in our family search file."

"OK," answered Carmen, "Daddy (calling her husband by her favorite pet name) jump in anytime. . ."

"You're doing great, dear; keep going."

"AJ, I never really knew your grandfather, my beloved papa, until I was in my early teens. His name was Manuel Jesus Rojas; my mother, or ma-ma, was a stranger the first time I met her. Her name was Maria Carmen de la Torre-Rojas. I remember the first time I saw her she was very beautiful but looked so tired."

"Dad said they smuggled you out of Cuba when you were only six months old, HOW?"

"Well, honestly, I don't remember, but the tio and tia who raised me as their own have told the story. [Tio, Uncle – Tia, Aunt] Their names were Mateo y Mirabella Rojas – my tio went by the English Matt for his gringo friends. He was my father's younger brother = he had escaped Cuba as a "Pedro pan" boy. He was very, very bright; he learned English quickly and went to middle and high school in Miami, living with an adopted Cuban family. It was a very common story for the Pedro Pan kids. Then he the University of Florida in Gainesville. From there he went to Harvard and earned a joint JD/MBA degree. Early in his career, he did all the legal work for a little more than minimum wage for a tech company in Silicon Valley. He had agreed to work for next to nothing, but realizing he was essential to the success of their start-up, the two brilliant entrepreneurs offered him a 10% share of the company stock - if he could get them launched with full regulatory approval. Tio Mateo had not met my tia at that time, and he was wondering how he would make enough to pay off a mountain of student loans for grad school. With no other offers on the table, he said yes."

AJ's eyes were growing huge as he asked, "So did it work out?"

Tio moved to San Jose, California, and there, with the high cost of living, he continued to live like a poor grad student for almost two years. But he stayed with those two young boy wonders of the Valley—the company launched a very successful IPO. One year later, his stock was worth 789 million dollars. When he died one year after we came out of witness protection, his estate was valued at 3.7 billion.

"You grew up RICH?!" AJ asked in amazement.

"I grew up very comfortable; my Tio was never flashy with his wealth, but let's say I had the best schools, the best clothes, a nice car from the time I was sixteen, and never worried about money. He was very generous with huge amounts of cash being quietly slipped back into Cuba to care for his family, including my pa-pa and ma-ma. I might also add that even though it was not necessary, I was expected to work and had a part-time job from the time I was 14 years old, and like YOU, I still had to do my own laundry, make my bed, and take out the trash every night. Even though we always had a least one maid – sometimes more. Usually, anytime anyone in the community needed work, they came to Tio. I loved him so.

"Why didn't your mom and dad find a way to leave – Uncle Matt got out, and they got you out; why did they stay?"

Alex added, "If I didn't really explain it this afternoon

– your grandfather couldn't leave. He hated what Castro had become – but he owed his life to him..."

"AJ," Carmen quietly whispered, "my pa-pa was a true hero of the Revolution. While there were a lot of rich people in Cuba, el presidente, a dictator named Batista was a very bad man. He took bribes, he stole from his own people, he didn't care if the peasants starved – and there were far more peasants than rich people. Castro wasn't bad when my pa-pa joined him and the revolution – the power turned Castro evil. My pa-pa would have died to fulfill the dreams of the revolution. Pa-pa was a teenager with a bold hope for a better life for all Cubans – he would have died for that cause, and without Castro saving his life when he was seriously wounded in a battle with Batista's thugs, he would have spilled his last drop of blood for the revolution. Castro broke his heart when he turned bad and then turned to the Russians – but that loyalty to the man who saved his life could never be shaken." By now, Carmen's voice was shaking with emotion, and tears were welling up in her eyes. Alex moved in to comfort his wife and said, "We will discuss this more in the days to come – but right now, you need to get to bed also – your seven o'clock Seminary class comes awful early. Good night."

Still trying to process all he had heard, both earlier and now, he quickly went over and kissed his mom, hugged his dad, and said, "Good night. I love you guys."

"We love you too, Aaaj" chimed in both parents.

Sleep was somewhat elusive for AJ as he tried to keep track of all the new information he had gleaned over the past 24 hours since discovering the "Gap Years" box in the family attack. When he finally fell asleep, his dreams replayed the same event that he dwelled upon while he was awake.

Far too soon his alarm clock sounded at 6:15 reminding him regardless of his parents' exciting past lives – he still had six more weeks of school in his sophomore year, which included a 7:00 AM religion class called Seminary, prior to the start of his regular school day at 8:30. He was grateful the class was held in the Church building barely a quarter mile from the school. Likewise, he was happy that his school day didn't start until 8:30 so the religion class could start at 7:00 AM – not like 6:30 or even 6:00 for some other kids whose schools started much earlier.

When he headed downstairs for a quick grab-and-go breakfast, his mom was waiting, as always, with a warm good morning and a kiss on the top of his head. She looked at him and asked, "Not much sleep—it shows in your eyes?"

"A lot to think about Mom, I, I, I'm, I don't know what I am this morning. You guys are still my amazing parents, but so much has happened to you, which we never had any idea how different your life used to be. . ."

"You didn't need to know until you were old enough to understand how complex the world can really be. We will have this conversation with the twins in a few years – but for now, I need to ask you to keep this part of your parents' lives within the walls of our home. No one, but no one needs to know these details. We will give you more details as the story unfolds, but for now – no one, and I mean no one outside these walls, needs to know."

The firm tone of his mother's voice left no doubt – and knowing what he did now, he knew about his mom, plus knowing "that tone," he replied, "Yes, Ma'am."

His dad walked in and said, "Let's say prayer, and then I'll run you to church—next year, you may get to drive there yourself." Like they did every morning before they left the home, they said a quick prayer and headed for the door. Just before her two "men" left, AJ turned to his mother and asked, "You told me a lot about your Tio—what about his wife, Tia Maribelly?"

All three froze for a moment – and then Carmen replied, "Your Tia was the first mom I ever knew – she loved me as her own daughter. She was a brave woman who had her own story of an escape from Cuba. Unlike my Tio, she preferred to work silently in the background. She was beautiful in her own way, very quiet and very unassuming...and yet, her strength of character was as great as anyone I have ever known. I will tell you more, but NOW off to class and school – go!" Again, her tone meant the conversation was over. Alex smiled as he thought to himself, "All these years and some things have never changed."

The two-mile ride to Church was quiet as AJ and his dad pondered the events of the past 15 hours. AJ was simply overwhelmed, and his dad was reliving some of those life-changing experiences from decades past. "We can talk some more after school if you are ready," Alex offered.

"Sure Dad, will mom be home?"

"I'm sure she will be. The twins are being picked up by another mom for some after-school museum trip – your mom told me last night she was not going on that one."

In the Church parking lot they said a quick goodbye. After a Seminary in which he totally zoned out, AJ and four others walked the short distance to Salisbury High School. His dad was heading to college to do some prep work before his 8:00 American History class on the "Gilded Age."

Both went through the motions of doing all that needed

to be done at school, work, church, or the classroom – and both were still lost in the events of the night before. As was Carmen as she busied herself around the home, making mental lists of the countless tasks that never seemed to get finished for busy American families. She had left the day-to-day workplace when the twins were born 10 years earlier. Her days were now filled with her roles as Wife, Mom, and a community/school volunteer on too many worthwhile (but time-consuming causes).

CHAPTER FOUR

When a high school sophomore is forced to absorb in one setting that his parents, whom he previously had considered good and respectable – but totally boring by comparison to his classmates, had a past filled with intrigue, it completely changes a host of his perspectives. So, it was with young Alex Barton, Junior. That day at school he had been distracted – he found himself going through the motions but far from his normal outgoing self. Judy, a freshman who shared his afternoon art class (who had a secret crush on him), finally quietly asked as he stared off into space instead of focusing on the pencil sketch in front of him, "AJ, what gives?"

No response. She repeated, "AJ, is anyone home?"

He looked up and said, "I'm sorry, what did you say?"

"I asked, what gives – you've been staring at the same blank sheet of paper for ten minutes," she whispered.

"Heavy stuff at home. I guess it's on my mind?"

"Is anything wrong? You, OK? Your parents? My parents have discussions and then get really quiet a lot of the time. I don't think they're like getting a divorce, just adult weird stuff..."

AJ immediately shook his head, "No, no, my parents are great, just, it's just stuff."

The art teacher, Mrs. Johanson, a serious artist in her own right who got along well with her students but expected them to always be working on the class assignment, cleared her throat and looked in the direction of their table. "Alex, Judy, it's independent time—did you need something?"

"No, ma'am, I was just asking Judy about shading..."

"I'm glad when students can work together, but it's independent time; save the collaboration for after class."

"Yes, ma'am," they both silently replied. AJ liked Mrs. Johanson; she was thirty-something, a tall blonde with a sense of style. Her wardrobe practically shouted, "I love art." Her own artwork was amazing and her passion for the subject was seldom seen, at least in his two years of high school, with most teachers. After the revelations of his own parents' past lives he now wondered about every adult he knew – how many more of them had a side they never showed to anyone?

When the bell rang and they left the classroom, Judy

ADVENTURES AT THE BOAT SHOW

asked again, "You're sure you are, OK? You have my cell number if you ever want to talk. . ." Hint, hint she thought to herself, how can boys be so smart and so dense at the same time?"

"OK, maybe later," was his half-hearted reply. Judy was a nice girl, very bright for a freshman; she was cute with shoulder-length strawberry blonde hair, she didn't go to his Church, but it had a least once crossed his mind to ask her what church she went to – she was a year older than most freshmen, he hadn't found out why. . .but all these jumbled thoughts got pushed to the back of his mind as he thought about what else he would find out about his parents when he got home.

Mercifully, art was the last class of the day. His school was only a 15-minute walk from his home, and so still in somewhat of a fog, he left most of his books in his locker and headed for the exit. To his surprise, Judy was walking out at the same time.

"Hi, again. My mom texted me—she can't pick me up; I've got to walk. What about you?"

Leaving his thoughts behind, he answered, "I always walk – where do you live?"

"Elm and 7th across from the little league fields."

"Really, that's just about 10 minutes past my house, and I'll walk with you."

Little did AJ realize that Judy had hoped for that text from her mom. There was something different about AJ—she had watched him from her first day at Salisbury High School. She knew his dad was a professor at Catawba and that he had twin siblings a few years younger than him. What she didn't know was why, of all the young men in her school, she felt so drawn to him.

Judy was adopted, her father was a lawyer, and her mom was a nurse at Rowan Memorial – the local hospital. She had never known her biological parents, all she knew was she thought she was originally born in Germany. where something had happened to her parents, and she was sent to an orphanage until she was three years old. When a professional couple from America adopted her and brought her to the United States, she knew very little English. She had started kindergarten at six and was always a year behind the other students. She picked up English quickly, and her adopted dad spoke German, so she became fluent in both languages.

AJ had never known her story but got a good snapshot in the fifteen-minute walk to his home. In a way, it was a welcome diversion to meet someone his own age, who had "a story" about parents she had never known. He couldn't tell her that right now; he was feeling the same way about his own parents. They were still the same people who had loved and raised him for fifteen years, but their revelations of their "past" made him wonder, did he really know them?

The teens became so engaged in their conversation that they walked past AJ's home without slowing down. Carmen glanced from the window, did a double take, saw her son with a girl, took a deep breath, and remembered Alex had reminded her he was going on 16—yes, girls would be on his mind. She could not know how intertwined her life was and would become with the young woman she just saw.

As they approached Judy's house, AJ realized that he had simply walked past his own home without even noticing where he was. He blushed and said, "I'm glad we walked together, but I passed my house about 10 minutes ago... she looked down, smiled, giggled, and replied, "Next time I'll remind you – or maybe I won't." She hugged him quickly and left him standing on the sidewalk as she went into her house.

For a moment, AJ's mind flashed back to his dad's description of how his first meeting with Carmen left him totally bewildered – his 15-year-old mind now had an idea of how a chance meeting with a girl could leave a guy completely confused. He also realized he needed to get home, and at that moment, his phone buzzed. It was his mom.

"AJ, you, OK? You walked right by the house...with a girl."

"Just a friend from school, we were talking and I just kept walking."

"I see – are you coming home now?"

"Yes ma'am. Be there in just a few minutes."

As he jogged back to his own home, he realized that he really hadn't thought much about his parents while he was walking with Judy. He had never really had a girlfriend – just friends, both boys and girls, many of whom he had grown up with in Church. But as he turned on to his block the questions from the night before flooded back into his mind. Alex was pulling into the driveway as he arrived. His dad called out, "Home a little late?"

"I was walking a friend home and lost track of time..."

Smiling as he answered, his dad replied, "I know – your

mother called me."

AJ blushed and laughed it off, "Just a friend, a new girl in our school; she's only a freshman but the same age as I am – I never knew she lived so close."

"Hmmm," was the only reply from his dad.

The door opened and Carmen ushered them in, kissing AJ on the head and her husband quickly on his cheek. "I have cookies and milk; I suspect AJ has some more questions."

Did he ever – but first, he wondered if he was going to get grilled on "who was that girl?"

It was the question Carmen wanted to ask, but her husband had already warned her, "They were just walking. Let him tell us when he's ready—IF there is anything to tell." She would follow his advice but was bursting out to know about the first girl she had ever seen with her first-born son. Carmen brought out the cookies, and they made their way to the covered lanai just off the family room.

Seeing his parents together, AJ's mind was again flooded with questions. If he thought the night before had been the surprise of his young life, what he was about to hear stunned him even more. He began, "I get it – neither of you had the stable, happy childhood that you've given me and the twins. And I just want/need, I guess, to figure out what happened after you turned over the diaries back so many years ago in Miami – when was that?"

Alex was a historian—he knew the day and even the day of the week—but he paused, "Well, a rough timeline looks like this—it was mid 1990s...we went into witness protection for

12 years and a few months; we made the decision to leave the program a year before you were born; and here we are now coming out of a pandemic in 2022."

"Were you scared?"

"We were in what was called close protection during that time. The world changed a lot, but it was still a big step – we could have stayed in the program – well, forever. We were in our 30s by that time and knew if we wanted to have a family and not be like Abraham and Sarah, we needed to start almost immediately. I was 37 when you were born."

"And I was 35," piped in Carmen.

"Wow, then you guys were past 40 when the twins were born…" said AJ almost in awe.

"We planned on keeping our kids closer together in age – but it didn't work out that way," answered Carmen.

"None the less," replied Alex, "we are truly blessed with three wonderful, healthy children."

"Tell me about Witness Protection, I've heard the term on cop shows – and that's all I know."

Carmen looked to her husband, "I had been briefed and had only an idea they could get me out of Miami. Then I met your dad – and life got complicated. He told you about how he found out at the Boat Show on Friday night. I had taken a real leap of faith and told my handlers at the FBI that IF I got the diaries, there might be two of us. I so wanted your dad to be by my side – I never wanted to lose him, but I knew or was afraid that he would run as fast as he could when I told him my story..." her voice faded.

"AJ," his dad continued, "as I told you last night – I had fallen totally in love with your mom and at that moment was at the song say, 'I was willing to walk into hell for a heavenly cause.' She was my heavenly cause – when she said that at a moment's notice, I was leaving my school, my job, my very identity, and becoming a different person, I was stunned. But my gut said you have met the love of your life – she is your destiny, and you are hers."

All three nibbled on their chocolate chip cookies before AJ broke the silence, "Last night, Dad gave me a fast and furious version, but to hear both of you sit here and calmly discuss such an amazing decision is almost too much to get my head around.

"AJ," his dad replied, "it is why we teach you to live life in such a way as to always be prepared to make the right choice on a moment's notice."

"Dad, mom, jump ahead – you have a chase scene out of a Hollywood movie, you deliver the diaries to the HEAD OF THE FBI and then get spirited off in a private jet heading where, how, what, I don't even know what to ask."

"Well, sit back, son," began Alex, "this may take a while..."

"Dear, how much are you going to share," asked Carmen.

"He knows the story – let's give him the details."

"OK, you're the historian – share some of our history

with him. . ."

"Aaaj, as a third-year law student, I had studied some cases where what the government likes to call people "material witnesses" who would be in danger of being killed before their testimony could be heard – and well, forever once their testimonies became public."

"Did you and mom ever have to testify?"

"We weren't worried about facing the bad guys in a court of law. The Castro Diaries were the implicating instrument – not us; the authorities were worried that so many people might be caught in the net that some of them would seek revenge for our role – really your mom's efforts in bringing them into the picture."

"Wow."

"Your mom had already been briefed that she was eligible for witness protection; when she made the commitment to deliver the diaries, she broke the news to her handlers about a young law student who was helping her – and if she were to pull it off, he would need to be part of the protection. I didn't know this, so she was planning my future – and by extension, yours. She had read me correctly, and my love for her was great enough to go through with the plan once she told me about that fateful night at the Boat Show. . ."

"Did you ever even think about something like this when you guys were dating?" Asked AJ.

"No," replied his dad, "if you remember my first question was 'is it drugs?'"

"Why ask that? Mom had told you not to do drugs," AJ looked puzzled as he responded.

"Because Aaaj," Carmen interrupted, "the smart money drug people don't use the stuff. In the circle, I had to travel in Miami, drugs, especially cocaine in that era, was everywhere!"

"She's not kidding, son; it wasn't sold in vending machines, but back then, it was so easy to get if you knew the right people, it might as well have been – it would have added a whole new meaning to "Coke machine," Alex said with a laugh.

"But drugs are still everywhere – I knew kids who were doing meth when I was in middle school here in this sleepy little town."

"Yes," continued his dad, "but Miami in that crazy era was something else. There was once a case that I was assigned to watch in court in downtown Miami. A man was charged with possession of cocaine. The state's attorney had a lot of circumstantial evidence but no cocaine. His strongest piece of physical evidence was a $20 bill. Back then, son, the 20, rolled into a tight mini funnel and became the snorting device for a line of cocaine."

"Dear!" Carmen said with an alarmed tone.

"He's not going to do drugs, and the kids today wouldn't know what to do with a $20 dollar bill since they all have debit cards."

AJ stiffled a laugh as his mother shook her head and said, "Go on dear."

The attorney for the state presented the 20-dollar bill, with lab findings as evidence. The defense attorney then asked "for the state's indulgence and asked the judge, the court reporter, the bailiff, and the jury how many happened to have a 20-dollar bill on them…between the judge, the officers of the court and member of the jury he collected 13 twenty dollar bills and then asked for a recess to have the money, turned over to the bailiff for safe keeping, to be tested for drug residue. The state's attorney protested, but the judge allowed it and called for a one-hour recess."

"When the court resumed, the defense attorney presented the findings from the Metro-Dade police lab: 11 of the 13 bills had drug residue. It was determined that there was so much cocaine being sniffed up the nose in greater Miami that almost all 20-dollar bills in circulation would have cocaine residue. The man, who was a drug user and small-time dealer walked."

That his parents had been this close to real, hard street drugs was surprising enough, but then the rest of the story started to unfold...

"So that was why my first question was about drugs?"

"But then you asked was it illegal," AJ added, "what else were you worried she might be involved in?"

Carmen was just shaking her head, remembering those crazy days. "Probably," she added, "since I looked wealthy and he didn't know the source of my money and didn't know the wealth of my Tio, his next guess would be. " She paused for her husband to pick up the story.

"Money laundering," Alex added, "and not washing cash in a machine. Even if you were not directly involved with drugs, other 'dirty money' was often funneled through Miami banks to various Caribbean Island nations where the banking laws allowed for a lot of privacy."

"Once she assured me it wasn't that kind of illegal, and gave me the snapshot, I just knew, if this was her cause, she was clean, and at that moment, I was ready to follow her to the ends of the earth – I just didn't know the details of what witness protection was really all about. . ."

"He's right, Aaaj. We were hustled out of the back of the Miami Herald building and down a loading dock to a waiting black government-looking car, with a Miami-Dade police car waiting to lead us to the airport. I never saw my Mercedes again. The police escort took us not to the Miami International Airport but to a general aviation terminal in Opa Locka."

"Opa what?" queried AJ

Alex smiled, "Opa Locka is a city just north of Miami in the same county. It's a very Hispanic part of town. They have an airport, and it's a great place for private jets."

"Remember son," Carmen resumed the story, "we were leaving with the clothes on our back. I had my ID and passport – that I would no longer need – in my purse; your dad had his wallet. Going into hiding involves a lot of trust that the government will really be there for you. The car took us to the tarmac, bypassing all security checkpoints. My handler was on the plane, along with an agent from the U.S. Marshall's office, which handles the protection of all what we were now considered, 'high-valued government assets.'"

At this point, AJ was slack-jawed, as the full magnitude of his parents' 'other life' was sinking in; the day before, it was almost a romanticized story. Now, as the story unfolded, he was even more stunned—but not as much as he would be as more and more details were revealed.

Carmen and Alex paused and looked at their son. AJ was soaking in every word, and since he didn't know what to ask next, there was a period of silence. Carmen broke the silence by passing around the plate of cookies and saying, "Let us fill you in on what happened in route to what would be our home for the next two months. Go ahead, dear; your memory has always been better than mine..."

"I will, but I think you are downplaying your own abilities here," he said with a smile. "Mom's handler was a man whose name was easy for me to remember, well at least the name we knew him as Jeff Davis. The U.S. Marshall was a woman in her mid-30's. Intense, very bright. She, like your mom, was a Cuban American – but she was an ABC..."

"America Born Cuban, I was smuggled in as a baby, Nicole, we called her Nikki, was born of parents who had come over right after Castro took over in 1959..."

"Jeff explained he would be our FBI contact until a field agent was assigned in whatever part of the country we would end up, but that Nicole would be our U.S. Marshall handler until we were firmly placed in a 'safe location.' He then explained we were heading for Colorado Springs, Colorado – home of the United States Air Force Academy and, though lesser known, HQ for witness protection orientation and placement for North America. Even as a law student, I never really thought about all the logistics of being in witness protection – nor did I even know how many 'high-value assets' the agents of the U.S. Marshall's office were assigned to watch over and protect. At any given time, the number, though the exact number is a closely guarded secret, is between 18 and 20 thousand people spread primarily across the United States – but quite a few in other countries as well."

'I can't even imagine," AJ offered in disbelief.

"Honestly, son, up until that moment, I would never have guessed how big the program is or the world we were getting ready to enter."

Carmen took over the narrative, "Nikki then explained what the next six weeks would look like for us. The WPPC, or 'Witness Protection Processing Center,' was located just outside the Airforce Academy proper, but still on secure protected land. It was a large complex with a four-story office building, a first-class medical facility, a commissary, and 35 residential units. They varied in size from one-bedroom apartments to four-bedroom units."

"Why anything so big?" AJ wondered out loud.

"Because" as Alex interjected, "witness protection sometimes involves whole families, not just soon-to-be-married young couples."

"But good question," added Carmen, "we were told that we would be given new names, a new history, new documentations, appearance changes – some people even had plastic surgery to alter their looks; new wardrobes; coaching on what would be the best places to begin our new lives and 'career opportunity choices...'"

"And yes son," added his dad, "the part about us being

already married was already in the script – yes, I suspect your mom had that part planned."

"I plead the 5th,"

"Anyway, yes, after the initial briefing, we had a small private ceremony at 29,000 feet. The pilot was a licensed minister of some Church in Colorado; the marriage license was issued for El Paso County Colorado – in our 'new names.'"

"You didn't keep Alex and Carmen?" AJ asked almost in disbelief.

"No," Alex answered, "for the next 12 years or so, we were, Aaron and Cathy Baker. It is also true that Gulfstream has a small cabin with a bed in the back of the airplane. We were then legally husband and wife – your mother's promise to her pa-pa had been kept. By that time, when we did go into the private part of the cabin, we simply collapsed and fell asleep for the balance of the flight. . .About four hours later Nikki gently knocked on the door and announced.

"Mr. and Mrs. Baker, let's go see your new temporary home..."

We sheepishly emerged from the back of the plane and then made our way down the plane's steps onto the tarmac at the Academy's airport, Davis Field. It was February, and for two Floridians, it was stunning and very cold...

As that part of the story concluded, the front door burst open, and the twins, with their usual enthusiasm, let the entire family know – they were home!

Carmen stood up and said, "I think we all need to eat. We can talk more after dinner."

****

Anticipating the discussions that she and Alex would have with their son, Carmen had one of her favorite "one-dish" casserole meals timed to cook in the oven, and she heard the timer signal just as the twins were arriving home. As was to be expected, Sam and Jon-Mark were bubbling with enthusiasm over their visit to the new "hands-on" interactive displays at the Discover Place Children's Science Museum in Charlotte. However, Jon-Mark was disappointed that the "hands-on" part didn't include touching the dinosaur bones. Alex and Carmen acknowledged that while they enjoyed the "small town life" of Salisbury, it was nice to have a major city with so many diverse activities less than an hour to the South of them, straight down Interstate 85.

Like so many moms, she was able to juggle and compartmentalize the serious discussion she was having with her older son while listening intensively as the younger ones related their field trip. After dinner was served and everyone helped with cleaning up, with the dishwasher running she shooed the little ones to the family room to spend some time with their homework before bed and bath. Then switching gears again, she joined her husband and oldest child in Alex's study.

Sensing the anticipation in AJ's demeanor, she asked, "Where did we leave off?"

AJ smiled and replied, "Mr. and Mrs. Baker arriving in the cold in Colorado..."

"It was very cold. We left Miami around 11:00 pm on that fateful night," she began.

Alex continued, "There is a two-hour time difference, and so with the travel time, it was somewhere between 3:00 and 4:00 in the morning local time. And, it was very cold, somewhere like 19 degrees..."

"They had coats for us on the plane," explained Carmen, "but we were still wearing the boat show staff clothes that we changed into back at the convention center – it had been 78 degrees that day on Miami Beach.

"Mercifully, they quickly took us to what would be our 'home' for the next six weeks," explained Alex. "It was a very nice one-bedroom apartment, fully furnished with some necessities, including what Nikki referred to as a starter wardrobe: Jeans and sweatshirts, underwear, pjs, shoes and socks, sweaters, some serious winter coats, and basic toiletries. The witness protection people do their jobs very well. Everything fit perfectly. There was cereal, bread, milk, soft drinks, lunch meat and some brown 'n serve meals in the fridge. As a college student, it was better equipped than my student apartment..."

"And, as a somewhat pampered child from a very nice home in the Gables, I was just happy that your dad and I were now "newlyweds," that we were safe, and the mission that I had trained for years was completed. Jeff reached Tio and Tia on their private line and while he couldn't tell them where we were, he sent my love and assured them we were safe. It would be over a year before it would be safe for me to talk to them – they knew this and were so relieved as well as proud that the mission was over. That morning when I left for the

Convention Center, we had an emotional farewell. They knew that if all went as it had, they would not hear from me for a long time. They were safe because their home was basically in a totally secure compound in a very private, owner-only access community, in Coral Gables. I never knew how much I would miss them until the morning I woke up in bed with my husband – and realized it might be years or never before I saw them again."

"Wow. I can't imagine just leaving my family, you, dad, the twins, friends and…" AJ's voice trailed away.

"Your mother made the choice to bring to light a story that had been whispered, but never with any proof. It had taken years to plan. Your grandfather and grandmother knew they were asking their only child to undertake a task that could cost them and her their lives."

AJ sat in stunned silence as his mother and father's story unfolded, and then asked, "What was next? This had to be like moving to another world."

"Well, our world had certainly and immediately changed. The law school dean was visited the next day and told by federal agents that Alex Barton was 'withdrawing from school,' and all of his grades and records were to be sealed."

Carmen picked up the story, "Nikki, our handler, called the Boat Show office and relayed to Mrs. Curtis a wild story that she was my cousin from Cuba and I had eloped with 'some boy,' and no one knew where she was headed, but to please call her number if she heard from me – she then gave a number to the switchboard in the U.S. Marshall's South Miami office. It was a generic number that was given to intercept anyone who might be looking for me."

"Fortunately for us," Alex continued, "Saturday is the busiest day of the show – Gary, the security chief for the Boat Show, had the local Miami Beach PD take the two thugs into custody; Gary had too many other things to worry about than ever finishing the report he had planned to write later. The Marshall's office picked them up that night at the jail, and they also "disappeared." The two CIA types that went into the drink after the drawbridge stunt got out alive – but were apprehended by FBI agents with warrants for their arrest. The new CIA head knew he had rogue agents somewhere and cooperated with the FBI to make sure they were secure.' We never heard, we never asked."

"Nikki called us the next day around noon. We had just woken up and stared at our new life. She said she wanted to drop by and take us out for a late brunch. I guess neither one of us realized we had been running on pure adrenaline, and other than snacks on the plane – we hadn't eaten in almost 24 hours. She was, at that time, our link to the outside world," explained Alex.

"In addition to brunch, she took us to a mall in Colorado Springs and basically outfitted us with a new winter wardrobe. I think we were at Macy's, but that day was somewhat of a blur..."

Carmen continued, "So that's how your parents' honeymoon began. New names, new surroundings, and without any idea of what was going to happen next. It's been almost 30 years since that new beginning, but I will never forget those first few weeks..."

"WHAT DID HAPPEN?" asked AJ still with a tone of unbelief.

Alex summarized the following six weeks, "First there were extensive debriefings and interviews with the FBI, the CIA, and the U.S. Marshalls. Carmen related the backstory of how she became involved with the whole plot to reveal the diaries from her first meeting with her parents in Cuba as a young teen. The majority of the information they wanted came from your mom. You could tell they were almost amused that I had been a unknowingly part of the plan for several months; and that I walked away from Law School without any plan other than to help your mom pull off this adventure.

But after all these details were discussed, hashed over and rehashed as only government agents can do, then it was time to plan 'our new lives.'"

"And this son," began Carmen, "is where life took so many more different twists. We met with psychologists who wanted to prepare us for what it is like to suddenly be "different people." They went over every word in our new bios – which we were expected to study, learn and be able to recite backward and forward."

"Then your mom and I met with 'appearance experts.' The government spared no expense on these new identities. We learned in the medical center were highly trained professional plastic surgeons who could literally alter our physical appearance. Neither one of us wanted that drastic of a change, so we focused on things like a complete hair change..."

"You mean Mom's short blonde hair and your shaggy over-the-ears look?" AJ asked.

"Yes, among other ideas. They had your mom try out

different shades of red before settling on the short blonde look. In my case it is where the mustache came into play – and it is one thing I have had ever since," reflected Alex.

"Once the different ideas were thrown around about how we should look, how to make sure we knew our new stories completely and could tell them without even a pause, the next question was 'now what?' We were in our mid 20's, we both had Bachelor's degrees, and I was a semester away from completing law school. The "department," as we learned to call the program, the plan was they would fund us for the next six weeks – and set us up with jobs and housing for six months – but, in that time, we were supposed to figure out how to make it financially on the paying jobs they would arrange for us. Since we were debt-free, it wasn't a bad gig – except what were we going to do with our lives??"

Carmen interrupted, "Not to get ahead of the story, but it took a lot longer than the six months to every find "what we were going to do with the rest of our lives..."

"What happened" asked AJ.

Alex smiled and added, "Let's say there were some extenuating circumstances that no one had foreseen and so our six months or so stretched for the better part of 12 years..."

AJ studied his toes for a few minutes and asked, "Is this where the pictures come in?"

Carmen and Alex exchanged looks and then he spoke, "Some of them – I had not made the decision to come back to Church; your mom was raised Catholic, like any good Catholic young woman, she attended catechism, took First Communion and attended Mass as often as she could with her Tio y Tia...but, religion and commitment to certain standards wasn't high our personal list during this era. So, yes, that explains some of the pictures – why don't you get them out, and we'll see if we remember them."

"You want me to go back up in the attic and get them?" asked AJ.

Carmen went to the closet in the study and brought out the box, "You don't have to go get them, I brought them down this morning when everyone left. I've spent a lot of the day going through them – some were great memories. Others I shook my head and asked myself, 'THAT was us!?"

The next hour was spent as AJ absorbed seeing pictures of his parents' adventures, which he would learn over the next few days stretched literally all over the Western hemisphere to the islands of the South Pacific, Australia, and finally New Zealand – before finally settling on North Carolina as home. It was almost too much to comprehend. As the noise in the family room indicated that any pretense of doing homework was over, Carmen said, "AJ, your dad and I are so grateful for the many blessings in our lives – I know this is a lot to absorb, and we will fill in a lot of the gaps as we keep unfolding the story to you…"

"MOM!" rang out in unison from the twins as they headed to the study.

"But for now son," interjected Alex, "let's get everyone to bed. Seminary is still coming at 7:00 in the morning."

AJ nodded in agreement and joined his parents and the twins for family prayer before heading to his room. He knew there was much to add to his journal, but for now, he just needed to try and process even a small amount of all that had been shared with him.

CHAPTER FIVE

For the rest of the evening, the Barton family was too occupied with the current demands of a home with a teenager – two tweens – a college professor dad, and an over-involved-in too-many projects mom. When the evening rituals were finished, and everyone was finally in bed, Carmen turned to her husband as they were ready to turn off the lights and said, "All in all, that went well."

"You mean by that our oldest is accepting that we are not 'stuffy old fuddy duddies'?"

"Among other things – just wondering, it seems like such another lifetime – did it trigger any memories or thoughts?"

"A host of them!"

"Did it bother you that we gave so much, and it really didn't change the world.?"

"Oh, but we did change the world."

"Castro stayed in power until he died. Who knows what the CIA is still doing. And the Mafia is still entrenched," responded Carmen.

Alex smiled, "I heard General Walters speak once when were in Miami…"

"Wasn't he like a number two guy in the Pentagon and an acting head of the CIA?"

"That's the one – it was when I was a law student and somehow got invited to a AFIO meeting held up in Palm Beach – one of my profs knew a lot of what he called, 'ex-spooks.'"

"Spooks?"

"You've been a homemaker too long and forgotten some of the stuff we did learn – spooks, spies."

"Go on. And AF..what?"

"AFIO – the Association of Former Intelligence Officers. Evidently, South Florida is where many of them chose to retire because they have a huge chapter there. I met this one guy there who claimed to be the nephew of Bill Casey."

"Reagan's CIA Director!?"

"You do remember…"

"Some of it I have chosen to forget – but, yes, at one time, between my Tio and his buddies, I heard a lot of names. What did this guy say?"

"I suspect he was somewhat of a Washington hanger-on type. I was waiting with my prof to shake hands with General Walters, and he sort of cuts in front of us and introduces himself as Bill Casey's nephew."

"Gutsy."

"For sure. Anyway, General Walters looks at him and said, and I quote, 'Your uncle designed the plan that changed the world.'"

"Wow."

"Yes, wow – how does it apply to us? Casey was gone by then; we gave the FBI a treasure trove of data, which I am sure they shared with a lot of intel people. General Walters commented in his after-lunch speech, which has stuck with me, addressing the former Intelligence offices, said, 'Your successes may never be known, but your failures will be shouted from the rooftops.' We provided a first-hand account of both good people doing bad things and bad people doing good things. We really don't know for sure how all that intel was used. But we did what was right."

Carmen snuggled up under her husband's arm, laid her head on his chest and said, "We did what needed to be done, and I could not have done it without you by my side."

Alex kissed his wife, turned off his light, and said, "With you by my side, there is no mountain that I am not willing to climb. Good night, love you." Within moments, he was sound asleep. Carmen listened to his breathing as he soon fell into a deep sleep. It always amazed her that he could fall asleep so quickly.

That night in her dreams, she re-lived some of those more carefree moments when she was a girl with short blonde hair, backpacking across the Pacific islands, along with many of the scary moments as well. Those moments caused her to wake up in a cold sweat, and she was grateful that they were in her distant rear-view mirror; she could never in her wildest imagination have dreamed of the life she was now leading but she was truly grateful to be living it with Alex.

****

The alarm clock went off too early in AJ's room – he also had been replaying the conversation of the night before in his brain most of the night. It had influenced his dreams as in his mind, he started picturing his young parents, living under an assumed identity, looking so much different than the way he had always known them. They were the same people, but he saw them with such a broader view. He quickly got up, dressed, and went downstairs to get his breakfast. and head out for his 7:00 Seminary class.

In many ways, it was also surreal for AJ. They went through all the normal morning rituals, and yet he kept wondering, "How did they do and see so much and yet look so normal?" He had crossed "boring" out of the words he used to describe his parents, but they looked just "normal."

On the way to school, AJ finally broke down and asked his dad, "Was it hard to be in hiding for so long and then return to this 'normal' life?"

"Aaaj," he began, "life is filled with transitions. Think about a soldier who goes to war and then comes home and becomes a factory worker. A professional athlete who plays in front of 50,000 people and then comes home to a wife and baby that needs a diaper changed."

"You are right – discovering it in my own home is just a shock. I really want to know everything you can tell me – and I really want to know how the Church became so much a part of your life," AJ replied.

"Good observations – and fair questions – actually, I think your mom and I are glad to share it with you so that at least someone that we love knows the details – but we are at Church and this conversation will have 'to be continued,'" he said with a wink and smile.

Alex ruffled his son's hair and said, "Out, before you're late."

"I forgot. It's Friday, the teacher always brings doughnuts! There is a softball game after school, and a friend of mine is playing. Can I stay and watch?" he replied.

"A girl?"

"How did you know?"

"Well, if it would have been a boy, you would have said, 'Tommy's got a game, can I stay and watch?' And, in high school most softball teams are girls, the boys usually play baseball."

"Her name's Judy, and she's just a friend."

"Yes, you can stay but, be sure you call when you are on your way."

After his class at Church, he and the other kids walked the ten minutes to Salisbury High. Rushing up to meet him on the front walk was Judy. He smiled when he saw her coming, funny until yesterday he hadn't noticed she really was cute.

"Did you?" she immediately asked.

"Did I?"

She looked a little crest-fallen, "Did you ask your parents if you could stay for my game?"

The honest answer was, "Yes, I did." He had not planned on telling his dad that there was a girl on the softball team who had asked him to watch her play. Truth be told. He was not sure why his dad had to pull it out of him; maybe last night's conversation had so blown him away that he didn't remember until right before he got out of the car. Maybe.

Judy asked, "So can you stay for the whole game – it should be over by 4:30?"

"I think so, I'll text my parents when I my way home and let them know."

"Thank you! I'm pitching Varsity today – for the first time, and I need to be able to look up and see a friendly face."

"Will your parents be there?" AJ asked as he thought back to when he played T-ball, Coach Pitch and two seasons of

Little League. One or both parents were at every game. When he was in his last year of Little League, his mom even brought the twins when they were babies.

"They can't – they both have to work."

"Bummer."

"Can I talk to you at lunch?" Judy asked in a quiet voice.

"Yeah, sure, they're letting us outside on the patio now – maybe one of the picnic tables?"

"Do you mind if we find a quiet corner inside – I need to talk to someone and I want to do it before the game."

"Sure," AJ answered and wondered what was up. Judy often ate with the girls on the softball team, and he sat at what was often called 'the reading table.' He and two or three others who preferred to actually read rather than scroll through TikTok had claimed a spot.

The bell rang, and Judy called out, "I'll see you lunch!"
AJ had girls as "friends" ever since grade school. A couple of cheerleaders were in his English class, but they looked so mature and confident that he seldom said more than "Hi" in passing to them. Judy was the first girl he had ever gotten so engrossed in conversation that he could walk past his own house and not even notice. He found himself looking forward to lunch.

The bell for the lunch hour rang at 11:47. The 'hour' was really 45 minutes as the bell for 5th period rang sharply at 12:42 – since his 4th-period geometry class was across the hall from the lunchroom, he made it a habit to be one of the first three people in line. Though he never knew why. The food was "OK" – predictable, but "OK." Hamburgers and fries on Monday, spaghetti and meat sauce on Tuesday, meatloaf on Thursday, and fish sandwiches on Friday. The only variation was turkey on the Wednesday before Thanksgiving and the last day of school before Christmas break. The fish on Friday dates back to when Catholics were not supposed to eat meat on Fridays. That commandment had been lifted almost 50 years prior, but the menu remained the same.

Today he really wasn't interested in the fish sandwiches, his own concerns about his parents 'other life' had been pushed to the back of his mind as he wondered what was worrying Judy. She appeared only one minute after him. They got their trays, went by, and she greeted warmly each lady on the serving line. AJ noticed because while he often at least said, "thank you," he seldom even noticed the women who served him food 180 days a year. Judy smiled and greeted each one, and they, in turn, showed her the biggest smile of appreciation. AJ was sensing that Judy was different than many kids in his school.

They found an almost empty table in the back corner of the room because at least half the students were eating outside while enjoying the beautiful spring day. AJ quickly put the tartar sauce on his sandwich and the ketchup on his tater tots. Judy carefully cut her sandwich in half and nibbled gingerly on a tater tot. She paused for a moment and then made the sign of the cross before picking up her sandwich. AJ didn't say anything – his family always said grace before a family meal, but if he "returned thanks" in the cafeteria, it was so quick that no one would have ever noticed.

"AJ, I don't why I find it so easy to talk to you," Judy

blurted out, "but I've already told you things that nobody else knows, and you listened, you really listened; maybe I'm babbling, maybe you are just being kind, I'm babbling aren't I?"

"Well, you've certainly shared what Mrs. Trotter (an English teacher from 5th grade) would have called a 'run-on sentence,'" he offered with a smile.

She laughed, "Thank you." She also answered with a quiet shy voice, "Let me tell you what I've been trying to figure out how to tell anybody for the past six months."

AJ calmly replied, not knowing what to expect. "I'm all ears."

"I told you I was adopted?"

"Yes, how old were you when your parents told you?"

"I had just turned 15…"

"Wait a minute we are the same age – I knew there is some reason why you are a freshman, but I didn't want to ask."

"I did; at the start of the school year when it hit me: I was a year older than all the other freshmen girls. I guess I never paid much attention until then. I just thought in elementary and even middle school that I was, you know, 'big for my age,' and then there is all that stuff that they teach in health about girls maturing sooner than boys, so we might be bigger than the guys in middle school, and…I'm doing it again," she said sheepishly.

"Yes, but I get it."

"Well, for six months, it has been eating on me – who were my real parents, why didn't they want me, why didn't my adopted mom and dad tell me? AJ, do you have any idea what it is like to find out that your parents aren't really the people you always thought they were?" She asked with such painful sincerity that it made him wince.

AJ thought out his answer. His first impulse was to respond, "If you only knew." But he knew that would open a discussion he was not ready to have outside the family. So instead, he asked, "What were they able, or I guess willing, to tell you?"

If they knew all the details, they couldn't share much. They were over 40, and so traditional adoption was closed for them. Dad is a lawyer and had a friend who had contacts with an adoption agency in Central Europe – where adoptions can be arranged for a fee. Mom was almost crying as she told me how much they wanted a child, how they had tried for years and now it seemed nearly too late even to adopt. When Dad told her about an agency with an office in Atlanta that could 'arrange' an adoption, they made an appointment and flew down the next day."

She sniffled a sob, and AJ instinctively reached over and took her hand. He looked into her eyes, which were welling with tears, and told her, "It's OK—but first think about it. They wanted a child, and they found a way to adopt you—have you ever doubted they love you?"

She choked back another tear and shook her head, "No. I know they love me, and I don't want to hurt them, I want to know more about them – but I want more details - like I really want to know, who am I…is that so wrong, to love my parents who have given me a wonderful life as well as to know the parent who first gave me life?

For a moment AJ was torn between the pain he saw on Judy's face and the angst in her voice with his own complex emotions about his parents' revelations. He also knew the answer he had given Judy applied to him – their parents only wanted the best for their children. The curiosity they both had to learn more about the details of their parents' lives was normal, but it didn't change the love they had for their offspring. As they sat in silence for a moment, their contemplation was interrupted by the bell signaling the end of lunch and the start of the 5th period.

Judy's face brightened as she said, "AJ, thanks for being a good friend and just listening to a girl rattle on – I'm so glad you're coming to the game – I think I told you, it will be the first time I've ever pitched varsity, I'm really scared, but Coach Cato thinks I'm ready, ooops I'm doing it again, aren't I?"

"Yes, you are," he said with a wide grin, "but it's really cute. And I can't wait to watch you play. I'll be your good luck charm!" He grabbed both of their trays and as she left, Judy turned and said, "I mean it. Thank you. See you in Art class."

CHAPTER SIX

AJ always considered it fortunate that his last two classes of the day were also his favorite. Mr. Smith, a good friend of his dad, was his World History teacher, and then there was Art class—he originally picked it because it was an easy elective, and he had at least a passing interest in drawing and sketching. Over the past couple of days, his budding friendship with Judy gave him one more reason to look forward to the final class of the day.

As they approached the end of the school year, World History was dealing with the turbulent years after World War 2 until the present day. Between his dad, Mr. Smith, and his own keen interest, this was a very exciting period to study. Both his dad and Mr. Smith had lived through much of it and could share their perspectives on what it was like to come of age in the Cold War, the Civil Rights movement, as well as the wars in Korea and Vietnam. And while it seemed to be distant history to his generation, clearly, everyone over 35 remembered the events of 9/11 as if they were yesterday.

When the bell sounded to end the fourth period, Mr. Smith called out his name: "Alex, AJ, sorry. Could I speak to you for a moment?"

"Sure, Mr. Smith, what's up?"

"I was going to ask you the same question – you are the brightest kid in my class and normally the most engaging – you keep me on my toes with your youthful vision of history – especially now in what everyone in your age considers the 50's to be about the same time as the Civil War. Your mind really appeared to be somewhere else today."

AJ studied his shoes and awkwardly replied, "I guess I have a lot on my mind – my mom and dad have been going over some family history stuff with me, and then at lunch, a friend laid some heavy stuff on me that she's handling. . ."

"She?" he asked with a smile.

"Just a friend, but we were talking right before your class and I was not really dialed in today, I'll catch it in the reading tonight. Honest."

"Relax, AJ. You are the last student I worry will not 'get it.' I just wanted to make sure you were OK because it was so not like you."

"I'll be alright, but thanks for checking."

"You have a good day, and I'll see you tomorrow."

AJ headed to his Art Class, shaking his head – he was carrying a 104% in Mr. Smith's class; he must have really been off his game for a teacher to notice. But then again, he remembered Mr. Smith and his dad were good friends, so he was more under a microscope than some of the other kids in the class.

Judy's face lit up the moment he walked into the room, and she whispered, "You were almost late. Anything wrong?"

"No, Mr. Smith just wanted to talk to me after class – it is the downside of being a history prof's kid in a class being taught by another history teacher who is in the running club with my dad."

Mrs. Johanson put three prompts on the smart board and told her class to pick two objects, sketch the first one, and then switch their paper with a partner to do the second. She added that you and your partner might want to agree who will sketch which one first, because the objective is to make a coherent sketch, with two objects completed by two different artists…"

It was a different kind of project for sure. The objects to choose from were an apple, a bicycle, and a tree. AJ turned to Judy and said, "Partner?"

She smiled, "For sure – what are you thinking?"

"The apple falling from the tree" he suggested.

"Or" she replied, "the bike leaning against the tree."

"How about the apple sitting in a wire basket on the

front of the bike," suggested AJ.

"Too hard. Remember we both are drawing—wait a minute, you are right—you draw the apple, and I'll draw the basket around it and the bike. I'll draw the bike, and you draw the apple IN the basket!

"Deal." The budding artists immediately started working on their first collaborative project. Neither could have known it would be the start of so many more.

****

Class time practically flew by as Judy and AJ immediately went to work on their joint project. They exchanged their first part of the project with 20 minutes to go in the class, and Judy was finishing her rendition of the bike, now with the apple in the basket, when the classroom PA squawked, "Teachers, pardon the interruption, but could members of the girls' softball team, Varsity and JV, report to the locker rooms for today's game?"

Judy smiled and said, "That's me – hand in our work, and I'll look for you in the stands – JV plays first and then I get to pitch for Varsity."

A few minutes later the final bell of the day sounded. Alex put the finishing touches on his part of the work and handed it to Mrs. Johanson. He grabbed his backpack, dropped off what he didn't need at his locker, and headed to the softball field – honestly, he had never actually watched a girls' softball game – but he loved baseball, and he suddenly had a reason for a renewed interest in the "girl's version" of the game.

Girls' softball has never been a game to draw large

crowds. There were a few parents, and a few other students – most of the parents had come to see their child play. Most of the other students were there to meet friends and really didn't care that much about the game. AJ watched the warm-ups and saw Judy in action for the first time. She really looked like she could put some serious heat on her throws. He was impressed.

Then an umpire came out and called, "Play ball." His jaw dropped; the umpire was Mr. Smith, his history teacher. As the players took their positions, the umpire turned to look at the few people in the stands, recognized him, and waved to AJ. Still surprised, he waved back – who knew one of his teachers would see him here? Who even knew teachers could be umpires for Youth sports? But then he remembered his own parents had certainly handed him a lot of surprises this week.

Judy seemed to take on a different persona as she stood on the mound waiting for the first batter. Her first two pitches were called "balls," the batter swung and missed the next two and then patiently waited for what was all three. With the count 3 balls and 2 strikes, AJ found himself holding his breath. Judy wound up and fired what to AJ looked like what should have been a strike. The umpire called out, "Ball FOUR, take your base." AJ was on his feet and realized, now was not the time to yell at the umpire and quickly sat down.

This was a breakthrough game for Judy the freshman. She walked around the mount and kicked dirt out of her cleats and seemed to be shutting out the whole world. Even AJ could see this incredible look of determination on her face. The leadoff batter, who was on first for the walk, would be the only baserunner of the game. Judy struck out the next three batters on five or fewer pitches. In the bottom of the first inning, the Lady SHS Hornets scored six runs – they batted around, and Judy got a double and drove in two of the six runs,

AJ found himself cheering as loud as he had when he and his dad took a road trip to Atlanta to see the Braves play. In the top of the second Judy struck out the side on a total of 10 pitches. She was in the zone, and it was an amazing thing to watch. In the bottom of the second, SHS scored three more runs, pushing the score to 9-0. Judy was unfazed as she took the mound in the top of the third. The first batter hit a lazy pop fly on her first pitch. The second struck out on three pitches. The third and final batter of the inning hit a slow roller back to the mound. Judy fielded it cleanly and fired to first for the third out.

In the bottom of the third, the Lady Hornets' first two runners reached base, the first on a soft single to right field, the second on a clean bunt that put runners on first second. Judy came up to bat for only the second time and her solid hit got past the center fielder and rolled all the way to the fence. Both runs scored as Judy pulled into second with a stand-up double. With the score now 11-0, Mr. Smith stepped from behind the plate and enforced the mercy rule that calls for the game to end after three innings if one team has a 10-run lead. Coach Cato was in awe of her young freshman – she had watched her pitch and hit in practice and knew she had good fundamentals – but her focus once she took the mound or stood at the plate was beyond her expectations. When the game was called, the team mobbed Judy at second base, and AJ's voice was almost gone from his cheering.

As the teams filed into the locker rooms, Judy made a dash to the stands. In sheer exuberance, she threw her arms around AJ and exclaimed, "You are my GOOD luck charm! Thank you for being here!"

"Thank me? THANK YOU! This was one of the most

amazing games I have ever seen! Do you KNOW what you just did?

"Yes! AJ, we won the first varsity game I got to pitch! Wasn't the team awesome?"

"Judy, you are the hero – you only faced 10 batters and pitched a no-hitter in your first high school varsity game. Do you have any idea how rare something like this is?"

"It was a no-hitter?"

"You're serious?" AJ asked, almost in disbelief. "The first batter reached first on what I thought was a bad call, and then then you put nine down in order – without a ball even getting out of the infield….and for good measure you got two hits and drove in 4 of the 11 runs!"

"I just focused on each batter, and when it was my turn to hit, I just made contact. I don't think I even knew the score until Mr. Smith called the game."

"You are amazing," was AJ's only reply as he hugged her again.

"Coach Cato Is taking the team out for pizza – I wish my mom, and dad could have been here. Dad was stuck in depositions in Charlotte, and the hospital asked Mom to pull a 12-hour shift because someone on her floor called in sick."

"I'm sorry, but you got my word, I'll be at every game you play."

Judy reached up and kissed him again on the cheek and

said, "You're too sweet. You're awesome. Thank you. I've got to get changed and go meet the rest of the team. Call me tomorrow, please."

"Count on it." As she ran towards the locker room, the emotions in his heart, mind, and soul were again creating turmoil that he had never felt in his 15 years. She was really special, and he was growing fonder of her every day.

His thoughts were interrupted by the vibrating phone in his pocket. It was his mom. "Are you OK, AJ?" she asked with concern in her voice.

"Sure, Mom, I was just about to call – didn't Dad tell you I was staying to watch my friend play softball?"

"He did, but I've called five time, and it went to voice mail…"

"My bad. My phone is on Do Not Disturb at school – and I was watching the game and didn't feel vibrate until this time. The game just got over and I'll be home in ten minutes."

"Did you get to watch your little friend play?"

"Her name is Judy. She's a freshman, but my age. That's a long story. In fact, her life is a long story, but Mom was awesome in the game"

"An awesome girl softball player."

"The team won 11-0. She pitched a no-hitter, got two hits, and drove in 4 of the runs her team scored. She was AMAZING."

Carmen detected the sheer enthusiasm in her son's voice and knew it wasn't just about the girl's athletic performance:" She sounds very interesting. Do I know her parents?"

"Not sure – they live about 10 minutes away at 7th and Elm."

"Oh, what is their last name?"

AJ had to think for a moment, "Uhh, Roland. Her dad's a lawyer and her mom's a nurse at the hospital."

"Are they in our Ward?" [LDS term for a local congregation)
]   "She's Catholic."

"Why don't you come home and tell me about this young woman, she sounds very interesting."

AJ knew the tone and knew there would be more questions when he got home, and that was OK; he really couldn't wait for his mom to find out that Judy was adopted but born in Cuba.

"OK, Mom, I'll be home in 10 minutes."

****

Carmen had learned to read her older son very well through the tone of his voice and the number of pauses in any given sentence; what she didn't realize was that he, too, had learned to read his mom with the same techniques. Neither had consciously thought about it, it was simply a natural intuitive ability that had been developed by their mutual observations. Because of this, AJ decided a sprint home was better than a leisurely stroll. Consequently, the 10-minute walk took only 6 minutes, and he burst through the front door breathing hard.

The twins greeted him with, "Yeah! AJ's home, can we eat!?"

Carmen heard the twins' announcement and walked out of the kitchen. Seeing her son breathing hard, she asked, "You ran home from school with that heavy backpack?"

"Sure, Mom," he said as she gave him a quick kiss on his cheek.

As was quite common in the Miami Hispanic community in which she grew up, kissing as a greeting was very common. What was called 'air kisses' for more casual friends and a quick peck on the cheek for closer friends and relatives.

"I didn't know if Dad had told you about the game, and you seemed a little concerned when you called."

"He told me, I was concerned when you didn't answer your phone," she replied.

When a child got their first phone, it was the cardinal rule in their home—if a parent calls or texts, you are to respond immediately. Both Carmen and Alex knew his schedule and never reached out to him during school hours, but Carmen always called and checked on him immediately after school. The knowledge that there was a 'girl' in the picture, and he wouldn't answer the phone had sent her into high alert 'mom mode.'

"Tell me about Judy."

"We have art class together. She is my partner on 'pair/share' assignments. I didn't know much about her until a couple of days ago when we walked home and got to talking – I mean, after all, she's a freshman..."

"Meaning?"

"I don't know, Mom, girls my age and older sort of scare me, and the freshmen girls just seem like 8th graders trying to act older," he explained.

"Girls your age, scare you?"

AJ stammered, "It's complicated, Mom—let's just say Judy seems different. When I heard her story and then saw her play today, it was like, 'WOW, she is different.'"

Carmen smiled. The unbridled enthusiasm told her instantly that the seeds of young love were planted and already bursting into bloom. She forced herself to slow down her questioning, realizing that her son was opening up and talking and that pushing too much would cause him to defensively shut down.

"She sounds very interesting. What do you mean her story?"

AJ then blurted out the summary – yes, she's adopted but didn't find out the details until she started high school this year.

"The details?"

"Yeah, Mom, that is what I've wanted to tell you since I first heard it!"

"What?"

"Mom, she thought because she can speak German and came from what she thought was a German orphanage she must have been born in Germany!"

"And she wasn't?" Carmen asked with a puzzled tone.

"No, mom. She was born in Cuba – her bio-mom was Cuban, her bio-dad's parents had moved to Cuba from East Germany."

Startled, Carmen asked, "Did she know where in Cuba she was born?"

"She said Santiago. Where is that?"

"It's the second largest city in Cuba on the far eastern side of the island. My Tio, my pa-pa and much of my family are originally from there. I was born there."

"Wow, her bio-parents might have known yours."

That thought crossed Carmen's mind as well. What were the odds that two young people from such totally different backgrounds could have such an unusual connection in a small town like Salisbury? She didn't let her mind dwell on it, or wouldn't right now; that would come later. Instead, she replied, "Why don't you go wash up and do some homework – Dad will be home shortly, and we can eat."

The twins who were listening in the background shouted, "YEAH – Let's eat!"

Carmen reverted to Spanish, "Silencio niños, haced los deberes." [Quiet children, do your homework]

Sam and Jon-Mark giggled but, like their big brother, knew the conversation was over.

Alex often referred to Carmen's switch to her native tongue as 'the conversation-ender.'

The twins retreated to their homework corner, AJ to his room, and Carmen to the kitchen to finish dinner when the phone rang. With her mind still on the conversation with AJ, she absentmindedly picked up the landline and said, "Hola."

"Hi is this Mrs. Barton?" came a girl's voice.

"Si, I mean, yes, this is Carmen Barton."

"My name's Judy Roland. I'm a friend of AJ from school, and I just tried to call his phone and went directly to voice mail…"

"Judy, AJ was just telling us about your amazing game —he's probably still got it on Do Not Disturb. I couldn't get through to him when he was at your game. I'll have him call you, but how did you get our number? We don't get many calls on our landline."

"I googled it, and I knew he was called AJ because he's a

junior and there is only one Alex Barton listed in the Rowan County directory."

Carmen's first thought was, 'Quick, young lady, her thoughts were to the story AJ had shared about Judy's biological parents. Before she could say anything, Judy added, "AJ mentioned you were born in Cuba – I would love to talk to someone else who was born there…may I come by your house to say hello this weekend?"

Judy was the only child of adoptive parents who had fostered her independence and strong-willed all her life. Almost immediately, Carmen saw a little of herself in this young woman and replied, "Yes, Mr. Barton, and I would love to meet you as well. After his dad gets home, I'll have AJ give you a call when we see how our weekend is shaping up."

"Thanks Mrs. Barton, it'll be a while before I get home – the team just got just to Pizza Hut, Coach Cato is taking us out to celebrate the game."

"You enjoy it – according to AJ, you and the team deserve to celebrate."

"Yes, Ma'am. Bye."

As Carmen returned the cordless phone to its base station, many thoughts flooded her mind: She had been very concerned about even the idea of AJ being distracted by girls, and now the very first one he had mentioned seemed to be a very bright young woman—with a past that she would soon discover had a connection, if not intertwinement, with her own story.

Just as the timer went off for the bread in the oven, she

heard the garage door open, and Alex's familiar voice called out, "Hi, Beautiful. I'm home and starved—let's eat!"

Within moments, they were sitting around the kitchen table, laughing and talking about the week. For the parents, it had been a week of reliving many of their lives' most colorful moments. For AJ, it had been an amazing week of discovery. For the twins, it had been a great week with end-of-the-year field trips.

CHAPTER SEVEN

Dinner was over, the dishes had been washed, the kitchen was cleaned, and the twins had won a concession to stay up later because it was Friday night so that they could see the latest Disney film screening on the Disney channel. In addition to discussing weekend plans, much of the conversation was about AJ relating the amazing softball game and his friend's performance earlier in the day. It was Jon-Mark, playing the role of the inquisitive little brother, who asked, "Is Judy going to be AJ's girlfriend?" An innocent question provoked all eyes to turn to AJ for his response.

"She's a neat girl, but she's just a friend – I've been in art class with her since the start of this semester, but we've only been really talking much this week," AJ replied with a tone that showed even he wasn't sure if he believed in what he was saying.

"Guys, give your brother a break," interjected Alex. We want all of you to have boys and girls who are your friends. It is perfectly natural for teens to start noticing the type of people they click with—and that is what eventually dating is all about."

AJ protested, "Dad, I haven't thought about dating anybody – she's just a really nice girl, and we enjoy talking to each other."

It was Sam's turn to play little sister and ask the question that would only cross the mind of a ten-year-old girl, well at least before her ten-year-old twin would think of such a thing, "Have you kissed her?"

"Samantha Jo, that is a highly inappropriate question!" barked Carmen. Then Carmen caught that AJ suddenly blushed and looked away. At that moment, she knew the answer and it was not the time to discuss it. "Sammy, I didn't mean to sound so harsh," she replied in a much softer voice.

"OK, I just wanted to know cause, in the movies, that's what boyfriends and girlfriends usually do," she replied innocently.

"We haven't kissed," AJ replied, "but she did give a quick kiss on the cheek right after the game. No big deal."

"OK," answered Sam, "can we watch the movie now?"

Carmen smiled at the innocence of a 10-year-old, who would simply ask what was on her mind without any filters – at the same moment made a mental note of the difference between 'casual kissing,' such as in the Hispanic culture, and the hormonal-driven kissing of youth.

Alex turned on the television in the family room, opened the Disney channel, and found the twins' favorite movie of the month – sometimes, they could watch the same film four times in a row and then never want to see it again. Carmen made popcorn and made everyone comfortable. AJ then asked, "While they are watching the movie, can we talk some more?"

For Carmen and Alex, the diversion of AJ's friend had come at a welcome time as they were unpacking both memories and the contents of the 'Gap years box.' Alex nodded and motioned for her and AJ to follow him into the study off the family room.

They left the door ajar to monitor the twins and see if they got bored with the movie. Carmen took a deep breath and asked, "More 'gap year questions?'"

"Yes, I want to hear more. We barely scratched the surface a couple of days ago."

"OK," Alex began. I think we left with Nikki and our time at the Air Force Academy witness protection processing center."

"How long were you there?

Carmen smiled, "In real time, or dog years?"

AJ giggled, "Real-time works, and where did you go again from there first?"

"In real time we were there 29 full days. They were packed full days. Haircuts. Wardrobe accessories. Backpacking strategies. Financial planning – we needed to live a lifestyle that looked like we were on some sort of fellowship grant – not rich, but not poor. Studying every aspect of our new identities. Voice coaching on how if we spent time in Missouri we needed to sound more like mid-west – not southern or South Florida," explained Alex.

"And, probably at least 100 other things that we never considered when we first agreed to enter the program," Carmen added, "we really did become 'different people."

"So, after your 'training,'" AJ asked, "when did you head out? Was Hawai'i your first stop?"

The thought of it brought a smile to both Alex and Carmen. "Your mother and I were more than ready to leave. Our heads were so crammed with our new lives; sometimes, we would spend 8 hours straight practicing answering every question that could be asked us – we had to know our 'new past,' as well as sound believable as we described something that was often pure fiction."

"Did you think about it as 'lying'?" AJ said with a puzzled tone.

"I think I can answer for both me and your dad. It was lying, but it was part of the role we had to play because of the path we chose to follow in our part of bringing to light information our country needed to know."

"Nikki coached us about what she hoped was every possible scenario that we would encounter," explained Alex. She brought out the travel plans for our stop. Oahu is the most populous of the Hawai'ian islands. The details were staggering."

As Alex was searching for a way to explain that first stop – Carmen reached into the box and pulled out a file labeled "Hawaii."

"Here it is here, dear, Nikki's spreadsheet," offered Carmen.

"Thanks, Beautiful," he said as he opened the file with different labeled sheets:

- Travel: Departure: March 24- Alaska Air to LAX; Hawaiian Air to Honolulu
- Accommodations: Week 1: Youth Hostel on Waikiki Beach (7 nights/prepaid room)
- Transportation: two scooters (prepaid)
- Luggage: two duffle bags; 2 oversized backpacks
- Assorted clothing for tropical climate
- 2 Dell notebook computers
- 1 dial up modem 56 kbs
- Nokia Cell phone /1000 minutes per month. Int'l roaming – government issued/paid.
- 2 rechargeable pagers
- Five hundred dollars in U.S currency – in $20 bills
- A Visa Debit card issued by Bank of Hawai'i– it was to be reloaded with $1,000 US

    dollars on the first of each month for most of the time we were to be in the protection program – though the card would be changed based on where you will be stationed.

- Men/Women's toiletries and bathroom essentials (they knew all our brands)

ADVENTURES AT THE BOAT SHOW

- Maps of the islands
- Highlights of "Island location"
- University of Hawaii Indigenous people prof*
- Tour guide*
- Safe House North/South sides of the island
- Catholic Bible / Book of Mormon

Carmen explained as AJ was looking over the list, "Nikki told us she would travel on the plane with us, as would a plain-clothes air marshal. Both would be armed, but they didn't expect any trouble. She apologized that the Youth hostel wasn't the best setting for newlyweds, but our bio had us being married since before we graduated – not just a month earlier."

AJ was studying the list with bewilderment, "You had a cell phone and computers."

"It was the first generation of Dell notebooks that weighed slightly less than a ton; they had internet back in those dark ages, but it was something called, "dial up…:

"We have some at our school?!"

"Really," Carmen asked in a shocked time.

"We have a tech museum – that's also where I saw the polaroid camera..."

Alex and Carmen just smiled suddenly feeling old that their son had seen their "state of the art" tech equipment in a tech museum.

Then AJ asked, "So what did you do? Your cover was grad students doing some sort of research, so didn't you really need to, you know, research something?"

"First things first," replied Alex "the flight was uneventful, though after flying on a private Gulfstream to Colorado, leaving in coach on a 737 was somewhat of stepdown. But everything in our life needed to match our cover."

Carmen continued the story, "We saw and knew who the air marshal was, but we never spoke to her or even acknowledged she was on the plane. This was our real first taste of the cloak and dagger stuff in public."

"When we arrived at the Honolulu airport, they still met flights with flower leis at the airport – remember this was pre 9/11" interjected Alex. With the Debit card and the cash, we had the ability to live comfortably but not exorbitantly. We got our baggage, such as it was, and headed for the taxi line."

"Why didn't you just take an Uber?" AJ asked.

Carmen and Alex both smiled, and she replied, "Because it hadn't been invented yet."

AJ looked puzzled, but his dad continued, "So we took the taxi to the hostel. It was clean and more like a dormitory than a hotel. We shared a large common area with two other couples. Both about our age, both with well-worn backpacks. The beds were these oversized bunk beds – almost full-size mattress top and bottom. It was a shot of realism when we realized our "new roommates were couples, that weren't married. They were shocked to find out that we were."

"It was, different, for sure," added Carmen.

"We had been practicing for weeks calling each other Cathy and Aaron. Our Missouri drivers' licenses were completely legit – except of course being creations of the tech wizards in the program. If we were pulled over for any reason they would come back as legit – but flagged, call a confidential number. Any law enforcement person who got that far would be told: Extend all courtesies – do NOT hold under any circumstances – where are they are currently located?"

Carmen then added, "It was at this point that life was becoming very real. In Colorado Springs we were almost on a working vacation. Now, we are in a real-world situation where they might be people who would just as soon see us dead."

AJ stared first at his mom and then his dad. The serious tone of that statement rocked his little world. Your parents running from bad guys and assuming new identities while living a life as backpacking-free spirits sounded like a movie script. Realizing they had come face-to-face with the idea that people might want to kill them was not part of the story he had ever entertained.

"Wow. I'm sort of like at a loss for words. What happened next?"

"Well, we checked in the hostel, found our giant dorm room, met our new roommates, who really were the backpacking hippie types that we were supposed to be – but were totally cool people. Then the cell phone rang. Since nobody knew the number, we hoped the 'blocked call' was from Nikki," explained Alex.

"Your dad answered the call but didn't even say hello until he heard Nikki's voice, "Hi it's your friend Nikki, I thought I saw you on this flight but didn't get a chance to catch up with you when you got off the flight."

Playing along, your dad said, "Oh Nikki, you were on the same flight."

"Yes, can we meet for drinks – there's a funky little restaurant close to the beach – where are you staying?"

Carmen explained, "Now, since she planned the trip, she knew even what room we were in, but from this point on, we always assumed someone might be listening or watching. She gave your dad the address, and he said it was close to us, and we'd walk there in 15 minutes."

"But she interrupted me," Alex explained, "and said take the cab – it's too hot to walk. We learned that too hot, wasn't just about the air temp. It was a word of caution we had studied back in Colorado. In fact, we had practiced this exact conversation many times."

Alex related what they found when they arrived, "We found ourselves in this tourist dive on the older end of the beach. It was classic Waikiki, the restaurant/bar opened directly onto the beach. There was the usual mix of midwestern tourists with sandals and black socks; the beautiful people in mini bikinis. . ."

AJ interrupted, "I saw the pictures." Carmen blushed – the suit she wore then wasn't certainly not what a proper LDS young woman would wear, much less a mother of three. "I was young and not a member of the Church then either," was her reply in protest.

Moving on Alex also described the tanned Hawai'ians

manning the rentals of beach chairs, tubes, boogie and surf boards. Almost any question to them was followed with a short answer and the 'thumb and finger' gesture followed by "hang loose bro." Nikki was there in the back of the restaurant away from the beach side when they arrived. She looked like a well-healed tourist, wearing modest shorts, stylish sandals, a polo shirt with her hair pulled into a tight ponytail.

Seeing them approach she called out, "Aaron, Cathy, over here."

By now they were getting used to their 'new names,' and usually called each other by them, even in private. They had changed into cargo short pants and University of Missouri t-shirts. They wore flip flops and not the short study hiking boots which were also part of their 'uniform.'

"I know it's not the Hilton," she began, but how are the new digs."

"Well," replied Carmen who had been very accustomed to upper class style, "it certainly fits our cover story. I've never even had a roommate – but right now we are still in the adventure stage. It works, I'm OK."

"Aaron?"

"I've been a poor college student for so long it seems normal," he said with a grin.

"I will be on the island for the first week just to make sure you have everything you need and are getting ready to start the 'working part' of the cover story. But the Director thought you like to hear an update on everything that went down in Miami."

"We're all ears," answered Carmen.

Nikki smiled and began her report which included the details of their 'escape' from the boat show with many missing pieces filled in – she was also able to add a perspective that even living in Miami neither Carmen nor Alex had any real knowledge. "Let's start," she began by acknowledging that South Florida in general, and Miami / Miami Beach specifically have always had an allure for shall we say, 'the dark side.'"

"How so?" queried Alex, who as a law student had seen his share of legal history involving Miami and Miami-Dade County.

"In the late 1800's a railroad magnate started building railroads up and down the east coast. According to local lore, a woman named Julia Tuttle helped convince him to extend the railroad from Jacksonville – then the largest city on Florida's Atlantic Coast by sending him fresh oranges and orange blossoms in the dead of winter," explained Nikki. "Once it was easy to get to Miami and the beaches by direct train from the Northeast and people found out just how mild the winters were, South Florida – especially Miami Beach became a winter home for the rich, famous and infamous."

"Rich, famous, and *infamous?*" asked Carmen with a questioning tone.

"Oh yes, some of the legit robber barons had winter mansions built directly on the beach. Things took off in the roaring 20's – the depression caused the market to collapse – but as the nation clawed out of the depression, the money came back – clean and dirty. Al Capone died there after he was released from Alcatraz."

"Then came the hotels," she continued, in the 50's and the 60's various 'families,' rumored to be Sicilian mobsters started setting up shop there for a host of different illegal activities. The Eden Rock hotel was at least by the locals thought to be a mob owned hotel."

"So, Mafia types appearing at the show isn't even that unusual?" asked Carmen.

"Miami turned big time to drug trade in the 1980's – remember the old TV show, *Miami Vice?* The Miami Boat Show became a shopping place for the expensive "go fast" boats of that crazy era. DEA calculated that if the drug runners could complete one successful run in boats costing up to $500,000, they broke even. Two or more runs, even if the boats and drugs, especially cocaine, were confiscated and the drug lords had turned a major profit."

Alex and Carmen were shaking their heads in disbelief. Alex had studied in law school, and Carmen had lived around in all her life but stayed clear of the drugs to focus on her mission to get the diaries out. What she didn't know *The Castro Diaries* did more than implicated the NY families in political assassinations – it also tied the drug trade directly to Castro who was using his island as staging ground for much of the cocaine coming into Miami. There were many reasons the people that Carmen referred to as men with Italian surnames didn't want those personal notes of Castro to ever seen the light of day.

Nikki continued the story – evidently after Alex and Carmen fled the scene, Gary Burns, the head of Boat Show security who by accident, had intercepted the bad guys on the loading dock because he thought he was protecting Boat Show staff. An ex-cop he soon had one Cuban and one New York 'family man' cuffed and waiting for Miami Beach PD in the security office. What he didn't know was that the two staffers whose badges said they were Michelle and Bob were in the center of the diary retrieval. Nor did he know about the car that immediately started following Alex and Carmen as soon as they left the Convention Center secured north parking lot.

"What about the car that was chasing us across the causeway on our way to the Miami Herald?" asked Alex. It looked like an unmarked police car or government sedan."

"Former, Florida Highway Patrol car, two former 'operatives' roughly linked to the CIA," explained Nikki. "The CIA went through some really turbulent years after the collapse of the Soviet Union in the '80's and through the early 90's. President Clinton was trying to find the right man to right the CIA Ship and redefine the agency's mission."

"Was it really that bad?" asked Carmen, who knew from her father and uncle that intelligence agencies often dealt with the darker side.

"It was," replied Nikki, "too many of their most trusted agents were double or triple agents. And in one of the biggest intelligence failures ever – in the period you were putting together the plan to get the diaries to the U.S. the CIA had a mole working at their highest levels of clearance, on Cuban Intelligence. Her name was Ana Belen Montes – she was an American born Cuban – spoke flawless Spanish and English. For close to 20 years, she fed her Cuban handlers in the United States details on all of the CIA's work on the island – including who were American spies. The Castro Diaries helped collaborate her involvement – but, since the Director who finally brought some stability back their work, George Tenant, wanted to catch her contacts – the arrest was delayed until

2001 – right after 9/11"

"They let her keep working even though they knew she was a spy?" asked Carmen in disbelief.

"Yes, but she was constantly given wrong information to feed to her handlers. The 'spy world' is about as crazy as you see in the movies – well, maybe a little worse. So back to your exit from Miami a few months ago," continued Nikki.

"Is Tio still safe?"

"Yes, your aunt and uncle are under a watchful eye – both ours and their private security. They are safe and considered major patrons of the Cuban cause – we don't feel that Castro would try anything against them."

"How was our, escape, if we can call it that explained?" asked Alex.

Nikki smiled, "Honestly, after Gary got rid of the bad guys, he had more than enough to worry about the 120,000 people who would flock through the doors over the five days after your event. It was written off as just another one of those 'crazy things' that happen in and around Miami Beach."

Nikki continued, "The Marshall's 'whitewash' team was on it the next morning. The two bad guys were released to the federal marshals – Miami Beach PD didn't really have any reason to hold them. The Cuban was a Cuban National who was deported immediately to Havana – he didn't complain. The New Yorker was sent to Sicily – where he met up with some distant family members and decide to stay 'for a while.' He wasn't a high enough interest for us to keep track of him.

"The two former CIA 'contractors' had outstanding warrants for some petty crimes. Tenant disavowed them as being part of the Agency. They went to trial in Palm Beach and were sentenced to a year in the Palm Beach County jail. Again, no one we felt a need to keep tracking."

Carmen then turned to AJ and explained, "At first, we were totally relieved. It looked like we had made a clean getaway – Nikki explained how my disappearance from my various "part-time gigs" that I had been working would not ever raise an eyebrow. Your dad leaving law school three months before graduation was a bigger one. His coursework had been completed; his internship was the final part of his degree. People known to us only as "government officials" called on and met with the President of the UM Law School. They were, of course, surprised that one of their Ace students was also an 'undercover government agent whose assignment had been so secretive that he was now in 'witness protection.' The president agreed that in the best interest of national security, his records would be sealed and his graduation put on hold until it could be safe for him to resurface."

AJ shook his head, "The law school thought you were a SPY?"

"They didn't know what to think until they were contacted a few years later by an intermediary requesting my transcripts and my diploma – so that I could take the bar exam."

"So, if your getaway was that clean – why DID you stay 'underground for so long?"

"That was our question for Nikki?" answered Carmen,

"and then she told us the rest of the story. This time, it wasn't about political intrigue and assassination or even embarrassing government agencies; it was drugs and drug lords."

"The DEA was using some of the information in the diaries to throw huge monkey wrenches into the Cartel's South Florida operation," Nikki explained, "they were picking up 'chatter' from sources that we were on more than one list of 'bad guys' who wanted payback for the millions of dollars if not lost, at least disrupted income."

"I remember," Alex continued, "Nikki getting very serious and explaining, based on our best intel, that there are some angry top men out there. Also, we did a good job of a diversion getting you out of South Florida. You didn't know, but when your agents left downtown Miami and headed to Opa Locka, two other caravans with a young couple that were good had been your doubles left simultaneously. One went to MIA, Miami's main airport; the other went a few miles north to Fort Lauderdale. They were decoys – one flight plan went to suburban DC – we have a witness processing center there and one in upstate New York. Those flight plans were less guarded – yours was never posted anywhere. It didn't happen."

She continued, "Nikki and her bosses felt we would remain hot for 3-5 years. All the chatter had them speculating we were going to be hiding somewhere between DC and Maine. The bad guys were speculating we would be "hid in plain sight" in a city where our Spanish would be an asset. And that our current plan was not showing up in the 'chatter' anywhere. We were sort of relieved. . ."

In unison, the twins called out, "MOMMY, the movies are over. Can we watch another one? It's Friday night!!"

Alex grinned at his son and offered, "Enough for one night. Let's go to ice cream and get the twins to bed. There is obviously a lot more—are you sure you want to hear this long tale?"

AJ's instantly and sincerely replied, "Oh yeah – I am very sure."

CHAPTER EIGHT

His parents' story took so many twists that it was sometimes difficult to follow. AJ would have probably been willing to stay up and talk for a few hours more, but he knew that he, his dad, and some other boys from his youth group were meeting at Church at 8:00 AM to work on a service project. In his Church and in the Barton household, "service to your fellow man" was a given. There was a widow in his ward whose yard had become overcome with weeds because of the spring rains. Did he want to get up early to go do yard work (especially since there would be their own yard to tend to in the afternoon)? No, but he and his friends would get the job done quickly, and their reward would be hot Krispy Kreme doughnuts! After the bedtime snacks, the twins were herded to bed, he and his dad did the last-minute planning for the morning, and then he too headed for his room.

After family prayer and all their kids were safely asleep – or at least in their rooms Carmen and Alex sat down in his study. Staring into space, she asked, "Are we giving him too much, too fast?"

"He's a smart kid and seems to be enthralled with the story – as I look at our lives now, it's hard to remember those difficult days. That meeting with Nikki where she recapped the Miami escape and then the news – that indeed our actions may have put our very lives in danger."

Carmen continued to look into the distance as she was replaying that conversation – but there were a lot of other thoughts running through her mind. One that kept popping to the surface was Judy. Sure, she was more than curious about the first girl that her first-born had ever even mentioned, much less showed such interest. Like most moms, this would been enough to delve into and find out more details – but the odd coincidence of her being born not only in Cuba but also in her hometown and winding up in Salisbury, North Carolina, was almost too difficult to imagine.

Hesitantly, she broached, "Did AJ mention a girl named Judy?"

"He did, said she's an amazing softball player – he told me when I dropped him off at Church this morning wanted to see her play..."

"And??"

"Oh, he said she pitched a no-hitter – which in girls' softball is somewhat unusual."

At times, Carmen marveled that her husband, who was

quick on the uptake of so many things, could still be oblivious to many others. "And that is all you remember?"

"It is unusual for sure – plus he said she got two hits and drove in four runs."

"Alex," she sighed in disbelief, "the boy has a crush on this girl – and she is just a little, er, forward."

"How so?"

"She called the house this afternoon looking for AJ..."

"And that means?

Again, sighing in frustration, "When our phone rings, it is a salesman, a political survey, or a wrong number – almost everyone we know calls our cell phone – I don't even know why we still have a landline!"

"Because our internet, cable, and phone line are cheaper when they are in the same bundle."

It was getting late, and Carmen could see she was not getting her point across, "I don't care that we have a landline. It's just Judy had to go to the trouble of googling it to find the number – she knew you were a senior and that A J stands for Alex Junior. And she was, we she was..."

"Rude?"

"Oh gosh no, she was incredibly polite with a strong, confident voice."

"I'm lost."

Carmen let out a sound of exasperation, "I've told you I'm not ready for dating, girls, and the craziness that comes with teens who think they are in love!"

"He went to her softball game – he didn't propose…"

"Dear, dear, dear, a woman can usually read another woman – especially when she is young enough to be my daughter. There is something in her voice that tells me she is very interested in our son – and more importantly, there is something in AJ's voice that tells me he is smitten with this girl."

"OK, I admit, I haven't gone this far down that road – but right now, let's just make sure they keep it on what they call an 'age-appropriate' relationship."

"Meaning??"

"Correct me if I'm wrong, but we've always agreed our standard would be "friends" and group activities at 14 or 15, but no dating until at least 16, and then preferable in double dating or group settings. Yes?"

Carmen took a deep breath, "I guess I just want to make sure we were still on the same page – it is the first time we've had to read this book," she said with a laugh. "But there is something else, it may be just one of the weirdest coincidences in the world, but I can't get it out of my mind."

"What is it Beautiful?"

"She is adopted."

"So, she is a lucky kid because her parents live around here, and she goes to Salisbury High."

Carmen thought out what part of the information was on the top of her mind, and what order she wanted to discuss it. "AJ said her dad's a lawyer, mom's a nurse at Rowan Memorial – they live close by over at 7th and Elm – they are Catholic…"

"I know we don't encourage our youth to date outside their faith – but so far, all that has happened is he went to her softball game."

"There is one other thing, that's the strange coincidence…"

"I'm listening."

"Alex, she was born in Cuba and ended up in an orphanage in Germany, where her parents found her and adopted her."

"Wow. She is one lucky girl – what are the odds of someone else Cuban born so close to us."

"It's more than that, Alex – she was born in Santiago. Her parents or at least her family would have been there the same time as were my parents – remember before I was smuggled out of Cuba as a baby, that is my hometown."

Truthfully, Alex had forgotten – he knew Carmen had told him her birth city at some point, but she grew up in

Miami and maybe visited Santiago once or twice. However, like his wife, he found it remarkable, almost to the point of being strange. "Well, all I can say, is she is anything like my favorite girl born in Santiago and then raised someplace else, she probably is an amazing young woman – and not just at softball," he added with a grin.

****

When AJ retired to his room, like normal, he always read before he went to bed – part of being a college professor's kid – there were always books to read from the time he was 3 years old. He listened on Audible to various subjects, but still enjoyed just turning the pages of a good book. He had just started on a Grisham novel, a writer his dad claimed had mastered "quality trashy fiction," when his phone beeped for an incoming message. Odd, he thought, who would be texting him at this time?

"U up?" it was from Judy

"Y, whatsup?"

"Just thinking about the game today? Can u tlk?"

He hit the call button, and Judy answered, "Hi, I didn't know if you'd be awake."

"Won't be for long – Dad and I and bunch of guys from my church are going over to do 'community service.'?"

"Wow. Are you in trouble," she asked with a concerned tone.

"What?!"

"You know, like when you've done something, and you make restitution for it through, like, community service."

"No, Judy," he said with a laugh – thinking she must have seen him as one of those people out picking up trash on the highway wearing the orange jumpsuits, "No, in our church, we do it as a way of giving back to the community – not as a punishment."

"That's totally amazing – I do some volunteer work too, but many kids our age don't."

"Cool, really, what do you do?" he asked with genuine interest, finding this smart and athletic young woman even more interesting.

"My mom's a nurse at the hospital, and I'm," she giggled, "a candy striper – we wear this red and white top that makes us look like a candy stripe."

"I'm impressed. I've gone to the hospital with my dad to visit people in our ward and saw a girl about our age, dressed like that – had no idea why she was there."

"We help the nurses, we read to the patients, go get things from the cafeteria or gift shop for them – stuff like that. Sometimes we must empty bedpans – that's not a fun part of the job. What's a ward?"

"Sorry, LDS term, it's what we call our local congregations.

"LSD?" she replied with a puzzled tone.

"LDS, Latter-day Saint, many people still call us Mormons. The full name is The Church of Latter-day Saints – but that's a real mouthful. I know you are Catholic; do you go to the Catholic Church of the Sacred Heart – out past 601?"

"It's the only one in Salisbury," she said with a sigh. How did you know I was Catholic?"

"You blessed your food at lunch and then made the sign of the Cross."

There was a pause before Judy replied, with some degree of surprise, "You noticed?"

AJ thought a moment as well before he offered a soft reply, "We always bless the food at our home, but sometimes I do it quickly and quietly at school – or sometimes not at all. But, for you, it looked completely natural. I was impressed."

In the modern high school era, religion was not something often discussed. AJ and Judy both knew a lot of their friends went to Church, but there weren't that many Catholics that Judy knew at school, and AJ, only a handful of his friends from the Salisbury Ward. Like the Catholics, there was only one LDS building in town as well. Both were strong believers in their parents' chosen faith. Likewise, both had grown up in their respective religions and had rarely even been inside the Church of a different denomination. At the time neither realized what an interesting position it put them in being united with a Christian faith, but on the surface worlds apart.

AJ glanced at his phone and realized they had been talking for close to 30 minutes and he really needed to get to sleep if he was going to pull weeds with him and his friends in the morning. Reluctantly he said, "I sort of gotta go – we're getting up early, way too early for Saturday, in the morning."

"I hear you, and I just wanted to mention that I talked to your mom."

"You talked to my mom?" AJ asked with a tone that reflected surprise.

"Yeah, I wanted to know if I could come by and meet her tomorrow – can you believe we were born in the same city in Cuba?"

"I had almost forgotten – we'll be through with our service project by lunch – can I tell her you'd like to come by around 2:00?" All the while thinking, 'I got to get home to take a shower before she gets here.'"

"That would be perfect! You need to get some sleep – see you tomorrow. Don't work too hard. Good night."

"Sleep will be good – see you then, good night."

As he stared at the phone, he realized he had just had the longest phone conversation with a girl in his entire young life. For a moment, he closed his eyes to picture her, first on the mound throwing the last pitch of her first game and then at the lunchroom, ever so quietly blessing her food before making the sign of the Cross. She was different than any girl he knew, and he realized he was growing fonder of her with every encounter.

****

AJ's phone's alarm went off far too early for a Saturday morning; he quickly dressed and met his day in the kitchen, where they both enjoyed a Jimmy Dean Sauage biscuit. Carmen limited their consumption to one day a week – IF they were planning on leaving before a real breakfast. This "southern delicacy" was not her idea of either proper or healthy – but neither were the doughnuts that she knew Alex would be treating the boys on the way home.

"Quick prayer, son, and then let's get the service work done."

Prayers in the Barton household were just a part of their normal lives. AJ and his siblings never even thought about it – it happened every morning, every evening, and every meal. While he never said anything when he was visiting a friend's home, he did notice that prayer wasn't as much of a lot of home as it was at the Bartons. On the other hand, he still felt self-conscious to be seen saying a prayer over this food in the lunchroom. However, on more than one occasion at school, he had thought to himself – if we are to eat this, it needs to be blessed.

Alex, AJ, and the other boys from his Church all arrived at the home of Sarah Jenkins. "Sister Jenkins," as the boys and everyone else in the Ward called her, lived alone in a home that she and her husband Tom had built when he came home from Vietnam in 1968. That was the year he said enough. Tom had enlisted in the Army at 17 in 1943. He had served in three wars and made the Army his life. He was good to the Army, and the Army was good for him. By the end of World War two he had been promoted to staff sergeant right before his 19th birthday.

Along the way, between wars and various assignments around the world, he finished high school, earned a bachelor's degree in political science, a master's degree in military strategy from the Army War College, and rose to the rank of full Colonel.

Colonel Tom's father, like Alex Sr., had been a history professor at Catawba. To his father's dismay and pride, his son dropped out of then Bowden High School to join the Army. Dr. Jenkins, the professor, and his wife, the elementary school teacher, simply prayed for their son's safe return home from the war. When he left at the end of his junior year in high school, it was with a lot of trepidation by his parents. They assumed if they didn't become a dreaded Gold Star family that, Tom would return home, finish high school and college, and perhaps follow his parents as educators. It didn't work out that way. After World War two came Korea, and then Tom served three tours in Vietnam before announcing his retirement shortly after the Tet offensive in early 1968. As a career Army officer and military historian, he recognized early that Vietnam was a war that wouldn't be won.

Salisbury was his hometown, but one filled with bitter memories. During a tuberculosis outbreak in 1947, his mother contracted the then-almost-fatal disease and passed away – she was only 47. Her husband was heartbroken and put off building their dream home on a plot of land near the high school. He remarried and passed away the year before Tom decided to retire. His second wife had died earlier the same year. Tom's return for each of the funerals brought sadness but created an inner draw that when he did retire and leave the Army, he would finally come home.

While he had been away from his "hometown" longer than he lived there as a child, he was nevertheless a "hometown hero." The local newspaper, *The Salisbury Post*, covered his military career with a photo and story of every promotion, commendation, medal, and college degree. Stories like this were the bread and butter for local papers that kept their circulation high, and their advertisers satisfied. So, while Colonel Tom Jenkins's return home was a greatly anticipated event, with the mayor calling for a presentation of the "keys to the city" for our local hero, no one anticipated that he would not be returning as the solider married to the Army, and a perpetual bachelor. A welcoming committee was waiting for him when his plane touched down at Douglas Airport in Charlotte. The local high school band, the mayor, several members of the City Council, and various ladies' auxiliaries were all hand. As the passengers walked down the steps and onto the tarmac, the excitement was building as the hometown hero emerged from the Eastern Airlines Lockheed Electra. A mighty cheer went up, and then a collective gasp. On Colonel Jenkins' arm was a very beautiful and clearly younger Asian woman – who, as all would soon learn, was now Mrs. Jenkins – she was the first native-born Vietnamese ever seen by most of the on-lookers. The crowd stood in silence and soaked up the scene, their own Colonel Tom had brought home a war bride. Her name was Hein Hoang, but she had adopted as her name Diana. She and Tom had been married in a traditional Vietnamese wedding ceremony shortly before his tour in Vietnam ended. A decorated war hero marrying the daughter of a prominent South Vietnamese official, her paperwork for immigration to the United States had been expedited.

When they married, it was a combination Buddhist/Catholic ceremony as many ranking Vietnamese officials were, at least in public, converts to Catholicism due to the influence of the French during the years that Vietnam was a colony of France. Tom's parents had been good Southern Baptists, but he had attended Church sporadically during his 25 years in the service. Like all men who had been in battle, he prayed fervently during some heated firefights on the field of battle. Arriving in Charlotte after traveling almost 10,000 miles, they only wanted a comfortable and quiet homecoming. The town had other ideas. The local Cadillac dealer had provided a new Fleetwood Sedan and a driver; in addition, there were many other private cars, the school bus for the band, and the escort by the Salisbury Police and Rowan County sheriff's department. The high school gym had been decked in red, white, and blue bunting. The event was catered by three local BBQ restaurants, and Tom and Diana were seated as guests of honor next to the mayor and his wife.

As they made their way to the head table he quietly whispered to Diana, "I really wasn't expecting this..."

She smiled and whispered to him in French (one of three languages he had learned in the service), "Chut, ils t'aiment." [Shhh, they love you.]

Tom had a wave of relief; his new wife would be fine. She had been brought up in the best schools in Saigon. In addition to her native tongue, she also spoke French and English fluently. At 22 she had earned a Vietnamese equivalent of master's degree in communication. Salisbury would be another world for both, and a nice quiet change from the years of war and turmoil. The speeches, the keys to the city, and the dinner seemed to go on forever before they were finally taken to what had been his parents' home. He had paid older veteran Sam Jones to watch after the home, keep the grass cut, and start up his dad's car at least once a week. Sam's wife had come in the day before their arrival and ensured the home was neat, tidy and dust free. It was a nice home, which would do for a few months while they planned their future. He and Diana had already agreed to build their own home on the land on which the father-in-law, that she had never met, had planned on building his dream home.

And build it they did. They were married for over 40 years before Tom passed away in 2009 at the age of 83. They had two sons, who, like their father, joined the Army and were making in their career. Both boys, unlike their dad, had married in their early 20s after completing a mission and college. Both were stationed overseas, one in Japan and one in Korea – they had given them 5 beautiful grandchildren. Diana missed them and while she could well afford to have her yard professionally cared for, she had accepted then Bishop Barton's request to let the young men of the Ward help her take of her home. Now 73, she was still very active and truly enjoyed the Saturday morning service projects. The boys enjoyed her as well. She was filled with wonderful stories, and fresh Vietnamese treats and lemonade would always be waiting for them at their break.

AJ had often wondered how this Vietnamese woman had ever found her way to this part of the United States and how she ever joined the Church. As a very young child he barely remembered seeing her with a very old man. He never knew how old she was because, like many Asian women, she didn't show her age. His dad always respectfully referred to her as Sister Jenkins, though many times she had said, "Bishop, Diana is fine." With so many unanswered questions going on in his life, this, too, was just one more mystery.

For whatever reason, that morning at their first break, as Diana brought out the lemonade and treats, AJ asked, "Sister Jenkins, how long have you been a member of The Church?"

She smiled at his simply boyish curiosity and replied, "Well, Tom and I joined The Church in 1969, less than a year after he retired, and we moved to Salisbury..."

"Wow." AJ said, "There couldn't have been that many members back then…"

"No, there wasn't. We met in an old Church that we shared with the 7th Day Adventists, they met on Saturday, we met on Sunday – it worked out well for both of us…"

"Did you know about the Church in Vietnam?"

"We were officially Catholic back then – though my mom clung to some of her Buddhist roots. Tom had grown up a Baptist – like so many people in the South. When he was on his last tour in Vietnam, he was in command of a brigade in the 101st Airborne – his executive officer was a major from Utah, Charley Redman. Charley was a Mormon and one of the most decent men I've ever known. He and Tom not only commanded the brigade, but they also became like brothers. On the night before we left Saigon, Charley gave Tom a copy of The Book of Mormon. We had been married for less than a week and were scrambling to get ready to leave for the States. Tom promised Charley, he would read it sometime when he got home.

When we finally got settled and unpacked, Tom found the book with some of the other items he had brought back from Vietnam. He tossed it on the nightstand, and that night he started reading it at 3:00 a.m. I was sound asleep when he turned off the light and muttered something. The next day he called Charley and told him he wanted to hear about his Church. The next day two young men appeared at our door. Tom invited them in and we sat down to listen to them. I didn't say much – Tom was on his personal road of discovery until that moment I was a very content Catholic. Tom went to Rufty's General Store the next day, and I picked up the book.

When the Mormon missionaries returned the next day, I asked for my own copy. Three weeks later, Charley flew out and baptized my Tom. A week later, Tom was allowed to baptize me. That was in 1969 – five years later, when the Washington DC Temple was dedicated, we were one of the first couples to be sealed there.

A tear ran down her cheek. AJ felt a tear in his eyes. He reached over, took her hand, and simply said, "Thank you."

Diana quickly composed herself and answered, "Oh, thank you for letting me tell you that story about my wonderful Tom, but you need to get back to work, or your dad will think I've kept you too long."

"Yes, Ma'am."

Diana smiled as he hurried out the door. Then she made a mental note to make sure that Alex knew she would again fund the Scouts' summer camp expenses. That little contribution was one that only she and the Bishops of the Ward ever knew about.

An hour after their break, the work was done. Everyone thanked Sister Jenkins for the treats. She praised their work and with the help of two other dads, the boys all headed for the second treat...warm Krispy Kreme doughnuts.

CHAPTER NINE

After the doughnuts, Alex noticed that his son was unusually quiet, so he asked, "Ajee, what's on your mind? You seem awful quiet—I saw you and Sister Jenkins had a nice talk."

"I guess I never thought about it. She seems like a nice older lady; I mean, I know she's Asian – er, Vietnamese, but her story is so amazing – I don't really remember her husband. She said he was 20 years older than her and a war hero."

"That he was son," he passed away when you were only about three years old; we were new to the ward and new back to our real life – but I swapped a few stories with him. Quite an old codger, was sharp as a tack until the day he died."

"Dad, I have never really thought about it, I've been a

member of the Church all my life, but he and Sister Jenkins didn't even join the Church until they were, well in his case, old..."

"AJ, he was in his early 40s and still had a lot of life in front of him...remember your dad is in his fifties," Alex said with a laugh.

"Sorry, didn't mean it that way. Anyway, it just got me thinking about why I believe what I believe."

"As you should, son, we can teach you the doctrines and beliefs of our faith – but you must find out for yourself; it is the life-altering question."

"What do you mean, Dad?"

"Perhaps the question that we all must answer is, 'What is truth?'"

After all that had transpired over the past week, it was a heavy question: a work project and four doughnuts. Carmen would have frowned over so much sugar; Alex made a mental note not to mention that little detail when he got home – and he knew that AJ knew better as well. When they walked into the kitchen, the twins were having a late lunch, and Carmen was cleaning up the kitchen. She greeted both with a quick kiss and asked, "Did my two Scouts go do their daily good deed?"

"Yes dear."

"Sure, Mom, I gotta go take a shower; I want to clean up.'

Carmen winked at Alex and asked her son, "Really, I

thought you might want to tackle part of our yard?"

"Uh, it was really a lot over at Sister Jenkins; I think our yard can wait till I get home on Monday after school; what do you think, Dad?"

"Hmm, well, I guess so."

Carmen was enjoying watching her son squirm, and her husband was totally lost when she added, with a smile, "I forgot. We are having company. Isn't Judy dropping by this afternoon?"

Probably for the first time in his young life, AJ blushed and muttered, "Yes ma'am, she said she would stop off around two o'clock." He then quickly added, "Er, she said she is really excited to meet another person born in Cuba."

"I heard," Carmen replied, again smiling, "go clean up—I have some chocolate chip cookies in the oven."

AJ darted out of the room, and Alex glanced between his son and his wife, "Did I miss something?"

Carmen smiled, "Oh dear, you often miss some of the little things. This little girl that he has been talking to and about and going to watch her play is coming over to the house. She asked me first, and I told her it was OK, plus I agreed. I want to meet another Cuban-born person as well. With the two of us in one house, it will probably be the largest gathering of native-born Cubans in the entire city."

"That, dear, is very true; well, if we are going to have a guest, I'll go clean up as well."

The twins, who had been very quiet, chimed in with a singsong voice that only ten-year-olds can pull off, "AJ's gotta girlfriend, and she's comin' to our house!"

"Silenco, clean up and go play," she said playfully, touching the back of their heads as she walked out of the room.

AJ showered quickly and dressed, looking down at his palms sweating. "Why," he thought," just a friend coming over to meet my family. As he was getting ready to walk downstairs, he heard the doorbell and the twins rushing to answer it. "Good grief," he murmured to himself, "this is turning into a family event."

Fortunately for both Judy and AJ, his mom was also at the door and accepted Judy's most polite introduction and ushered her into the family room as AJ made his appearance, "Hi," he said, trying to sound as nonchalant as humanly possible. Judy was dressed in nice jeans (with no holes or tears as so many girls seemed to like to wear), a simple t-shirt with a Carowinds Park logo, and strap sandals. Seeing that she was the only one wearing shoes, she immediately slipped them off, just smiled and turned to Carmen and gushed, "We never wear shoes in our house either, and you do have a beautiful home; and AJ, you didn't tell me your little brother and sister were so cute."

Looking back he wasn't sure he had even mentioned his siblings – he knew she was an only child so it must have come up, "They keep our family on our toes."

Carmen said, "I have hot chocolate chip cookies just coming out of the oven, with a glass of cold milk and I want to hear about the girl born in my hometown."

Alex was lost in what had happened on this day in history in his study, but Judy, AJ, and the twins immediately followed Carmen to the kitchen. She looked at Judy and offered, "I have regular milk, oat, soy, and almond if you would prefer non-dairy."

"Oh my gosh," AJ thought, " She's going to go on a health kick, even serving us cookies." Wise beyond his almost 16 years, he simply said, "I'll take the almond."

"Me too," echoed Judy.

"We want the real stuff," exclaimed the twins in unison.

After the milk was poured and a huge plate of cookies was set on the table, the two teens joined Carmen at the table – with milk in spill-proof cups and cookies on a tray, Carmen let the twins take their snack outside. The aroma of the cookies filled the house, and a few minutes later, Alex joined them, nodding his head in greeting Judy, who immediately stood up to offer her hand. She had, in 5 minutes, also won over the parents – she already had AJ's heart – even if he may not have truly known it at that moment.

The next hour passed quickly as Judy related her discovery of being adopted and then found out from Germany, at least on her bio-mom's side, that she was Cuban. Carmen had at least been back to the town of her birth in her early teens and had heard many of the stories of pre-Castro Cuba from her Tio y Tia. Judy soaked up the information on the town of her birth like a sponge. "No," unlike Carmen, Alex, and their children she knew little Spanish." But because her father had been some kind of missionary in Germany, he spoke fluent German and had taught it to her since she was adopted at age 3 or 4.

The remark of "some kind of a missionary," caught Alex and Carmen's attention. Carmen asked, "I thought I remember AJ saying your family are Catholics."

"We are; I was brought up Catholic, was baptized after I was adopted, did catechism and first communion, and still go to Mass every Sunday – with my mom. My dad is more of a C and E and HDO Catholic," Judy explained.

"I know the terms C and E – Christmas and Easter – I don't know HDO," Alex said with a look of puzzlement.

"Holy Day of Obligation," answered Judy, "besides Christmas and Easter, there are 16 more. Dad says being at Church 18 days a year is enough for him – he doesn't talk much about religion, I think he converted to Catholicism before I was adopted, but I don't know what sort of missionary he might have been."

The former Bishop's part of Alex's mind kicked in to make a note to find out.

Judy then remarked, "I feel guilty, I've talked a lot about me, and other than what AJ has shared, I don't know too much about you guys. There must be a story about leaving Cuba as a baby and being raised by your Aunt and Uncle..."

"Oh, there is," answered Alex, "as a matter of coincidence, Mrs. Barton and I are just now digging into some family history about our lives before the children – maybe someday Alex will share some of it with you."

Glancing down at her Apple watch, she again practically gushed, "That would be awesome, but I just saw the time. Mom and I are going shopping for a new outfit—AJ, can you call me later?"

"Count on it."

"And, Mr. and Mrs. Barton, thanks for such a wonderful afternoon and those amazing cookies!"

"Any time, Nina, any time, come here and let me show you how a proper Cuban says goodbye." She took Judy in her arms, touched first her left cheek and then right to Judy's, and kissed the air both times. [girl]

Judy shook her head and said, "Thank you! I feel like a real Cuban family member or how do you…"

"Amiga," answered AJ, "friend, feminine."

He walked her to the door, and she turned and said, "If I am an amiga, you are?"

"An amigo."

As she turned to open the door, she quickly touched his left and then right cheek to hers, kissed the air, and said, "Bye amigo. See you later."

"Si, hasta luego," he called in response. [Yes, see you later]

Carmen and Alex watched the scene from the hallway

and realized their lives were going to change.

****

AJ walked back down the hall and turned to his dad to ask, "Remember what we were talking about this morning about how and why people joined the Church or, for that matter, any church?"

"I do; you have a follow-up?"

"I don't know it's weird, you joined the Church, served a mission, and then really wasn't that active…Mom, turning to Carmen, was raised like Judy, a Catholic, and at some point, joins the Church. The Jenkins didn't join the Church until after they got married. Why so different ways, and how, I'm just feeling confused."

Carmen spoke up, "Let's go back to the den – some of the answers, at least as far as your parents are concerned in are in the box of memories we have been exploring."

Alex jerked his head around not quite sure where this discussion was headed, but said, "OK, I guess."

Carmen brought in three drinks, and they all took a place around the desk as Alex brought out "the gap years box." He began, "You remember us telling you how the first place in our witness protection place outside of Colorado took us to the island of Oahu and the city of Honolulu?"

"Yeah, that was crazy, it's where you learned for the first time that mafia guys might be holding a grudge for a long time."

"Yes," Carmen inserted, "Nikki gave us the full run down, made sure we had everything we needed, but then gave us instructions that almost contradicted each other."

"How so?"

"First, she told us to take a couple of tourist days and then start our undercover world as grad students exploring indigenous cultures," answered Alex.

"That seemed obvious to us," continued Carmen, "but then she threw in that you must never draw any attention to yourselves as you never know who might be watching."

"Wait a minute," AJ interjected. You were to be seen and conspicuous, but be seen and inconspicuous?"

Carmen and Alex both laughed as he responded, "That was our first reaction as well."

"So, what did you guys do?"

"First, we asked Nikki for some complete guidelines on exactly how we were to do this," Carmen said.

Alex and Carmen then dug the memory box and pulled out pictures of them at Diamond Head, Pearl Harbor, the war memorials, the Royal Palace, and an amusement park called the Polynesian Cultural Center. Holding up the picture of them as a carefree and very different-looking young couple attending a Luau—an island tradition for all tourists—she paused for a moment.

"That was a fun night!" Alex said with a smile.

"It was an EVENTFUL night in so many ways," Carmen said wistfully looking into the distance, "it was the night we got the first warning call from Nikki."

"Warning?" AJ asked with a curious tone.

"The day before, when we toured the Royal Palace, which is where the last Queen of Hawaii was held as virtual captive when the Marines invaded the island, it seemed like a good place to start if we were going to study the Indigenous people of the islands as part of our cover."

"And, it was," continued Alex, "we had taken a cab from our youth hostel, we had our cameras and notebooks and pocket recorders so we could play the investigative part well, and then I slipped and called your mom, 'Carmen,' not Cathy – your mom gave me a quick elbow, but we didn't think anything about it. When we got to the Royal Palace, I paid the driver, who was very friendly and talkative. I noticed his name was Miguel Russo. I didn't think anything of it. But then..."

"Then, right after the luau, the phone rang in my pocket," said Carmen, "since nobody but Nikki knew the number, it startled us. She immediately asked where we were and where we had been. We told her about the trip to the Royal Palace and how we took our scooters around the island to the PCC and had just finished a luau."

"Was something wrong with going there?" AJ asked.

"Not there, Nikki told us to lock the scooters and meet her at the side entrance in 20 minutes," explained Alex.

"WHY?" AJ almost shouted.

Alex then opened a story of how sometimes a large world can still have a lot of small connections. When Alex was serving his mission in Paraguay, he had a mission companion for six months, and they grew very close – the missionary serving with him was from Hawaii; his name was Steven Russo. Elder Russo was the only member in his family, and at times, in quiet conversation, he had hinted that his father and brother were "involved" in some things he didn't want to talk about. His brother's name was Mike – the cab driver that day, "Miguel," was Steven's brother.

"Honestly," Alex explained, "so much had happened over a few short weeks that I completely forgot that Steven would give me a call about once a month and we'd just talk – he was in grad school at U.H. and told me he was trying to stay away from the family business."

"What do you think the business was?" asked AJ.

"I never pushed – but we know now there is a 'Sicilian connection,' in Hawaii. Nikki filled us in on the details when she picked us up. The 'cab driving gig,' was a cover for a lot of different deliveries that Miguel made on the island. He had seen a picture of me with his brother when we were on our mission. To make matters worse, I had talked to Steven in early February and mentioned that I was seeing this amazing Cuban gal named Carmen."

"Wow," was all AJ could say.

"Nikki's friends from various law enforcement agencies had picked up some chatter about the possibility that the Cuban girl and her gringo boyfriend were in hiding – and suddenly one of their lower-level drivers had seen us in

Honolulu," explained Alex.

"Were you guys, like, totally scared?"

Carmen smiled and replied, "Well, it certainly reminded us that we had not really left our actions and our past lives in Miami. The irony was that night was almost my first real exposure to the Church. Your dad and I never talked much about religion – he was what some would call a 'wayward Mormon,' and while I have been raised a devout Catholic, I never gave any thought to what effect our sudden change would make on my life."

AJ sat silently and absorbed this latest revelation. Like most of the other adults in his life, the parents he had known for the past 15+ years seemed to place the Church at the center of everything they did. His father, an inactive returned missionary, and his mom, a 'non-member,' were things he was having trouble processing in his young mind. "So, what does seeing your cover might have been blown have to do with the Church?" he asked.

Alex and Carmen smiled at each other and Alex replied, "It should have prompted both of us to think about praying…"

"Honestly, while I never talked about it, I always kept my Rosary close during these times – and your dad doesn't talk about it much – but many times when we were in a difficult situation, I noticed he got quiet and just for a few moments closed his eyes…"

"You knew I was praying?" Alex replied.

"Yes, but to answer your question AJ – the Polynesian Culture Center is directly adjacent to the BYU-Hawaii campus, and next to the campus on the other side is the Hawaiian LDS Temple. It was the first time I had knowingly been around so many Mormons and Mormon things in my life. Your dad took me for a walk around the Temple grounds before we went to the Luau – I think it was the first time he openly discussed how important the Church had been to him and how he missed it."

"Wow. This had to be one crazy night, what did your friend Nikki want you guys to do?" asked AJ.

Alex shook his head and said, "She had two suggestions. The first was that they could get our stuff from the hostel and get us off the island within an hour—which, considering how crazy our life had been up until this point, didn't seem like a half-bad idea."

"It was my first thought as well, but tell him the second one—to this day, I shake my head in amazement that we agreed to it."

AJ's gaze darted back and forth between his parents, and he blurted out, "And that was?"

Alex just shook his and replied, "Nikki suggested this was the first break that any agency had on this particular 'family,' if you want to call them that in a long time. She said her bosses wanted to propose that we continue to hide but in plain sight. It would be risky, but they would protect us, and following Miguel or Mike, might lead them higher up the food chain."

"Our first reaction," Carmen explained, "was they were nuts, but then Nikki went into some detail. The Hawaiian Islands are interesting in that one island, to this day, is still privately owned; Niihau was purchased by a private citizen named Elizabeth Sinclair from the King of Hawaii in the middle of the 1800s. It is still owned by her family. There are many native Hawaiians who work and live on the island. It is unspoiled and keeping with our cover, it would be a perfect place for grad students researching Indigenous people to do research."

Alex continued, "And because it is privately owned, access is tightly controlled. She explained they would work with the owners; we would be given very comfortable quarters, and we would have 24-hour security our entire time on the island. They wanted to monitor all the chatter and see if it could lead them further up the food chain of this organized crime family."

"And I guess you guys said, YES?" AJ asked in almost disbelief.

Carmen smiled and replied, "We were young, we didn't have children or a much-extended family to think of. We had already taken on Castro's representatives, some New York families, and rogue CIA agents—it didn't seem that crazy at the time."

By this time AJ was practically shaking his head in disbelief. First, his straight-arrow, strict LDS parents hadn't always been active or, in the case of his mom, even a member. The whole story of how they met, the adventures at the boat show, and then going into witness protection totally blew away any image of his parents as boring people. To him, it was as if every new shared memory was an eye-popping adventure. That fact, then getting close to and learning Judy's story almost simultaneously at times left him almost in a state of bewilderment – which was not the best state to be in with less than 4 weeks of school and finals looming on the horizon.

"AJ, Aaaj," Carmen said in a tender mom voice, "Are you OK? You are just sitting there staring."

"Sorry, Mom, I'm just trying to absorb it all – you guys are so much braver than I could have ever imagined, and I don't know if anyone who knows you would have ever guessed how exciting a life you guys led before settling down to be parents here in a small town."

"Son, never confuse an exciting life as the only measure of a meaningful accomplishment," replied Alex. "I think your mom will agree there is really nothing more exciting in our lives than the day we welcomed first you and then the twins into our lives."

"Your dad Is right – and of all of what you know, think of as 'amazing things,'" she continued with air quotes, "and after deciding to leave witness protection and then enter the Temple and to be sealed for eternity tops all our adventures."

"Wow." I know you and all the leaders talk a lot about the Temple, and I'm really glad when I get to go with the other youth, but I've never heard any stronger statement about its importance than what Mom just said."

Alex stood and said, "I think it's enough for tonight…do you want to explore the lost years anymore, or have you heard enough?"

AJ almost laughed out loud, "No way are we stopping now – you guys continue to amaze me, but I want to hear it all!"

AJ hugged his parents, kissed his mom, and headed for his room. Carmen embraced her husband and in a flood of emotion burst into tears and quietly sobbed, "I love you Alex

Barton, we have truly been blessed."

CHAPTER TEN

C

In his room, AJ sat on the side of his bed and simply pondered how many things could have turned his life upside down in just a few short days. So many things were still clearly the same – and so many things seemed so different. He was trying to imagine his parents as 20-somethings in Hawaii, being watched over by federal agents who were using them as bait to try and catch some sort of Sicilian gangsters. Glancing at the clock he saw it was almost 6:00 in the evening. He thought about Judy and the amazing set of coincidences that had brought them together and seemingly interwoven their families. Starting with the service project through the latest tale of what he now called his parents' 'Boat Show Adventures,' it had been a full day.

Then he glanced at the calendar on his phone and sighed – he was giving a talk in Sacrament tomorrow at Church. One thing LDS youth learn early is being a lay Church, there would be a lot of opportunities for public speaking. Scrolling down he smiled at the assigned topic, "Family history and my family." Thankfully, he was just a youth speaker, and it would only need to be 5-7 minutes – but, how in the world could he even begin to give a talk about his past week? As he was trying to wrap his mind around what safe things he could say the phone dinged with a message. It was Judy; he scrolled down, "Some of the team are going over for some impromptu batting practice; want to come to watch?"

"Wow," was his first thought, eat dinner, watch a Disney flick with his siblings, prepare a talk, or go watch Judy in practice."

He texted his reply, "How lng is practice?"

"About an hour – done before 7:30"

"BRB"

He made his way down the hall and found his parents had adjourned to the kitchen where Carmen was fixing a light soup and sandwich supper. How to ask the question, he decided not to aim at either parent, "Judy wants me to go watch her pitch batting practice – I can be home by 7:30. . ."

Carmen asked, "Don't you have a talk tomorrow?"

"Yeah, but I can still get it done by bedtime. Church isn't until 10 tomorrow."

Alex surprised AJ and his wife, "I'd like to see this young lady pitch too…"

Carmen almost instinctively shot her husband "the look" but immediately softened and said, "That could be fun – I'll feed the twins and save you two some food."

AJ stammered, "Sure, I guess. Can I ask if we can give her a ride to school?"

"Sure, son."

This was a direction that AJ had not expected, but after he left them in the study, they both agreed. First, she really seemed like a nice girl and would be a good friend. Equally, it was much easier to watch them than to worry if they would try and find ways to be together.

AJ called Judy and gave her the news. To his additional surprise, she was excited to have his dad along as well. No, they didn't need to pick her up – her dad was taking her to the field, he could meet AJ's dad.

So it was that 15 minutes later, the two dads, a scattering of other parents, and AJ were sitting on the bleachers at the SHS softball field watching the team take batting practice. Judy was to pitch to the first round of practice. Coach Cato went to the mound and told her freshman pitcher, "Slow it down – this is batting practice, save the fast stuff for the games – OK maybe just a couple, I'll give you a sign, I want a couple of our power hitters to see what it is like to swing at your fastball."

Before taking the field, Judy quickly introduced her father to Alex with a short, "Dad, this is Mr. Barton. His wife is the lady I told you about from Santiago, and AJ here is my partner in art class and designated cheerleader," she said with a lilt in her voice. She then kissed her dad on the cheek and went out to take the mound.

AJ sat on the bottom row as close as he could to the backstop. Alex and Mr. Roland went to the top row of the bleachers. Alex extended his hand and said, "Alex, not Mr. Barton. I'm a prof over at Catawba."

"Brian Roland, an attorney with Fisher & Boyd out of Charlotte, but I also have an office in the Plaza Building downtown."

"That's a landmark; for years, it was called the Wallace Building."

"So, I'm told," replied Brian.

Alex was racking his brain on where to take the conversation. He was meeting the father of the first girl his son had ever shown an interest in. He had several questions. The former Bishop in him wanted to ask about what kind of mission he served in Germany. Specifically, was he now or a former LDS? The Dad in him, though impressed with young Judy, wondered to what standards she had been raised. He was mulling over these and a few other thoughts when Brian opened the conversation.

"Isn't it Dr. Barton? You are a college professor."

Alex was somewhat taken aback, "Catawba hired me with a master's degree as an adjunct. When I finally get around to defending my dissertation, it will be Dr., but I'm not big on titles."

Brian smiled, "I know what you mean, but you have another title that I guess I really need to acknowledge."

Looking puzzled, he glanced to see the number three hitter in the lineup, a fan on three pitches. "Wow, your daughter has an arm. What other title? Dad is one of my favorites."

Brian chuckled as he replied, "She does have an amazing arm for a freshman – she's been pitching since she was nine and we have always tried to keep her from throwing too fast too soon, but Alex, I should say Bishop Barton."

"I am an ordained Bishop," Alex replied, "but I was released last year after serving for almost six years."

"I know."

"How?"

Brian looked down, studied the bleachers, and, looking toward the mound, called out, "Looking good, Judy. We moved here about six years ago, and, as I've done in every place we've lived, I checked the meeting house locator and saw your name."

"You are a member?" Alex said quietly.

"Lifer, great great or more grandparents walked across the plains only a few weeks behind Brigham and the first company."

"And you served a mission in Germany."

"Yeah," Brian replied quietly as a tear ran down his cheek.

" What happened?"

"Bishop, I've been putting off this conversation for so long," he replied while trying to steady his voice.

"Brian, I'm not the Bishop; you can go with Alex – but I'm here, and I will help any way I can."

"Oh, it's a long story; I served a mission in a tough country but loved every minute of it. I came home to St. George, but after seeing Europe, Southern Utah, especially then, seemed so small and 95% LDS. I was getting a lot of pressure to go the "Y" or at least start at Dixie and then go the "Y." [BYU – Brigham Young University]

"Wow. I am a convert – joined the Church in my teens and served my mission in Paraguay. I was from the South, no pressure to go out west, Alabama undergrad and then UM Law School in Miami."

"I know."

Alex again looked surprised as he first responded with a shout of encouragement as Judy wrapped up her time on the mound, "How do you know?"

"I don't blame you for not remembering. USF in Tampa offered me a baseball scholarship. I jumped on the idea of moving to Florida, playing ball all year, and finally being away from Utah and the rigor of a mission. I graduated in three years and then went across Tampa Bay to Stetson Law School. In my first year, I got to go in support of the mock trial team."

"You did mock trial in Florida against other schools."

"Yeah, my freshman year, the UM team destroyed us in the courtroom – you were the 3rd year superstar."

"Oh, my goodness!" exclaimed Alex in total shock. We were in Florida at the same time!"

"We were," Brian answered, "and I was totally blown away thinking, I hope I never ever have to go up against this guy in court. That was in the fall of my freshman year. When it came time for competition in the Spring, we again had to go up against UM – the whole team was dreading facing you guys again. Then we got there, and there was no Alex Barton – we were relieved. BTW. We won that round."

Alex was still trying to decide what to say next. As Carmen observed, he closed his eyes and answered, "I'm glad you guys got the win. The one in the fall was my last major mock trial event before I left law school."

"You were in your third year; I'm betting you had a good gig already lined up after graduation, and then you just left?" Brian said in almost disbelief.

"That, my friend, is a long story—it will have to wait for another time. I know what it was like with me in Miami. There was no time to go to Church, I was studying all the time, and I did Expresso to pull all-night reads—you remember your first year of law school," said Alex.

"Oh yeah – I do."

Alex continued, "Anyway, I met Carmen shortly after that tourney – it was a whirlwind of many kinds. By then, I had packed the Church in a box in the back of my mind, with the idea that someday I'd go back. You?"

"Well," Brian offered, "I made it through law school. I got a job clerking for a federal judge in Washington, then a position with a big firm in DC. I met Maria there at a Georgetown function, she was a senior, and I was smitten at first glance. Yeah, and like you, between the night scene in Ybor City in Tampa, and DC hot spots, the Church was way back in the back of my mind. My mom called every Saturday night to ask if I would attend Church the next day. Sometimes I made excuses; sometimes, I just lied. Not my finest hour."

The two men sat silently for a few minutes and watched Judy take her turn at bat. The other best pitcher on the team threw an outside fastball, then one low, and then all her speed right down the middle of the plate. Judy connected, and the ball landed deep in center field. Alex and Brian joined AJ with a loud cheer. Somewhat embarrassed, Judy turned to look at the bleachers and waved her hands while mouthing, "Not now."

For a minute, the serious talk of their past lives and drifting away from the Church turned to sports. Brian played baseball at USF and was given a chance to try out for the Marlins but turned it down to go to law school. Like many in the South, Alex was a lifelong Atlanta Braves fan. After a few war stories of great games they had witnessed, Alex finally asked, "So what has kept you away for so long?"

Brian bit his lip and said, "Pride. Maria and her family have been Catholics forever. One of the conditions for us to get married was I had to promise to raise any children in the Catholic faith – even if I didn't become one myself. I tried to take what we call their discussions, but I couldn't go that far. So, I promised myself I would support my wife and raise any children as Catholics. It wasn't a concern for the first 10 or 12 years because try as we might, no pregnancy,"

"Judy told us you didn't give her the details until this school year."

Again, shaking his head, he replied, "She was so young, barely three years old, and we fell in love with her the moment we saw her in that German orphanage in Poland. She was meant to be our daughter. So, I kept my word. She was baptized, their version, as soon as we could legally. Did all the right things to raise a good little Catholic girl. I couldn't just tell her that I was faking it all these years when I knew so much better."

Alex's heart ached for his new friend at that moment, "I'm not your Bishop, but this is in confidence between us. But, more importantly, I hope I can be your friend. I have walked some difficult roads to come back to Church as well. When you are ready, know you have someone who will walk with you."

At that moment, Coach Cato blew her whistle to signal the end of practice. Judy ran over, quickly hugged AJ, and then asked, "Dad, can AJ come over for an ice cream sandwich? Mom promised me one after practice."

Brian turned to Alex who looked just bewildered.

"Please, Dad," Judy continued, "I want Mom to meet AJ—he can even bring his dad!"

"Alex, you up for an ice cream sandwich?" asked Brian.

"Short visit, AJ's got a talk in the morning – but I think we should touch base with our wives," he said as both men reached for their phones.

AJ turned to Judy and whispered, "Dad always says, happy wife, happy life, and if momma's not happy, nobody is happy."

Judy sniffled a giggle.

Brian spoke first, "Clear at my house."

"Likewise," said Alex. Both men knew there would be explaining to do after their impromptu dessert.

****

Maria Roland was still wearing scrubs from the hospital. She was a very fit-looking woman with reddish blonde hair who wore her 53 years very well. She was very gracious as she hugged her daughter, kissed her husband, and then turned to AJ and Alex, "So this is the young man and his dad that my daughter has said so much about?"

"MOM!"

AJ grinned and said, "Yes ma'am, I'm AJ Barton, and this is my dad..."

"Alex," his father answered, "we are pleased to have now met the whole family. Judy was at our home this afternoon and Brian and I got to know each other at practice."

"All good impressions, I hope?" asked Maria.

"Very good," replied Alex. It seems my wife and your daughter were both born in Santiago, Cuba—and while I didn't remember it, in another lifetime, Brian and I were in the same mock trial together."

Judy motioned for Alex to pick up the ice cream bar in the bowl on the kitchen island and for him to follow her to the dining room, softly saying as they left, "We'll eat in here." (AJ thought while this Meet the Parents episode plays out – but was grateful to be out of the center of the conversation.")

"That's fascinating!" exclaimed Maria, "when we found out that Judy had been born in Cuba before her parents fled to Europe, I was taken back – you see, my great-grandfather was also born in Santiago. I always thought of us only as Italians, but this grandfather moved to Ybor City at the end of the 1800s when that part of Tampa Bay was the world's cigar capital – outside of Cuba. He married an Italian/American and became completely assimilated. I never even knew of my Cuban heritage until my mom told me when I was a teenager."

Alex's mind was spinning as he tried to keep track of the many ways their lives and now their children's lives had crossed paths. The chance of the two families winding up in a small town only a few miles from each other with such connections had to be astronomically small (and that was not even factoring in the Church connection.)

"Wow," was about all Alex could utter, "Coincidences like these are what reminds us that no matter how big the world gets, we all are more connected than we think."

In the dining room, Judy innocently asked, "Are you like talking in your Church tomorrow?"

"Yeah, I'm the designated youth speaker it will only be about 5-7 minutes."

"Wow, you mean like in front of your whole church?"

"It's not that big of a Church just a couple hundred people on a good Sunday."

"You have to speak in front of 200 people!?"

"Well, in our religion, we grow up giving talks first with kids our own age starting at 3 or 4, so I've been doing it all my life – I guess I never thought of it as a big thing."

Judy sat quietly studying her young friend. She had known there was something different about him from the first time they met in Art Class. The more she found out, the more she wanted to know about him. "What time does your Church meet?" she asked.

"The main church part is at 10:00 – then we have youth and adult classes in the second hour."

"I think I said we're Catholic, we go to first mass at 8:00, but tomorrow we don't have youth Sunday School – could I, like, er, come watch you talk? You came to my game."

AJ grinned, "I got to cheer at your game. I just want people to stay awake during my talk. It would be great, but you need to ask your parents."

In the kitchen, as the adults were comparing places they had lived and how they ended up in Salisbury – Alex only mentioned in passing that he and Carmen had 'traveled abroad a lot' when they first married and that after Law School, he had decided to go into education. The Rolands had lived in Florida, DC, Maryland, and Pennsylvania but had decided to settle in Salisbury when Judy was in middle school. It was close enough to Brian's main office in Charlotte, but he could do much work at the Salisbury branch. Maria loved Rowan Memorial and was the lead Charge Nurse in Labor and Delivery.

Seeing it was a few minutes past 8:00 and he had told Carmen he would try and be home by 8:15, he started to say, "We've got to all get together…" when Judy and AJ entered the kitchen with their now empty ice cream bowls.

Judy turned to her mom (who she knew was the decision maker) and asked, "AJ is giving a talk in his Church tomorrow at 10:00. Since we are going to the first Mass tomorrow, may I go hear him talk? It seems only fair—he came to my game."

Alex and Brian both looked surprised.

Maria asked, "Oh, that's nice – his Church lets the youth have their own service. What Church is it?

Alex replied, "Although we are members of the Church of Jesus Christ of Latter-day Saints, many people still use the term Mormons."

"Oh," Maria replied, "I've heard about them – love their choir – I saw them once in what you call it, the tabernacle in Salt Lake City – I was there for a nurses' convention at the U of U hospital. One of my nurses, Sharma Fuller is a Mormon."

"Yes, she is," answered AJ, "one of my Sunday School teachers."

"Mom," Judy said in almost a whisper, "he's going to be talking in front of the whole church, not just the youth."

Maria turned to Brian and said, "That is impressive. I don't see anything wrong with Judy going anywhere where Christ is taught." And, as I said, "I love their Choir."

Alex softly answered, "We'd love to have her join us or the whole family if you want, but when we sing, we probably won't sound as good as the Choir in Salt Lake."

Alex was trying to sound nonchalant. He knew this was a difficult time as Brian was facing so many of his questions about where he stood with the faith that ran so deep in his blood. Brian had put on his best attorney's face, trying to remember – he knew he had told Maria that he had served as a missionary for "his church" – in the past," but had never shown any signs of interest. She knew that he was a lukewarm Catholic for the sake of her and Judy, but he had always kept his word on raising Judy in the Catholic Church. Maria had nothing but positive impressions of the Church and no idea of the thoughts dashing across the minds of either Alex or Brian. Judy and AJ thought it would be neat to have another excuse to be together.

Brian decided to plunge in and said, "It's a great idea – Judy, I'll be glad to drop you off, but if your mom wants to go hear AJ, I'll be glad to go too – what's the address?" He knew the Church was. He had driven past it a hundred times since they moved to Salisbury almost six years earlier.

"1255 Julian Road," answered Alex.

"It sounds like fun," replied Maria. I want to hear a young man with enough confidence to speak in front of his church. We'll all come—we'll be out of Mass a little after 9:00. We can get some doughnuts and coffee on the way and look for you guys a little before ten."

"I'll be waiting for you guys near the front; you can sit with us – and I promise my 10-year-old siblings will behave," AJ said with as much conviction as he could manage.

"Great, then it's all set – now let me get this guy home so he can make sure it's a good talk," Alex said with a smile.

Judy gave AJ a very quick hug and mouthed, "See you tomorrow."

The adults shook hands, and as they walked towards their car, both Alex and Brian wondered, "What just happened?" In Alex's mind, one thought kept racing across his brain: "Coincidences are miracles in which God chooses to remain anonymous."

****

When they walked into their home ten minutes later AJ turned to his mom and said, "I'm taking a shower and then working on my talk – call me when it's time for prayer." Before she could respond, he kissed her on the cheek and fled the room.

"What was that all about?" Carmen asked inquisitively.

"Oh, it's a real long story," Alex replied.

"OK, I have some baking to do, and I want to make a casserole for tomorrow's lunch. Will you give me the digest version?"

"Sure," he replied, "Judy is an amazing softball player; her dad is an inactive RM who has known where the Church is located since they moved here years ago; he knew I was the former Bishop; he knew me because my UM team defeated his Stetson Law team in Mock Trial debate about a month before I met you; his wife, Maria also has ties to Santiago; she loves the choir because she saw them in the Tabernacle when she was at a nurses' convention at the U in Salt Lake; She is the lead charge nurse in Labor and Delivery and is Sharma Fuller's supervisor."

"Wow, and that's the digest version. Did you leave anything out?"

"Yes – their whole family is coming to Church tomorrow to hear AJ speak – their Mass ends at nine, and they are stopping for coffee and doughnuts at Krispy Kreme on the way."

Carmen put down her cookbook and said, "Why don't you get the twins ready for bed? After prayer, you can come in the kitchen and give me what you would call the rest of the story."

CHAPTER ELEVEN

It is doubtful that many youth speakers in any church have prepared as much as AJ did for his 5–7-minute talk to be given the following Sunday morning. Yes, having a girl he was growing fonder of each day and her family in attendance certainly contributed to his need to get it as close to perfect as possible. Meanwhile, in his parents' bedroom, the pillow talk continued with the conversation that had started in the kitchen.

"Alex," his wife began, "WHY? I mean, you've told me as many of the details as you can, but why would such an unusual family be placed in our lives right now?"

"Not sure dear," why did I buy flowers for a girl I didn't know in Miami so many years ago?"

"Dear," she replied, "you are the one who first taught me there a no coincidences…"

"I know, and I've thought about it many times; it's almost as if, for some reason, they are being placed in our lives for us to help them – or them to help us. I'll think about it; maybe I will get some insight in the morning."

In his room, AJ polished his remarks, practiced several times to come in at exactly six minutes, read it three more times, and finally, just before midnight, turned off his light.

Only a few miles away at the Roland home, there were three different emotions at play. Judy was excited for any chance to see AJ – she imagined what it would be like to say, "That's my boyfriend, AJ."

Maria wasn't that concerned about hearing a young man speak in another Church. She had been raised by strict Catholic parents and was very comfortable in her faith – but since they had often lived in places where there were many other Churches, she had friends of all stripes and denominations. This included a few other Mormons, Baptists, a couple of 7th Day Adventists, a nice Mennonite couple, and a few Jewish and even Buddhist friends. Her antenna was up because Judy had crushes on boy band stars since she was ten, and this one was her first real boy. She would keep her eyes open, but he appeared to be a nice boy from a good family.

Brian, on the other hand, was having a gut-wrenching session. Other than one out-of-town business trip he took by himself almost ten years ago, he had not stepped inside "his Church," indeed the Church of his family for multiple generations, since he left Utah to go to college.

When he went with Maria and Judy to Mass he like others in the congregation. did not go up to receive communion on any given Sunday – no one even seemed to notice. He knew the Sacrament of the Bread and Water would be passed to his entire family. He had managed to put these feelings off for so long – how come they were striking him? He halfway wished he hadn't told Alex as much as he had, then the other half was so glad to finally get something that weighed so heavily on his mind off his chest. He kissed his wife and closed his eyes; tomorrow would be here soon enough.

For the Barton family, it appeared to be a normal Sunday morning. Alex made his famous pancakes, each one in the shape of the given child's first initial. There was a quick review of this week's "Come follow me" lesson and a lot of good-natured ribbing from the twins when they learned that Judy and her family were coming to Church to hear AJ's talk.

Samantha started it with, "AJ's GIRLFRIEND is coming to Church!"

With Jon-Mark adding the sing-song, "Girlfriend, girlfriend, AJ's gotta girlfriend…"

"Silenco ninos! Es sufficente!" barked Carmen – and as usual, the dropping into Spanish silenced the unwanted serenade. [Silence children! Enough!]

AJ shook his head, "I'm going to run through my talk one more time and then we need to get there a few minutes early so I can help prepare the Sacrament."

"Deep breath, son," offered Alex. It'll be fine—we do that every Sunday, and you've given a lot of talks."

"I know, Dad," he said as nonchalantly as possible, "just want to make a good impression. I think I would have been fine if it was just Judy, but her mom and dad?"

Alex grinned; Carmen shook her head. The full impact of the teen years was now upon her, and it happened so fast!

At 9:40, the family loaded into Carmen's Rav4 and headed for Church. It was a trip they had taken almost every Sunday morning since arriving in Salisbury. She remembered what Sundays looked like in another lifetime when they were still in the witness protection program. It was in that 12-year period that she learned so much about the Church; at different times, they even visited LDS Chapels in Hawaii, across Canada, the Western United States, Mexico, Central and South America, as well as Tonga, Australia, and then all the pieces finally fitting together in New Zealand. Those were surreal times when a tremendous amount of her knowledge of the Doctrines of the Church was first acquired, yet she always felt uncomfortable. It wasn't Alex and Carmen visiting a far-flung Ward of the Church; it was strangers, Aaron and Cathy, undercover as grad students. Now, long behind them, she looked at her husband and three children. So distant a memory, and yet with 'family history,' being AJ's talk – so close to the surface.

Arriving at Church, they parked in their "regular spot," AJ rushed in to help the other boys of his age prepare the bread and water for Sacrament. As with any Church service, LDS or otherwise, the Sunday Meeting was a time for what good Baptists often call "fellowshipping." AJ was trying his best to simply focus on the basics. One and a half slices of bread on each tray, another boy from his class, Trey, was filling the water cups. AJ straighten the white tablecloth on the

Sacrament table at least three times more than normal. Trey finally asked, "AJ, you OK? You seem jumpy this morning."

"No, no I'm fine."

"I saw the program, you're the designated youth speaker, better you than me." Trey said with a smile.

"I'm OK. There's going to be a family here to listen this morning, and I hadn't expected it."

"Out of towners?"

"No, they are from Salisbury, Mr. and Mrs. Roland and their daughter…"

"Judy?" Trey said with a little surprise.

"You know her?" Alex asked, and then it clicked: "Trey Fuller was Sister Fuller's boy, his age."

"Her mom works at the hospital with my mom," Trey added, "isn't she a freshman?"

"She is, she's my partner in Art Class. I was at the girls' softball game the other night, and somehow, it came up that I was giving a talk. The next thing I knew her whole family was coming to Church this morning." AJ realized he was intentionally leaving out a lot of details but sometimes wished Salisbury wasn't this small of town - where everybody seemed to know everybody.

AJ's downplayed intro seemed to satisfy Trey, who simply replied, "That's cool. Good luck with the talk, man. You are in good company today; Elder Jones of the Area Presidency is on the Stand." Having grown up as a BK "Bishop's kid," he was quite comfortable being around the important leaders of the Church but speaking on the same Sunday with one added just one more twist to this unusual day.

AJ took his place sitting with the other young men who would pass the Sacrament shortly after the meeting started but kept glancing to the rear of the Chapel – at 9:55, his family, followed by the Rolands, walked in together. AJ caught Judy's eye, and she immediately smiled and waved. He breathed a sigh of relief when he saw they were dressed like everyone else, as he knew some churches dressed a lot more casually on Sunday mornings. Judy's Catholic church attire more closely matched his own, what the old people still called, Sunday Best. He then noticed it was the first time he had even seen her in a dress. For a moment, he felt his heart flutter; he had never really thought about Judy or any girl being pretty, but at that moment, Judy was simply beautiful in his young eyes. Quickly he shook the thoughts out of his mind.

The prelude music had started and a few minutes past 10:00, Bishop Barnes stood and opened the meeting. Alex had explained to the Rolands who were sitting with them, the Sacrament procedure since he knew it was quite different than their own faith and that partaking of the bread and water was totally optionally, they could choose; the only counsel was that, like the Sacrament in their own faith it was to remember the sacrifice of Jesus Christ. Alex caught Brian's eye and gave him a reassuring look that conveyed "It's ok either way."

As it happened, when it was time to pass the Sacrament to the Congregation, the row on which they were seated was one to which AJ would pass the tray. Judy looked at him, and for her, it was the first time she had seen AJ in a white shirt and tie. In her young eyes, he simply glowed. She quickly took a piece of bread and passed the tray to her mother and father, who did likewise.

For Judy and Maria it was a totally different way of partaking of the Lord's Supper, while different it did not necessarily seem strange to them; but, for Brian, it was bringing back a flood of emotions, from his own youth when he had passed the Sacrament so many Sunday mornings in their Ward in St. George, Utah, to his mission days; and then the empty feeling the day he first chose to skip Church and slip in after leaving Utah for college. He quietly took the bread, and a tear ran down his cheek. Maria saw it, squeezed his hand, and wondered what had provoked such an emotion.

The water was then passed [in the LDS Faith, water is used in lieu of wine or grape juice to signify the blood of Christ], the young men returned to their positions, and they were dismissed to sit with their families. AJ instead took a place on the stand as the program was introduced. He heard his name, "Alex Barton, Jr. or AJ as we call him," announced Bishop Barnes. AJ tuned out the rest of the announcements as he glanced at the printed copy of his talk that he had polished so much the night before. He heard the Bishop turn to him and say, "AJ, your turn."

The next voice in his head was so profound that he almost shook his head in disbelief: "Speak from the heart, AJ. Speak from the heart."

He went to the pulpit, laid the talk in front of him, closed his eyes for a real quick prayer, and began, "Good morning, Brothers and Sisters, I have a talk which I prepared and will share most of it with you, but I must first say that I feel prompted to say –When I was assigned to talk on the importance of family history, my first thought was talking about the Mormon pioneers and how I had read about some of my father's relatives who had crossed the plains and built the Church in the Valley of the Great Salt Lake – and I realized, to know my family history, I really needed to know more about my own parents."

Carmen shot Alex a look to say, 'Where is he going with this??'

"To be honest, while I love my parents and even my sometimes annoying little brother and sister, it seemed like we were one of the most boring families on earth."

The Congregation laughed politely.

"While going through some of our family files, I discovered that my parents were not only the wholesome adults who are doing such an amazing job raising my siblings and me but have also had many adventures that I would never have dreamed possible. Their sacrifice and persistence in doing what is right are amazing lessons for which I will forever be grateful. Thank you, Mom and Dad. I love you."

AJ then reverted to his prepared talk on how family history allowed us to see that we are so much more than our nuclear family and that, in reality, we are all one large family, even the family of loving heavenly parents. He again thanked his parents and then paused to say, "And, I am truly appreciative that my friend from school and her parents were able to join us this morning." He caught Judy's eye, who simultaneously smiled and blushed.

The rest of the meeting progressed as announced, with the congregation proving Alex's warning to Maria correct, the local ward did not sound as good as the Choir in Salt Lake. It was a fourth Sunday, and the Rolands were invited to stay for the second hour. Brian was surprised when Maria suggested she would love to join Carmen in the women's meeting. The youth were having a joint meeting that day, so Judy and AJ certainly didn't mind. Brian was wrestling with attendance at the adult Priesthood meeting, which he had not attended in over two decades.

When their respective meetings were over, the Bartons and Rolands walked together to the parking lot. Maria, with genuine enthusiasm, thanked them for letting her family join them that day. To AJ, she turned and said, "I was very impressed. Your remarks and insight were so much beyond your years."

Judy gushed, "I thought you were amazing."

It was AJ's turn to blush as replied, "Thank you, and thanks for being here. It's always good to have friends who are more than family supporting you."

"You did a great job, son," added Alex.

"Better than you will you know, young man," said Brian, "better than you will ever know – you touched my heart today as well."

Alex was the only one beside Brian who realized the depth of his remarks and knew his new friend was having a soul-searching experience. The Hispanic came out in Carmen as she hugged her new friends, kissed Judy, and whispered to Maria, "Call me; we need to get together soon."

Judy gave AJ a quick hug and mouthed the same message to him, "Call me."

The twins observed it all, trying to stifle their giggles. It had truly been an interesting Sunday morning for both families.

When they arrived home, Carmen's casserole had just finished cooking from the pre-set time when she left for Church. The family gathered, as always, for lunch and a discussion of "What did we learn at Church today?"

Sammy popped up with, "AJ gave a good talk and Judy is cute."

AJ shook his head as his dad added, "Thank you, Sam. I'm glad you got that in the right order. What else?"

"We will be 11 this year, which means next year is the year we will turn 12, so we get to be in Young Men/Young Women," added Jon-Mark.

AJ shook his head almost in disbelief when he realized his primary-age siblings would be in the same program as him next January.

Carmen's contribution, "What a wonderful family the Rolands are – Maria and I had a great talk after Relief Society. She admitted to having many Mormon friends, and she and Sharma got to talk to each other as well. She told me that somehow she suddenly just felt comfortable being with us in Church. Even though it is so different than her own faith."

"It was a good Sunday. The Rolands are a good family. AJ, you must be doing something right at school to attract good friends. Judy does seem like an exceptional young woman."

"You are right, Dad – she is amazing. I'm glad that fate brought us together in Art Class cause normally, as a freshman, I would never have had a chance to know her. But, on another subject, about what I said this morning, I meant that, but I want to hear more."

Carmen replied, "For the first time I realized that in many ways it is as important for us to share the story, as it is for you to hear it. We'll talk later. But let's clean up first."

****

On the way home Judy asked, "Can we eat at that place with a nice salad bar?" Without even thinking Maria replied, "Not a bad idea, I don't really want to cook, what about you dear?"

When her husband did not respond, she repeated the suggestion, "Dear, Judy asked if we could eat at the Chanticleer —she wants the salad bar."

Snapping back to consciousness, Brian, who had been deep in thought, finally replied, "Sure, that sounds great."

At the restaurant all three decided to order the rather elaborate Sunday Salad Bar and were soon at the buffet building their personal feast. When they were again seated, Brian offered a blessing on the food, and all three made the sign of the cross after amen. For Brian, it was a reminder of how far, and yet how close he still was to the faith of his fathers.

Judy, whose tone clearly showed some starstruck feelings, asked, "Wasn't AJ awesome? I mean, to be my age and get up and give a talk like that to an entire Church—I don't even like to stand in front of my class."

"He was very impressive," agreed Maria.

Brian pondered, remembering his own childhood of giving talks in Church, and he offered, "LDS kids get the opportunity to speak young and often; they don't have any paid ministry."

"LDS?" Judy asked in a quizzical tone, "What's LDS?"

"Mormon shorthand," replied her dad, "their full name is The Church of Jesus Christ of Latter-day Saints...hence the LDS for Latter-day Saints."

"Oh yeah," Judy responded, "I remember AJ saying that when he told me what Church he went to."

"You know, dear," Maria began, "I almost forgot you were born in Utah – you've really talked about religion. Were you ever a Mormon?"

Brian paused; he had managed to avoid the question for over 25 years. He had simply gone with Maria to the Catholic Church, told them he was a Christian and had never officially become a Catholic, but promised to raise any children in the Catholic faith so he could be married to his wife. And now, the two most important people to him in the world were staring at him, waiting for an answer.

He took a deep breath, smiled, and punted, "That is a short answer with a long explanation. Let's finish our food, then tackle the fresh apple pie at the end of the buffet, and we can enjoy both our food and the answer."

His surprisingly chipper, though avoidant, answer

bought him the time he needed to best frame his response. Indeed, when the meal was finished and the apple pie was consumed, his lawyer training and presentation skills were ready to go. Judy started simply with, "You were raised a Mormon, weren't you?"

His daughter's perception amazed him as he watched both her and Maria waiting for his answer. "The answer would be yes, but why are you so certain?"

"Because, looking at AJ and his dad, you have that same look."

That response caught him a little off guard in that he hadn't been accused of 'looking like a Mormon,' since his mission days in Germany. But he quickly recovered and decided that the truth, or as close as he could come to it, was the best way forward. He began, "My family, which I know you've never met dear," he said, looking at his wife, "trace our roots to the first Mormon settlers who walked across the plains. I was raised in The Church of Jesus Christ of Latter-day Saints. The missionary work that I have only mentioned as if it was just something I did one summer was two years in what was then known as West Germany."

"Why didn't you ever tell me?" asked Maria.

"You were so much stronger in your faith than I was then. After my mission, I left Utah; I was from St. George, it was a little Mormon enclave in the desert of Southern Utah. I had been a good 'Mormon boy' all my life, the mission was great – but I saw so much of Germany that I just wanted to see not only the Mormon world but the rest of the world."

"You thought I was strong in my faith?" Maria queried.

"You were, you were unabashedly Catholic from the day we met. I was the one who stepped away from my faith, and at that point, I wasn't looking back – the fact that Catholics could drink wine didn't hurt either," he said with a smile and a half attempt at humor.

"Daddy, you've always been a good Christian, regardless of whether you were Catholic or Mormon. You are a good person," Judy said with a pained look on her face.

"Let me set the record as straight as I can," Brian replied, "Yes, dear, you are a much stronger Catholic than I ever was a Mormon. And, yes, I accepted the responsibility of raising our daughter as a Catholic as the promise I made to marry you – a decision I have never regretted. The two of you are what has helped me be the man I am today. And, maybe Judy just nailed it on the head – it isn't about being a good Catholic, Mormon, or Baptist -it's by being a good follower of the Good Shepherd."

Judy smiled, got up and walked over to her dad and simply said, "I love you."

Maria reached over and grabbed his hand and echoed the same, "I love you, and our daughter is wise beyond her years. We are very fortunate to have so much love in our family and to be able to now have friends like the Bartons. I am, for one, glad that AJ is our daughter's Art partner, so we could meet him and his family. But let's go home—it's time for a nice Sunday afternoon nap.

At the end of that long day, both the Bartons and the Rolands knew that somehow, life was changing because of a friendship that had started simply enough with their two oldest children. The adults each pondered the events and where life would go from there. Judy and AJ were high school sophomores – high school crushes could end as soon as they started, but the new wrinkles of Brian's past relationship with the LDS Church were there to stay regardless.

Brian, even for all of his reassurance to his family, knew he had to confront his past and his faith. His own parents had died in a car crash shortly after he graduated from Stetson – the next year, he had met Maria, and after being away from the Church for several years and his parent's death, the course he had taken then seemed so much simpler.

Maria pondered in her own heart: Had Brian really given up his faith for hers, or were there more layers of this onion yet to unpeel? Regardless, she knew now more than ever that he was indeed a great man and was glad they were in this time of decision together.

Alex reminded himself that his role was to support his new friend but that he was not his Bishop, and he must let Brian choose his next move.

Carmen saw so much of her own life in Maria—she, too, had been raised as a good Catholic girl. Where would their lives have been if Alex had not opened up to her that night in Hawaii and just kept those feelings to himself for more than two decades? She closed her eyes before she went to sleep and said her own silent prayer of thanksgiving.

CHAPTER TWELVE

AJ had told his parents that he was anxious to hear more. Carmen acknowledged that she realized telling this story and passing it down to her firstborn was, in many ways, as important to her Alex as it was for AJ. The twins went to bed at 8:00. AJ and his parents talked until almost 11:00 when the "mom" in Carmen kicked in, and she insisted AJ needed to get to bed so he could get to his Seminary class on time Monday morning.

Since the first time he and his dad had talked only a week earlier, he had come away from every session wondering if this story could take any other twists and turns. So far, the answer was, "Yes." Judy had texted to say goodnight at 10:00—both parents saw him glance at the phone, and Carmen asked, "Judy?"

"She was just saying she loved the day and wishing us a good night."

Carmen smiled, "Send her a short, good night."

Then their story continued. When AJ finally retired to his room, sleep was the farthest thing from his mind. He showered quickly, threw on his PJ bottoms and a t-shirt, then opened his MacBook for his journal entry. He wrote for 45 minutes almost non-stop. Hitting the high points of what he had been told, he wanted to make sure he kept it all straight in his mind. The entry read:

> My parents really opened up to me about their life in Hawaii after they were outed and agreed to be used as bait. I couldn't believe it. They were transported to this private Hawaiian Island called, Niihau by a registered Hawaiian ferry craft. The island was a perfect place if they really had been grad students researching indigenous people because the Hawaiian natives living there were indeed preserving native traditions. Almost all of them had lived there all their lives, some were quite old and had relatives who had told them the story of the white woman who bought the island from the king of Hawaii in 1864.
>
> Mom went into detail about this one lady, who turned out to be a member of the Church, who was still working in the kitchen at the main house at the age of 94. Mom said she was incredibly spry for a person of her age – indeed would have been considered very active if she had been 25 years younger. Her name, and I probably haven't got the spelling right was Akela. Mom said she never knew her last name, the other natives called her Tūtū wahine Akela– and I know I butchered this one. I'll ask mom later – she said it means Grandma in Hawaiian. To dad

the fascinating thing was that Akela's grandmother had lived to be over 100 and was there when the island was first sold!

For me, that would have been amazing enough – but, then Dad made the story even better. The reason that Akela was a Mormon was because her grandmother was one of the early converts to the Church in the 1850's. Akela told them the story of how a young white boy had been sent to be a missionary. He was only a teenager – about 16 years old. I thought wait a minute I've heard this story. Then Akela told them the young boy's name was Joseph F. Smith – the nephew of Joseph Smith who was on his first mission, and his first trip to the islands of Hawaii. Mom told me that after first meeting the Hawaiian grandma, she had to ask Dad a lot of questions about the Church. There were so many terms that were familiar and yet strange to her. Growing up Catholic, she had heard of the Apostles all her life. But they only had first names, like Peter, Paul, John, and Matthew, and they all had the added title of Saint. Now she was discovering her husband belonged to a Church where all the members were called "saints," and their apostles weren't men who had been dead for 2,000 years.

This all started to make even more sense to her when Akela told her grandmother's tale of a man who was "not good." He was a white man and for a while took over the Church and ran it like he owned it he made the natives enter his home, which was the best one in their village, on his hands and knees. That is when young Joseph and two apostles from Salt Lake City came out and helped bring the Church back in order and again were following the prophet Brigham Young. She told how young Joseph had helped the Church buy a large tract of land on the north shore of Oahu – right where the school, the culture center and most important the Temple still sit to this day. Mom admitted, talking about prophets was even stranger than talking about apostles, but dad related it to how her faith has the Pope.

These stories alone would have had me shaking my head in wonder, but then dad grew very serious and explained that Nikki had been correct, we were being watched and we had to start being very careful. We thought we would be safe on Niihau because it was isolated, private and protected. Nikki told them they were for the "next few nights" going to have a security team stationed on the island, just to be safe. Mom said initially she didn't like the idea, but that Nikki promised her they would be in the shadows, and she would probably never see them.

Suddenly, Mom and Dad were back in real cloak-and-dagger stuff – and as they related, two nights later, they were in real danger. Dad said they had spent the day talking to a lot of the old workers on the island that Akela had been kind enough to introduce to them. He explained that this was a real door opener to get Native Hawaiians, some of whom were still really suspicious of white people from the mainland, to talk openly to them. That night they went to bed when suddenly a brick came through their window, followed by a gasoline bomb. Mom said she screamed! And the door burst open, followed by two men wearing flak jackets that said FEDERAL AGENT. To their relief, they smothered the flames. Dad and Mom admitted they were both beyond terrified. In the distance, they heard an exchange of automatic gunfire, and then the agent's radio squawked, "Targets neutralized, all clear."

Dad explained that according to their rescuers, two hit men must have been dropped off by a fishing boat, and they made their way silently to the island in a rubber raft. If the feds hadn't picked them up, but when the brick and the gas bomb came through their window, they knew the MO immediately. The projectiles were thrown that would cause a fire, and then when they ran outside, they were waiting to gun them down.

Mom buried her head in her hands as Dad told the details; I was stunned. There were four men watching their little guest house. Two came in the back to secure them and the house. The other two picked up the bad guys with night vision glasses. The agents had fired a short round to draw fire – and the moment it did, as the radio indicated the bad guys were "neutralized."

Which diary is why I am still up – how does one go to sleep hearing your parents tell a story like that? Mom promised more details tomorrow, but she said, "We were evacuated to a safer SAFE House at first light."

****

Needless to say, when AJ and Alex left for Seminary the next morning, he was very tired and still amazed. Only Alex was in the kitchen and explained, "Your mom had a hard night, that experience on Niihau was one of, if not the worst, night of our lives. She's OK, but I just let her sleep."

"Dad, how do you go on when something like that happens? Didn't it just shake your whole world, like is the witness whole protection gig going to work?"

"Yes, and no son. It worked – it terrified us in the process, but the protection held. But let's get you out the door."

On the way to church, AJ broached the question that Carmen and Alex expected was coming, "Dad, I don't want to share the why or much of the details, but can I at least share some of this with Judy? We talk every day and I just, I, I…"

"Son," Alex began, "We, especially your mom, feel you need to know this story, not because it's scary, but because it reminds us that we are all put here on earth for a purpose. Our story simply verifies that there is a shield placed on all of us—we will be protected in order to fulfill that purpose."

"Uhh, you've sort of told me this before, but what about Judy?"

Alex chuckled, "The Rolands are in our life for a purpose as well. You and Judy are young, but a connection is forming. Yeah, talk to her – no real details other than your parents are far more 'exciting' than you had ever imagined."

"That's an understatement dad. Class is starting. Judy has practice after school and no games, so I'll be home about the regular time. Love you."

"Love you too son, remember –"

"I know, remember who I am." AJ smiled, hopped out of the car and headed for his class.

After the class, on the way to school, he was joined in the walk by his friend Trey, who had called out to him, "Hey, wait up!"

"Sure Trey, another Monday, right."

"For sure – hey what's up with all of Judy's family coming to hear you at Church? My mom was like blown away seeing her boss in Relief Society."

"I told you I sort of went to her game. We are partners in Art Class, and when I let it slip, I was talking, and the next thing I knew, the whole family was coming too."

"Are you guys dating?"

"Trey, like you, I won't be 16 until later this summer—my dad was a bishop, and my mom's an overprotective Cuban mom. Do you think I will just start dating?"

"I've never gone to a girls' softball game or had a girl come to hear me talk – just saying if it walks like a duck."

"OK, I like her a lot. She has some real interesting ties to our family history."

"What?"

"She was born in Cuba in the same city that my mom was born."

"For real??"

"She's adopted. Her dad was German, and for whatever reason, she was adopted out of Germany from some orphanage in Poland. German was her first language, and her dad speaks German, so she is bilingual."

"Wow, and she's not bad to look at either – when will she be 16?"

"Later this summer."

Trey laughed and poked his friend, "I see a first date in your future, later this summer. And a lot of 'group activity' between now and then." [Yes, in LDS tradition youth often go on what can best be described as group dates at 14-15, but traditional dating is usually reserved for 16 and older]

When they walked up to the front of the school, Judy was waiting. AJ blushed as she called out, "AJ, over here!"

Trey punched his friend, "Your future is calling," he said with a smile.

Judy ran up to him and, without any hesitation, gave him a quick hug, exclaiming, "Yesterday was wonderful – you were amazing – your church was wonderful, but something else amazing happened."

As she spoke the first bell rang, "Can you meet me for lunch? I really want to talk about what happened yesterday!"

"Sure," AJ replied quickly.

"Great," she replied, and then, without notice, she gave him a quick kiss on the cheek, "See you after the third period."

Trey walked up and joined AJ as they headed to first-period Geometry. He put his arms around AJ's shoulder and simply offered, "Wow. It's a good thing you are not dating."

AJ, somewhat embarrassed and somewhat bemused, was thinking of a comeback remark when he simply blurted out, "I told you, she's Cuban, and they kiss all the time."

****

The morning classes seemed to drag longer than normal, and when the lunch bell finally sounded, he was not surprised to see Judy waiting for him at the tray line. Lunch was the predictable hamburger, fries, and corn with peanut butter cookies for dessert—not gourmet food, but not bad for a high school lunchroom.

Judy practically gushed as he walked up, "Wait until I tell you what I found out yesterday!"

They made it through the lunch line and decided to sit at one of the outside tables on the patio. This time they both took a moment to quietly bless their food. As soon as Judy finished with the sign of the Cross, she practically blurted out, "AJ, my Dad is a Mormon!"

"What??"

"Yeah, it came out Sunday when the family went to the Chanticleer for Sunday lunch," she began, "he started to explain something about your religion, and it dawned on me – he talks a lot like you and your dad."

"I'm confused, Judy; what do you mean he talks like me and Dad?"

She looked down and studied her food before responding, "I mean, since the first time when we really talked and then after I met your mom and dad, there was just something different; I don't even know how to explain it; your countenance is different. But then I began thinking, where have I seen this? And then, when I was listening to Dad talk at lunch yesterday, it clicked!"

"So, what did you do?"

"Dad's a lawyer, I have always been taught, if you want to

find out something, ASK. So I asked."

"What did you ask?"

"I asked him if he was raised a Mormon."

"And??"

"He was like totally stunned, but then it all came out, he was born and raised LDS. His ancestors walked across the plains with someone called Brigham..."

"Brigham Young?"

"That sounds right, the way he said it I guess he thought we'd know he was someone important."

AJ paused and smiled for a moment. Of course, he had heard of Brigham Young all his life. He knew from his dad that the Prophet Brigham Young had led the Saints to the Utah valley, but in addition to being an important Church leader, as the head of the Mormon Pioneers, he had played a major role in the westward expansion of the United States—something Judy and other Freshmen wouldn't learn from the classroom until their junior year in U.S. History.

"Brigham Young played a big part in the Church history. Where did your dad say he grew up?"

"Some town called St. George. He admitted that after spending two whole years – can you believe that, when he was like 19, he went and taught about the Church in what he called, West Germany,"

"Did he say why he stopped going to Church?"

Between bites, the story unfolded, "Dad seemed embarrassed to admit it – but he said he was tired of all the rules, and after spending time in Germany, he just wanted to really experience the rest of the world. He moved to Florida to go to college, stopped going to church, and after his parents died, he went to DC, met my mom, and decided she was a stronger Catholic than he was a Mormon. When he married her, if he wasn't going to convert, he had to promise to raise any children in the Catholic faith."

"Wow. That's like nothing I could have imagined. How are you handling it?"

Judy reached across the table, touched his hand, and said, "I am very happy in the many things I have learned about Christ in my Church; and I'm proud of my dad for finally being able to tell us, and, and, one other thing."

AJ looked with a quizzical look into Judy's eyes, "What else?"

"AJ, I'm glad your family, and especially you came into my life. It makes me feel warm all over just knowing such a great guy and his wonderful family."

At a loss for words, he finally blurted out, "Judy, I am just happy that I met you. Dad has always taught that coincidences are miracles where God chooses to remain anonymous."

As he spoke, the bell rang. Judy grabbed her tray and impulsively kissed him again. She said, "I have practice right after school. Talk when I get home? Call me. I have to get to the other side of campus. I got to run."

AJ gathered up his tray and sat silently wondering, "Where is this miracle going to take us?"

Lunch went by too fast – the rest of classes went by too slow, and when the final bell sounded, AJ was more than ready to head home to try and sort out the many twists and turns his life was taking in the final part of his sophomore year.

Walking home with his thoughts he was glad to see his mom's car in the driveway. He bound in and found her in the kitchen. She greeted him with her standard, "Hola mi hijo primogénito. ¿Qué pasó en la escuela hoy?" [Hi first-born son, what happened in school today]

"Nada, well actually a lot…" [Notihing]

"Digma – tell me son!"

With that, the whole story of his conversation with Judy unfolded. Carmen kept quiet, not telling her son that she and his dad already knew this part of the story. She could tell by the emotion in his voice that his thoughts were jumbled so when he finally blurted out, "Mom, why are so many things happening in my life all at once? First finding out the many things about you and dad that I never dreamed – then meeting the first girl I've really liked and then finding out that her dad is or has been a member of the Church. Mom this is all in a week's time!"

"Ah son, life can be like that – sometimes it seems like the same old same old day in and day out, and then a thousand things seem to happen all at once. Then the mom's voice kicked in, "You really like Judy, don't you?"

AJ felt his face flush, and he stammered, "Uhh, well, yes – we're not dating or anything; we're just friends."

Carmen smiled and, in a reassuring, answered, "I like her too – her mom and dad seem like great people; it's OK to first say you really like her and to have really good friends. Do what you are supposed to do, as you always have, and it will all fall into place."

And then, as often happens in what could be a tender moment, the kitchen door flew open with the twins' arrival from school and the chorus of, "MOM! We're hungry. Can we have a snack—HI AJ!"

Carmen and AJ both smiled as she offered him a reassuring, "We'll talk more later."

CHAPTER THIRTEEN

Monday night at the Barton home was reserved for "family night." For years in the church, it was the only night in which no activities, other than "family events," were planned. Leadership in the Church recognized that with the changing world that "a specific night" reserved for families was more practical than saying it was required to happen exclusively on Mondays. As long as they had been parents, for Alex and Carmen, it was Monday night, and so the change never affected their family. The indication that things might be changing came when Carmen had to call AJ to the family room three times – because he and Judy were comparing notes of how school had gone for them that day.

This was family game night – and so after several rounds of "Apples to Apples," and an evening prayer, Carmen announced, "Snack time," and everyone adjourned to the kitchen for hot fudge sundaes. After cleaning up, the twins headed for a bath and bed. AJ turned to his mom and asked, "Can we talk about what happened after you were rescued when you were targeted by the bad guys on Niihau?"

"In the study," Alex nodded. The three then adjourned for what would be another night of discovery for AJ.

AJ with anticipation in his voice asked, "So the Federal agents killed the people who were going to kill you?"

Alex watched his wife wipe away a tear and replied, "Yes, son. We hate that anyone had to die because they were told to hurt us – it took us a while to come to terms with that. Fortunately, we were immediately whisked off the island."

"Where did you go?"

"That night," Carmen explained, "we were taken to a safe house on the Big Island. The next day, our belongings were gathered and brought to a private airstrip. A government Lear Jet was waiting, and that was the end of our Hawaiian research project."

"But where did they take you?"

"Nikki explained they wanted us back under deep protection and no longer being 'hidden in plain sight,'" answered Alex. "So, they flew us to San Diego."

"Why San Diego?"

"Actually, a very special area near San Diego, Naval Amphibious Base Coronado, home to the training facility for the U.S. Navy Seals," explained Alex.

"No, no, no," stuttered AJ. "You and Mom didn't become SEALS in this crazy adventure?"

Carmen smiled, "No, we didn't become SEALS and learn to blow up things and take out bad guys ourselves. But there is a little-known detail about that base – the witness protection program uses some of the same instructors who train the SEALS in self-defense to train people under protection, who might need to know how to protect and defend themselves."

"No," Alex replied almost hesitantly.

"MY PARENTS were trained by the same people, at the same place, that Navy trains the men who run special dark ops for the government – like taking out Osama bid Laden??"

"Slow down, son," asked Alex. Being trained in self-defense by experts does not mean we trained as assassins. We trained more on how to watch for trouble and, if we were in a situation where our lives or safety were in danger, how to defend ourselves.

"Like what, what did you learn?"

Carmen smiled and replied with a grin, "Well duck and cover…"

"How do hide under a desk?" asked AJ.

"A little more complicated than that," Carmen continued, "in addition to various evasive procedures based on if we were in a car, on foot, on public transit, in public and so forth – what to do, and more importantly, what not to do."

"Soooo," AJ asked with somewhat of a puzzled expression, "you really didn't get in to down-to-down fighting?"

"She didn't say that," Alex interjected with a serious tone. We were taught that flight was usually safer than fighting, but if we had to fight, as if our lives depended on it, how to do just that."

Alex's shift in tone took a lot of air out of the room before AJ finally asked, "So what type of fighting?"

Carmen looked down and tried to sound more or less nonchalant, "Primarily various forms of martial arts."

"What, you mean kung-fu and karate stuff?"

"Yes," Carmen replied, "but more defense than offense, it was a blend of various techniques, heavy into both judo and aikido because they both have a wide range of defensive moves."

Still trying to absorb these new revelations AJ asked, "So how long was this training?"

"A lot longer than we had ever thought we would need," answered Alex.

For almost the next hour AJ peppered his parents with questions seeking more details and clarity. Alex and Carmen told how their training and planning for their next "assignment" stretched from what was planned to last 3-6 weeks to just under 7 months. During this time, they were practicing with multiple-degree black belts in judo, karate, and aikido, and they became very proficient. They trained with both basic recruits and, at times, with new SEALS classes.

In addition to the physical martial arts training, they studied many scenarios they might be forced to encounter someday. Various locations and adaptations of their cover were planned and finetuned. The near miss in Hawaii had shown the top brass in the Witness Protection Program that it might be more difficult to keep Carmen and Alex safe than they had first planned. Nonetheless, they were confident their record of never losing a protected witness would remain intact.

As their skills became very developed, after practicing as many as 6-8 hours a day, the lead instructor asked if they would like to have a mock test as if they were testing for various ranks. He explained he could not officially award belts, but that he would put them through the same tests that his private students took at an off-base Dojo for various rank advancements.

"WOW! You guys got to test like you were going for the belts we see in Karate classes?"

Carmen and Alex smiled at each other and Alex answered, "Something like that. Our Sensi was arguably one of the best in the world. Hence why he was hired to train SEALS. We don't know if we really were expected to train as much as we did – but when it became clear that we were going to be there for a while, we decided to make the best of it."

"How good, when you say, 'one of the best in the world?"

"Quite literally, just what your Dad said, he was trained in multiple disciplines of martial arts and was like an 8th-degree dan black belt in Taekwondo."

"What does that mean?" asked AJ sincerely.

"9th degree dan in Taekwondo is the highest rank in the world. He was one of the few holding 8th degree, and maybe the only one qualified in 4 other forms of martial arts."

"OK, Mom and Dad, you guys have asked me about every test I have ever taken...how did you do."

Alex studied Carmen's face for a reaction before asking, "Should we tell him – we really haven't even thought about it that much since leaving that life behind us."

"OK, dad, please!"

"Your dad did very well – Sensi Brooks said if it had been a real-life test, your dad would have earned a brown belt – which is quite an accomplishment for about 7 months of training."

"I'll say," said AJ, "there's a boy in my class who has been taking karate for five years, and he told me last week that next month he will be testing for his brown belt. What about you, Mom—are you as good as Dad?"

Alex chuckled, "Better. Sensi Brooks said she was the most natural he had ever taught."

"Wow, so you both would have been brown belts."

"Not quite, son. Your mom would have earned a black belt. She was that good."

AJ sat stunned, looking at his mother, whom he had

always known was amazing, and seeing her in yet another light. He shook his head in somewhat disbelief before finally responding, "Every time you guys open up, I think it can't be any more—but then it is and so much more."

Carmen walked over and kissed her son on the top of his head and said, "And, probably more than enough for tonight. You need to get to bed." AJ agreed but knew his journal entry would again be a long one.

"I guess so, love you guys." He walked over and kissed both parents good night before heading for his room, knowing sleep was still some time off.

In his room his phone beeped indicating a text message – it was from Judy, "still up?"

He immediately replied. "Sure but heading for bed."

"�� me 2, but just wanted to say goodnight a c u 2morow."

Instead of responding, he dialed the number. In a hushed tone, Judy answered, "I didn't mean you had to call."

He replied, "I didn't have to, I wanted to. Just to say good night to you too."

"You're sweet – thank you. I'll see you in the morning."

"Count on it. Good night, my mom always says, "Don't let the bed bugs bite when she says good night to the twins."

"That's too sweet," Judy replied. " Let's talk tomorrow.

Thank you. Good night, bye for now."

"You too," he replied.

As she turned out the light her almost 16-year-old mind could hear herself saying not just 'good night,' but 'good night, and I love you.' The thought made her smile, and she closed her eyes to drift into the world of sleep.

AJ stared for a moment at his phone, marveling at the many things in his life that he had never known or dreamed of but now was front and center of his young world. He reached for his journal and prepared another long entry.

****

Brian and Maria Roland were having an interesting conversation of their own after Judy kissed them good night and headed to her room – to say good night to AJ. As she walked out of the room Brian turned to Maria and said, "Our daughter is amazing - I've read too many stories on adopted children when they become teenagers having all sorts of desires to find their real parents' and often give the parents who have loved them all their life a lot of grief."

"We are blessed, and from the day we brought her home, she has always been and will always be our daughter."

There was a moment of silence as they both considered the depth of their thoughts and then Maria spoke hesitantly, "I've thought a lot about the discussion in the restaurant. . ."

"Me too."

"Dear, the interesting thing is I've never thought about being a 'good Catholic.' I went to Catholic schools, learned all the information I was supposed to learn from the nuns and the priests and just accepted that is the way life was supposed to be...maybe I was being the 'good Catholic girl,' like you were being a 'good Mormon boy.' The only difference is I never saw a reason to seek out 'whatever the other side is...' I guess we don't have as many 'thou shall nots' as the Mormons."

"But you stayed strong in your beliefs; I didn't want to risk losing you if you couldn't accept mine... you were the strong one. I accept full responsibility for my decision."

"Brian, I saw the look on your face when we walked into the Barton's church on Sunday – you were both scared and looked like a man walking into his home. Do you want to go back?"

Brian had thought of ways to bring up the subject – he never expected Maria to raise the question. Judy had taken it in stride. He had kept his promise to raise his daughter but with a question that was paining his very soul, "had he kept the promises he made to his Lord, his Savior, and his Church?" He sat very silent for several minutes. Maria did not talk – she knew this was the way her husband processed any deep question. She also sensed she had asked him the deepest question of his adult life.

After what seemed like an eternity he answered, "I will never do anything to hurt you or Judy and your faith."

"Brian, I already know that - my question is, do YOU want to go back? If you do, we will support you, just as you have done Judy and me for all these years. I know it's hard, but there are plenty of successful marriages that embrace two religions – hey, I'm thankful that we are both Christians. It would be a lot harder if you were Jewish," she added with an impish grin.

At that moment, the dam broke, and a feeling of relief so overpowered him that Brian burst into tears, followed by long, quiet sobs; Maria went over, pulled him to his feet, and wept as they hugged and cried together in the kitchen.

She quietly whispered, "I love you; we will make it work – I think our God's tent is big enough for all of his children." Neither knew what really lay in store, but through their love of each other and the Savior, they knew somehow it would work out.

For the first time, in a long time, Brian openly prayed before going to bed, with Maria kneeling beside him, he begged the Lord to show him and Maria the way to better serve him and bring their family even closer together.

CHAPTER FOURTEEN

An amazing phenomenon happens during the second semester after the winter holidays at most schools across the country. It is as if the clock is running faster, and the days simply fly by. The last full marking period is perhaps the swiftest of them all as teachers and students deal with a host of year-end activities: final exams, spring sports, dances, transitions for those graduating, and schedules for the next school year. For the Rolands and the Bartons, it was no exception. In the case of the Barton household, there was the high school sophomore who would be a junior, the twins who would be entering middle school, and Alex's classes at college preparing for finals before the end of the school year.

The Rolands, with only one child, still had an extra load in that Judy's softball team had made district playoffs, and if they did well there, it would be on to state – Judy was a straight-

A student and even as a freshman, was now one of the most dominant players on the team. Her schedule was beyond busy. While both she and AJ were maintaining, "We are great friends and partners in Art Class," even the most casual observer could see the chemistry between these two almost 16-year-olds was growing more each day. They managed to talk several times every day – and always finished the night off with a good night call. Carmen was spending almost every day at the Twins school as the PTA Mom of the year for the 5th graders who would soon be moving up to Salisbury Middle School. It would not be until Thursday night, after staying for Judy's game, a quick family dinner and getting the twins off to bed before AJ again was able to corner his parents for what happened after San Diego.

The meeting in his dad's den again stretched for almost an hour and a half after Sam and Jon-Mark went to bed at 8:00 p.m. When it was over, he was again left shaking his head as he learned another of his parents' amazing adventures. Kissing both goodnight, he took a short shower and saw his phone buzzing the moment he walked into his bedroom. "Hi Judy, I just got out of the shower. I was going to call you—you had another great game!"

"We won; since we are already in the playoffs, Coach Cato was worried we might lose some edge."

"Judy, you pitched a two-hitter, went 4 for 5, and drove in half the team's runs; I don't think you guys missed a beat."

"I had that many RBI's?"

"You're too much," AJ said with a half-laugh. Yeah, girl, you did, and you are that good."

If he had been on Facetime, he would have seen Judy

blush. Though she loved the confidence that he always showed her and depended on him for the game stats, she just focused on every batter and connected with the ball when she was at the plate.

"Thank you, AJ. You are kind, and I appreciate you so much. I just wanted to say good night because I have a paper due tomorrow."

"You are more than welcome; I'm just glad to be your cheerleader and stats man. I gotta run too – finished with homework but just had another talk with my parents, and it will be another long diary entry."

"OK...AJ...I mean it, thank you – see you in the morning."

"Me too. Night."

Both teens stared at the phones. Judy heard herself again quietly whispering, "Good night, I love you." AJ was still trying to figure out how to say something more than good night. But then boys are usually slower on the uptake than girls their own age.

He picked up his journal and began to write what turned into a very long entry as he tried to recall what his parents had shared with him in detail over the past two sessions:

Dear Diary,

I have given up being surprised on whatever my parents lay on me next – tonight was no exception. After absorbing on Monday that my mom could be a black belt in martial arts and is actually better than my dad after training with the Navy SEALS they gave me the details of what happened after they left San Diego.

After spending several months hiding and training, their next stop was the next extreme. They were to keep their cover of studying indigenous people. In fact, they pulled out the book they wrote – it was published under the pseudonyms they used while in protection. It was accepted by two Universities as being the equivalent of a doctoral dissertation on the subject. Mom explained since they were doing it as a cover, anyway, why not go ahead and do the research.

That was surprising enough, but nowhere near as surprising as where they went to do their next research. While they had only been in Hawaii for a short time, they had some good notes from the Hawaiian natives and stories of how the LDS missionaries had left a lasting impact on the island and the native population. It is hard to imagine a greater extreme, but their first stop after San Diego was ALASKA!

This was almost too much – South Florida to Hawaii to Alaska all in the same year. Dad recounted how they left San Diego and flew by government Lear jet to a base in Fairbanks. It was mid-fall by then, and the days were already getting shorter. And it was getting colder. It was the traditional perfect 75 degrees when they left San Diego, but it was only 2 degrees when they landed almost 7 hours later in Fairbanks – Mom added, "That was a shock to the system, fortunately, they had outfitted us with an Alaska winter wardrobe – for a girl from Miami this was cold!"

Dad said they got used to some different things real quick. Their driver from the airport was an Air Force non-com who, when they complained about the cold, assured them – this was mild – it would get worse. Dad, trying to strike up a conversation, asked him if he was an Alaskan Native. Hawaii has a distinct racial and

ADVENTURES AT THE BOAT SHOW

cultural identity with Hawaiian Natives, so the Airman's response, "Half native," took him off-guard. The man then explained his mother was a Yupik full native and his father had been stationed at Elmendorf AFB over 25 years ago – they had married, and when he retired, he returned to Alaska. He said there are over 200 federally recognized Alaskan Native Tribes, but most natives identify with one of the 12 major tribes. Dad said he decided to think before his next question; since he was supposed to be studying Indigenous people, they better start learning a lot.

When I asked how long they stayed there they both looked away and said, "in months or winters?"

Even though I knew this it sounded strange to describe just how big Alaska really is – he pointed out, "If they cut Alaska in half, Texas becomes the third largest state. Even more was there only one true city in Alaska – Anchorage. The next two large towns, Juneau and Fairbanks, only have about 25,000 residents. Of Alaska's 700,000 people, nearly 80% live within 100 miles of Anchorage. They discovered the land was huge, vast and sparsely populated.

The next question led to another amazing part of their adventure. They were "sent" by an official-sounding college grant program to the Village of St. Michael, which was way up close to the Artic Circle, to study and live with the Yupik people. This blew my mind because they said that there were only 335 people in the village, there were no roads, and you got there by plane, boat, or snow machine. [Dad explained that the Alaskans referred to what we could call a snowmobile as a snow machine]. Then the scary stat - of the 335 people in the village, all seemed related by blood, marriage or both.

Mom explained, "To say we stood out would be an understatement. The village population is over 90% Yupik a sprinkling of mixed races, 4% white, leaving me the lone Latina in a 1,000 miles. It was also the farthest we have ever been away from The Church – in Hawaii, it seemed I ran into LDS people everywhere. I learned much later there wasn't a branch or ward within hundreds of miles of us."

I guess mom or dad weren't really thinking about the Church at that point. I asked if they felt safe while they were there. Dad explained that even as isolated as it was, there was a government presence in that the official "weather station" was actually a CIA listening point because of its closeness to Russia. Just when their story couldn't get any weirder – it kept doing it. The CIA agents there doubled as their contact with witness protection – evidently, this wasn't the first time the government had stashed people in a truly remote place.

What amazed me was that mom and dad decided to make the best of it – they met the local leaders, found there was a library with occasionally working internet since everything was dial up at that point. They studied the history and then went out, with the help of their "friends" at the weather station and went about their role as grad students investigating native people in far flung parts of the world. Dad added the locals were taken with mom in they had never met a Cuban or probably any Hispanic.

They both said it was a bittersweet time. Once the people started trusting them, they were invited into sometimes humble homes. After the first few times, they learned to only go for lunch because, sadly, any gathering after an evening meal turned into a drinking session – which would end when many of the party passed out on the floor or couch. The other sad fact was, according to what they discovered, almost every child who had been born in their village in the last 50 years had some form of fetal alcohol syndrome. I guess growing up in my small town with LDS parents I didn't know that so many women in poor areas drink when they are expecting babies.

They were there for most of the entire winter – unlike what I had heard it isn't either dark all the time or the sun never sets – instead they are gaining or losing about 8 minutes a day – by December they said the sun barely showed at all and then quickly dropped under the horizon. On the other hand by the time they left in early June the sun seldom set getting gray for about 90 minutes at 4:00 in the morning and then coming back up before 6:00 AM – that must have been weird.

So, I asked, "at least you felt safe?"

Mom and dad both smiled and then said, "Well from bad guys that wanted to shoot us we felt very safe...but,"

When I looked puzzled mom told of how by March when the days were getting longer again, they put on snowshoes to walk around town – it had been covered with snow since they arrived. It was fun, she said, and when they got on the outskirts of the village, they saw a moose and her calf. Mom wanted to get close enough to take a picture. Suddenly a unseen bull moose charged from out of nowhere. Mom screamed and ran towards dad then they heard a loud gun shot and the moose was startled. A local marksman told them he put the shell to within one inch of the bull's ear. The shot scared the animal away.

I of course wanted to know if the guy was a marksman why he didn't kill the moose. Dad explained the natives have tremendous respect for the animals. The bull was protecting his young and it was still mating season. Yes, they often harvested males in the late fall to fill their freezers for the winter – but never killed unless it was for food or protection. The man chose to protect them and spare the moose at the same time.

I gulped and figured I had more than enough to write about, but now it's late, I'm tired and going to bed. My mom and dad are amazing.

AJ turned off his light and within moments was having in his dreams his own Alaskan adventure – one that would be interrupted a few hours later with the alarm clock greeting him for yet another day. It was Friday and the school days were getting down to the final weeks – but early morning Seminary would continue until the final week of school. With great reluctance he pulled himself out of bed a quick prayer and then off to start the day. At that moment his phone buzzed. It was Judy, who texted, R U up?

He replied: Sure – I got that early morning Church class

Judy: I know. My dad said he would drop me at your Church if I could go see what your class is like

Looked at the phone in stunned disbelief - after all, LDS kids went because they were expected to go, not because they necessarily wanted to be there, but he quickly replied: Sure – It starts @ 7:00 and out by 7:50 – Trey and I walk to school from there. You can walk with us.

Judy: Grt – c u at 7:00 bye

AJ hit: K and then stared at his phone.

Judy stared at her phone in equal disbelief – she invited herself to a religion class of another Church. Her dad had mentioned it, but she really hadn't told him she wanted to see what it was like to go to a religion class that early in the morning. Quickly she grabbed her robe and called out as she walked towards her parents' bedroom, "DAD…can we talk.?"

Brian turned over in bed and saw it was 6:05 AM – Maria was still asleep. He threw on a robe and walked out into the hall to see what his daughter needed so early in the morning.

"Daddy," she began, in her best daddy's girl voice, "you know how I said I'd like to know what makes you, Mr. Barton, and AJ so special? AJ said it was OK to go to that religion class at his church this morning. It starts at 7:00. Can you take me? AJ said I could walk to school from there with him and his friend Trey. Please." She managed to roll out the entire request and explanation without taking a breath. Long ago she learned that if humanly possible her father would meet any request if he could.

Brian stood bewildered and finally muttered, "Sure kitten, anything for my little girl. Grab a bite, get dressed, and I'll drop you off."

"Thanks, Daddy, I'll get dressed, but I remember AJ saying they have doughnuts on Friday – I'll start the day with a sugar rush," she said with a grin and quickly kissed her still-confused dad on the cheek.

Alex was an equally puzzled dad when his son announced on the way to Church that morning, "Oh, Judy said she wants to see my Seminary class—I told her OK. Do you think Sister Williams will mind?"

"Uhmm, no, when did you find out – did she ask her parents?"

"She texted me this morning and said her dad was going to bring her, so I guess she must have told them."

"OK, AJ, just remember who you are, and that both of

you are only 15…"

"Dad, it's not a date – she just wants to see why I get up and go to a Church class so early in the morning."

Both dads arrived in the Church parking lot at the same time. The teens jumped out and headed for the door, leaving Brian and Alex still shaking their heads in the parking lot

CHAPTER FIFTEEN

When AJ and Judy went in for their first Seminary Class, her father parked his car and went out to say hello to Alex. Both were feeling a little awkward for reasons they couldn't describe. Alex got out and met Brian and said, "Good morning. This was a surprise."

"For both of us," answered Brian, "Judy had talked about AJ going to some class every morning before school, and I told her it was Seminary – that when I was in high school, it was across the street, and we took it as a forced elective."

"I joined the Church in my teens, but if we had it in the deep south, I never heard of it, so I missed that elective. But having experienced it as a teacher and for the past two years every school day morning bringing AJ to Church - I'm just glad the school is within walking distance."

"Alex, have you got a few minutes? I need to talk this out."

"Sure, but let's go to Krispy Kreme and grab a doughnut—the kids will be eating theirs in Church, so we might as well have a Seminary breakfast as well," answered Alex.

"Good idea, plus, I don't want Judy to think I'm spying on her – we really like AJ, but I'm a dad. I really trust her, but…"

"Brian, it's OK – we have both been young – I have an almost 11-year-old daughter at home, and I'm dreading the first time a boy, any boy, shows up in the picture."

Both men laughed, got in their cars, and drove to one of Salisbury's favorite places – West Innes Street's original Krispy Kreme doughnut shop. The store had become an institution in town. It was barely a mile from the College Campus, and had been there for almost 40 years. The locals told the story of how when Salisbury was a much smaller town, their now favorite doughnut shop had been under construction with no signs of opening for almost two years. Then, one morning, an A-frame sign appeared in front of the store reading, "NOW OPEN - Hot Doughnuts." According to local legend, the traffic jam was so bad by nightfall that a Rowan County Deputy was assigned to handle the flow in and out of the parking lot. The town had grown a lot over those 40 years – but the love for doughnuts had remained the same.

They parked, went inside and both men ordered two hot doughnuts and cups of hot chocolate. Coffee was one of the specialties; Alex, as a long-time member, didn't drink coffee – Brian, even with years of being outside the Church, had never developed a taste for it either. That morning, he was glad as he was sitting down with a Bishop, even a former Bishop, that at least he wouldn't have to have that part of the Word of Wisdom discussion – the wine and beer would keep for another day.

Once seated, Brian opened his heart. He told Alex of the conversations he and Maria had on religion; how he was surprised, almost shocked, to hear her say that if he wanted to return to his childhood faith, she would support him. How Maria was surprised to learn he had used their relationship as the reason he had been away for so many years. Finally, he quietly whispered, "Alex, I love my wife and daughter more than anything on earth – their Catholic faith has truly brought us together as a family. But, last Sunday, I realized I want to come home – I've been away too long - BUT, and it's a big BUT, I can't do anything that will hurt Maria or Judy's belief in the Catholic Church. I need some advice – how, what, I, I, don't know where to start."

Though no longer a sitting Bishop, it was now a true ministering opportunity for a brother in the Priesthood who was staring over his doughnut, looking at him for counsel. Alex closed his eyes, took a deep breath, and said a silent prayer before responding, "You are a blessed man. The Lord wants his children to be happy. You have a wonderful wife and daughter, my first blush advice is to always remember this and cherish them for what they are, like you, children of our Heavenly Father – not Catholics, not Latter-day Saints, fellow children of our Father in heaven."

A tear rolled down Brian's face.

Alex continued, "I didn't say it, but a prophet of the Lord did, 'the greatest work you will ever do is within the walls of your own home."

"Harold B. Lee," answered Brian, "my dad quoted it many times."

"OK, this is not an overnight solution," said Alex, "first, I am tempted to ask the same question that Nephi asked his brothers…"

"Have I inquired of the Lord?" replied Brian with a smile, "I pulled out a copy of the Book of Mormon and have been reading it at work on my lunch break. I guess my roots are a lot deeper even than I realized."

This time, it was Alex's face upon which a tear appeared as he said, "Sometimes we give up on the Lord, thankfully for both of us; he has never given up on us. You have a lot to think about, but I'm willing to guess that you have been quietly living a Christ-like life for your entire marriage – it is why your wife is so supportive and why Judy wants to find out more about the Church – it's not just AJ. Your example through the years is why this opportunity has been placed before you, well, you, your family, and mine as well. We both probably need to get ready for work – let's talk again soon."

"You can count on it, my friend," replied Brian, "you can count on it – let me have your number, and I'll call you later."

The two men finished their doughnuts, threw away the wrappers and headed for their cars – both realizing that life was taking a very important turn.

****

Seminary that morning was an amazing experience for Judy, who had grown up in her very Catholic world; she had attended Catholic Schools until this year; she had dutifully attended catechism preparing for First Communion, and as she remembered, it was always being taught a strict dogma and very well scripted response to any religious setting. That morning in AJ's Seminary class, after warming up with doughnuts and OJ, the teacher – who for some reason was called Sister Williams (though she didn't look like any of the nuns from her Catholic School experience) led the students in an open discussion on the Priesthood. Again, it left her somewhat confused even though her dad and AJ had told her that in the LDS world, all boys were eligible to be ordained Priests in something called the Aaronic Priesthood the year they turned 16.

One of the other girls in the class, who Judy recognized as a senior cheerleader, talked about how her father gave her a Priesthood blessing before every Cheer Competition and how it helped give her courage to go and give her all even when the pressure was on. The other students nodded in agreement on the number of times they had received these 'Priesthood blessings' in their young lives. When the meeting was over Sister Williams had come over and talked to Judy and told her while there were only two weeks of school left, she was welcome to attend anytime. Her warmth was so warm and genuine that it immediately put her at ease.

When it was time to leave, AJ's friend Trey gave a closing prayer, and then all 12 students filed out to make the 10-minute walk to school. Trey joined Judy and AJ, asking, "So Judy, AJ dragged you to our morning class," he said with a grin.

Judy and Trey didn't have any classes together, but she had learned that her mom and his mom both worked at the hospital – and, of course, the whole school thought of her as AJ's girlfriend. Judy smiled and replied, "Actually, it was my idea – my dad grew up Mormon; I'm sorry, you guys don't call yourselves that anymore; anyway, he told me that when he was growing up in Utah, he walked across the street for Seminary, and it was a graded elective. So, I asked AJ if I could come watch."

Trey looked confused, "You WANTED to get up this early to go talk about Church?"

"Yes, why not?"

As a lifelong member, now in his second year of Seminary, it was always just an understood thing that LDS kids 'had to do.' That someone who wasn't even a member might WANT to go was difficult for him to grasp.

"Forgive my friend," AJ interjected, "I guess many of us just think it's what's expected, and we don't think of it as that much of an option – some mornings after a late-night studying, sleep would probably be all our first option."

"I can see that," Judy replied. I guess I've always been a morning person, and for me, the class today was fascinating. I've been in my faith's religion training classes for years—and we are told what we believe—seeing you guys have this open discussion with the lady, Sister?"

"Sister Williams" replied Trey.

"OK, I gotta get used to that too – all the sisters in my life were nuns. Anyway, just the way she engaged you guys, and you all shared these personal experiences was amazing."

Both boys were silent for a moment. Unlike Judy, they

had grown up with wonderful teachers like Sister Williams for their entire lives. To them, what she found amazing was simply routine. AJ finally added, "You got us on a good day. First doughnuts help the discussion with any lesson, and Sister Williams is arguably one of the best teachers any of us have ever had—she teaches at Catawba. She is a sociology professor."

Judy looked stunned. "She isn't hired for this. Is she a college professor? For real?"

AJ smiled, "for real."

"Is this like a part-time gig she does in addition to teaching in college?" Judy asked inquisitively.

"It's what is known as a calling or church assignment," Trey answered.

"They have a college professor who gets up to teach high school students a religion class at 7:00 in the morning and she doesn't get paid??"

"In our Church," explained AJ, "we don't have paid ministers or staff – we all have a responsibility and just do it as part of being members."

Judy let the thought settle in; in the Catholic faith, the Priests and the nuns were often unpaid but had all their living expenses covered, and their full-time job was to serve the Church. That she got. But the idea that members with real jobs also volunteered to do what she had experienced with Sister Williams took her by surprise. "AJ, can we talk more about this at lunch? I must check in with Coach Cato before school starts, but there is something else I need to talk to you about. Trey, you can join us if you want."

Trey answered, "Actually, I'd love to, but you guys have a different lunch – this one is all yours AJ."

"Lunch works for me," he said as they walked onto the school grounds. Before he could say anything else, Judy reached up, gave him a quick kiss on the cheek, and said, "Great! Meet you at our table."

As Judy ran off towards the locker rooms Trey turned and gave his friend a smirk, "Not dating. And just a goodbye kiss?"

"I told you, she's part Cuban; they kiss all the time," he replied, trying to downplay the exchange. Truth be told, he truly enjoyed it and wished he was brave enough to return the kiss.

The morning classes seemed to fly by as teachers were trying their best to make sure they had covered all the material that would be on the upcoming finals; when AJ and Judy's bell rang for lunch, they were first in line for the traditional Friday fare, "Fish sandwiches, fries and a salad." Another beautiful late spring day found them again eating at what had become "their table" on the courtyard.

As now had become a routine in which they both were comfortable, both teens bowed their heads for a quiet private blessing on the food. Judy still made the sign of the Cross when she was finished and then they dug in, AJ towards his fish sandwich, Judy with the question that had been on her mind since the morning's seminary lesson.

"AJ, you know how your friend in class this morning,

the senior who is like our head cheerleader, said her dad gave her what you call a Priesthood blessing before she went for a competition."

"I remember."

"Has your dad ever done that for you?" she asked.

"Well, I've never gone to a Cheer Competition" he said with a quick smile.

"No silly, I mean for something really important."

"Sure, actually, every year since kindergarten, I have gotten a father's blessing at the start of the school year…and a couple of times, if I was struggling before a big test, he would give me one as well – LDS kids just sort of take getting blessings for granted."

"Wow. In our Church, we get some high points, like when a baby is baptized, and we take first communion – but, it is important, but something the Priests does – we never think about our dad doing something like that."

"I guess it's another one of those things LDS kids grow up taking for granted," he said with a shrug.

"AJ, you know we have a district final playoff tomorrow?" Judy asked.

"Of course, I'm going – you're pitching, aren't you?"

"AJ, for the first time this season, I'm scared – this was the only team that beat us badly at the start of the season…"

AJ interrupted, "You were still playing JV – it was the start of the season. The team has lost one game out of the last 12 since you cracked the line-up."

"True, but we were playing teams that were good, but not great – East Rowan has 7 seniors in their starting 10; six of them have already committed to D-1 programs for the freshman year in college. I'm a HIGH SCHOOL freshman…"

AJ never ceased to marvel that Judy simply didn't know how good of a ball player she had become. Coach Cato built the team around her. When she didn't pitch, she was playing center field and always batted third or clean-up. He knew there were college scouts already watching this freshman phenom. Judy took every game, every pitch, and every at-bat in stride. He replied, "You will do what you always do – your best."

Judy smiled, "Thanks, AJ. I told you that you are my good luck charm. Since that day you came to watch me pitch my first Varsity game, I have looked up at the stands to see you there for my team."

"I wish you could believe how good you really are…"

"AJ, would your dad be able to give me a good little Catholic girl one of your priesthood blessings to help calm my stomach?"

The request caught AJ totally off guard – it would be perfectly normal for any LDS youth to make such a request, but as she called herself, she was a "good little Catholic girl."

His silence caught Judy by surprise, and she thought she may have asked something wrong. "I know you said he had been a Bishop, so he has what you guys call the Priesthood."

"Yes, he does and I'm sure he'd be honored. Why don't I walk you home after practice and you can ask him."

"AJ, one more favor...will you ask him for me – I'll be there – but I'm not sure what to say."

"Sure, I will," he replied, "just trying to figure out how to begin." At that moment, the bell rang for the start of the next period. He grabbed her lunch tray and said, "I got it, see you in Art class."

Judy gave him another quick kiss and said, "Thank you! See you then."

On his way to class, he texted his dad, "I'm walking Judy home after her practice. She wants to ask you for a p'hood blessing. Big game tomorrow."

Alex was in his office at the college when his phone chirped with a message – he read it, and knew it was a window of opportunity if Brian really wanted to come back to Church. He replied, "K. stop at our house on the way home."

******

That afternoon, Alex's theory that "coincidences are where God chooses to remain anonymous" received additional verification. About five minutes before AJ and Judy were expected to arrive from practice, Brian Roland pulled into his driveway.

Alex greeted him at the door with, "You have great timing."

"I was just on my way home – we got through a little early today, and I figured I might actually make it home in time to have dinner with Judy and Maria – what do you mean, great timing?"

"Well," Alex offered, "your daughter and AJ are on the way here right now – the Seminary lesson must have hit some cord with Judy."

Brian looked confused and asked, "Has seminary changed that much – we just ate doughnuts and chilled back in my day."

"I don't know if they had a lesson or what – but I got just a text from AJ that he was walking Judy home, and she wanted to ask for a blessing because of a big game tomorrow."

"She's pitching in the district finals tomorrow, I knew she was a little on edge because East Rowan is the only team that beat them soundly this year, but I didn't know she even knew what a priesthood blessing is – doesn't get much discussion in the Catholic world," he said warily.

"Brian, I didn't even know how I was going to respond – I would never offer to bless another man's kiddo without the parents knowing about it – when she asks, why don't you offer to give her one?"

"Alex, I haven't given a blessing since I was a missionary – I've been totally inactive for decades – how could I give anyone, much less my own daughter, a blessing."

Alex smiled and thought momentarily, "I don't think the Lord has forgotten you were ordained an Elder in His

Priesthood, but equally important, you or any FATHER is free to give their child a father's blessing at any time."

Alex let his words sink in, and Brian pondered what he had just said. AJ and Judy walked into the home at that moment.

Seeing her father standing and talking to Alex's dad, Judy said excitedly, "Daddy, how did you know I was going to be here – in the church class this morning, Mrs er, Sister Williams had the kids talking about priesthood blessings. And this one girl in our school – she is like our head cheerleader, said her dad gives her a blessing before a competition." Judy breathed and continued to gush, "So, with tomorrow's game being such an important thing for me and the team, I was going to ask AJ's dad for a blessing because I knew he was what they call a priesthood holder."

AJ stayed quiet, not knowing who should say what next.

Alex smiled and walked over and put his hand on Judy's shoulder, "Ahh, young lady, you are an amazing young woman, but let me ask you a question – why not ask your dad?"

Judy looked like the idea surprised her and she asked, "Daddy did you ever hold the priesthood?"

Everyone except Judy knew that every LDS Missionary is an ordained Priesthood holder. Brian looked at his daughter and gently said, "I was ordained as an Elder in the Priesthood as part of my calling to serve as a Missionary for the Church so many years ago. I haven't given a blessing in a long time, but I would be honored, especially if Alex would give me a quick refresher to give my daughter," he said with his voice cracking with emotion, "a blessing. But let's see if Mom's home so she can be there too." With that, he wrapped his arms around Judy and kissed the top of her head.

Alex quickly wiped a tear from his own eyes – as did AJ, Judy, and Brian.

"Well, I guess we have that question asked and answered," said Alex. Judy and AJ, give us a moment, and Mr. Roland and I will figure out how to get everyone together."

"Sure, Dad," Judy said, practically beaming. I need to ask AJ a couple of things. We'll be on the front porch if I can ride home with you."

"That works daughter, let me get a brief refresher course."

For the next several minutes, Alex patiently went over the details of a father's blessing combined with a priesthood blessing. He reminded Brian that he was still an Elder, still a good father who loved the Lord, his wife, and his child, and half-jokingly said, "It's not quite the same as riding a bicycle, but just listen and let the Holy Ghost prompt you—you'll be fine. The question is, "How will Maria respond?"

"Well," replied Brian with a smile, "she has always had my back and said if I wanted to return to my faith, she would support me – I'm not trying to change our daughter – just help her feel calm and do her best in an important ball game."

It would be an eventful evening for both families, Judy was excited as she and her dad rode home to break the news to her mother. Brian had some trepidation, worrying if his wife would think this would be a distraction to Judy's Catholic upbringing. This was quickly dispelled when arriving home she burst into the kitchen where Maria was finishing a pasta dinner salad and announced, "Mom! Dad has agreed to give me a father's blessing to help me play better tomorrow."

Maria looked confused and Brian explained, "You remember how I told you Judy went to the religion class this morning over at the Barton's church?"

"Yeeess...."

"Evidently, there was a discussion, and one of Judy's classmates was a cheerleader. She told the group that her dad had given her a blessing before a cheer competition."

"And," Brian continued, "she was going to ask Alex if he could give her a blessing – not knowing that even though I haven't been active for years, any dad can give his child a blessing. I had asked Alex something about their meeting schedule, and he told me that AJ and Judy were on the way to his house – he was happy I had dropped by unannounced because he would never have given Judy a blessing without talking to us first."

"What's a blessing?" Maria asked with a totally confused look on her face.

"If you are comfortable with it, I will simply put my hands on her head and, like a prayer, invoke the Lord's blessing on her to perform at her best and be ready for tomorrow's game. Though I haven't done it in years, I am still an ordained Elder in my Church."

The terminologies and concepts sounded completely strange to her, but the enthusiasm in her daughter's voice, the personal struggle that she knew her husband was going through facing his decision to return to his faith—along with the sure knowledge that Brian was a man of his word and wasn't trying to convince Judy of anything about either faith—led her to close her eyes, take a deep breath, and say, "I trust you. Can I be there when you give her this blessing?"

As the words came from her mouth, the phone rang. It was Carmen. "Maria, I heard that Brian is talking about giving Judy a blessing for tomorrow's game. We are going to have ice cream after supper. I would love for our family to see this. Will you guys come over and honor us by doing it here in our home?"

While it was hitting her all at once, Carmen's sincere tone and the comfort she had felt attending their Church and watching how clearly they supported her daughter, a feeling of peace came over her, and she quietly whispered, "What time? OK, 7:30 would be perfect."

"Brian, I told you," she began, "that I saw in your eyes how much attending Church meant to you. For all these years, you have kept your faith bottled up, supporting first me, then Judy, and myself. I can't say I know what this blessing is, but I trust you and the Bartons. I will be glad to be there for you and Judy.

At the Barton household, Carmen laid down the law for the twins to make sure the family room was neat and orderly, and she said with special emphasis, "THERE WILL BE NO TEASING, NO AJ'S GOT A GIRLFRIEND, NO NONESENSE! Niños ¿me entendéis? [Children do you understand me]

Sam and Jon-Mark piped in, "Si Mama, SI!"

At 7:30 sharp, the Rolands joined the Bartons in the

family room. Brian had surprised Judy and Maria by not changing out of the shirt and tie he had been wearing at the office. Maria was also surprised to see that Alex was wearing a white shirt and tie on a Friday evening. Alex expressed his appreciation for the Rolands being willing to include their family in this special first blessing for Judy. Prior to leaving that afternoon, Alex had gone over the mechanical details and reminded him of the words to use as he started the actual blessing. It was decided that since it was a father's blessing and not one of healing there was not a need for anointing with oil – though Alex assured him he had some if needed.

Alex brought over a straight-back chair into the family room and asked Judy to sit down while Brian took his place behind her. Brian looked over and asked, "Alex, join me please." Though it was a common sight for the Bartons but totally new for Judy and her mom, the two men gently placed their hands on Judy's head as Brian took a deep breath and said, "Judith Ann Roland, as a priesthood holder in Christ's church and as your father I join with Bishop Barton to give you this blessing…"

Then, with a sincere, quiet voice, he blessed his daughter with a spirit of calm, additional strength, both mental and physical, and the ability to perform at her very best during the game tomorrow while invoking safety and the desire for fair play for her, her teammates and the players from East Rowan. As he closed in the name of Jesus Christ, a tear ran down his cheek; Judy got up and threw her arms around Brian and softly sobbed, "Daddy, I love you so much, thank you." Then she hugged Alex saying, "Mr. Barton, thank you and your wonderful family." Maria walked over and hugged her daughter and, through tears, whispered, "I am so proud of you and glad you had the courage to ask for this blessing. It is one of the most beautiful things I have ever seen."

AJ was standing awkwardly to one side, and Judy walked over and hugged him while whispering in his ear, "AJ, because of you I have just had one of the most amazing experiences of my life. Thank you," She then ever so quickly and discretely kissed him on the cheek.

The room practically glowed with the warmth and love that was being felt by all. The Bartons knew it was a very spiritual moment. Brian felt at home with his faith for the first time in over two decades. Judy and Maria didn't know at that moment it was a life-changing event. Carmen knew the twin's behavior threshold was close to being reached and quietly suggested, "Let's have some ice cream."

Spiritual moment or not, there was no need for a second suggestion for ice cream.

****

After the ice cream, the Rolands begged off so Judy could get some sleep before the big game. Unlike in the past when her stomach was tied in knots the night before she was going to pitch, that night she dropped into a deep peaceful sleep very quickly. The game was scheduled for ten AM, with the teams reporting at nine. Judy was up, dressed and ready to go by 8:30. Since it was a district playoff game it was held at Catawba College's softball field instead of either team's home field.

The game itself turned into a combination of a defensive battle and pitchers' duel. Judy, the freshman phenom, held her own against East Rowan's ace, who had already signed a national letter of intent to play for the Florida State Seminoles next fall. In the top of the 7th inning, Judy walked the first player of the inning and then gave up only her third hit of the day – unfortunately, it was an inside-the-park home run, and suddenly Salisbury was down by 2 to 0, and down to their last three outs. All who were there on the field and in the stands for a long time will remember what happened next.

The Lady Hornet's number 9 player beat out a blooper that dropped in left field; the number 10 player struck out. One out and one on. The leadoff hitter laid down a perfect bunt down the 3rd base side, and by the time the third baseman fielded the ball, both runners were safe at first and second with only one out. Salisbury's number two batter worked the count full but went down swinging on a low fastball. Two outs, two on, and Judy was at bat. She looked up and saw AJ, her parents, Carmen and Alex. AJ gave her a thumbs up. She looked skyward, closed her eyes, and remembered her dad's blessing from the night before.

The game was on the line. For a change, Judy knew exactly what was riding on her at that moment. Not just this game but the entire season would come down to this time at bat. She put on the batting helmet, looked skyward, and, as she did with every at-bat, made the sign of the Cross before stepping into the batter's box.

The East Rowan girl was throwing nothing but heat. After six pitches, two of which Judy had got just enough of them to send them foul, the count was 3-2; Instinctively, she knew the pitcher was not going to throw her a bad pitch, which would load the bases. For a moment, time seemed to stand still. She stepped out of the batter's box, took two practice swings, and then stared at the other pitcher. Their eyes were locked on each other. The wind-up, the delivery, the pitch. Judy was cool and ready with her mantra of 'just make contact.' The ball soared high down the left field line over the 200' sign and was fair by 3 feet as it cleared the left field fence. Judy tossed her bat back toward the dugout, savoring her first out-of-the-park home run. She made sure to touch every base and was mobbed by her teammates. The Lady Hornets had won 3 – 2. The Salisbury fans were going wild; much to Coach Cato's chagrin, the cheerleaders were leading the crowd with "Damn straight! We're headed to STATE!

Judy found her parents, the Bartons, and hugged AJ, simply saying, "I can't believe it. We beat the best. We're going to State."

AJ hugged her and said, "Yes, you did. You are amazing and quickly kissed her on the cheek. It was his first kiss. It would not be his last.

CHAPTER SIXTEEN

Major shared events are what tend to bond individuals, families, and even nations together. Salisbury High School's dramatic finish in the District Championship affected the Bartons and the Rolands. Of course, Maria and Brian were there to watch Judy's team come from behind in the bottom of the last inning to win the game with their daughter's walk-off home run, but so was the entire Barton clan.

At the end of the game, after the tears and cheers as the players did the traditional "good game" walk, Judy sought out her support group of the two families. When it finally sank in she dissolved in tears in Brian's arms. Getting her tears under control, she said, "This is unbelievable. I just wanted to make contact, and then when it left my bat, I saw it going over the fence. I couldn't believe it." Turning to AJ, she threw her arms around him and said, "I told you, you're my good luck charm."

"No," he replied, "I told you that you really don't believe how good you are."

Coach Cato walked over and joined the group and announced, "One of the player's dads owns Pizza Inn and has invited the team and the families to join us for a celebration lunch—you guys wanna come?"

Jon-Mark and Sam immediately chimed in, "We wanta go for Pizza!"

"Sheeh," hissed Carmen, "she said players and family."

Judy immediately replied, "Coach this is my family."

Coach Cato smiled, "I've seen AJ at every game and every practice – I think we have room for the Bartons as well." Then she added, "I know you are all proud of Judy – after I saw her pitch that no-hitter in her first Varsity game, I wondered why I hadn't put her on the Varsity roster sooner. She's a great softball player and even a better student – we all love her."

Judy blushed and offered a quiet, "Thanks Coach, you made us the best team ever."

With the celebration plans solidified Judy headed for the locker room to change. Leaving the adults and the Barton kids waiting. Brian took Alex aside and told him, "Thank you for yesterday. It may have been one of the most important blessings I have ever been asked to give."

"Your daughter's amazing, and not just because of the fast or long ball. She is special."

"I know, and I know I need to be the best dad I can be."

AJ was invited to ride with the Rolands to Pizza Inn; the twins, Carmen and Alex, followed in their car. The restaurant had set aside half the tables for the celebration. After more pizzas than can be imagined were eaten and gallons of soft drinks consumed the families headed for their homes. As they were leaving Judy took AJ aside and said, "I'm going to Mass in my Church tomorrow, but if it's OK with my parents, I'd love to come to your Church after that."

"You are always welcome at our Church, but can I join your family for Mass tomorrow – I've never been to a Catholic service."

"I'll talk to my parents, but I'm sure it will be alright. Dad's waiting in the car – I'll call you," she said as she quickly kissed his cheek, "Bye.'

They didn't know it then, but what started as just a curiosity about the others' beliefs would have a strong impact on their own faith—and eventually, their destiny.

The Bartons stopped at the home of the twins' friends, who had been invited to see a movie that afternoon. That left Carmen and Alex finally alone with AJ. His mom spoke first, "Wow, that was quite a moment. Judy seemed so quiet and unassuming at first, but she looked like she owned the field. And the blessing her dad gave her last night was amazing."

Alex added, half-laughing, "If Coach Cato knew she might want Brian to bless her entire team, I would agree with your mom. They are special people. Brian was almost shocked when I suggested he should give her a blessing, but he has a strong spirit—he just needed a nudge to wake it up."

AJ asked, "Do you think he will come back to Church someday?"

"Yes, I am almost certain of it – he may be the instrument that brings his whole family to the Church. But our job is to just love them and support them as they work through their own complex situation.

The mother instinct kicked in for Camren, who added, "Judy is a wonderful young woman, but please remember the two of you are not even 16 yet."

"I know, Mom. She is too special for me, too, anything that would ever hurt her or her friendship." He would ask later about attending Mass—right now, he was just reliving the moment when Judy gave up the home run and then followed the next inning with the walk-off home run to propel her team into the state championship tournament.

Then he flashed back to the last time he and his parents had talked about "the gap years." So, he asked, "Mom, Dad, we left off with you in Alaska...can we talk some more this afternoon?"

Carmen smiled at Alex, who replied, "Sure, son; I guess we left you when things were just about to get even more exciting."

The idea startled AJ, and he repeated, "Just about. I thought it was already pretty exciting."

****

So, after a few housekeeping errands, Alex, Carmen, and

AJ found themselves in the study, again unpacking the "gap years box." Carmen began, "Our time in Alaska, especially that cold winter, was one where we could see the often negative impact that happens when one civilization clashes with another."

"How so?" asked AJ.

Alex explained, "Unlike the Native populations of the rest of North, South, and Central America, who were greatly influenced by Europeans, starting with Columbus, the Native Alaskans' first contact was often Russian fur traders, who in many cases brought a disruptive ingredient—vodka."

"Wow, but Russians have been drinking vodka since the beginning of the Tsars," replied AJ.

"True," answered Carmen, "but very much like Native Americans here in the lower 48 and the First Nation throughout Canada, evidently, they have a genetic predisposition to alcoholism. Throw in the long cold winters, the subsistence lifestyle, and later social programs designed to help after a couple of hundred years. You have massive poverty, broken families, and sadly, too many Native children born with Fetal Alcohol Spectrum Disorder. In some of the villages we visited, close to 90% of the children were born in the village in the last 50 years."

"Almost nine out of ten?" AJ asked in disbelief.

Alex shook his head and added, "Some think its higher – almost 100%"

"We loved the people. The pure beauty of the state defies even putting into words – but we felt ourselves mentally slipping. And so, we came up with a plan."

"A plan?" asked AJ

"Your dad actually came up with it – it took some convincing of first me and the Program."

"And?" repeated AJ.

"It sounds crazy now, but I suggested since they were having to keep us out of sight – why not do something productive," explained Alex.

"Productive?" AJ said with a puzzled look.

Carmen then explained Alex's plan, which the agency eventually accepted. When Spring arrived, they would be outfitted with a Class A motor home and with a "grant" paid for by the government but fronted by the National Institute of Health. They would first visit representatives of the 12 most populous tribes in Alaska and conduct a survey on just how many of the youth were showing FASD symptoms.

AJ looked stunned, "And the government bought and paid for this idea?"

"It took some talking, but your dad has spent almost four years prepaying to be a lawyer – so he was use to talking – a lot," Carmen explained with a smile. She explained how they were flown to the University of Alaska in Fairbanks and given a crash two-week course on the tell-tale signs of FASD, that while there is no definitive test to determine how serious the disease is on the Fetal Alcohol Spectrum after you've seen it a few hundred times, you can spot it quick. Because of the high percentage of babies born with it in Alaska, the state is one of the leading research centers for FASD. Indeed, people of all races move to Alaska because of the research being done on the disorder.

Your dad's idea was actually first just a different cover for us – but, before it was over it was a study published, under pseudonyms, by the FASD Association. She explained how they started in Southern Alaska, where the spring thaw, known as the breakup, started before the northern part of the state.

"Alaska is a big place son," continued Alex, "we put almost 5,000 miles on the RV in three months and then..."

"And then a lot of people, including me at first," stated Carmen, "thought your dad had lost his mind!"

"What?" AJ asked with the most confused tone possible.

"When I was about your age, we had a geography class in which the textbook was called, "From Baffin Bay to Papageno" – so I suggested what if we took our Motor home on a little trip..."

"A little trip – how far is that isn't that like the far ends of North and South America?" AJ asked with a strong tone of disbelief in his voice. "How far is that??"

"As the crow flies," said Alex, "about 19,000 miles. Since we were searching for different groups of Indigenous peoples, we made a lot of side trips," Alex responded.

"Be more specific dear," instructed Carmen.

"Yes, dad, please."

"Well, after driving across Alaska and halfway across Canada before heading south…we drove closer to 40,000 miles – not quite two times around the Earth."

"And the government paid for all this?" again with disbelief in his voice.

"Yes," Alex replied, "but actually, compared to paying for housing and creating jobs for us somewhere in middle America, it was cheaper and probably safer."

Carmen spoke up softly, "It was also a time of great discovery and allowed us to create a bond that few people on this planet will ever have. From an academic standpoint, the books we published, though we never asked for any royalties, are still in college libraries worldwide. Its why your dad teaches at the college level still without formal recognition of a Ph.D."

"How long did this trip take," AJ asked quietly.

"Almost two years," answered Alex, "we tried to time the seasons to avoid driving in the winter months in cold climates. After we made it halfway across Canada, we headed south back to the U.S. We stayed clear of the eastern part of the country because we didn't want to flag any of our "old friends.""

"You mean the people who wanted to kill us?" Carmen said with a smile.

"Yeah, those. We visited the 12 major tribes in Alaska, 19 more First Nation tribes in Canada and then every state west of the Mississippi River – and almost every Native American Reservation in every state."

Carmen pulled out their travel log and noted every state, every Canadian providence, every city, and every Indigenous tribe. In many cases, there was also a summary of estimated cases of FASD and, when possible, a visit with an oral historian (for any tribe that had one who would be willing to be interviewed). This was a treasure trove because, in many cases, the Oral historian could relate the first contact with Europeans – and sadly, many of the atrocities that had befallen them at the hands of the White man.

Carmen was very solemn as she explained this to Alex. She began, "As a Cuban, like many of what we call fair-skinned Cubanos, we can trace our heritage to the Castilian region of Spain. However, there was a large Negro population brought in to work the sugar plantations." [AJ noted she used the Spanish pronunciation for Black even though the American word has fallen into a non-use status]

"And," she added, "there is a small remnant of the 'first natives" of Cuba, the Taino Indians, who were a subgroup from South America. Like so many of the peoples who were on the Americas when Columbus found them – their populations were decimated within less than 100 years. So, I bear both the European heritage, and the angst for which some of my people caused and the pain that they felt. Our treatment of the Negros was not much better than this country. The king of Spain finally outlawed slavery in 1886 – twenty years after the American Civil War fought about the same subject. Our travels brought us great joy and sometimes great sorrow."

It caused AJ to really ponder a moment—his mom was so fair-skinned that he never really considered "Hispanic" to be a difference and never thought of himself or his siblings as bi-racial. At that moment, he had an adult thought and blurted out, "I guess you and Dad have done a good job—I never really think about racial makeup."

"We try, son, we try – it is easier from mom than for me growing up in the deep south – especially Alabama, or even now in parts of North Carolina," replied Alex.

"There is something else that your mom and I started doing on this 40,000-mile adventure," he continued.

"You mean besides becoming experts in anthropology of Native Americans and the impact of alcohol and other bad white man habits?" AJ asked with a puzzled look on his face.

Carmen laughed as she replied, "Yes, I think I know where your dad is going – it was arguably a very important part of our journey – other than staying alive."

Another puzzled look and, "What do you mean?"

"You tell him," replied Carmen.

"After we started traveling, we stopped every Saturday night if we were on the road and went to Church," Alex explained.

"Cool, is that when Dad decided to become active, and you decided to convert from being a Catholic?" AJ asked.

"Not exactly," both parents said at the same moment.

They then laid out their worship schedule – such as it was. They went to a Church every Sunday but alternated between a Catholic Mass and an LDS Sacrament meeting.

Carmen explained that she, like Maria and Judy, had been raised a good Catholic all her life. She knew the Church was important to Alex, but if he wasn't willing to come out as a member, she wasn't ready to consider switching her faith – though thinking back to Hawaii, she remembered the powerful sensations she felt talking to the members after walking on the Temple Grounds at Laie.

Alex told his narrative as well. He had never denied the truthfulness of the Gospel but knew he hadn't and possibly wasn't willing to live up to the Covenants he had made when he was called as a missionary. He explained he wasn't guilty of any serious sins—he and Carmen had kept the law of chastity before marriage and had been fully faithful to each other after they married.

"But," Alex added, "I guess I had one habit I didn't want to think about. I developed a taste for good wine, and your mom's church saw nothing wrong with it."

"It's true," explained Carmen, "my beloved Tio was a wine connoisseur. I had been allowed to drink a glass of wine with my meals since I was 8 years old. I too loved a good wine – it wasn't hard to convince your dad."

"Sorry to burst any bubbles, son, but your parents were totally human with this frailty," explained Alex. "So, we alternated going back and forth LDS to Catholic. I knew in my heart that I was a member of the Lord's Church – and I knew while I loved the pageantry of the Catholics, I could never walk away from my faith.

"And son," added Carmen, "I knew long before I told your dad that I needed to join the Church – but if he wasn't ready to go back…well, I guess we both just kept saying we'll do our best but not worry about Church right now."

"I don't know what to say," said AJ.

"Son, I would never tell anyone it's OK to stay away from Church for any reason – I was wrong, and my example kept your mother out of the waters of baptism for a long time. Perhaps it is why I try so hard to set the example of the right things for you and the twins."

Carmen softly added, "While we were wandering, there is something else that we did, that your dad seemed to make sure of…"

"What?" asked AJ.

"You tell him dear," replied Carmen.

"When we visited any city with a Temple, I took your mother on a walk around the Temple grounds – it left me so torn because I knew we couldn't go in, and yet, I so much wanted your mom to know what I knew, to feel what I had felt within the walls of the Temple. No, I can't tell you what kept us on the outside for so long."

"You were on the road for almost two years – you didn't work, how did you live?"

Alex explained that the government grant continued to replenish their debit card at midnight every Thursday at midnight while they traveled. They budgeted well and always had plenty for gas, food, accommodation, and other needs. Before the trip was finished, we had planned on visiting all the countries of Central and South America. That would have included sending the motor home by ferry at the Darien Gap between Panama and Columbia. It is an area with such high mountains and dense jungles that there is no road on which you can drive heading into South America. We did get to all those countries, but not always with the motor home.

Carmen interrupted Alex's narrative: "You are getting ahead of yourself – just keep going with how it all started out."

Alex nodded and added, "In every country except Brazil, their ability to speak Spanish proved to be very valuable in finding the best directions and being accepted by the locals.

In every major city Alex had the motor home checked from end to end, with all necessary maintenance and repairs. In addition, they carried an extensive emergency kit but no weapons, especially after leaving the United States. They were routinely stopped by the police or national guard often – but their official papers from the U.S. Department of State explaining their research travel opened doors no matter where they went.

By this time AJ's head was again spinning as yet another layer of his parents' past was shared. Adding all the excitement of his first girlfriend and the end of the school year kept his mind constantly asking, "What else can they possibly have done?"

Carmen was just starting to explain, "Wait until we tell you about one of our adventures in Mexico, which is where there were some changes in our plans." The front door opened, and the twins shouted in unison, "MOM, we're home!"

The two excited tweens stuck their heads in the door, and Alex said, "Hey guys, go wash up and give us a few minutes."

"OK!" was the response in the favorite tween volume."

"Oh! Dad and Mom, I forgot to tell you," added Alex, "Judy wants to come to Church tomorrow – and I want to go see what her Mass is like."

Carmen took a deep breath – how could you say anything when she and her husband just admitted they had attended each other's church for two years? But then they were grown and married, not 15, almost 16 and high school students. "I see," Carmen replied, "let me make sure it's OK with her mom and dad."

****

As Carmen reached for the phone, it started to ring. Glancing at the caller ID, she saw the name Maria Roland (Cell), and she quickly answered with a cheery, "Hi, if this is Maria, this is Carmen. I was just picking up the phone to call you…"

"What another coincidence," replied Maria. It may be about the same thing—Judy and Brian are planning on visiting your church after Mass tomorrow, and I told Brian I'll support him if he wants to attend his church, so I will be there too. But I wanted to talk to you about AJ coming to Mass. Are you OK with that?"

"Of course, Maria!" Carmen replied, hoping her voice didn't show any concern, "Our kids have always been allowed to learn about other faiths."

"It is certainly OK with us – I never complain when a young person wants to go to Church, but Judy swears that AJ asked on his own without any prompting from anyone."

"Maria, I promise you it's OK with both Alex and me—we were concerned that you might be worried about it."

With that, Maria laughed and said, "I guess we both were concerned for no real reason. They are good kids, and they could certainly ask to go places worse than a church."

"For sure, we'll look forward to seeing all of you tomorrow – oh, what time is Mass?"

"We will be going to 8:00 tomorrow to make sure we get through in time to go to your meeting. If it's OK, we can pick AJ up around 7:45 on our way."

"Thanks, Maria, I'll have him ready. See you tomorrow. Good night."

"You too."

Carmen hung up the phone and stared at it just for a moment, smiling she said to herself, "I guess we will let God prevail."

****

It was the start of a multi-family religious odyssey that, over the next several weeks, would see some combination of the Bartons and the Rolands at each other's Sunday services, with the exception of the following week. While both teens came away from their visits with genuine interest and questions, for Judy, it was the week to prep for a leave for the State High School Softball Championship Tournament in Raleigh. The double-elimination tournament started Thursday afternoon and concluded with the Championship game on Sunday.

Coach Cato would have the team do an extended practice on Monday and Tuesday, and they would leave on Charter bus for the 2-hour drive to Raleigh after school on Wednesday. She was incredibly proud of her team just making it to State. She did her best to prepare her girls so that now that they were some of the best, they would play nothing but the best. Schools with much larger programs and much deeper pockets for all the extras that help make a good team even better. Salisbury High had a good program, but nowhere near the major schools in Winston, Charlotte, and Raleigh-Durham.

Wednesday morning, Judy asked for and got another father's blessing. This time, both she and Dad were better prepared. As he said, "Amen," she felt a calm come over her tense nerves and knew—win or lose—she would be able to do her best.

By the time AJ asked, his mom and dad had already decided they would take him and his siblings out of school on Friday to spend the weekend in Raleigh and hopefully stay until Sunday afternoon to watch Judy and her team play.

It was the boost Judy needed because the tournament started on a sour note. She played well in the first game, though not as the pitcher – she did get two hits and drove in three runs, but it was not enough as it turned into a slugfest, which they lost 9 to 7 – sending them to the "loser's bracket." Which meant they couldn't lose another game if they wanted to make it to the finals. And they didn't. With both families in attendance for Friday's game, Judy pitched a 3-hit shutout, and the Lady Hornets won 2-0. Playing center field the next day, Judy's glove in the field saved the day as she leaped high and took an almost certain home run away from a power hitter in the bottom of the last inning to preserve a 2-1 victory. The second win then put them into the Championship game on Sunday afternoon.

Saturday night both families went out to Chillis as a break from the pizza celebrations. The family was buzzed with the excitement of the team's 2 wins after the disappointing first-round loss. Judy, half-joking, half-serious, told AJ, you are my good luck charm, and you couldn't be there Thursday – but I'm really glad you're here now. Alex offered a little road trip to the nearby city of Apex as a chance to show them something special. The two families piled into their cars, with AJ joining Judy with her parents. Alex drove the 17-minute trip to the grounds of the Raleigh Temple of The Church of Jesus Christ of Latter-day Saints. He explained, "We sometimes love to come to the Temple grounds just because it such a peaceful place."

The Bartons had been many times. Brian knew there was a Temple in the Raleigh area, but simply wrestling with going back to Church the Temple hadn't crossed his mind. Judy and Maria were struck with the simple beauty of the building, and as Judy observed, "It's almost like the building whispers peace. I don't know how else to describe it, its, its," and at that moment, an unexpected tear rolled down her cheeks." Maria hugged her daughter and turned to ask Carmen, "Can we go inside?"

It was an innocent enough question for a practicing Catholic to ask—the great Catholic Cathedrals of the world are open daily almost as tourist attractions. Carmen gently sidestepped the question with, "Not tonight. The Temple is closed on Saturday evenings—it's a little more complicated than that, but we can talk more later."

"I would like that," answered Maria.

"But right now," interjected Brian, "we need to get tomorrow's pitcher back to the team hotel. The coach has a nine o'clock curfew for all her players. She let the players who had families come over go out for dinner but strongly reminded us to have the girls back on time.

The Rolands and the Bartons were staying at the team hotel – a Courtyard Marriott only five minutes from Campus. The team was going to have breakfast at 8:00, a short chapel service presided over by the father of one of the players who was a local minister, followed by a team meeting, a light lunch and then heading for the field for warm-ups at 12. The game time was 2:00 PM.

Brian and Maria indicated they would be attending Mass at a local Church; the Bartons found a Ward with a 10:00 AM Sacrament Meeting and they agreed to meet back at the hotel for lunch at a nearby Bob Evans. Alex and Carmen did not eat out on Sundays unless they were out of town. Alex reminded Carmen that even the Apostles eat out when they are on the road, whether justified or otherwise.

She reminded him, "Yes, but they are on the Lord's errand." To which Alex replied, "I feel we are as well."

Regardless, after church, chapel services, meeting breakfast, and lunch, players and fans alike were ready for the game. The National Anthem was played before almost 1,000 people—a sizeable crowd for girls' softball—and the umpire yelled, "PLAY BALL."

The Lady Hornets' opponent, who was designated as the Home Team since they won every game in the winner's bracket, was Raleigh Country Day. It was a large, well-funded private school that was allowed to compete with the public schools because of some twist in the guidelines. They came into the tournament with a record of 17-2—with their three tournament wins, they were now on a 14-game win streak.

Like the Hornets, they had an overpowering pitcher - who, unlike Judy, was a Senior and already committed to play for the University of Miami and expected to start in college as a freshman. Three years older than Judy and well-seasoned she set the first three Salisbury players down while only throwing 12 pitches.

Judy took the mound, turned and faced the outfield, made the sign of the Cross, looked up to the stands to spot AJ and her family, and then tuned out the rest of the world. Nine pitches later, she sat down on the bench, having struck out their first three batters. A pitching duel was on. After four innings, going into the top of the 5th inning neither side had got the ball out of the infield. Judy had struck out eight; her opponent, Rachel had struck out nine of the Hornets. Judy gave up her first hit in the bottom of the 5th – but the threat ended with a perfect double play. In the top of the sixth inning, the Hornets leadoff hitter got a solid hit on a ball that seemed to have eyes as it skirted between the shortstop and the short fielder. With a runner on first Judy came to bat with everyone expecting her to swing for the fences. Catching Coach Cato's eye, she nodded and laid down the perfect bunt that rolled slowly down the 1st baseline. Somehow, she beat out the play at first which allowed the runner to go all the way to third. After a strikeout, the Hornets second best hitter got hold of a fly ball, which went deep to center. The runner on third scored, and Judy went to second, where she stayed as the next batter also struck out. Raleigh failed to score in the bottom of the sixth and Salisbury went down in order in the top of the 7th.

The last half of the 7th inning is one that will be remembered and talked about for a long time. Judy had said a quick prayer as she walked to the mound. Again, she made the sign of the Cross, smiled at AJ, and went to work. She was still at her best, striking out the first two players and holding a one-run lead in the bottom of the last inning with one out to go. The next batter hit several foul balls and took three close pitches for balls. AJ and both dads were ready to shout boos at the umpire when their wives pulled them to their seats. Ball four had both moms as angry as their husbands. Judy's opposing pitcher, Rachel, who was also a power hitter, stared at her, and the two competitive young warriors made eye contact. With the count at 3-2 with two outs Judy put everything she had left on her fastball. Rachel tattooed it to deep center field. The runner on first scored easily, tying the game. Rachel was rounding second as the throw was being made from center field to home, the third base coach waved the runner. Judy was backing up the catcher but the perfect throw from center arrived a split second after Rachel slid under the tag. The game was over. Raleigh Country Day and Salisbury High School had just played one of the best games in North Carolina High School Sports annals.

Judy dropped her glove, ran to the plate, extended her hand to Rachel, pulled her up as she dusted off her pants leg, and threw her arms around her. Both girls cried. They knew it was a very special moment in both of their lives.

Salisbury had finished second in the State; they didn't win the Championship, but their coach could not have been prouder of her young team and their efforts. Nor could she have been any happier than her prospects for the next season. Unlike the teams they had beaten, who had most all seniors in their starting line-up, she had two seniors, two juniors, five sophomores, and probably the best freshman player in the state, maybe the nation.

CHAPTER SEVENTEEN

To say that the weekend in Raleigh was filled with exorbitant high emotions would be an understatement for all the Bartons and the Rolands. Judy was understandably torn between the pride in the way her team had performed and how close they had come to winning the State Championship. In a way that showed an inner character far beyond her years was her gratitude for being part of the team – never seeing herself as one of the primary reasons they got as far as even being in the championship game. In fact, the thought never entered her mind. When AJ had suggested as much to her it came as a complete surprise that anyone would see it that way, especially her levelheaded boyfriend (a title she was now comfortable using.)

However, no matter how great the weekend was, Monday still followed Sunday, and it was back to school for students and student-athletes alike. After seeing the twins off to school, Alex, as was their arrangement, had taken AJ to Seminary – and was only slightly surprised to see Brian driving into the parking lot to bring Judy to class as he and Alex approached. He nudged AJ, who was still groggy from the late-night return from Raleigh, and said, "Looks like Judy may become a regular seminary student if she can make it here after yesterday."

AJ only grinned as he thought to himself, "My girlfriend (a term he was now very comfortable with as well) is quite a girl – and I'm a lucky guy."

That morning Carmen was enjoying a cup of her favorite herbal tea while listening to a morning update on Alexa when her cell phone rang – it was Maria.

"Hi Maria – good Monday morning, you guys must be exhausted."

"We are, but to both mine and Brian's surprise, Judy was up and wanted to go to that religion class that AJ goes to every morning," she said.

"Seminary," Carmen said, "even many of our Church kids are not excited about getting up for one more class, but AJ has told me that even when he would rather sleep, it gives him a good start to his day."

"Judy came home raving about it – that's why she asked Brian for the father's blessing thing. I will never say no to a teen these days who wants to build a better spiritual foundation."

"Amen to that," replied Carmen.

"Carmen, are you busy this morning? I work three 12s, so today is one of my days off," Maria explained.

"I was just going to decompress some after the weekend. I have errands this afternoon, but I'm not doing anything all morning. I'm having a cup of my favorite peach tea. Why don't you come over? My house is empty right now."

"Thank you. I was hoping we could get together. This weekend caused me to think about a lot of things besides just Judy's game," she replied, "I'll be over in a few minutes.

Carmen got up to make some more tea and pondered to herself all that had transpired since her son first told her about a girl named Judy. Her initial concern and even a little angst about her soon-to-be 16-year-old son's first expressed interest in a young woman. She chided herself a little on being judgmental because Judy was not a member of their church. Then the unfolding of the stream of amazing coincidences of the way the separate lives and backgrounds of both families seemed to be interwoven. Both she and Alex had already accepted this "chance meeting," was not accidental, that indeed there was some 'greater purpose.' She silently prayed that she would be receptive to promptings from the Spirit to be an instrument in the Lord's hands – regardless of whatever that purpose might be.

Her thoughts were interrupted with the doorbell and a few moments later she welcomed Maria into the warm kitchen and handed her a freshly brewed cup of heavenly peach herbal tea. Maria graciously accepted and said, "Brian reminded me that LDS don't drink coffee so I wasn't going to ask if you have any decaf."

Both women laughed as Carmen replied, "I was raised

by a traditional Cuban Aunt and Uncle, I was drinking Cuban coffee and expresso in kindergarten – it was one of the things I truly had to get over when I made the decision to join the Church years ago."

"Carmen," she asked with a hesitant voice, "can we talk? I mean really talk. There are so many questions in my head as I try to navigate the changes in our lives over the past few weeks. I need someone who can listen and answer me. Please."

There was a pause and then Carmen reached across the table and put her hand on Maria's hand and said, "Of course. In many ways, I have walked a path that you are now just beginning. In many ways, trust me, it was far different – but in being a life-long Catholic and then falling in love with a man, more of a boy than a man, who was a member far from his faith, I think I can relate."

Maria, at that moment, was overcome with emotion and softly sobbed, "Oh Carmen, thank you," she said between tears as she continued, "my parents, my grandparents all the way back to my great, great grandparents who came from Italy to America were devout Catholic. My family brought our Catholic faith with them from Italy almost 200 years ago. Along the way they married primarily with other Italians, or in one of my grandparents' case, a Cuban, but if they were not Italians they were usually Irish immigrants."

Let me guess replied Carmen, "The common tie was of course they were…"

"You got it," replied Maria, "they too were Catholic. I am the first person in at least 50 years to marry a non-Catholic. I had no idea of Brian's LDS faith because he wasn't attending any Church, his parents had been killed in a car crash, and he never even mentioned his Utah roots. When I pressed him about what religion he would claim to be he simply said, 'Christian.'

"Wow, though I can't say that initially Alex really talked about being what we commonly called a 'Mormon' when we met years ago," explained Carmen.

"Brian won over my parents and my priest by promising to study Catholicism, and regardless of if he ever decided to join, he would support my faith and, equally important, raise any children as Catholics," continued Maria. "So, you can see the turmoil that is in my heart. Brian has more than kept his word, but I sense just how much it would mean to him to start attending the faith of his youth again."

Carmen got up and cut a piece of pound cake for both her and Maria, "Well, I perhaps understand more than anyone you'll ever meet. I didn't wake up one morning and say, I think I'll ditch my faith and become a Mormon. My conversion was a process that took years."

"Any regrets," asked Maria.

"No," Carmen replied softly," No, because my Catholic faith led me to know my Savior. I did not leave Jesus behind, just found, for me, another way to follow and serve him."

Maria then added I was named Maria after my great, great grandmother – at times, I have considered simply changing it to Mary because now it sounds so Hispanic – I'm sorry, no offense."

Carmen laughed and broke the tension, "I am very well aware that I am Hispanic and that most Americans can't tell a

Mexican from a Cuban from a Brazilian!"

Both women laughed as Carmen continued, "But, first and foremost I think we are sisters of the same Father in heaven and then Americans. Hispanic is a man-made title."

Maria breathed a sigh of relief and said, "I think we are going to get along great. May ask some of the questions that are bouncing around my head?"

"Sure, fire away."

"Well, I have been thinking about this one since Saturday night. Why was the Temple closed, and why is so different from just your Church only a couple of miles away?"

Carmen thought for a moment, closed her eyes, said a quick prayer, and then answered, "Let's start with how the Temple is different from our Chapels." Carmen then explained how Temples were where the Church's most sacred, not secret, ordinances were performed. How Temples have always been since Biblical days, holy places of instruction for the Lord's people – she reminded Maria of the Children of Israel's tabernacle in the wilderness, Solomon's temple, and how Jesus himself worshipped in the Temple in Jerusalem. She trod lightly on the need for a Recommend to enter the Temple that it was only open to members who were living the standards of the faith. When she did Maria looked confused and asked, "You have to tell someone that you are doing something that your faith says you are supposed to be doing?"

Carmen smiled and her previous Catholic faith gave her an answer that Maria immediately grasped, "Well, it isn't quite going into the confessional and talking through the wall to the Priest," she said with a grin, "but I guess for me growing up and telling the Priest when I had broken a commandment, I could see the parallel."

Maria smiled, and her mind flashed back to similar experiences talking to her Priest. She replied, "We may have more in common than I would have first thought—we can discuss this what your faith calls worthiness another time. You mentioned being married for all time. Aren't we all married that way?"

"What does the Priest say when after you exchange wedding vows? Asked Carmen.

"He pronounces you 'husband and wife, until death do you part...'" her voice trailed off as she finished the sentence.

"I know, it had never hit me until years later when I first began to learn about the Church after Alex and I had been married for several years, and he explained how marriages in the Temple were 'for all time and eternity.' In other words an Eternal Marriage – both in this world and the next."

Maria sat very still and then asked, "So you and Alex weren't married in the Temple?"

"Not at first – that's a long story that will keep for another day, but we were married by the pilot on a government jet – who was also an ordained Baptist Minister at about 30,000 feet."

"What!?" Maria asked almost in disbelief!

"As I said, it is a very long story, but several years later – after Alex and I had literally traveled much of the world, and

I attended Church with him, and he attended Mass with me, I decided that I knew my faith, but I needed to know what made Alex tick."

Again, Maria was stunned, "So you did what Brian and I are just starting to do? And, for several years?"

"Yes, to both questions. I wasn't ready to give up a faith that my family had followed for almost 200 years; and yet, I saw something in Alex, even when he wasn't going to Church that made him so different."

Carmen got up and poured them both another cup of tea and then continued, "It wasn't easy to make what many considered such a drastic change of something as important as my relationship with my God. I spent a lot of time on my knees, praying for the right choice. Alex would never have pressured me to join the Church. He would have continued to support and love me as a Catholic. He knew the decision had to be mine and mine alone."

Maria sat quietly, studying her tea, and asked, "But you didn't have any children then?"

"No, AJ arrived after I had been a member of the Church for a few years. By then Alex and I had been sealed in the Temple."

"The one we visited last Saturday?" asked Maria.

Carmen smiled. It was a wonderful memory, but she knew the answer would raise yet another question: "No, we were married in the Temple in Hamilton, New Zealand."

"Wow! How in the world did that happen?"

Carmen decided the best answer was the truth, without a lot of the back story, so she replied, "When Alex and I got married we were both just out of college (sort of true) and we stumbled (sort of true) on a grant proposal to let us travel and study the impact on Indigenous people when exposed to the traditions, religions, and cultures of primarily Europeans or at least Eurasians."

"And, that included New Zealand, the Māori?" asked Maria.

"Yes, you are one of the few people I have ever met that have heard of the Māori."

"I was an anthropology major before I decided to go into nursing, I had this dream of traveling the world and studying different cultures – it sounds like you did. Where beside New Zealand?"

Carmen looked down at her cup and smiled again, "Hawaii, Alaska, the western half of Canada, and the western half of the United States, Mexico, Central America, South America, Tonga, and Australia before we reached the end of the Earth in New Zealand."

"How long did it take?"

Carmen looked away into the distance. It seemed so far away, and the reason that they were literally hiding for their lives seemed like such a bad dream, but the adventures and the discoveries shaped their lives. She quietly answered, "More than a decade, 11 or 12 years."

"It sounds like you guys lived a life and a half even before your kids were born," Maria answered softly, "half of me wants to ask so many questions, beginning with 'why'"

"That is certainly understandable. We really haven't shared this with a lot of people. The members in our Ward just thought we moved around a lot and settled down when Alex started teaching at Catawba. Which is true, with a lot of gaps," added Carmen with a smile. "But you came to talk to me with questions, not hear my narrative."

"I'm touched and honored you shared this much with me," replied Maria. "And I can't begin to express knowing that you have walked some of the roads I am walking now, how, reassuring I guess is the word, to know that someone else has faced these same decisions. I thought I must be all alone."

Carmen smiled and added, "I don't think our God ever leaves His children all alone – it's just sometimes we don't turn to the people he has put in our path. Tell me how Judy came into your life – what a blessing she must be."

Maria then unfolded the story of how she and Brian wanted a child, prayed for a child, and spent a small fortune trying to get pregnant. How they knew at some point they would be too old for traditional adoption agencies, and then Brian heard of a contact who had a friend who knew nuns in a Polish orphanage. The trip to Poland, the discovery of this scared 3-year-old girl who only spoke German. Maria explained that when Brian spoke to her in German, he said, "Hallo Kleines, hab keine Angst " [Hi little one, don't be afraid] that Judy's eyes lit up, her face melted into a smile, and she ran to us saying, "Papa! Mama! " [Daddy! Mommy!] They never knew if she thought we were her parents or just so glad to hear someone speak the only language she knew.

"My heart as well melted on the spot as she attached herself to Brian's leg," explained Maria, "and Brian was wrapped from that moment around her little finger."

Maria continued that the adoption, the red tape, and all that went with it cost a small fortune. They were very glad that Brian was a partner in the law firm at that time and they had the resources to pull it off. It took 6 weeks in Poland and Germany to get all the paperwork done and to live with their new daughter. When they returned to the United States they came back to DC until Judy was in the 3rd grade. They wanted a slower pace than the craziness of Washington. A position came open in North Carolina. They moved to Salisbury and enrolled Judy in Sacred Heart Catholic School about six years ago; but decided to let her go to Salisbury High School, primarily because Christ the King High school was at least 30 minutes away on the other side of Concord.

"Brian was a man of his word," offered Maria, "I now know how much he was aching to reconnect with his own faith – but he had promised me and the Priest that when we had children, they would be raised in the Catholic faith."

"Been there," spoke Carmen, "and good Catholic girls go to Catholic schools. Mine was the Our Lady of Lourdes Academy in Coral Gables. The same school that Gloria Estafan had attended at least a decade before me."

Both women smiled at the memories of the Catholic School education, complete with nuns, rulers and daily Mass.

"If I would have asked, or even more if Judy would have asked, we would have made Christ the King work, but now I am so grateful that we went with Salisbury High," said Maria.

"We all are. What can I do or say to help you?" Carmen asked with all sincerity.

Maria reached out and took Carmen's hand, "You have already done more than you will ever know."

Carmen replied, "Let's agree that we will be there to support you along this journey. It is your family's journey as well. It is my hope that whether they become, or I guess I should say stay, boyfriend and girlfriend, they will always be close. Clearly, they bring out the best in each other."

Maria replied, "Carmen, your family brings out the best in us. I admit when AJ first entered the picture, I, too, was nervous. Judy is one year older than most freshmen girls and so I was expecting it a lot sooner. But he's a wonderful young man and always welcome in our home."

Carmen smiled as she replied, "We both have been blessed with very good children. Regardless of where the journey takes us, let's just take it one step at a time. But know, when you need a listening ear, or have the questions that I can promise you will have, I am here for you."

"Oh!" exclaimed Maria, "You have already left a big impression on Judy!"

"How so?"

"You taught her the Cubans often greet their friends with air kisses or pecks on the cheek for close friends. She has never been shy about kissing us, but now she makes sure she does it what she calls 'Cuban style.'" She has insisted since meeting someone born in her bio-mom's city in Cuba that she can claim her Cuban heritage."

Carmen almost blushed and said, "I hope you are not upset."

"Oh, heavens no," replied Maria. Not only is it cute, but we love that she embraces her Cuban, German, and American heritage so fully. Again, thank you for everything, but especially for your friendship and all that you shared this morning."

They stood up and Camen insisted, "Since in many ways we feel practically sisters, we must do this goodbye, Cuban style. The two women shared what would be the first of many Cuban-style hello and goodbye kisses.

CHAPTER EIGHTEEN

Monday afternoon, as Carmen was returning from her afternoon errands, getting ready to prepare cupcakes for the twins' classroom party, thinking about all that she and Maria had discussed and doing it all while preparing dinner, the kitchen door opened with AJ and Judy in tow.

"Hi, Mom!"

"Hi Mrs. or Sister or Barton," stammered Judy.

Both quickly kissed Carmen, who answered, "Either one is fine; you guys are home early."

"Softball season is over," Judy began, "and AJ volunteered to go over my Geography for a test tomorrow; he said he had Mrs. Goldman last year and has a good idea of what she will be asking. Do you mind if we study here for a little bit?"

"Not at all, did you ask your mom?" she asked.

"I did, it was her day off and they called her in to cover half a shift because another nurse was sick. And dad won't be home until late because he's in litigation. So, I'm sort of a latchkey kid," she said with a sigh and a grin.

Silently she was glad that AJ remembered one of the family rules, 'No visiting in anyone else's home if the parents aren't home.' Maybe Brian and Maria had the same rule or maybe not, but she was sure they would rather have them study here than in the house alone. "You and Alex can certainly study here – use the dining room because the twins will take over the family room in a few minutes. Send your mom and text that I said it was fine with me, and if she is getting home late, please plan to stay for dinner."

"Sure thing, and thanks. I really didn't want to fix something for just myself. Dad will eat something on his way home, and Mom will grab something at the hospital."

Carmen took a deep breath, and remembered, "You would always rather have your kids feel comfortable bringing their friends to their home." She threw in two more burgers and added some fries to her plans, it was going to be burger night in the Barton home. By 5:30, when Alex got home, the twins. as well as Judy and Alex, had finished their homework – and everyone was ready for dinner. Other than eating at the restaurant, it was the first time Judy had dined with the family – and the first time without her parents. She so immediately fit into their dinner routine she could have been a Barton that night. At the end of the meal, it was Judy who volunteered, "Can AJ and I do clean-up in the kitchen? The meal was great, and it's the least I can do."

Alex started to say, "Judy, we don't make our guests work for their supper…"

When Carmen interrupted, "Offer accepted," she said with a smile, "AJ knows his way around the kitchen and I'm sure the two of you can get it done in half the time. I need to check the twins' homework."

Alex sighed, "And I've got some papers to grade before family time– so I too am grateful for some help this evening!"

"No problem," Mr. or Brother, or, "it's OK, Judy. I understand," he replied with a grin.

The twins cleared the table, and AJ and Judy rinsed and loaded the dishwasher. They put away the food, and Judy turned to AJ and asked, "Do we mop the floor or just sweep it?"

"Uhh, sweep," AJ asked with a questioning tone.

Judy heard the hesitancy in their voice and said, "Sweeping isn't normally your chore, is it?"

"No, I guess we are spoiled, my mom is an incredible housekeeper, there is seldom anything left like that to do."

"Mine is too," replied Judy, "but I've been doing kitchen chores, I think, since I first got to America when Dad had to translate what sweep was from German to English."

A little before seven, with dinner over, papers were at least partially graded, the twins' homework was checked, and Alex called everyone to the family room for family night. Judy just seemed to immediately fit in. She texted her mom to ask if she could stay. The reply came back, "Yes, Dad should be home by 8:00; he will pick you up from the Bartons. Judy loved being part of the larger Barton family; the twins loved the addition of what seemed like a big sister. AJ loved having his girlfriend and his family together, while Alex and Carmen marveled at how normal it seemed.

Alex's lesson was taken from the parable of The Good Samaritan. A story that all, including Judy, knew well. The twins loved Alex's retelling of the story with some modern twists and turns. When it came time for the family prayer, Judy's hand joined with the family as Carmen offered a prayer and blessing on the refreshments that were to follow. It was the first time AJ would hold Judy's hand – it would not be the last.

Just as they were finishing the ice cream sundaes, Brian arrived. He was very tired but happy to see that Judy had been with the Bartons and not home alone. "Hey, sweetheart!" he said as she ran over and gave him what Carmen knew the Rolands called a 'Cuban-style kiss.'

"Daddy, we had great burgers, and Mr. and er, Brother Barton just did a great lesson for family night."

Brian beamed as memories of his own family home evenings buried deep in his memory came to the surface. He really hated these few times a month when both he and Maria were not at home when Judy got through at school. And he could not have imagined a better place for her to be. "Thank you, Carmen and Alex, for letting Judy join you—it means a lot, but are you ready, Babe? Your old man is tired."

Judy shot back with a smile, "You are NOT old, daddy,

but yes—we need to get home." With that, she gave a "Cuban-style" goodbye kiss to all the Bartons, perhaps just a little lingering with AJ. The twins hugged her tight when she left, and she promised, "Sammy and Jon-Mark, I'll be back—I love your family."

As the twins prepared to head for bath and bed, AJ asked, "Mom, you mentioned Mexico. Do you have time to share a little after the twins are in bed?" Carmen turned to Alex and asked, with a twinkle in her eye, "Do we, dear?"

He responded, "I don't have a morning class, I guess we can take AJ a little bit farther down the road on our ultimate road trip."

******

Later that night, when they met in Alex's office, which had now become a place where nothing could really surprise him as his parents' adventures unfolded, Carmen began with an explanation of how her faith and decision to join the Church had unfolded on their journey of over a decade.

"AJ," she began with a slight hesitation in her voice, ", what I guess we didn't say, is not only did we attend as many Catholic Churches as we did LDS Wards, but we also visited as many, if not more Catholic Cathedrals as we did Temples. My conversion to the Church, or away from Catholicism conversion wasn't a blinding revelation. There was no Moroni at the foot of my bed." She paused for a moment to gather her thoughts, "I knew that I felt a peaceful and safe feeling on every Temple Ground, which after the first year or so, safety was still very important. I realized that it was a warm and calm feeling, but there were many things along our journey that led to my conversion.

"Correct me if I am misquoting you dear," interjected Alex, "but I have heard you compare it both to the gradual light that comes with a sunrise or the falling of an evening dew."

"I think I realized that speaks to my conversion after I heard an Apostle say it in a Conference," Carmen replied ruefully, "but it so true. The light doesn't go from dawn to blinding sun instantly, it's a process. For me Mexico was so much a part of that process."

Alex added, "And, as I saw a Gospel spark in your mom's eyes grow brighter, I too felt my responsibility not to so much teach, as to really start living all that I had pushed to the background for so long. We didn't really speak about it openly that often, but I felt something each time I could tell a new ray of light was shining through-your mom's conversion was very mine as well."

Since AJ had never known his parents as anything but model faithful members of the LDS faith, even after seeing the pictures, and hearing the stories that boggled his imagination, the part about them being basically converts and reconverts was difficult for him to process. Which led him to ask, "So how does Mexico get into the picture, by then you had crisscrossed North America, had been to the islands of Hawaii and almost to the Artic Circle. What made Mexico so different?"

Carmen smiled, turned to Alex and asked, "Where do I begin?"

"How about El Paso and then Juarez?" He replied.

AJ looked puzzled and said, "Why those two places."

Carmen smiled and answered, "They sit on the Mexico and U.S. Border – they are perhaps two of the most classic border towns in America. Our travels had taken us through New Mexico, and we had spent some time in Ruidoso, New Mexico. While there we stayed with members of the Mescalero Apache Tribe, who have a fascinating history of their own, but that's another story. That whole part of the great Southwest, in many ways, still has strong ties to Mexico."

"In both language, culture, and food," added Alex with a smile.

"So, when we left Ruidoso, it is about a 3-hour drive across the White Sands Desert, where the Space Shuttle has landed, and into Texas. El Paso is this large city that just jumps up at you out of the desert. It was the last week of December 1999," she paused and smiled as she added, "and so we thought it might be better to spend that New Year's Day in a large city."

"Why?" asked AJ in a puzzled tone.

"Believe it or not, son," Alex explained, "there was a lot of angst – almost worldwide on how the computers would handle the move out of the 20th century. It was called, "the Y2K" issue or problem."

"We studied that in great American hoaxes!" burst out AJ.

"Well, at the time," Alex patiently explained, "the media had done a good enough job that there was real concern on if the electrical grid would shut down, if ATMs would work, and what our home computers, such as there were, would do."

"I know, I know, for kids your age," said Carmen, "who have completely grown up in the computer world it seems strange – but for two of us, living in our unusual – to say the least circumstance – it was at least a concern. So, a big, still in the United States, city seemed to be a safe bet."

"And it was! Obviously, New Year's Day came, the world went on, and so we set up the camper and actually stayed just a little over a month in El Paso. Weather was mild, and it gave us time to organize pages and pages of notes on our travels throughout the Western part of the United States."

"I'm just a little confused," interjected AJ, "how does this fit into Mom's conversion story?"

"It's a fair question," replied Carmen, "but you needed a little background. While there, we plotted out our next month's travel – which included spending some time in Juarez and looking specifically for any natives who might trace their ancestors back to the Aztecs or Mayans. These were two groups we wanted to do some deep dives into as our research unfolded."

"Your mom's right," Alex continued, "by now, the 'cover' of being grad students doing research had become our real-life profession. It was no longer part of the whole we were hiding in Witness Protection, it was our real 'job' so to speak. But your question of where the Church comes in is what happened next. You remember studying Gordon B. Hinckley in Seminary?"

"Of course," AJ replied, "Sister Williams told us how she met him once and how he was the Prophet who started the modern day building of Temples."

"Very correct," answered Alex, "when I was a teen, there were only about 30 Temples in the entire world, but then President Hinckley announced this ambitious goal to have 100 Temples built, announced, or under construction by January 1, 2000. At the time the Church gasped in amazement at this incredible expansion plan – and here is the tie to our story. One of those Temples was in Juarez, Mexico – it was to be dedicated in February."

"When your dad found out, and there was a Temple Open House scheduled the week before the dedication he announced we had to go," continued Carmen.

"Son remember," explained Alex, "while I had taken your mom to numerous Temple grounds, that I hadn't held a Recommend since I left the mission…"

"And I didn't even know what a Temple Recommend was," piped up Carmen.

"But I knew," Alex continued, "that we didn't need a Recommend going through the Temple during an Open House."

"So, we crossed the border and found an RV Park in Juarez, not far from the Temple. Rented a little car so we could get around for a few days – we had one in El Paso, but it couldn't be driven across the border, and I got the dates and times for the Open House," Alex said with his voice cracking with emotion.

AJ asked, "Wait a minute – you just decided to go into Mexico? I know you said you were planning on driving all the way to the end of South America, but I, I, weren't the drug cartels even worse then? Didn't that bother you?"

Alex smiled as he regained some composure, "AJ, by this time we had sort of put a lot of fear behind us. Miami was terrifying. Being chased through the city of Miami Beach I can't even begin to fathom now. The shooting and firebombing in Hawaii, fleeing back to the mainland, and then because we had spent almost two years in obscurity with Native Alaskans and Native Americans, I guess we thought the things that once scared us so much were in our distant rear-view mirror."

"You thought?" asked AJ.

Carmen reached over and took Alex's hand, "We're getting ahead of the story. There was danger, perhaps especially in Mexico which we hadn't counted on. We'll get to that. Your first question was how Juarez moved me closer to conversion."

"OK," replied AJ with a grin, "I think I sense another story that is going to blow me away, but let's stay on the Juarez Temple visit."

Carmen too smiled as she continued, "Your dad had explained a lot about the Temple, but since I had never been inside the Temple it was hard to imagine. Remember Catholic Cathedrals are huge sanctuaries designed for a thousand or more people to sit in a worship service. I didn't know what to expect, but then..." her voice also trailed off as the emotional memory touched her deeply.

Alex continued, "When we got to the Temple site, it was late in the afternoon; there were still a lot of people, but nowhere near as many evidently had been there earlier in the day. Most of the people were either Mexican Saints or friends who had heard about the Temple and wanted to see what was inside. Like other open houses, there were a lot of LDS Youth helping to slip on shoe covers to go inside, as well as more Missionaries, Elders, and Sisters than you'll normally see in one place."

"A set of Sister Missionaries came up and first asked your dad if he spoke Spanish," began Carmen, "he answered, sounding like a gringo, that we both did but that we both spoke English as well. Then he was asked the question that immediately captured their attention."

"What?" asked AJ.

"Oh, are you guys both members?" asked by what I immediately took to be a Utah Mormon, Carmen explained, "and then you gave the answer."

"I'm an RM. I served my mission in Paraguay, but my wife is Catholic."

"They were fully stunned for a moment or two and then quickly regained their footing by asking, 'Can we share with you why we're here?'" Carmen related, "I smiled and told them Aaron and I had a lot of talks on religion and had visited a lot of Temple sites, but please share with us."

The two young sisters, one was indeed from West Jordan, Utah, the other who was Guadalajara, bore their testimonies of The Church, how they had both gone to college and then felt the call to be missionaries. In a friendly non-combative tone, they then gave (what Alex recognized immediately as an abbreviated version of the first discussion) focusing on Joseph Smith. Gently, without being pushy, they encouraged "Aaron" and "Cathy" since they had given them their WP names to take the self-guided Temple tour, and they would love to hear what we thought at the end.

"I was excited about finally seeing the inside of a Temple," Carmen then commented, "but with some apprehension. Your dad really didn't talk much about the Church, except to answer some of the questions that had come up in Hawaii. I guess we both put our religion on the back burner. We visited Churches, but he had not been to a Sacrament Meeting in years. And, I had not gone to confession or taken Communion since we went undercover," she explained with her voice trailing off.

AJ looked puzzled and asked, "I know how important Church is to you now – why do you think, you were able to visit Churches and even Temple sites and not want more? You had been an active Catholic. Dad was a returned missionary?"

"In my case," responded Alex, "it was the old story of when a single log is taken out of the fire it burns less and less and tell it loses heat and light. I drifted away from The Church, and then with the adventures your mom and I were having, I was just too distracted – and that's only half true. I wasn't prepared to make the changes in my life I knew I would have to make to return."

"I was a Catholic girl who had finished a quest I had worked on since I was a teen and was sometimes running for my life – with the love of my life. I still said my rosary every night and often, without thinking, made the sign of the Cross before I ate."

"I know," replied Alex, "I saw, but was proud that you were keeping more in touch with your faith than I was. I still prayed daily, but quietly so no one would notice. Well, except when were being chased by bad guys."

"Sooooooooo," AJ asked, "you both still believed in your faith – just kept it yourself?"

"I think he nailed it," answered Carmen as Alex nodded his head in agreement. "But inside the temple made the spark of interest just a little stronger."

"How, what happened?" AJ asked.

Carmen looked at her son and answered, "You were about 12 when the Raleigh Temple was re-dedicated, when we took you and the twins through the Open House and,"

"And then a month later all the youth got to go to the Temple to do baptisms!" AJ said excitedly.

"Do you remember how you felt the first time you were able to walk into the Temple."

"Oh yeah," AJ answered, "it was exciting and a little scary since I didn't know what to expect, but when we were there for the Open House and walked into the Celestial Room, I just started crying, and I didn't know why."

"Let's just say," Carmen replied, "when I walked into the Celestial Room that day long ago in Juarez I had the same reaction – and like you I couldn't describe why."

AJ looked very serious and asked his mom, "Is that when you decided to join the Church?"

Carmen smiled only slightly and replied, "No, while I was aware that I was in a holy and spiritual place, and it was different from anything I had ever felt in any Church anywhere, my Catholic roots run very deep."

She then looked at Alex and said, "Your dad held my hand and kissed me softly on the forehead as he whispered, 'One more room I want you to see again.' This time he took us back to a ceiling room and said, ever so softly, 'one day, Beautiful, one day." Carmen reached and took Alex's hand, smiled, and said, "It was quite a proposal. And, one day it did happen – but that is a different time and place."

"But Mom, what was holding you back?"

"Well, son, at that time, the Church, our Church, had been around for about 165 years – as Catholics, we had been proclaiming to be the Lord's true church for almost 2,000 years. Your dad and, more importantly, the Lord was very patient with me," she answered.

"I'm glad you and Dad made the right choice," replied AJ. Then, in a throwback to his dad's sense of humor, he added, " Plus, I don't think I would have liked being an Altar boy."

All three of them laughed at AJ's off-the-cuff remark, and Alex replied, "I don't know, you do a great job passing the Sacrament at Church – I think any Catholic Priest would be happy to have you assist him as an Altar Boy."

AJ wanted to get his parents back on the story track and it was getting late so he gently asked, "You mentioned or hinted that things did get dangerous. What happened?"

"We took our first Mexican road trip," Alex began. We wanted to see the most famous Mayan Temple, El Castillo or Temple of Kukulcan, in Chichen Itza on the Yucatan peninsula.

It was a long drive, and we also decided to see the leading Mexican tourist city, Cancun, on our way."

"And, that son," interrupted Carmen, "is where things go dicey and we realized we didn't know if we could ever feel real safe again. In Mexico, it is quite common to see Mexican soldiers riding up and down the main roads, with their M-16 in their arms. I think it is designed to show the tourists it is safe because of a strong military presence."

"Did it?" asked AJ.

"Yes and no," replied Alex. Since we were not used to seeing armed troops on a regular basis in our travels across the US and Canada, it could be unnerving as well."

"Your dad is being gentle, the problem wasn't the armed soldiers that you could see, it was the powerful members of the Cartels that were in the shadows, and some of them had links to the bad guys we hoped we had left far behind us," inserted Carmen.

Glancing at the clock Alex then added, "And that story is a somewhat of a long one and will have to keep for another night."

"DAD! Really, you are going to drop that part of it and say, later?" Asked AJ in sheer exasperation.

"Your dad is right; you still have another week of Seminary, and it is way past time for you to be asleep."

AJ stood shaking his head and said, "OK, OK, but tomorrow – deal?"

Both parents said, "Deal, go to bed."

AJ kissed his parents goodnight, but knew he would have a hard time getting this part of the story out of his head before he finally slept.

Later, as AJ reluctantly climbed into bed, he checked his phone and saw a missed call and text from Judy: " Sorry. I meant to call earlier, but I was working on homework and just saw the time. I miss you. Call you tomorrow."

He immediately replied, "me2 – long talk w parents. U won't believe some of it. more 2morrow."

CHAPTER NINETEEN

That night, quietly talking as they lay in bed, Alex asked, "So how do you think AJ is taking it as we keep peeling this onion?"

"He seems to be at the point of 'what else can they possibly have done that I could never have imagined? But our story tonight brought back a lot of memories – along with my talk with Maria this morning," replied Carmen.

"Oh yeah, I was wondering how that went."

Carmen thought for a moment and then replied, "The similarity in our stories is so profound. I can truly know how she felt when confronted with the choice of something outside the Catholic faith."

"What did you say?" Alex asked.

"I listened a lot more than I talked, like me, she'll need time. Like me, she is a lifelong Catholic, as is everyone in her family for the past 400 years. We both agreed on something that is very important."

"How so?"

If Alex could have seen his wife's eyes in the dark, he would have seen a twinkle in them when she replied, "Oh, we both agreed we are daughters of God...and married to special husbands. But that walk down memory lane wore me out—let's talk in the morning." As they had done for many years, they kissed and said, "Good night, and I love you."

****

The next morning, when Alex and AJ pulled into the Church parking lot, they were no longer surprised as Brian Roland was pulling out just as they arrived. AJ smiled and said, "She's always early."

"Good trait," replied Alex, "quite a nice young woman."

Later, after Seminary, as Trey, Judy, and AJ walked to school, the topics turned to finals and the last two weeks of school activities. Well, they talked about generic things until Trey headed to class. Judy went first, "We must have a long time. Mom asked me how I felt when I came to Church with you. She didn't sound angry, just like she wanted to know what I was feeling."

"What did you tell her?"

"The truth, silly, is that I have been a Catholic Christian all my life. I love my Savior. Sister Williams is an amazing teacher. And you guys are neat to hang with," she replied with a coy smile.

"Well, at least you got to answer a question – all I got was 'we'll tell you later to MY questions."

Judy asked with a puzzled smile, "What did you talk about that your mom and dad wouldn't answer?"

"It's a long story – I can tell you more at lunch, but it was weird. It involved their first trip to Mexico, the LDS Temple in Juarez and drug cartels," he answered.

"Seriously??"

"Yes, I'm serious, but we have to get to class."

"OK," she said as he gave her a quick hug and she kissed his cheek, "but I want to hear more."

After the morning flew by, they met up for the Tuesday same old/same old spaghetti with meat sauce, salad, and Texas toast lunch. AJ gave her the narrative about the conversation of how and why Mexico, hit briefly on the Temple, and then talked about why he wondered that his parents hadn't thought about the drug cartels when they ventured into Mexico. The week prior, following his dad's OK, he told how, as grad students, his parents cris-crossed North America doing a research project on Native Americans. He didn't go into the details of how it started out as cover because they were in Witness Protection. Which is, to him, why the subject of the cartels would be even more troubling. Judy absorbed it with wide-eyed wonder as if she were dropping in on the middle of an action or spy movie. AJ was thinking, "Wow, if she only knew the rest of this crazy adventure."

"But tell me why you think your mom is asking you about the Church?" AJ asked.

"I guess because, in reality, for both mom and me, Catholicism is the only thing we have ever known. Finding out that dad is a Mormon, er, LDS and all the time attending Church just to be with us has caused us both to think a lot about Church things," she replied.

"And for me, I have always been an LDS and so going to Mass with you has reminded me that we are all Christians. I am willing to talk about it any time you are ready."

"Not yet," Judy replied, "I'm sort of organizing my questions in my head – while trying to focus on finals. How about by Friday night?"

The bell rang and he said, "Meet after school."

"Coach Cato is calling a meeting to discuss a summer league," she replied, "but I'll call you when I get home."

"Great," AJ replied, grabbing her tray. She gave him a quick kiss, and they headed for class.

****

AJ made it home after walking Judy to her softball team meeting. He discovered his mom in the kitchen working on the night's dinner, his dad in his study working on the next day's

"This Day in History with Alex Barton," the twins working on, or at least pretending, to be working on their homework. Remembering the pending finals and his research paper for History, he greeted them all and headed for some serious study time in his room.

Buried deep in his notebook, Carmen had to call him three times for dinner. The twins began teasing him the moment he sat down, with Sam first saying, "He was probably talking to Judy and forgot about eating." This was immediately followed by Jon-Mark, "Do you think you and Judy will get married?"

"Silenco," barked Carmen, "Uno, son demasiado jóvenes; dos, no una conversación durante la cena." [Silence! One, they are too young; two, not a conversation over dinner."]

Even if they weren't a bilingual family, the twins knew that subject was closed.

"Anything good at school today?" asked Alex.

"Not really. We are all dealing with upcoming finals and final reports. Judy's coach is organizing a summer team for her American Legion league—she's sure she will be invited, though it's usually only for Juniors and Seniors to impress college scouts."

Alex sighed and replied, "I suspect a lot of colleges will be watching her over the next three years. Hey Jon-Mark, Sammy are you guys getting excited about going to middle school next year?"

AJ was grateful that the conversation about him and Judy had quickly been changed. Carmen looked at her offspring and marveled at how fast they were growing up. She had just adjusted to AJ being in high school last year and the twins getting close to the end of Elementary. Such as it is with their kind of age spread in the kids there were always conflicting events at this time of year. What had never crossed Carmen's mind until a few weeks ago was the addition of a "girlfriend" to the mix – and even more complicated the aspect of the girl's father being a less-active LDS.

AJ stayed very quiet through dinner, thinking both about Judy and the conversation he hoped to have with his parents in an hour or so. The twins chattered throughout the meal, and that was fine with him that it engaged his parents so he could think about what to ask next. When the meal was over, the five Bartons all knew their respective roles, and the table was quickly cleared; the leftovers – such as they were, very little food was left over with three hungry kids, the dishwasher loaded, and the twins off to more homework and showers.

As things quieted down, AJ asked, "So can we pick up in Mexico in about an hour? I need to finish a section I'm writing. Alex looked up and turned to Carmen. She replied with a smile, "Sure, let me make sure the twins are getting everything done. We'll have an early family prayer and then we'll share more of our Mexican adventure."

As AJ retreated to his room, his phone rang. It was Judy, she began, "Can you believe it, I just got home!"

"Wow that must have been some meeting," answered AJ.

"It turned into a meeting and dinner. I had to call my parents to tell them I wouldn't make dinner. I wanted to call you, but my phone died as I was talking to Mom, and I had to borrow Coach's phone just to finish talking."

AJ chuckled, "It happens, I guess that's why it went to voice mail when I tried right before I went to dinner. What was the meeting about?"

"You were right; the summer league is normally only for college prospective Juniors and Seniors; I'm the only freshman invited to join the team," she replied.

"That's cool, but not surprising."

"AJ, I'm scared, I don't know if I'm that good. It won't just be the girls from our school. It will be county-wide, and I mean I am the ONLY freshman period. Am I really that good?"

AJ choked back a chuckle and said, "As your biggest cheerleader, I've watched all season and told you over and over you are 'that good.' I am so proud of you."

"And I am so grateful to have you not just as a fan, but a friend, well, a boyfriend; I'm the lucky one," she answered.

By now they were both comfortable acknowledging they were boyfriend/girlfriend. Neither know when the boy/girl was added to 'we are just friends,' but it came as no surprise to anyone who watched them as they had grown closer and closer together.

Judy then explained, "I really, really want to talk for a long time about Church and Churchy stuff. Is Churchy a word? Well, never mind, you know what I mean, but I have a ton to do, and I bet you haven't finished your history paper."

AJ marveled that she kept up with her crazy workload and knew his as well. He replied, "I haven't yet. I'm hearing more from Mom and Dad about Mexico. I think 'churchy' is a word—and yes, we will find the time to have that long talk."

"You are so sweet," she softly replied, "it's one of the things I love most about you."

There was a momentary pause, it was the first time the word 'love' had been in the conversation. The word seemed to hang in the air. ' Love' at 15 going on 16 or 50 going on sixty is intoxicating. First love is one of those magic moments that often seem to sneak up on teenagers.

"Judy," AJ said quietly and calmly, "you are special and it's why I love you."

Hearing it for the first time from AJ caused Judy's young heart to skip a beat, her practical side kicked in as she recovered quickly and said, "We both need to finish homework, I'll see you at Church in the morning. And, AJ?"

"Yes."

"I love you too. Good night, sweet dreams," she whispered.

"You too," he replied, realizing that three words can make a difference in any relationship. Later that night it would be a special journal entry. Glancing at his clock he decided to see if it was time to meet his parents.

****

They met in the family room. Alex led the family in their evening prayers. Carmen hustled Jon-Mark and Sammy to bed in their pajamas and joined her husband and son in Alex's office. "So where did we leave off?" she asked, sitting a pitcher of lemonade on the desk with three cups.

"Well," AJ began, "you covered your first time in an LDS Temple, why you were in Mexico and that you had decided to travel to the Yucatan to see a famous Myan temple and along the way ran into some people who might have been friends with the bad guys who had been chasing you."

"OK," began Alex while pouring three glasses of lemonade, "let me clear up some basic questions. First, yes, we were still driving our 'home on wheels.' In major cities, there are RV parks that, as Mexico goes, are fairly safe. Mexico gets a bad rap every time a tourist is kidnapped or worse. Does it happen? Yes, but usually, it is at the wrong place at the wrong time. We had planned the trip with Nikki, who by now had been our handler through thick and thin. She arranged for us to 'trade-in' our larger vehicle for a smaller one before we left the United States. It came with diplomatic plates which allowed us, along with diplomatic/educational issued passports, to cross freely at all borders in Central and South America.

We carried credentials from four different major universities explaining the purpose of our trip. Our debit cards had been updated to allow them to function outside the United States. We were given a government-issued gas card that was valid at all major petrol stations throughout the Americas. Additionally, we had an emergency kit, advanced life support first aid kit and the RV was equipped with a panic button that could bounce a signal to a satellite and give our exact location.

For 20 years ago this was advanced stuff.

AJ sat sort of slack jawed as his dad opened up about the details that had had never even crossed his teenage mind. He asked, "So how far is Juarez from Cancun?"

"A lot longer than I thought," replied Carmen, "driving across the United States and half of Canada we had put in a lot of miles. Being from Cuba, where a lot of people have traveled to Mexico I never thought of Mexico as being that big. I mean Cuba is not 800 miles wide. And from Cancun to Cuba is a couple hundred miles, but Juarez to Cancun was a lot more!"

"A lot more, meaning?" asked AJ.

"Over 2,000 miles," responded Alex. "We stayed on major highways, made sure we were in secure spots at night, and checked in with Nikki more in the 8-day drive than we had in most of the eight months prior to leaving the United States."

"So, it was safe?" AJ asked.

"It was safe, as long as we stayed safe," Alex answered, "you mentioned cartels. It's a scary word, because they are real, and they are a powerful force in Mexico. It is an irony, while it is not spoken of often, there is a strong suspicion that many of the luxury tourist hotels in the popular parts of the tourist areas are built by, owned by, or controlled indirectly by various criminal cartels."

"And the government allows it?" AJ asked almost in disbelief.

"Son," Carmen replied, "while Mexico has amazing resources, one of the leading economic engines is the tourist industry. It employs millions of locals; brings in billions of nice clean tourist dollars from the United States, Canada, and Europe."

"Which is one reason the tourist zones, and the main highways are relatively tourist safe," continued Alex, "both the government and cartels have an interest in keeping the tourist dollars flowing. As do the workers who simply want to earn a good living for their families."

"Wow. And you guys knew all this and still did this journey?" asked AJ.

Carmen and Alex smiled as she replied, "A, we were younger, and it was an adventure; B, much of it we learned AFTER we started our journey. It was an amazing trip. Along the way we drove through Guadalajara, which to us looked huge. It has a major university, which we stopped and added to our list of credentials. They were impressed and offered us all sorts of services."

"We thought," added Alex, "that it seemed huge after some of the smaller Mexican villages, and it's big, over a million people, the 2nd largest city in Mexico."

"As your dad said," interjected Carmen, "we thought it was big, and then we drove a day to the outskirts of Mexico City."

"I remember in Spanish class saying it is one of the largest cities in the world," added AJ.

"Twenty-one million people," said Alex, "or even more than New York City. It is an old city, built by the Aztecs as Tenochtitlan almost 200 years before being conquered by

Cortez as part of the Spanish invasion. It was almost destroyed and then rebuilt like a European City where it served as the colonial capitol until the Mexicans won their independence from Spain."

"Wow," was all that AJ could offer. It did not surprise him in the least that his dad would have a grasp on the history of Mexico or anyplace on their travels.

Alex and Carmen then took time explaining that so far all had gone as planned. They stayed a few weeks in Mexico City, again offering their credentials and receiving assistance of the National University of Mexico, the largest University in all Latin America with over 240,000 students. That number caused AJ to gasp as it was ten times larger than UNC Charlotte a few miles away. They could have spent a year doing research there, but Nikki advised it was not wise to ever stay in one area long enough for anyone to really start looking into their past – just in case there were any bad actors still out there. It was good counsel and one that was an eerie foreshadowing of what was to follow later in their journey.

"What do you mean, eerie foreshadowing," asked AJ.

Carmen took a deep breath and exhaled, "That's where Cancun and the Mayan Temple come into play and where things got dicey. I was really getting comfortable in Mexico City. We found a long-term RV park, had rented a small VW Golf and were going all over the area. We found the Mexico City Temple and visited the ground three different times. Each time I again felt that peaceful feeling but kept pushing it to the background because I wasn't ready. We attended Mass in a magnificent cathedral and one sacrament meeting in a Stake Center on the outskirts of the city.

Then Alex continued the narrative, explaining that after three weeks Nikki was getting anxious and kept reminding us in daily emails that we needed to quietly vanish and get back on the road. He explained they still were a thousand miles from Cancun. They turned in their rental car, made sure the RV was in tip-top shape, and with Willie Nelson (one of Alex's favorites – not Carmen's) playing "On the Road Again," they left the great Ciudad de Mexico heading for Cancun and the "Mexican Rivera."

"And we got careless," interjected Carmen, "we thought it might be fun to be just American tourists in one of those ritzy all-inclusive hotels that line the beach in Cancun. We floated the idea with Nikki who was hesitant but finally gave in admitting we had been on the road for a long time and never really spent as much money as the government thought they would have to spend to protect us."

"That shocked me!" exclaimed Alex. I thought we had spent a ton of Government money—evidently, when they set up a couple with jobs and apartments, it's more expensive than our nomadic wanderings."

"So, Nikki made some calls," continued Carmen, "and ended up booking us at this beautiful all-inclusive resort right on the main drag of Cancun with a private beach. It was called. 'Le Blanc,' and it was beyond amazing! Somehow, they had a government rate – maybe that is where they hid other people under protection. Anyway, we got a week on Uncle Sam and the rate card was $1,000/night!"

'SEVEN THOUSAND DOLLARS FOR ONE WEEK!" AJ almost shouted, "and they thought that was a bargain!"

"We didn't ask," replied Alex, "for seven days we ate magnificent food, lounged by the pool and the beach, we weren't, or at least I wasn't an active member, so I enjoyed a few pina coladas…"

Carmen almost snorted, "I'd say we enjoyed more than a few, and their wine list was amazing."

This left AJ shaking his head even though his now strict LDS uptight parents had admitted it was one of the things that held them back from becoming active sooner. So, he tried to take it in strife, "So when in Cancun, you did as other non-LDS tourist would do?"

Catching himself, Alex replied, "Yes, son, and not my finest hour. It might have also been what kept me from noticing that one of the bellmen looked familiar and seemed to be almost staring at us. Remember my hair was longer and probably bleached blonde for that time frame."

"Mine was short and red," added Carmen.

AJ just shook his head and said, "Go on."

"I put two and two together the day we left 'paradise.' We were going to check out and get back to our 'jobs' by starting with the RV, which had been parked in the Le Blanc parking lot since we arrived, and heading to the great Myan pyramid Chichén Itzá."

"Yeah, before you guys decided to play rich tourists isn't that where you were headed after you left Mexico City? Asked AJ.

Sheepishly, now wondering if the wine and pina coladas really should have been part of the story Alex replied, "Yes, that was our original destination when we headed to the Yucatan. We checked in with Nikki, thanked her for the amazing week and updated her on our route and next destination."

The bellman I mentioned was now working valet and he was tasked with bringing our RV to the front. When he got out and handed me the keys who looked straight at me an in Spanish asked, "Alex Barton, bist du das?" [Alex Barton, is this you] "I recognized him, and I was not sure if I could bluff my way out of it. He had been one of the few Mexican Elders sent to Paraguay – most stayed in Mexico. His family was able to support him, and for whatever reason, he was in the mission at the same time."

"Were you guys ever companions?" asked AJ.

"No, but he was the companion of my friend from Hawaii, and we probably went on a couple of three-way door knocking afternoons. So, I responded, "No soy yo amigo, soy Aaron y esta es mi esposa Cathy." [Not me friend, I am Aaron and my wife Cathy]

"Perdón señor, parece usted casi un viejo amigo." [Pardon sir, you look just like an old friend.]

Alex continued, sounding like a gringo or not, I was glad I spoke Spanish and replied, "No hay problema, dicen que todo el mundo tiene un gemelo, tal vez el mío sea este tal Alex." [No problem, they say everyone has a twin, maybe mine is this Alex person.]

He answered, "Tal vez sea así." [Maybe so]

Alex shook his head, "My hair was different, I was older, I tried to sound like a gringo, but I wasn't sure if he bought it. We drove away and I told your mom, 'Call Nikki on the hot line.'"

"And I did," continued Carmen, "Nikki seemed a little shook and surprised. She asked, "How many Mormon missionaries were there in Paraguay AND why do you keep finding them!?' I assured her I didn't know and didn't want to sound the alarm just wanted her to know. She thanked me and then, fortunately, ignored my attempt to sound calm."

"Why?" asked AJ.

"It's the part where it got a little dicey that we told you about last night," answered Alex. "It is a main road that runs to Chichén Itzá. As we already told you, in Mexico, it is not unusual to see open Army trucks with 6-10 soldiers armed with what looks like M-16s just cruising up and down the road. It's the government's way of saying, 'You are safe here,' because of this show of force. So. when a truck that looked just like that pulled up and motioned for us to pull over at first, we were surprised but not scared."

"I was scared, my tio had told me too many tales of bad troops in Cuba," added Carmen.

"OK, I wasn't scared at the moment," Alex continued, "I knew we had official diplomatic plates, visas, and real US Passports. A man came to the driver's side and said, 'Senor, please step out of the vehicle,' in heavily accented English.

"Your dad answered in Spanish, porque? [Why?] added Carmen.

"Then his tone turned nasty, and he shouted in Spanish,

'¡Ahora! Esto no es una petición, es una orden. Sal del vehículo y tírate al suelo boca abajo. La mujer también.' [Now! This is not a request. It is an order. Out of the vehicle and go face down on the ground. The woman also.]

"Trying to look and stay calm, I whispered under my breath to your mom, 'hit the panic button, these guys aren't army.' She discreetly hit the button on the dash as I stalled for a few minutes of time by saying, "Sí, sí señor, déjame buscar nuestros papeles. [Yes sir, let me get our papers.]

He screamed louder, "Sal ahora, al diablo con tus papeles!" [Get out now, screw your papers.}

AJ was sitting on the edge of his seat and almost screamed, "And, what happened!? Were you scared?"

Carmen chuckled, "I can laugh now, I was so far past scared that I couldn't even process what was going on."

"And, at that moment," continued Alex, "the calvary arrived. Real Mexican soldiers, in four trucks, two from each direction, surrounded us; as we were about to breathe a sigh of relief, then a fake soldier fired his weapon into our windshield. We both dove for the floor holding each other for dear life and praying in two languages at the same time."

"Other than the scare-the-moose shot in Alaska, we had not heard gunfire, or felt scared since we left Hawaii," Carmen continued, "nor had a shot come so close to us. The soldiers in the four trucks let out bursts of fire which seemed to last for hours, though it was only minutes. When it stopped, we just were laying on the floor sobbing."

Alex picked up the story and told how a real Mexican

officer opened the door to the RV and, in perfect English, explained we had almost been kidnapped by six low-level thugs who worked for one of the cartels. When I asked if it was safe to get out of the vehicle, he said yes, and we stepped out and saw the carnage. There were six bullet-ridden bodies on the ground. No real soldiers were shot. The bad guys had got off six more shots and our front window was totally shattered. As was our illusion that we had left the Miami issues in the rear-view mirror. Our RV Road trip was over.

"But you said you made it all the way to the Southern end of South America?" asked AJ.

"We did, but in a different fashion," Carmen said with a smile, "about ten minutes after the shooting stopped, two American CIA agents arrived in their car. They took us to the nearest airfield, where by then a US Government Lear Jet was standing by. We were flown to Guatemala and stayed at the American embassy in Guatemala City. This was a safe place but still in a dangerous part of the world."

"It also felt like we were in a very nice prison," she continued. "Nikki flew down the next day and we worked with operatives who came in from Mexico to try and figure out who the bad guys were. The former missionary who worked at Le Blanc had disappeared the same day we checked out. All the papers that he used to get hired were fake. The best guess is he was on the cartel payroll somewhere – maybe that is why his parents had seemed well off. There were too many gaps to say for sure who they were; best guess is some of the cartel's partners in the U.S. somehow, through the ex-missionary, had got a positive ID on us and were planning on either a kidnap for ransom or just a hit."

"We were very tired, scared and wondered if the

nightmare would ever end," stated Alex, we had been in protection with new identities the better part of four years, and.."

"And, ironically added Carmen, "we really were enjoying what at first had just been a convenient cover, and…"

"And, we didn't want to stop," added Alex.

"So, what happened then?" asked AJ.

"Let me just give you a quick recap of the next six months," answered Alex.

Alex then proceeded to give the narrative that, initially, Nikki had suggested a completely new cover. Both he and Carmen wanted to finish the planned North to South American project and get the opportunity to visit at least 8-10 countries in South America – it was deemed no more in Central America. They had already identified the native people in most of the South American countries they wanted to interview. Nikki shook her head, wondering what she had created with this cover. A compromise was reached. They would be able to fly from major city to major city. There they would be met by an American agent who would provide them with a car to take them to locations that could be scouted in advance and deemed safe. They had to submit their travel plans, the names of the tribes and were given six months to wrap up the Americas.

"So, after you finished South America, then what?"

"And that son," said Carmen with a smile is where the story gets interesting, but again its time for bed."

"NO, no way, are you doing this to me again without at least a hint of where it goes after you leave South America."

"OK, fair enough," replied Alex, glancing at Carmen who was frowning but not vetoing the request, "Nikki said her bosses realized that when we roamed the American and Canadian west, we went basically undiscovered, but when we went to big cities that might have ties to American crime families is when, as in Hawaii and Mexico…"

"All hell broke loose," interjected Carmen.

"Your mom's description is not that far off, so they suggested let's get you far away from where there will be ties to American criminal activities."

"Where in the world is THAT?" asked AJ.

"As your mom said, that's where the story gets interesting: Tonga, Australia, and finally, New Zealand," replied Alex, "now we kept our part – you to bed; I'll see you in the kitchen in too few hours."

At 10:45, AJ kissed his parents, threw on his PJ bottoms, and fell into bed. Just as his phone beeped, a message from Judy said, "Still up?"

He hit dial, and when she whispered hello, he said, "I just finished another wild tale from my parents…you'll never believe it."

"Actually, I'm sure I will. I just finished a chemistry project, and my brain is fried. Can we talk about it tomorrow?"

"Certainly," he replied, I'm glad you sent me a text, I was afraid you might be asleep."

Judy quietly replied, "Not until I heard how my boyfriend's meeting with your parents went."

The thought and the sound of boyfriend made him smile, "You are too good to me."

"No, I'm not, we are good for each other, but I'll see you tomorrow in Seminary, and AJ…"

"Yes?" he replied.

"I love you; good night again, sweet dreams," she quietly answered.

"I love you too; good night." He reached for his journal and made a short entry that said two things: Parents' wild adventure that started at a crazy boat show just got crazier."

And, btw, "I love that girl."

CHAPTER TWENTY

[Authors note: Einstein, perhaps the greatest physicist of his time, and perhaps of all time is well known for this theory of relativity in relation to time. Far from scientific, most high school students will also testify that time and the calendar's days move faster in the second half of the school year than before Christmas break. In addition, those hours and days seem to fly by even faster during the last two weeks of any school year.]

Since Judy usually did not have any practice or just a short planning meeting after school, they walked home almost every day after school. Their discussions ran the gamut from the food in the lunchroom, favorite classes, sports, politics, art, and music. They had quickly grown so close that they could often talk for what seemed like forever to both parents. Regardless of what subject they started, invariably it turned to religion – either LDS or Catholicism. For almost sixteen-year-olds, they were both well-schooled in their respective faiths. The conversations were always respectful as each tried to listen and understand how they had each gained the beliefs in their respective faiths.

Over the past week, AJ had noticed Judy was asking a lot more serious questions and knew that, at some point, it was going to turn into a much more in-depth discussion than what they could do in the 15–20-minute walk to her house (or AJ's if her parents were not home). On Friday afternoon Judy opened even stronger than before and asked, "AJ, do you believe, I mean really believe, in your heart of heart, soul of soul, that Joseph Smith was a prophet?"

Pausing only for a moment, he asked, "I do, but why do you ask with such intensity?"

"AJ, we've been sharing much about our faiths for almost a month. I have attended Seminary for that long and learned more about the LDS faith than I ever imagined. Sister Williams is amazing, and I have no doubt she believes, but I believe, or up until the last month, never questioned my own faith as being the correct way to worship the Christ…"

"Judy, you are one of the most Christ-like people I have ever met – I have no doubts about your sincerity."

"And," she replied, "Thank you, and I appreciate that—but if what I've been taught over the past month or so is really true, if Joseph Smith was a prophet and Russell er, I'm sorry I forgot, the current one?"

"Russell M. Nelson."

"Yes," she continued, "if Joseph was a prophet and President Nelson is a prophet, then in reality, they would be on the same level as we see Pope Francis, the Vicar of Christ."

At this moment they were closer to his house than Judy's, so he asked, "Are your parents home?"

Judy sighed and replied, "No, mom sent me a text, she had to go into cover a shift and will not be off until after 9:00 – dad is in New York doing some pre-trial work on a big case. I was going to ask if we could stop at your house, I really want to talk this through."

"My mom's home – she said you are welcome anytime," he said with a smile.

Judy burst into a grin and said, "Thank you. Let's go!"

A few minutes later, they were in the Barton kitchen, greetings and kisses all around, and fresh-baked chocolate chip cookies being served at the kitchen table. After enjoying the cookies and fresh almond milk, AJ asked, "Mom, Judy, and I are talking about Popes and Presidents of our Church—if we leave the door open, can we use Dad's study? The twins have on a Disney movie in the family room."

The topic caught Carmen slightly off guard, but she answered, "Certainly, but no cookies at Dad's desk."

Judy giggled and AJ smiled, promising no food in the study. They retreated to the study and sat in the two chairs in front of the desk – AJ could not bring himself to sit where his professor father sat during lessons and serious discussions; even though this was perhaps one of the more serious discussions in his young life.

AJ started first, "Judy, we are both young and have learned a lot about our faiths – but one thing I have truly learned is that studying it in a book or hearing even a great teacher explain it doesn't let you know if it's true."

"Then, how can we ever know?" she asked.

"May I share with you what I've been taught, well since I was able to read and understand?" he asked.

"Please do."

"You certainly know that we have another book of scripture, other than the Holy Bible?"

"The Book of Mormon," she replied.

"Yes. For many of us we call it the keystone of our religion. If it is true, Joseph was a prophet, and everything else falls into place."

"And, if it isn't," she asked with even greater sincerity.

"Then, we are one of the other 10,000 Christian sects. We have good people and good practices but can't claim that we are that different than the others."

"So, I guess the first question I really need to ask is 'do you believe in the Book of Mormon? That Joseph found gold plates and, with some almost magical instrument, translated the book?"

"You've been paying close attention in Seminary," AJ

smiled as he spoke.

"I told you; she is amazing, and yes, I have been paying attention, watching you, your parents, the other kids from our school in Seminary, studying a lot about the Church online and one other thing."

"There is a lot of stuff, good and bad online; what is the one other thing? Asked AJ."

"Sister Williams gave me a copy of the Book of Mormon after my second Seminary class."

"I remember," AJ replied.

"I finished it last night."

With a little astonishment, AJ asked, "You read the entire book in two weeks?"

"Two and a half," she replied, "I didn't read much when we were at State. I had that major project in geography, and I was taking some notes as I read."

AJ shook his head in disbelief: "It took me my entire freshman year to finish the Book of Mormon. Just how fast do you read?"

"Oh, I wasn't bragging," she answered. If you remember, I only spoke German when my parents adopted me. That was my primary language for the first couple of years here in the United States. When I started kindergarten at a Catholic school, the nuns held me back one year to make sure I was fluent in English."

"And, how, when, where did you get so fast?" he asked.

"By the end of the second year of kindergarten, I was reading English at a 3rd-grade level. Mom had me tested, and it came back that I was something called 'gifted.' So, from first grade on I have just read everything, and really fast."

"And, so where are you now in reading skills?" AJ asked still in somewhat disbelief.

"Last August, when I started at SHS, they said I was reading at a 2nd-year college level," she replied, "I never really think about it – it's sort of like my fastball; it's just something I do."

"How fast do you read?" still with disbelief in his voice.

"Er, I don't really know, the nuns tested me at the end of 8th grade, and I think I could hit 950 words a minute, but retention was only 55% - if I slowed down to between 500 and 600 words a minute I could hit like 98% retention," she answered without any trace of bragging.

AJ simply marveled. His girlfriend was talented, brilliant, unbelievably cute, and perhaps had the most tender soul he had ever known, with perhaps the exception of his own mom. Remembering they were both born in the same city in Cuba, he thought to himself, "There must be something in the water on that end of the island." What had started out as a simple question had shed a whole new light on Judy.

"Well, back to the question," he began, "what do you think about the Book of Mormon?"

"Well, just as someone who has read a lot of books, I don't believe it was possible to someone with so little education to have created such a complex story. I love that the entire book points to Jesus. Not really crazy about the wars and the gory parts. It answers a lot of questions – it causes a lot more. I found the verse in the last book that basically challenged people if they read the book to pray about it, and the Spirit would let them know if it was true," she said a serious quiet tone. "And that's where I need help."

"How so?" he asked almost with a laugh, "Catholics certainly pray a lot."

"Yes, we do," Judy replied, "in fact, we have a couple of different books, the Breviary and the Missal, which have the set prayers for every occasion in any Catholic worship service from birth to death…"

"But you don't pray just like you are talking to God or Jesus," AJ added.

"No, we usually, well in my life, almost never; it's what hit me so hard the first time I heard your dad pray; it was like he was talking to his dad," answered Judy.

"He was," replied AJ, "hence the 'Our father' at the start."

"AJ, I don't even know where to start to pray to find out about the Book of Mormon, your church, my church, or anything," Judy said, her voice filled with emotion.

AJ reached out and took her hand and calmly said, "It's OK, Heavenly Father loves us all. You could do what Joseph did…"

"I remember, I read about it in the Joseph Smith story; he read in James 1:5 that if you lack wisdom, ask of God."

"You do remember what you read," he replied with a smile. Here's an idea: Ask your dad for another father's blessing —tell him you want to learn how to best follow Jesus if you don't want to come out and say you are praying about the Book of Mormon."

"How did you know that!?" Judy asked with a surprised tone. "I know my mom and dad are wrestling with the whole where does our family go to Church thing, and I don't want them to make a decision because of me one way or the other."

"Still holding her hand he added, "I didn't know, but somehow I felt it – you know you are really spiritually incredible, and you are a great softball player!"

She took his hand in hers, and in perhaps one of the great moments of foreshadowing in her young life, she answered, "Thank you, but you and your family are the spiritually awesome ones; I think we will forever be grateful that our paths have become so intertwined."

That night, Alex surprised the family by stopping at Domino's on his way home. He walked in, kissed Carmen, and said, "Save tonight's meal for tomorrow. I have pizza for the kids, and you and I can catch the new film at the Terrace that we've wanted to see."

"It was going to be simple," she replied. It was some reconstituted leftovers, which will keep. AJ and the twins will always eat pizza. Did you bring enough for the twins and two teens?"

"Judy's here," Alex asked without the least hint of surprise.

"Her mom's covering a shift at the hospital, Brian is in New York for work."

"You know I always bring extra pizza, in case I want it for breakfast tomorrow," Alex replied, "are you OK with AJ and Judy being here alone?"

"With the twins, they will not be alone; you can ask if she minds helping AJ babysit, and I'll call Maria and find a good PG on Netflix for them all to watch," answered Carmen.

Alex always marveled at how quickly Carmen could place all of life's ups and downs into nice, neat compartments. Judy jumped at the chance, she had always been an only child and loved the idea of being around AJ and his younger siblings. Maria shared Carmen's confidence that it would be OK for her daughter to be at the Barton's until she got off work. And so, it was heading into the summer that another family tradition was born; many times, over the next few months, Judy would join the Barton youth while the parents, which often now included her parents as well, went out for an 'adult date night.'

****

For Brian, the opportunity to become a closer friend was very timely as he worked through his own decision on where the Church, his Church, fit into his family's life. When he returned from New York after that fateful night when AJ and Judy stayed home at the Barton's, he was hit Saturday morning with the conversation that pushed his decision onto the front burner.

That morning, he had gotten up earlier than Maria and Judy. Maria was exhausted from pulling an unexpected 12-hour shift at the hospital, and Alex and AJ had brought Judy home around ten minutes after he got home. He had been happy that Judy had not come home to an empty home, but he expected she would probably sleep in, as she often did on Saturday mornings. Instead, as he sat scanning the headlines on his computer, Judy bounded into the kitchen.

"Hi, Daddy! I wanted to talk last night, but honestly, I was tired!" she explained with teen age enthusiasm that often burst forth when she was excited or nervous."

"Long week at school – at least softball is over until the summer season starts," he said as Judy gave him a quick kiss on the cheek.

"That too, but it was so neat to be around AJ's twins, Sam and Jon-Mark. We watched a movie and then they wanted to play 'Apples to Apples,' which is a fun game, but they are high energy to say the least!"

"Too much?" Brian asked.

"Oh no! It was fun. In fact, AJ suggested that if you guys ever want to go on a double date with his parents, we can do it anytime," she replied.

The dad's brain for a moment caused him to think about his daughter and her boyfriend being in a home without parents, but then the idea that a) his daughter was perhaps the most level-headed teen he had ever known, and that AJ certainly knew the boundaries pushed it into the background. Judy continued, But Daddy, AJ, and I were talking about something important, and he said I should ask you."

Concern again went to the front of a dad's brain with a daughter, "And what was that."

Judy blurted out her answer, "I've been reading the Book of Mormon that Sister Williams gave me. I just finished Moroni, and I ask AJ about Moroni 10:5 – you remember that verse?"

"Oh yes, Judy, I remember, every missionary hopes to have someone read the Book of Mormon and then challenge them with that verse. What did AJ say?"

She continued, "I told him as a Catholic I know all of our prayers or where to find them in the prayer book, but I don't know how to just pray to ask God a question – will you give me another father's blessing to help me pray as I seek my own witness of the Book of Mormon?"

The request hit him surprisingly harder than he expected. Initially, he had been concerned that her interest in AJ, and the Bartons would cloud her thinking on her own faith – but he also knew that his daughter was very bright and her roots in her Catholic faith had been planted deeply. He thought back, though, on how many others he had known in the mission field that, when exposed to his Church, had also wanted to know the same answer that Judy was seeking: Is the Book of Mormon true? In all his time away from the Church he had never doubted the book's truthfulness – he simply buried his own testimony to keep harmony with his wife and daughter. Giving her a blessing before the big games had been the first time he had attempted to exercise the Priesthood since his mission – he had been truly grateful that Alex had been there to guide him.

"Daddy?" Judy's voice interrupted his thoughts.

"Yes, baby, I heard you. And, yes, if that is what you want—of course I will. As you recall, I'm a little rusty. Let me talk with Alex for a little guidance, AND let's talk to Mom."

"Of course, Daddy, I want Mom there for the blessing like the other times," she replied.

"Why don't you make both of us some of those famous chocolate chip pancakes of yours, and I'll give Alex a call to see how soon I can talk to him," Brian replied with a smile as he ruffled his daughter's hair.

While Judy started whipping up the pancakes, Brian stepped into the den and called Alex, who was also having a quiet Saturday morning before the twins woke up the house. "Alex," he began, "we need to talk if you have got some time later today."

"Sure, what's up?"

"Judy just asked for another father's blessing," replied Brian.

"Great – I love it when my kids ask that."

"I know, but you are not trying to figure out how to return to your faith – you already, and excuse the cliché, have been there and done that," answered Brian.

"Krispy Kreme later this morning?"

"Judy's making pancakes – how about sometime this

afternoon?" Brian asked.

"One-thirty?"

"That works, I'll meet you there," responded Brian.

In less than an hour, Judy had whipped up a batch of pancakes for the Roland family, and the three of them sat down to eat. Brian was pondering how to explain to Maria their daughter's request for a blessing to help her understand the Book of Mormon. Judy, as usual, was much more direct and started the conversation with, "Mom, I have asked Dad for another Father's blessing."

"Is there a tournament coming up that we haven't heard about?" Maria asked.

"Something different. You know how that the LDS Church has another book about Jesus called, "The Book of Mormon."

Maria smiled. After her conversations with Carmen and her husband, she looked into many of the different dimensions of the LDS faith, and she replied, "I am well aware of The Book of Mormon. AJ's mom and I had a long talk."

"You know that Sister Williams gave me a copy and that I've been reading it for the past couple of weeks."

"Yes, dear, I saw it on your bed," she replied.

Judy continued, "It means a lot to me to find out for myself if this book is true."

Brian injected, "And that's why she asked for a father's blessing. What are your feelings?"

Maria paused and looked at Judy and then Brian, "We have a very bright and spiritually entuned daughter. We have given her a solid foundation in our faith. Before I met the Bartons I might have had reservations, but Carmen and I have walked too many of the same roads – they are just a great family. From what I have read, their Book of Mormon is what they call 'another testament of Jesus Christ.' How can we not want Judy to study any book that teaches about our Savior?"

"Thanks, Mommy, " Judy replied. It is something I need to do for myself. I love our faith, and what I'm learning in Seminary is enriching my love for Jesus. If this book is what it claims to be, I must find out for myself."

Brian and Maria looked at their daughter and wondered how fortunate they were to have such an amazing child come into their lives – even under such incredible circumstances.

"I'm meeting up with Alex this afternoon – I just want some pointers on this because I'm really rusty, and I just need to talk to someone who, like me, was outside the Church for a long time," explained Brian.

"GREAT! Maybe we can do it tonight – or tomorrow after Church?" asked Judy.

Brian turned to Maria, who added, "We'll make it work."

Somehow Maria felt a calming influence come over her whole being. The idea of her husband and daughter growing closer to the LDS faith seemed to be reassuring and not threatening as it might have been only a few weeks earlier.

****

So, at one-thirty, Alex and Brian sat down in the Krispy Kreme doughnut shop for one of the most important conversations of their lives.

"Alex," it felt wonderful when I was giving my daughter a blessing to help her perform her best on the softball field – but this is deep. She is asking the question we both had always hoped an investigator would ask about the Book of Mormon – she quoted me Moroni 10:5 verbatim," explained Brian.

"She's a sharp girl, I guess the equally important question is, how do you feel about The Book of Mormon having been away from the Church for so long?"

Brian studied his doughnut and started his explanation, "Growing up in St. George, it was always just a part of my life. I gained my own testimony of the book in Germany. It was a hard mission with so few real converts, my companions and I threw ourselves into personal and companion study. It's what kept us going through some dark times."

"And now?"

"Judy is not the only one who has been reading it daily since our two families started getting to know each other. Alex, I want to come home, how and where do I start?" Brian asked in an almost pleading voice.

Alex smiled as he replied, "You have already started. Since I'm a good friend, and hopefully will be your "ministering brother" officially in the near future, but not your Bishop – why don't you start there? Cal, Bishop Barnes is great – you will love him."

"I will call him today. What about Judy's blessing?" Brian asked.

"I saw you give her your first blessing in years. You know the mechanics. Maybe a little prayer and fasting for the right words is in order, but you'll know what to say and do."

"Will you assist?" asked Brian.

"Of course, but only if Judy wants it – I think she wants it from her dad."

Brian felt a load lifting from his shoulders. He had finally said out loud the deepest feeling in his heart and soul. His choice of words was exactly what he meant, he wanted to come home. He turned to Alex and, with tears in his eyes, said, "I've wanted this moment for so long. I am going to talk to Bishop Barnes this afternoon – let's do the blessing tomorrow, will your family come over for lunch after Church?"

"We would be honored," replied Alex, "Now let me get a dozen doughnuts to take home – Carmen will not be totally pleased, but AJ and the twins would never forgive me if they knew I was at Krispy Kreme and didn't bring any doughnuts home."

Brian smiled and replied, "Not a bad idea, but there is only three of us, I think six will do."

The two men bought the doughnuts for their families

and headed home. Carmen was not pleased, but not unhappy and was thrilled to hear about Brian's decision. She expressed concern about Maria but felt she would continue her journey of discovery as Brian and Judy made theirs. The twins and AJ would have devoured the whole box of doughnuts, until Carmen gently, but firmly said, "Sólo dos por favor. " [Only two please]

At the Rolands' home, Brian surprised Maria and Judy with the doughnuts and then asked to speak to his wife alone. In every way, he was more concerned about speaking with her than the bishop. It was an unnecessary concern. When he told her he wanted to return to activity in the Church of his youth, she smiled and said, "Mormon or Catholic, you will always be the man I love."

"You are, OK?" he asked tentatively.

"Dear, we've been married a long time. I have known this was coming since the first time we went to church with the Bartons. You were home, it was all over your face," she said, squeezing his hand.

"I hope you don't mind," he said with almost a romance, "but I asked Alex to assist in the blessing tomorrow and invited the Bartons over for lunch after church – I should have asked."

"Actually," Maria replied, "I was thinking about calling Carmen and asking if they wanted to come over for lunch after church—we are on the same page, we always have been, and we always will be."

Brian hugged his wife and said quietly, "Thank you. I want to wait to tell Judy about my decision until after she has made hers on the Book of Mormon."

"That is also a good idea," replied Maria, "she is a bright girl with her own mind, but she's also daddy's girl."

"She has been my little princess since the day we found her in Poland, and the second most important person in my life," he said as he kissed his wife.

CHAPTER TWENTY-ONE

Sunday was another one of those Journal Entry days that the writers will remember for a long time. In what seemed unthinkable only a few months earlier, the entire Barton clan attended Mass on Sunday at 8:00 AM (the twins were not overjoyed about two Church services, with one beginning two hours earlier than normal, but by this time, they loved Judy as well). Judy and Maria both went forward to take the hoar and wine from the Priest. The Bartons and Brian stood in quiet reference. After Mass, they did not stop for doughnuts, but only because Maria had left early that morning to buy two dozen doughnuts to take with her family to Church. The twins suddenly felt much happier about attending what was such a totally different Church, two hours earlier. The two families used picnic benches in the school section of the Church complex for an impromptu breakfast (Maria had even thought of bringing almond milk and OJ in a cooler in their car).

After breakfast, the two-family entourage made their way to the Salisbury LDS Ward. By now, seeing some combination of Judy, her dad, and now mom seemed normal to a very tight-knit LDS congregation. Bishop Barton and his family had the love and support of the entire ward. Brian had indeed met with Bishop Barnes on Saturday evening in the Bishop's office. It was a heartfelt meeting in which tears were shared, and Brian felt like a prodigal son who was truly being welcome home. The Bishop explained Brian had done an excellent job hiding himself for years; but that his records could still be found, getting all the information he promised the search would begin as soon as he gave the data to his clerk on Sunday morning.

It was a wonderful service, in which all the Bartons and Rolands took the Sacrament when passing by the Aaronic Priesthood. Two young sister missionaries assigned to the Ward greeted the two couples after the Sacrament on their way to the youth and adult classes. "Hi, I'm Sister Young. This is my companion, Sister Tuttle. We've seen you here with the Bartons before. Are you visiting, or do you live in Salisbury?

Brian and Alex smiled. They were quietly wondering what had taken the missionaries so long to notice the new faces, who had been attending in some fashion for over a month.

"I'm Brian Roland, let's say I've known, or known of Alex for a long time. We do live in Salisbury; this is my wife Maria and my daughter Judy. She and AJ have some classes at Salisbury High together."

"Oh," said Sister Tuttle, "are you guys members?"

Brian flinched, though he knew the question was coming. Before he could answer, Judy spoke up, "My dad is. He served his mission in Germany. My mom and I are Catholic. We came several weeks ago to hear AJ's talk, and he has been going with us to Mass, and then I, or me and my parents, come to Sacrament."

Maria smiled and extended her hand, "I think our daughter gave a really good summary. Let's just say it is a time of discovery for both families."

Carmen sensed the need for a rescue and gently said, "Why don't we talk to the young sisters after Relief Society? We all need to get to our classes."

"Of course," said Sister Young, "Judy, do you know where the young women meet?"

"Sure, there are some girls I met in Seminary that I go to school with, they have always helped me find the right room."

The young Sisters' missionary minds were trying to absorb the information. A returned missionary suddenly appeared at Church, along with a non-member wife and daughter who were Catholic and a Catholic high school girl attending Seminary with girls from the Ward. It was a lot to process. With Carmen's guidance, the adults and the teens headed to Relief Society, Young Men/Young Women, and Priesthood. The twins headed for Primary as soon as the Amen was said in Sacrament.

The teens made their way to their respective youth

classes; Brian updated Alex about his meeting with the Bishop on Saturday night, and to no one's surprise, Sisters Young and Tuttle sat immediately behind Carmen and Maria in Relief Society. When the Relief Society meeting finished, Carmen turned to the young missionaries and said, "I know it sounds complicated, but our two families have found we have a lot in common and have grown very close in a short amount of time."

Maria added, "I think that's another great summary."

"Wow, it sure is – we are missionaries, and we are always available to answer any questions that anyone has about the Church, but honestly, you couldn't have found a better source of Church information than Bishop Barton and his family."

"You are too kind," replied Carmen.

"I don't think they are just being kind," added Maria. You have given me more insight about your faith than you will ever know—and I, like Judy, have fallen in love with AJ and the entire Barton clan."

"Well," said Sister Tuttle, "we just wanted to introduce ourselves. If you ever have any questions, please reach out to us or ask one of the Bartons. We love them too."

The Sisters had to use every ounce of missionary restraint in their young bodies not to try and immediately set appointments to teach and baptize to them what was an obviously golden family. Their genuine and welcoming style put Maria (and, to some degree, Carmen) immediately at ease.

Maria replied, "We'll have questions, and we will be more than happy to discuss them with perhaps you and the Bartons.

What she didn't say is that she had spent time online with both pro and con "Mormon info sites." The negative comments really didn't phase her because of how well the Bartons had treated them, along with the shared path that she and Carmen had traveled, albeit at different times. She knew that most converts to the Church in the United States often came from other denominations – they were seldom "unchurched." She had seen the statistics on the Church's world-wide missionary program and knew that instead of massive revival meetings that the Church had grown to more than 17 million members usually in quiet one-on-one meetings in people's homes. And knowing the direction that Brian had chosen she was also sure she would be attending, at least to gain a full understanding of what it meant to be a member of The Church of Jesus Christ of Latter-day Saints.

"Super!" both young Sisters replied, almost in unison.

Carmen the added, "We need to go round up our families. Maria did you want us to come over now, or after we change from Church?"

"Why don't you guys go get more comfortable, the twins can't be happy being dressed for Church for almost four hours – just come over in 30 minutes or so," answered Maria. The two moms and the two missionaries parted with all knowing they would meet again.

Less than an hour later, the Bartons, now dressed in comfortable Sunday afternoon clothes—not as strict as many LDS families, they did not stay dressed in Church clothes all day on the Sabbath—entered the Roland home and were met with a Sunday afternoon picnic of Hamburgers, hot dogs, salad, chilled watermelon, and apple pie for dessert. Maria also promised cookies later in the afternoon.

"Carmen," started Maria, "I know that Brian is going to give Judy a blessing in a little while, but your story of how you and Alex must have been such world travelers before you settled down here in Happy Valley, has intrigued me – would you mind filling in some of the details?"

"I'd love to, but I don't want to take away from Judy's blessing, and I'm not sure if the teens and twins would find that interesting," answered Carmen.

"I would, and we have this great Netflix for kids channel that I bet Sammy and Jon-Mark would love," added Judy."

"Hey, I'm in. I've been hearing this unfold for several weeks, and it never ceases to blow me away," piped in AJ, "Mom, Dad, please."

"I sense there is some really good information for all of us here," added Brian.

Carmen looked at Alex who shrugged his shoulders, "Sure, why not, when you get to New Zealand that is where the meat of where we are today really starts."

This remark took AJ completely off guard, and he thought to himself, "After all I've heard, New Zealand is the meat – whatever that means."

After Judy got the twins tuned to a Netflix-for-kids movie in the family room, the teens and adults moved to the living room where the story, which for AJ had left off with an ambush in Mexico, unfolded. Alex tactfully explained that after a very difficult experience in Mexico that the University that was funding their grant suggested perhaps a safer part of the world – the South Pacific. As he told the high points of the narrative it was also interwoven and where they found the legacy of the Church woven into the "isles of the Sea."

From Mexico, they first went to the island nation of Tonga; this was fascinating to everyone as even Brian, who was a lifetime member, had not known of the Church's remarkable growth in this tiny island nation. Though the missionary work began on the island in 1890, when the Church was under persecution in their own land and primarily a Utah-based faith, Church missionaries, as they had since the Church's founding, were being sent worldwide. In Tonga the progress was slow with barely 1,000 converts in the first twenty years. Two world wars and the lack of the Book of Mormon in the Tonga language further slowed the work. But, when the translation was finished, the work took off; by this year, in 2022, there were over 66,000 members in a nation of a little over 100,000 people. The Church has two Temples in Tonga with over 60% of the population identifying as Latter-day Saints.

"For me," started Carmen, "it was a spiritually touching experience as a non-member seeing the tremendous faith that these native Tongans, far from the rest of the world, felt. To them, they accepted that in the Book of Mormon when Jesus said, "He had other sheep, that were not of his fold, that they were indeed a part of those other sheep."

"I remember reading that," Judy said immediately, "and I wondered, WHO those people could be. I was still wrapping my head around Jesus being somewhere here in the Americas, but other people. This is amazing. Go on, please!"

Alex smiled and explained they had spent nearly a year on the island, their history, their often colorful and sometimes disturbing interaction, with first Europeans and then Americans. He explained how religion had always been an important part of their culture – one where, at times, various Christian missionaries took advantage of the sweet nature of the Tongan people. He admitted that for a time, there was concern that LDS missionaries were, like many of the other Christian faiths, trying to proselyte about this man called Jesus.

"We gained valuable information on the effects of religion, especially Christianity on indigenous peoples for what had become the focus of our work," explained Alex.

"That's true," added Carmen, "but for me, it was causing me more and more to examine what I believed and what I was anchoring my faith as I became older, so far from Cuba, Miami, and the rest of the Americas."

"How so?" asked Maria.

"When you grow up with everyone being more or less the same, you don't see as much of the big picture. By now, we had become close with natives of Hawaii and Alaska, numerous tribes across Canada and the United States, and then the assorted indigenous peoples throughout Mexico and Latin America. The isles of the sea, let me see, there was a great God for many, many people!"

"I am in awe of where you have been and done," Judy replied, "but Mom mentioned something happened that changed everything in New Zealand."

"That's true, but believe it or not, there was one more stop before there," she explained.

AJ having just been absorbing most of what was new to him as well asked in a questioning tone, "Australia"

Alex smiled and replied, "You are right, son, nine months with the Aboriginal and Torres Strait Islander peoples of the magnificent country of Australia."

"You guys were in Australia!?" Judy said with considerable enthusiasm.

AJ smiled just thinking to himself, "wait until the day she hears so much of the rest of this crazy story."

Carmen picked up the narrative, "It is an amazing country, well, continent, that is incredibly modern but with ties to antiquity that go back to the Stone Age. And it's big, very big!"

"How big is big?" asked Maria.

"Let me put in this way, if they cut Alaska in half, Texas would be the 3rd largest state...and, Australia is five times larger than Alaska," replied Carmen

"Oh, it's big and virtually uninhabited," continued Alex. It has 25 million people, and 90% of them live less than 100 miles from the ocean. All the major cities are on the coast, and what they call "the Outback starts less than an hour's drive from cities with between a million and five million people."

"And did you find the Church there too?" asked Judy

Carmen smiled and explained that the LDS missionaries

had first landed in Australia in 1840, seven years before the first Mormons made it to Utah. There was more or less a continual small band of Saints on that distant land from 1842 until 1960 when there were only 7,000 or so members spread across the vast distance. The Church started building permanent Chapels there in the 1950s and after that the membership grew to over 150,000 today with five temples, five separate missions and over 300 congregations.

"We were warmly welcomed by the Saints in the large cities, traveling the Outback, usually by bush plane we met some active LDS in distant parts of that vast land – they in turn took us in, shared their history and how they found the Church," explained Carmen, "I was again touched with their simple faith and again and understanding of believing they were 'the other sheep. It was humbling to say the least."

"It was dear," added Alex, "but we met such incredible people." He then, from memory with Carmen's help discussed some of them:

- **Lorna "Nanna Nungala" Fejo**: A Warumungu woman from the Northern Territory who was baptized into the LDS church in 1973. Fejo was an activist, health worker, and elder in her community.
- **Mulga Bore**: A remote Indigenous community where every resident is a Mormon.
- **Northern Territory**: LDS members from the Northern Territory have traveled to the Sydney Australia Temple to worship, some after waiting nearly 40 years.
- **Elyssa**: A member missionary who shares the gospel with her family in Maningrida.
- **Elder Kevin Jackson**: An American missionary who

spent time with Indigenous community members in Mulga Bore and surrounding areas

"These great Saints led faithful to the covenant lives in some of the most isolated places we have ever seen," Carmen explained as a tear rolled down her cheek.

Everyone sat in quiet amazement, for only a short time as Jon-mark and Samatha entered the room and seeing everyone in silence waited a moment before Sammy whispered, "Do you think they are praying?"

Judy smiled and reached out from where she was sitting on the floor and said, "No Sam, your mom was just sharing a story, is the movie over?"

"Uh huh," replied Jon-Mark, "didn't your mom mention cookies?"

Everyone broke into a laughter as Maria responded, "Yes, I did why don't we get some, take a break and after the cookies I think Daddy wants to give Judy a blessing."

The twins erupted into cheers, Judy smiled as she was now torn from hearing more from Alex and Carmen, having cookies with AJ, and getting the requested blessing. The cookies won out during the break. After everyone had enjoyed the chocolate chip and peanut butter cookies, they adjourned back to the living room and Brian said, "We all want to hear more, but on that spiritual note combined with my wife's cookies, I think we can move to the Priesthood blessing, "Alex, I would be honored if you would join me."

"No, I would be honored," Alex answered.

A chair was placed, the twins sat on the floor, AJ sat with Carmen on the couch, and Judy asked, "Mom, can you hold my hand while Daddy gives the blessing?"

Brian looked at Alex who had never heard the request before, but it seemed right, so he answered, "Sure."

Alex and Brian stood behind Judy, her mother knelt by her daughter's side, and everyone bowed their heads as the two fathers gently laid their hands on Judy's head with Brian pronouncing a father's blessing on his daughter that she might receive the wisdom and knowledge she sought to determine on the truthfulness of the Book of Mormon and the mission of the Prophet Joseph Smith.

At this point it was only the third Priesthood blessing Brian had given in almost three decades – no one listening would have ever known that fact. He spoke with a soft but confident voice, and when he said "Amen," there wasn't a dry eye in the room. Judy wept as she hugged her Mom and Dad. Carmen walked over and put her arm around her husband; the twins held hands as they shed tears, but they were not sure why. AJ stood in amazement at just being part of the moment. Judy saw him and went over embraced him, kissed him on the cheek and said, "I owe this all to you and that first game." They both cried.

When the tears were wiped away Judy asked, "But what about New Zealand?"

Carmen turned to Brian and said, "I think it's time to move the picnic to our home – Brian, are you in town tomorrow night, and Maria what time do you get off"

"I will be definitely in town tomorrow night," replied Brian.

"I'm off and will stay that way. If we get a call-out, I'll get someone to cover the shift. What time tomorrow?"

"Does six work for everyone?" Carmen asked.

With all heads nodding in agreement a most memorable joint family Sunday came to a close.

That night, after evening prayers, AJ adjourned to his room to check to make sure there was no homework and to record the day in his journal. As he was reaching for his phone to say good night to Judy, it rang and she immediately said, "It was the most spiritual day of my life – I could never imagine feeling the Spirit that I have heard you guys talk about in Seminary."

He replied, "Aside from my first time in the Temple, it was the most spiritual experience I have ever experienced. Judy, you are a very special person, as are your mom and dad."

"I also meant what I said, I owe this to our friendship – you and your family have become such an important part of my life. I could go on forever like this, but I called just to say, I have a short story to finish for English. See you in the morning at Seminary?" she asked.

AJ smiled to himself as he replied, "For sure."

"AJ, and one other thing I meant."

"I know."

"Know what?"

"I love you," he replied.

She giggled and said, "that's supposed to be my line, but good night, love you too, till the morning."

"Good night."

In her parents' bedroom down the hall, lying in bed for pillow talk, Maria said, "That was more powerful than I could have imagined. I, too, have a lot to think about. What did the Bishop say at your meeting."

"He told me that my records might be old and dusty, but I could still be found. I told him I wanted to wait for Judy to get the answer she was searching before I made my return official."

"Brian, I want you to go back. I saw the look in Judy's eyes. She has her answer. She may be the only good Catholic girl to join the Church, but there is no way she can deny what we all felt this afternoon."

"I know. What about you?" he asked.

"I think I have to find an answer to the question that I didn't want to ask. Let me pray and ponder first."

"Certainly," he replied, "good night and I love you and our daughter."

Across town, at the Bartons the parents were having a

similar discussion, and Carmen remarked, "I have never seen a mom of a teenager holding the kid's hand during a blessing."

And, as a former Bishop, "Neither had I, but it felt right. I had a mom hold a sick child when the child was getting a blessing, Judy wasn't sick, but she wanted to feel both her parents at that moment."

"It was powerful," she agreed, "I had to talk to the twins because they weren't sure why they were crying, gave me a good reason to explain that the Spirit often moves upon people that way. But to be honest, other than at our sealing in the New Zealand Temple or a baptism of one of our kids it was as strong as anything I have felt in a long time."

"I know," he said as he bent over and kissed his wife, "we have been blessed to be part of a miracle. Good night, Beautiful, love you."

"As I love you, handsome."

CHAPTER TWENTY-TWO

Monday, in the last week of any school year, is always overloaded with activities. For the students at Salisbury High and A.T. Allen Elementary, it was no exception. As the designated professional room mom for the twins who would be moving up to middle school next year, it was a packed week. For Judy and AJ, it was the last full week of Seminary as well. In typical Judy fashion, she had asked for and been given the entire curriculum for the majority of the year that she did not attend, and promised that if she wanted to complete it, Sister Williams would issue her a first-year certificate at the end of Summer. Alex's classes had ended the week before and now it was final exam week. For Brian and Maria, life as lawyers and nurses doesn't run on the school calendar year – but the family's social calendar still does.

Somehow, though, everyone did indeed complete their day's work/school/play. Carmen had put her crock pot and oven timer to work so that the meal would be finished and ready by 6:00 p.m. As she finished taking the chili out of the crock pot and a casserole out of the oven at 5:55 p.m., Alex walked into the kitchen and marveled how his wife, who had been on school errands all day, had a meal for eight ready to go exactly on time.

"Dear," she asked, "grab the salad out of the fridge and toss it; add some croutons, please," was Carmen's only request for assistance.

The twins ran from the family room to greet Judy and her family the moment the doorbell rang with shouts of "IT'S JUDY!"

AJ followed right behind and ushered them into the dining room as Carmen was setting the food on the table. "Great, you guys are so punctual—I just took the food out of the oven. It's been a crazy busy day, and we're starved, and I hope you guys are too," she said as she kissed Maria and Judy. Judy had already given AJ a quick Cuban-style kiss.

Carmen's chili and casserole were well received by everyone. The range was still working on an apple pie, which would be for dessert later. As is the case with four kids at the end of the school year, the conversation revolved around the events of the day and the week to come. However, what had been on everyone's mind—well, not as much on the twins, but everyone else—was where the story of New Zealand was going to take them this evening.

So after the teens and twins cleared the table and started

the dishwasher – by now Judy knew where everything was in the kitchen and didn't need to ask AJ, the kitchen was immaculate. Almost as clean as if Carmen had done it herself. The four younger ones joined the adults in the family room. Carmen had retrieved some of their New Zealand memorabilia. Some had been in the "gap years" box – others were in the parents' bedroom.

Alex turned to Carmen, "Where do we even start? AJ started this weeks ago when he was doing the work on family history, and it has been a time of a lot of reflection for all of us."

"Well, more for us, and AJ, we really hadn't brought Sammy and Jon-Mark as much into the discussions until yesterday. I know Judy and AJ have talked about it at school – well, I think Judy and AJ have talked about everything since they seem to be talking all the time," Carmen added with a smile.

"I have found it fascinating to what a man who was once my nemesis in law school is now a friend and a church member," added Brian.

"And Carmen," interjected Maria, "you will never know how much your story has helped me understand the many aspects and changes that are happening in our family over these past few months. You guys just pick up and tell us what was so special, what happened in New Zealand."

Alex stroked his chin and said, "Well here goes, New Zealand was and is to this day a stunningly beautiful island nation, also another former British colony – which still has a unique treaty arrangement with the Monarchy. Auckland, the capital of New Zealand is 1,300 miles from Australia, the closest continent. There are 5 million people, twenty-five million sheep, and about the same number of cattle The diverse topography make it a favorite movie filming location for things 'out of the normal world.'"

Carmen smiled and added, "They were filming the Harry Potter movies when were there."

"Yes, they were, but we went specifically to study the Māori people. A fierce, intense group of indigenous people who traveled by canoe from other islands in Polynesia. And another amazingly spiritual strong people," he added.

"With strong LDS ties," added Carmen, "it is where my testimony of the Gospel finally bloomed, after being planted for almost a decade." That remark left the room quiet, and all eyes were begging for more details.

"By now, we had volumes of research data and added almost as much as we had already gleaned from our travels because of our time with the Māori," continued Carmen. "Alex had a degree in history before law school and before our adventure began, so what was started as a special grant project had grown into what academia calls a non-terminal master's degree."

"But we needed stability. We needed a roof over our heads that didn't fly or have four wheels. We were tired of simply traveling so much."

Judy, who was always absorbing information faster than almost everyone in the room, asked, "So what happened?"

"Another twist in the narrative," replied Alex, "the grant we were working under had both university and government ties. It turns out that the University of Missouri had a working relationship with the University of Waikato..."

This time, AJ was caught off guard and blurted, "A wakey university?"

"The University of Waikato is in Hamilton, New Zealand, and they also have strong ties with the Māori and with the LDS Church," explained Carmen, "both of which became a significant part of our story."

"And?" Judy pushed. as her mother gave her a strong mom look.

Smiling Alex replied, "I was granted an adjunct professorship to teach one class on the United States Constitution and a budget to continue my writing on what became OUR master's thesis – Carmen is a co-author, when successfully defended, what will be OUR Ph.D. [What Alex couldn't explain was the interwoven government protection and that, at this time, they weren't Alex and Carmen, they were Aaron and Cathy.]

"I'm getting a little lost, Dad. At least now I know how you are teaching college with only a master's degree, but mom, you mentioned the Church—where does this all fit in?" asked AJ.

"Let your mom pick up the story, she saw the Church through new eyes, and I saw it through a restored vision of what I have known since I was a teen," said Alex.

Carmen then recapped the story of the Church in New Zealand, how missionaries had arrived there in 1851 only four years after the Saints entered the Salt Lake Valley. The early struggles, the translation of the Book of Mormon to the Māori language, and then some of the almost beyond-belief stories they were told by the oldest members of the local Māori Saints.

"How were they so beyond belief?" asked Maria.

"Oh, after listening to them, and feeling conversation heart-to-heart and spirit-to-spirit, I believe in them as sure as I'm sitting here," replied Carmen.

"Please share them with us," Maria replied most earnestly.

Carmen then detailed how the Church grew very strong in that southern part of the North Island of New Zealand. That the Church's 11th Temple opened in New Zealand of all places in 1955. How at one time the Church operated what was essentially a boarding high school called, The Church College of New Zealand, which operated for over 50 years educating thousands of Māori – many of which would go on to Hawaii to attend the BYU/Hawaii campus, or later when they proved to be such great football players, the Provo Campus.

"We met a couple who were visiting Hamilton with the man's elderly father who had been a missionary there before World War II – he was a former General Authority of the Church, they call it 'emeritus status," but he was still working at almost 90. His name was Glen Rudd, and his son and daughter-in-law were Charlie and Annette."

"Once they opened the doors to their Māori connections we were immediately adopted as well," and then the stories started to pour out!" explained Alex. He then added, "Your narrative, go ahead."

Carmen smiled and related a story that was interwoven

with her own. She told how Elder Rudd, as a young missionary in those pre-war years, served as the assistant to the Mission President, a man named Matthew Cowley, who would later become an Apostle of the Church. The Māori practically revered President and then Elder Cowley as sort of their patron saint among the Saints. The older locals who still remembered both Elder Cowley and later Glenn Rudd both as a missionary and his return as the Mission and then Temple president. She then added, pulling from her own handwritten journal, some of the stories we or I were told:

- Prior to the first LDS missionary's arrival, there had been other Christian missionaries. The locals wanted to know, what Joseph had wanted to know – which Church was true. There was a wise old Māori elder they went to for council. He stated he did not know, but he would fast, pray, and ponder until he had an answer. Three days later the old man emerged and said, "the true church is not yet here, but it is coming, it will be taught by people who come from afar, they will speak our language and when they pray they will raise their right hand to square – evidently, in the second half of the 19th century that was a common form of prayer for LDS Missionaries – none of which had ever been seen by a Māori

- On more than one occasion then, Mission President Cowley was present when a Māori man who had died and was being prepared for burial was given a Priesthood blessing, sat up, and said, "Call for the Elders. I don't feel well." According to the story the man brought back to life outlived the man who had pronounced the blessing upon him.

- Another time, President Cowley was asked to give a

small child a name and a blessing because his parents hadn't 'got around to it.' As President Cowley took the young man into his arms to give him a name and a blessing, the boy's parents added, "And will you bless him with his sight? He was born blind."

Carmen paused and said, "I was still wrapping my head around a man being raised from the dead, maybe he was just unconscious, but how could a blind baby even know he was being blessed to have his vision when it had been dark for him since the day he was born, I turned to Charlie and must have had a questioning look in my eye. He put his finger to lips and mouthed, 'I'll tell you later.'"

"And he did?" asked AJ

"He did; while his dad was resting, Charlie and Annette took us on this tour of Hamilton, where he explained a lot of Church history – his dad's relationship with Elder Cowley, which would continue for decades, the impact that both his dad and Elder Cowley had left on this people."

"Charlie sounds like he learned a lot from his dad," added AJ, now more blown away than before.

"Oh, he did, and as I said after we left he and Annette returned to preside over the same mission," continued Carmen, "and it was Charlie that we first told who we were, that Alex was a returned missionary, that I was a Catholic and how had now been running into the Church all over the world."

"He smiled," added Alex, put his arm around both of us and said, 'let me show you a house.' He then took us to a house located behind the Temple in a quiet neighborhood. He explained that the whole family came to New Zealand, well Charlie and a younger sister – his older brothers were on missions to the UK, when their dad had been called as the Mission president. He stopped and pointed at one house and said, "That was the house the boy who was blessed to receive his sight by Elder Cowley lived in. I met him when he was an old man, and he had perfect vision; he died only a few years ago."

"Sister Barton," Judy asked, "what, how did you process all this?"

"Charlie and Annette made us feel totally at ease, his only comment that sounded like a missionary statement was, 'the Lord must have put you on this path for a reason.'" Replied Carmen, "So that night I started reading, really reading a copy of the Book of Mormon that I had got in Hawaii – until then I had read "in it," but not really read for any understanding – I was scared, I loved my faith, but I had met so many of God's children now across the world, and so many whose lives had been changed by the Book of Mormon and the story of Joseph Smith."

Maria was wiping tears and asked, "Did you feel you had an answer?"

"I felt it was my responsibility to find out in such a way that my faith would become almost as sure as knowledge," Carmen replied.

Judy, who was trying to control her emotions, said, "And you did, but when did you know?"

"I went through the whole Book of Mormon; I prayed every night to myself and with Alex before he left for his teaching job at the uni. One day he had a long day with two classes and a faculty meeting, so I went to the Temple grounds and sat in the shadow of the Temple. That afternoon, my entire life, from my time in Cuba and Miami, unexpectedly meeting and falling in love with Alex, our journeys, and the people we met all flooded my mind. I felt calm and at peace as if a tiny, small voice was whispering, 'You have always known the truth, accept what you have been given, for in you there are yet many great works to finish.'"

The room was silent as Carmen continued, "As soon as Alex got home, I hugged him and told him it was time; I wanted him back in Church because I wanted him to baptize me."

Judy and Maria were softly sobbing. Alex and Brian were dabbing at their eyes. The twins again had tears rolling down their faces as Alex sat beside them and hugged them both.

Carmen took a deep breath and steadied herself, "Perhaps even more details than I had planned. We saw the Bishop that night, we had a lot to straighten out before Alex could baptize me."

"How come," asked AJ with an inquisitive tone.

"Alex, is it OK for me to give a short-form answer to that question," Carmen asked, looking toward her husband.

"Let me," he replied, "we left Miami because we were helping with some issues with the Cuban government. We had government protection during this time and had assumed names. They could have never found Alex Barton because we were Aaron and Cathy Brown—and other than AJ, we have never told anyone else who didn't have a need to know. It is no longer that big of a deal, but please keep this as our family's secret."

Judy practically gushed, "You guys are even more amazing than I could have ever imagined. Of course, we will be quiet—right, Mom and Dad."

"Right as always daughter," replied Brian and Maria with one voice.

"So, when did you get baptized?" asked Judy.

"It took about a month to track down records. Fortunately, the Church has people inside the government who were able to quietly give them the information they needed to find Alex. With approval from the First Presidency, we had our records flagged though Aaron baptized Cathy, with a need-to-know local Church leaders could see our real names in the Church's main MIS system," explained Alex, "I hadn't baptized anyone in over a decade…"

"And yet you got it right the first time," Carmen added, "and I was totally surprised that Charlie and Annette, who had been touring Australia, were able to come for my baptism – your dad and Charlie then confirmed me a member of the Church and pronounced the Holy Ghost on me.' Wow, that has fired up a lot of memories…but anyone up for some hot apple pie with vanilla ice cream?"

The twins shouted, "ME!" in unison and were off to the kitchen. Carmen took Alex's hand and whispered, "We have to get in there before they help themselves." Alex grinned; his wife knew their children very well.

Brian reached over and hugged his wife and said, "What a story, they have certainly been through a lot."

Maria's voice, still twinged with emotion replied, "Carmen had shared some of this, but her conversion part was like reading a book on my own life. I, too, have some praying to do."

Judy walked over to AJ and took his hand as they headed towards the excitement of the apple pie with the twins; she reached up and kissed him on the cheek, whispering, "We both have amazing parents; I can't believe all that your mom has been through and her tremendous courage."

"As long as I've been alive, I've known Mom has an awesome testimony. Tonight was the first time I ever heard the details of why," answered AJ, "but I want some pie—let's eat." Both teens grinned and headed to the kitchen, leaving Brian and Maria absorbed in their thoughts on the couch.

Both families felt they had grown closer that evening. After hugs, kisses, and expressions of gratitude, Maria finally asked, "So you were both now members – what happened? And how did you ever get your real lives back?"

"A story with a lot of details," replied Carmen, "but short version, we were in New Zealand for another 14 months; on the one-year anniversary of my baptism, we were sealed for time and eternity in Hamilton, New Zealand Temple by the President of the Temple. By that time, we had met with our handlers in the witness program, and they felt there was a reasonable degree of safety that we could, as they call it, 'come back in from the cold.'"

"True," added Alex, "the question was where do we go? Our master's thesis had been accepted, and the dissertation version was now under review. I didn't want to go back to law, and honestly being a college prof seemed to be a pretty good gig for me. Then there was one other ingredient."

"Which was?" asked Judy.

Carmen smiled, "Actually, there were two things: first the where and how, then we both accepted that we weren't getting any younger, and we wanted to start a family of our own."

AJ looked bewildered, "By now, you had traveled the world, survived the bad guys, met a lot of good guys, were working on your doctorate and you somehow picked SALISBURY, North Carolina as the place to start this new life?"

Carmen smiled at her son. Until a few weeks ago, she knew he had considered his parents boring people living in a boring town. Now, he knew his mom and dad already had enough pure excitement for a lifetime but wondered why they chose what he still considered a sleepy little town. "And, why Salisbury is a story for another night; we have four kiddos that still have school tomorrow."

CHAPTER TWENTY-THREE

After the pie was consumed, along with many hugs and kisses, as well as expressions of appreciation for a wonderful evening by both families, the Rolands adjourned to their home. The twins were exhausted, and it was easy for them to head to bed. AJ was still pondering, "My parents led such an amazing life from the time they met, and when they decided to start a family, they moved HERE? Why?" In essence that was the question he asked his parents right before heading for his own journal and bed.

Carmen put her arms around her son, who now stood three inches taller than her, and said, "There are so many ways to answer that question, but let me share one with you first – and I, we (turning to Alex) promise a lot more details will follow."

"OK, I'm listening," replied AJ.

Alex started, "Your mother and I were attending Sacrament at the Hamilton 3rd Ward while we were going through our options with Nikki, she had been our handler for close to 12 years. She had been promoted by that time and oversaw an entire department but insisted on being with us as long as we were in protection."

"Dear, you digress. He needs to get to bed. Short answer for now," Carmen interjected. Where your dad was going was that Sunday after we had been on a long, too long call with Nikki. We went to Church—still pondering what and where. The closing hymn was an old favorite but hit both of us like a ton of bricks."

"What was it?" asked AJ.

Alex smiled at his wife and quietly answered, "I'll go where you want me to go..."

"I'll do what you want me to do," added Carmen.

Then, in unison, both said, "I'll be what you want me to be."

AJ shook his head in somewhat disbelief, "The LORD wanted you in SALISBURY and for Dad to teach at Catawba?"

"You asked," replied Carmen nonchalantly, "you asked, and as I promised, more details later." With that, she kissed her son, and he left, murmuring, "I asked."

****

When AJ headed to his room, Alex turned to Carmen and said, "You know we left out quite a few chapters in that answer?"

"Yes, we did," she replied, "but we all needed to get to bed, and those chapters will keep, until at least tomorrow."

"True," Alex replied, "but it sure brought up a lot of memories."

The two of them sat down on the bed and, for almost an hour, ran through the process that got them from Hamilton, New Zealand, back to being Alex and Carmen and settling down in a small town in the South. There were many twists in the road that had led them to North Carolina. The first and biggest obstacle to confront was a long talk with Nikki on the threat level from the different areas of concern that had kept them looking over their shoulders for their decade of hiding?"

Nikki had her analysts do a lot of research. They reached the following conclusions:

- Castro had first been terminally ill and then turned the reins of power over to his brother Raul. The United States had dealt with a myriad of issues, and no one really wanted to drag up more investigation into the Kennedy assassination. Fidel's declining health, as well as any real influence on the world's communist stage, had all but evaporated. Raul knew the U.S. had his brother's diaries, but realized he needed to focus on the Cuban ship of state, which was everything he could do to keep it afloat. Most of the old-line hard-liners in Miami who might have been involved with the great diary escapade had passed on.

The young couple that had been in the center of it had vanished. The threat level from Castro's fading forces was deemed to be almost nothing.

- Through both Presidents Clinton and George W. Bush the CIA had substantially cleaned up their act, or at least hid much better some of their black ops – though the "War on Terror" brought on by the 9-11 attacks had raised some eyebrows on just who did what, and knew what in the CIA. Long and short again, IF there were rogue elements involved with the Kennedy assassination in the early 60's, they too had long since gone to their reward. The Agency simply had too many other hot irons in the fire to worry about what might have happened in their darker past. Threat level – zero.

- The Italian "families" – primarily the New York connection tied to drugs in Cuba had taken some hits, sometimes as a direct result of names in the Castro Diaries. It was believed this was the primary reasons for the attempts to assassinate the Bartons in Hawaii and then the ambush in Mexico. Interestingly, in both cases their attempts to take out Alex and Carmen had shown a spotlight on some of the mid-level and then next level up drug kingpins. This led to some serious arrests of individuals previously thought almost untouchable. Sadly, the Mexican cartels had in many ways grown even more powerful, but there was so much money flowing that all the analysts agreed the serious leaders now at the helms of the Cartels had no desire to bring any attention to themselves by taking out two, what they considered now 'bit players' in a 12-year-old bad choice by some of their predecessors.

Threat level, barely a 1 on a scale of 10 – especially, if Alex and Carmen decided to take a low-profile lifestyle in some small southern town.

Alex listened patiently as Carmen recapped the why and how of their decision to leave witness protection. Nikki had made it clear it was entirely their decision. Since Alex had secured a decent paying position, with US government help, they had voluntarily reduced their stipend equal to his New Zealand pay. They were still receiving a small housing allowance, but both Carmen and Alex realized it was time to start providing for themselves. Nikki had indicated they were costing the government so little nobody really cared – the total amount spent on them in the years in New Zealand was so small she had called it a rounding error in the overall scheme of things. As for Alex and Carmen, they had managed to save quite a large amount of money over the 11-plus years and knew they had more than enough for a good down payment on a house in the United States – IF he could secure a college professor slot, with a tenure track.

It was Alex who suggested Salisbury. He remembered Carmen had looked confused and asked, "There is a Salisbury in England, and I was disappointed as a child when told we were having Salisbury steak, and it turned out to be a wet hamburger."

Alex laughed and gave her some details, "Yes, Salisbury is a very British name; in addition to the one in North Carolina and England, there is also one in Maryland. It is a very small part of my life that I seldom think about," he continued. As their minds flashed back to a conversation over 16 years earlier when she had first heard about the town, she now called home.

Thinking that she knew just about everything about her

husband's past she had looked puzzled and asked, "How so?"

"You remember I went to a lot of schools and had multiple family settings while I was growing up?" he asked.

"Sure, are you going to tell me that somehow Salisbury, North Carolina is in this mix?"

He sort of grinned and said, "It's a short story that I usually block out, but yes, my father was a really interesting guy. The career criminal until he hooked up with my mother and they had me. Yes, I told you he went back to prison, he and Mom never made it back together, and hence why I went from pillar to post."

"I remember this part, it's when I asked, OK, I know this is going somewhere..."

"And I replied, sorry, I am wandering a lot, aren't I?"
"Yes, dear you were, and you are, and it's getting late. Can you remind me the short version, and the rest of the story tomorrow?" Carmen asked, running her fingers through is formerly dark now streaked with gray hair.

"Sure. Dad's 3rd or maybe 4th wife was a piece of work. They weren't together that long, but she convinced him his son, me, who was in the 4th grade at the time, should have a real dad and a new mom – her. They got hired at Rowan Manufacturing back when there was still a garment industry in the United States. They rented a home in Salisbury, and I went right where the twins are going now. A.T. Allen Elementary for the 5th grade. My class made several field trips to Catawba College, and I have always just looked back upon that weird year as the school and the college field trips with fond memories. Their marriage was a disaster from day one and I prayed nightly it would end so I could be shipped off someplace else. It did. Two days after school ended, I was on a plane out of Charlotte heading back to live with my elderly aunt."

"Wow, now I remember. You had never given me those details before that night in Hamilton so long ago. That's when you found the Church…"

"And my life changed, and I guess I had just blotted out a lot of what happened before then," he said ruefully.

Carmen and Alex simply sat there quietly for a few moments, reflecting on all that had happened, all the things that had 'fallen in place" over sixteen years. When they had broached the idea with Nikki, she liked the choice of the state and the city. It was a small town within an easy drive of an international airport, and there were several colleges in the area she was sure they would have a 'connection' she could work to get Alex the college job he was seeking.

They looked at the clock, it was getting late, and AJ would be up for seminary in a few hours, "Let's call it a night," Alex said, we can give AJ the high points tomorrow on how Salisbury must have been the place the Lord wanted us to go because of everything that happened to get us here."

"Wait until he hears about Dr. Singer and his ties to the agency which opened up so many doors to make your job possible," Carmen added with a smile before they had prayer, and she kissed him goodnight.

****

Of course, the next day was hectic from the time

everyone jumped out of bed. AJ really wanted the rest of the story on how Salisbury became his home, but he knew that it would have to wait. For both AJ, Judy, and most of the students at SHS, these final days were a blur. Judy did get a few words with AJ on the way to school and was still amazed at the story of his mom's conversion. AJ wanted to ask how she was feeling and if she felt any answers or inspiration, but his dad had wisely counseled him to let the Lord speak to her in His own way, and in His own time. The only hint Judy offered as they headed to class was, "Your mom is so brave, I hope I can have that much strength and courage as well."

He smiled and gave her a quick hug. She kissed him quickly on the cheek and they were off to separate classes. She had another softball meeting after school, so AJ headed home and was happy to see his dad's car in the driveway. He had forgotten that classes were over at Catawba; maybe the answers to the "why Salisbury" were coming sooner than he hoped.

"Hi, Dad, I'm home!" he announced, entering the front door.

"In the study," came the reply, "moms at the twins' school for an awards ceremony, or a PTA meeting, or a planning session for the kids going to middle school, or determining who will replace her as PTA President…"

AJ smiled, and remembered his mom had been a fixture as the most visible parent at A.T. Allen from the day he was there, she had also followed him to middle school, but her support was a little more distant after he finally got to high school.

"Dad," he began, "about last night's the 'why Salisbury,'

question."

"OK," Alex replied, "Pull up a chair; there is the rest of the story."

He related how he had never really shared with any of his kids, but he, too, in one of his many childhood homes, spent the 5th grade at A.T. Allen, where he had first visited Catawba College. Like so many other ingredients of his parents' story, this too took him by surprise, but at least it was no longer a shock.

"But dad, visiting a college when you are in 5th grade doesn't just open the door for you to walk in and start teaching thirty years later," he said with an inquisitive tone.

"True, especially for a master's degree only – at least officially – whose only college teaching is a college in New Zealand as an adjunct prof," answered Alex.

"Soooo."

"You remember son it has almost become a family motto that there are no coincidences in life…" answered Alex.

To which AJ replied, "they are only miracles in which God chooses to remain anonymous."

"Do you remember my department head, "Dr. Singer?"

"Sure," replied AJ, "when we go on those faculty family outings (which he really didn't care for), he always comes over, is really friendly, and seems to take a personal interest in our family."

"That's the one," Alex replied, "he's somewhat of a

legacy, though an unusual career path. His dad was chairman of the History Department at Catawba for over 25 years. His son, Anthony, now my boss chose not to follow, at least immediately, into academia. He got a history degree, then a master's in poly science, and then went to work for various agencies in the federal government in DC."

"There's a tie coming in here somewhere..." replied AJ.

"Yep, there is," Alex continued, "he was our handler's right-hand man in the witness protection program. He was one of the agents covering our home in Hawaii the night the bad guys first tried to take us out. He saved our lives."

"Wow."

Alex then unfolded the 'rest of the story.' Evidently while working for the government, he also pursued and received his PhD. In history from the American Military University. Despotism happens in academia, so one of his father's last hires at Catawba was his son Anthony as a new Associate Professor of History. That happened two years after the Hawaii incident. By then he had a family and being shot at and having to shoot other people had lost a lot of its appeal. During the time Alex and Carmen, or Aaron and Cathy, were in protection he rose through the ranks to full professor and then Chair of the department, the year before the Bartons moved to Salisbury.

When Alex had floated the idea of Catawba Nikki reached out and was stunned to find not only someone, she knew but someone who would understand the complexities of hiring Alex. Dr. Singer had reviewed Alex and Carmen's work and knew it would pass any Ph.D. defense; knew the character of Alex and Carmen and was more than willing to help his old boss at the agency. He took the hire to the President of the College and gave him enough details to get the doors opened.

"So," Alex concluded, "when we arrived in Salisbury, there was indeed a close friend, who had already taken very good care of our family waiting for us. If he seems to genuinely care about us, it is because he does."

AJ again just sat stunned. Every time he felt that there were no more surprises, yet another one was thrown his way. Alex continued the story, "I was hired as an Associate Professor. The housing market was somewhat soft, and with our downpayment money and a few right calls to the right people from both Nikki and the college, we got an all-time sweetheart mortgage. The salary was adequate, and for the next four years, until I hit the tenure track, the school received a government grant to allow me to continue our work on my yet still unofficially published dissertation. When my salary increased and a few other nuggets dropped our way, we were able to live a comfortable, safe, stable, and, as you have often thought, boring,' middle-class life."

"I will NEVER consider your life boring again," promised AJ.

"It's OK, son, it is the life your mother and I dreamed of for most of those years in protection."

"Are you every going to tell the twins?" AJ asked.

"Oh, they will find out someday, who knows maybe their big brother will narrate the tale by then," Alex replied with a smile. But, more importantly, are you ready for the last week of school – finals and the rest."

"I got one final left tomorrow. Judy's got two. The rest of the time is what you teachers like to call "enrichment," replied AJ.

"We don't make the rules – the state mandates 182 days of school – but after all the curriculum is taught, we must fill the day somehow. Let's go check the kitchen; mom left me instructions on what to turn on so dinner will be ready when she gets home. Speaking of Judy, any hints on where she is with The Book of Mormon and Church?" asked Alex.

"You told me to let her work it through on her on time – she's a smart girl, smarter than me for sure. The only thing she mentioned still was how blown away she was with mom's story."

"My advice still stands," said Alex, "if she wants to work it through with you out loud, she'll come to you. She's smart and not shy." Ruffling his son's hair he said, "but for us, the kitchen."

CHAPTER TWENTY-FOUR

While AJ was talking to his dad about the Salisbury decision, Judy was alone with her thoughts in the dugout of the SHS softball field. There was no practice, and the team meeting had ended 20 minutes earlier. So much in her life had changed over the past three months. Secretly she had a crush on AJ since the day they first met in Art class at the start of the second semester. She loved working with him, and when the classroom relationship grew into a boy/girl friendship and the first time she heard him speak in Church, she sensed he was so different.

Of course, little did she know that Sunday would open the doors of so many other questions about Church, God, and her own family. Add to this mix her emergence as one of the most promising young softball players in the state; she was grateful for her time in the early morning Seminary. Prayer, which had been a set group of words, had become so much more to her. Receiving Priesthood blessings from her dad made her realize just how lucky a girl she was to have been found by Brian and Maria Roland. Sure, sometimes she still wondered about her bio mom and dad, but even at her young age, she saw God's hand in placing her right where she was at this very moment in her life.

The blessing she had received on how to find out about the Book of Mormon had both strengthened and, to some degree, scared her. She had loved being a good Catholic girl all her life. She really wanted to pray for a simple prayer, have an angel appear and tell her an answer and then she'd know what to do.

Sister Williams must have known the struggle she was going through, and one morning, she got to the Seminary early. When she walked in, she heard, "Judy, I was just thinking about you when I remembered something that Joseph Smith's scribe, Oliver, dealt with years ago; it's in a book we call the Doctrine and Covenants. I'm sure AJ can show you the exact verse, but long and short, the Lord told Oliver to ponder it, sort it out in his mind and then ask the Lord for confirmation. Not exactly sure why I'm prompted to tell you, but you came to my mind when I read it."

She thanked Sister Williams for the advice and the words had bounced around in her head since then. She did ask AJ about it, and he found it for her and even more about "cast your mind back to other things the Lord had told him." So, sitting alone in the dugout, she decided now was as good of a time as any to ask with real intent, and for her, the softball diamond was almost as important as Church.

Trying to figure out how to pray reverently in the dugout, she didn't hear her dad's car pull into the parking lot. So, she had no way of knowing her dad had gotten off work early and that when he stopped at the house, her mom had told him she had sent a text she was still at school, thinking in the dugout.'

Kneeling seemed a little awkward, so she folded her arms the way she had seen so many LDS kids pray and, with heartfelt sincerity, poured out her heart. She expressed her love for Jesus, for being taught so many wonderful things by the nuns and priests while growing up, for meeting AJ and his family, and for learning about the Book of Mormon. Now almost pleading, she asked the question, "My heart tells me it is true, may my heart and mind be of one voice?"

Brian quietly walked up to the dugout and realized his daughter was alone. He prayed he heard her words, "My heart tells me it is true. May my heart and mind be of one voice?" The sincerity of her request and the maturity beyond her years left him stunned. As an almost 16-year-old decades ago, he grew up believing the Book of Mormon to be true, so he had never had this conversation with God.

Judy rocked quietly on the dugout bench, eyes still closed and let all that she had been taught over her life and the past three months flow through her body. Brian simply stood still and waited. As the memories flooded both of their minds, a tear ran down his cheek, and then he heard Judy begin to sob. Quietly, her dad entered the dugout and sat down beside her. His large arms engulfed his crying daughter, she looked up and realized the arms that had always comforted her were there at the moment she needed them most and through the tears whispered softly, "Daddy it's true, I can't deny what I know,

The Book of Mormon is true, Joesph is a prophet of God."

Father and daughter embraced in one of the most special moments in their lives. When the tears finally stopped, they again embraced, and Brian said, "Let's go find Mom."

It is observed the Lord works in mysterious ways and that His time is certainly not ours, so it was that afternoon. What neither Brian nor Judy knew was that since Maria had the day off from the hospital, she too had spent most of the day pondering the changes, the introduction of the Church into their lives, her husband's desire to return to Church, her daughter seeking for clarity on her relationship with God.

At first, she had been concerned that Judy's interest in the LDS Church was tied to her first boyfriend. Getting to know AJ and the Bartons and hearing Carmen's story had quelled that concern. Her silent struggle was how to deal with her own new knowledge and feelings – while supporting her husband and daughter. She, too, had finished her copy of the Book of Mormon, and that afternoon, since Brian had left to find their daughter, she decided to ask the same questions that Judy had asked. If Brian had been able to be in two places at the same time, he would have found his wife also pouring out her heart in their bedroom.

Maria had dried her own tears for a moment when she heard Judy and Brian enter the kitchen. She met them, knew they had been crying, and instantly knew why as the three immediately embraced. Tears again flowed and she finally was able to say, "I see we all got the same answer."

They adjourned to the living room and there they knelt and gave thanks to the powerful manifestation which they had all received.

CHAPTER TWENTY-FIVE

The last surprise, the unfolding of his parents' past life, was perhaps as big, if not bigger than all the rest. After he and his dad had ensured that dinner was ready, his mom and the twins arrived home. As they finished dinner, there was a knock on the door. Sam shouted, "It's JUDY and her parents!"

When they walked into the kitchen, even teenage AJ realized that Judy had initially been crying, but for the first time in his life, he thought he was actually seeing someone 'glow.'

With enthusiasm, Judy blurted, "We had something so big we had to share it with the most important family in our lives!"

Carmen got up quickly to greet Judy and her parents with a quick kiss and then ushered everyone to the family room, asking, "Share, please tell us!"

"You tell them mom," said Judy.

Fighting back tears of happiness, Maria replied, "This afternoon, our lives have changed forever. We didn't plan it, but we were all seeking the same answer, Judy and I want to be baptized; the Bishop called earlier, and Brian has been found. Your family was the key to us finding the Church."

Carmen rushed forward to hug Maria, Judy was hugging AJ, Brian and Alex embraced and the twins found a way to encircle everyone. There were tears of joy flowing in one of the most momentous multifamily celebrations one could ever imagine. The Krispy Kreme doughnuts planned for the twins' party at school the next day were reassigned as celebration food for the Bartons and Rolands. They laughed, talked and cried until it was past time for everyone to be in bed; it was a night they would all long remember.

****

Needless to say, the next day was a blur for everyone. When AJ and Judy walked home from school that afternoon, they saw an official government-looking sedan in the driveway. It was perhaps the final surprise in the tale of Alex and Carmen or Aaron and Cathy. AJ opened the door with Judy and called out, "Dad?"

His father answered, "In the study, there is someone I want you to meet."

He and Judy shed their backpacks and shoes and walked in to see Alex talking with an attractive but older woman who stood to greet them when they entered.

Facing the teens, he said, "AJ, Judy, I want you to Ms. Nicole Walker; she is a very old and dear friend."

"Aaron, sorry, Alex, I've been Nikki to you for close to thirty years, no need to get formal now," she said with a smile. "AJ, I have known your parents for a long time."

The name clicked in his mind, "You are THE Nikki?"

Judy looked puzzled. "I think I heard something when your mom was telling her story about New Zealand and someone in the government who was helping you guys."

"That would have been me," replied Nikki.

"Ms. Walker, Nikki, was a rising star in the witness protection program years ago; she took us under her wing, and even when she headed the entire department, she was still our point of contact. She saved our lives, moved us all over the world, and, when the time came, helped us settle here in Salisbury. I told you how my Catawba position came to pass, much because of her and Dr. Singer," explained Alex.

"Wow," was all that AJ could at first utter before finally blurting out, "but why are you here, I mean, I, we owe you everything for all that you did for my mom and dad, but they've been out of the protection program for years."

"Yes, they have AJ," Nikki answered, "but we always sort of keep one eye open on all our protectees – present and past. But today is sort of a wrap-up and social call all the same time.

I caught up with Carmen earlier today before she headed over to your siblings' school, but I wanted to share something with your dad that I already told your mom."

Nikki then gave a quick snapshot of her long career in government service. After Carmen and Alex had been safely placed in Salisbury, she transferred to historical support for the CIA. Keeping people alive who had helped the government for over 20 years had been just about 2 years too long. Like Alex, her degrees were in History, and when a position opened on 'the farm" to be an official historian for one of the most secretive organizations on the planet, she couldn't turn it down. She was also planning on retiring at the end of the year but had run across a journal entry by a top former acting CIA director that she felt she should share.

Nikki pulled out a document that had some heavy redacting, but then said, here is the part that I can share, "It was from the daily diary of General Vernon A. Walters. For years after he officially retired he still had Top Secret Security Clearance. During his long, long career of government service he was a trusted advisor to five presidents and CIA Directors. The General kept notes on everything and put them in classified status – hence why much of this document has been redacted, but I have authorization to share the part that is not, let me read it to you."

"Wait a minute," Alex replied, "I heard him speak when I was at UM Law School, you could just tell he loved his work and appreciated that the intelligence community would never get the respect they deserved. In fact, a few weeks ago, I told Carmen something I remembered him saying years ago, "Your successes will never be known; your failures will be shouted from the rooftops."

"That's our General," Nikki answered with a smile, "He may have not known the young law student that day, but he would eventually know of you and the work you and Carmen completed."

She then read the unredacted section of the document: Today, date redacted, I personally reviewed a document brought to us by the daughter of a top lieutenant in Castro's government. The document has been authenticated, and much, if not all, of it is written in perfect Spanish in the verified handwriting of Fidel Castro. Ms. Name Redacted, and Mr. Name Redacted of Miami were able to secure the document at a large marine trade show being held in Miami Beach. These two did so at the peril of their own lives. It is my understanding they have entered the witness protection program, and one can only wish them 'godspeed.' The information contained in this document will be reviewed and worked on by various government agencies for at least five years. Agents of the DEA have already secured indictments of 16 key individuals in the name redacted family of New York; the name redacted family in Miami and the name redacted family in Mexico City. As a result of their efforts, the CIA has also arrested name redacted, name redacted, name redacted and name redacted former contract CIA agents who were indeed working directly with Castro's government. There are other political activities documented, but for reasons of national security may never be fully utilized. It is safe to say this is one of the greatest treasure troves of knowledge this agency has ever received from a voluntary source. It has been a key instrument in solving so many questions – and, in the process, saving the lives of countless agents and assets of the CIA. Our nation owes this brave young couple a debt of gratitude. General V.A. Walters.

The room was silent. Alex finally spoke, "I don't know what to say."

Nikki smiled and added, "Carmen cried; she told me she often wondered if you two had really made a difference. I knew some of this, but not all of it, and when I found it, I had to go through a lot of channels to even get this much to you, but you deserve to know, and your kids deserve to know just how brave their parents really are, and the contribution they have made to keeping our nation safe."

Judy broke the ice, she went over to where Alex was sitting, and kissed him lightly on the cheek, and said, "I've always known you were a hero, and even if I had never heard this, I would have known you were great, you see, I know your children; you and Sister Barton are the greatest."

****

For Alex and Carmen, the revelations of General Walters through Nikki's visit had finally brought a full measure of closure to their lives hidden in the infamous "gap years" box tucked away in the attic of their home and their memories. For AJ it so broadened his understanding of the sacrifices his parents had made for their nation and then to ensure a normal life for their children.

Judy's young life, which had almost as many twists and turns as the Bartons and her parents, was now on an even more upward trajectory. Summer was upon them. Graduation exercises were held at Catawba College and for the Seniors at SHS. Both families attended both commencement exercises out of the tradition for the town they called home.

For the Rolands, an even more significant event occurred

the week following graduation. Judy and Maria were baptized as the newest members of the Salisbury Ward of The Church of Jesus Christ of Latter-day Saints. Bishop Barnes had cleared Brian to baptize his wife and daughter; but at her request, Judy was baptized by AJ, his first as a Priest in the Aaronic Priesthood. Judy and Maria were both confirmed by Brian with Alex and the Bishopric in the Confirmation Circle. In attendance, in addition to Sister Williams' full Seminary Class was Coach Cato and the entire SHS Girls' softball team.

Coach Cato led her Summer Travel team to the state championship over the next six weeks. The Rolands and Bartons were able to attend every game. During that eventful summer both Judy and AJ celebrated their 16th birthdays. Three days after Judy's birthday, AJ, now with a brand-new North Carolina Driver's license picked her up at her home for their first date, not at Church or the softball diamond. Dinner at the Chanticleer and a movie at the Cinemark Tinseltown Cinema. It was a solo date, sort of, as coincidence would have it, their parents (who had arrived separately) were enjoying a meal discussing all that had transpired on the other side of the restaurant. For the evening, Norm Cooper, a young professor in the Catawba History department, loaned AJ his Tesla Model S for the evening. Carmen had some trepidation about her son driving such an expensive car with a top speed of 200 mph but knew he had been driving safely with the family with his learner's permit for over a year.

Before the end of the summer, Judy, as promised, completed all her Freshman Seminary work and earned her Freshman certificate. A reevaluation of her test scores allowed her to start AP courses in her sophomore year. By mid-August, both families were ready to start another school year. Alex and Carmen defended their Dissertation/master's thesis before a special board of the University of Missouri. Because of his position as a College Professor, Alex was awarded his Ph.D., and Carmen was awarded a Master's in Sociology for their work. Though he never took the bar, Alex's grades were reviewed, and he was finally awarded his JD from the University of Miami. He continued to teach as now a full professor at Catawba. Carmen moved her professional PTA skills back to Salisbury Middle School, just as she had when AJ left A.T. Allen Elementary School.

Maria was promoted to the Director of the entire Nursing Department of Rowan Memorial Hospital. Brian was elevated to be a Senior Partner at his Charlotte-based law firm and still allowed the freedom to do most of his work from the Salisbury branch location.

In a break from softball, the Rolands and Bartons made a trip to Raleigh where they were able as a family to do baptismal work in the Raleigh LDS Temple. Leaving the Temple, Brian promised Maria and Judy they would return in less than a year to be sealed together as a family for all time and eternity. For their birthdays, since the relationship between Judy and AJ seemed to be growing ever stronger, their parents presented them with gold CTR rings and challenged them to always wear them and always remember the admonition of those letters: CHOOSE THE RIGHT.

Lying in bed that night, Carmen leaned over and kissed Alex and simply said, "Te amo." [I love you]

Made in the USA
Columbia, SC
13 April 2025